PRAISE FOR
RICHARD S. WHEELER
AND *GOLDFIELD*

Tor/Forge Books by Richard S. Wheeler

*forthcoming

GOLDFIELD

Richard S.
Wheeler

A TOM DOHERTY ASSOCIATES BOOK
NEW YORK

This is a work of fiction. All the characters and events portrayed in this book are fictitious, and any resemblance to real people or events is purely coincidental.

GOLDFIELD

Cover art by George Bush

A Forge Book
Published by Tom Doherty Associates, Inc.
175 Fifth Avenue
New York, NY 10010

Forge® is a registered trademark of Tom Doherty Associates, Inc.

ISBN: 0-812-54803-5
Library of Congress Card Catalog Number: 94-44451

First edition: April 1995
First mass market edition: April 1996

Printed in the United States of America

0 9 8 7 6 5 4 3 2 1

For Norman Zollinger,
with admiration

PART I

. . . .

The Last Bonanza

I see America not in the setting sun of a black night of despair ahead of us, I see America in the crimson light of a rising sun fresh from the burning, creative hand of God. I see great days ahead, great days possible to men and women of will and vision. . . .

—Carl Sandburg

For this is what America is all about. It is the uncrossed desert and the unclimbed ridge. It is the star that is not reached and the harvest that is sleeping in the unplowed ground.

—Lyndon Baines Johnson

CHAPTER 1

· · · · · · · · · · · · · · ·

Big Sam Jones mused that if cinders were food he wouldn't feel so hungry. He had swallowed a lot of cinders and a heap of dust standing in the aisle of the packed coach rattling along the narrow-gauge tracks of the Nevada and California Railroad.

Everyone else in the jammed coach hungered for gold but Sam had only beans on his mind. He feared he would spin to the grimy floor unless he found succor in Tonopah. He leaned into his hickory walking stick, trying to make a tripod of himself to keep from keeling over while the little train struggled up the last grade to the silver camp.

Jones would have stood even if the coach had been empty because of his bum leg. It had broken in four places when a horse rolled on it, and mended into an unbending pole. The injury had ended his life as an itinerant horse trader, a fact that still surprised him. He had expected a load of buckshot to end that career.

The green-lacquered coach was so jammed that if he fell, he'd take half a dozen gold-crazed fools with him. The rank smell of sweat and tobacco smote him in spite of the November cool and the open windows. Most of his fellow travelers were male but a few veiled harlots occupied wicker seats given up by men. Women were such a rare commodity that even these won courtly gestures from the men around them.

Tonopah would be the end of the line. There was talk of extending the railroad to the new gold camp twenty-five miles south but so far no one had laid any track. The financiers were waiting to see if Goldfield would go bust like most boom camps.

The clackety-clack of wheels slowed and Jones beheld buggies, mule wagons, freighters, horse teams, stagecoaches, and even several horseless carriages. All of them were primed, for a fancy price, to race the latest mob of fortune-hunters to the new Golconda. The entertaining thing about a bonanza camp was the several ways people got rich fast.

The train screeched to a halt under a billow of steam and cinders and even before the harassed brakeman had the footstool in place the sweaty mob bulled its way down the steps. A brute in a bowler shoved Jones aside, toppling him in the aisle. No one helped him up; instead, the fevered fortune-seekers stepped over him while Jones watched a forest of britches and a wave of crinoline wash over his inert carcass. He acquired an education in footwear and hosiery and greed. But he didn't think it'd help him any. He knew all there was to know about greed.

Getting up from the aisle floor, with one leg as stiff as a fence post, required monkey tactics but Jones had done it before. He hoisted himself up by the handles on the moveable seat backs, dusted the grime off his black britches and suit coat, smoothed the handles of his moustache and combed his dark hair with his fingers. His hair pomade had sponged up grime. He recovered his warbag from the rack above and limped off the coach into chaos.

The whores were shouting at a gent in a bowler, the proud possessor of a horseless carriage, who was raising his price every ten seconds. A gaggle of roughs—miners perhaps—had occupied a mud wagon and were fending off frantic men who wanted to climb to the roof. One dandy with a sleek yellow roadster was offering to take two people to Goldfield in the miraculous space of one hour—for fifty dollars each. A dozen proprietors of buggies, spring wagons, freight wagons, and one-horse shays were touting their low prices instead of their speed, and found plenty of takers. Beside the box cars, freight outfits were loading dray-age into their big tandem Murphys hooked to twenty-mule teams.

Dizzily, Jones watched the bedlam. One after another wagon and buggy started south, raising a screen of suffocating dust over those who followed. Two harlots in a Stevens-Duryea touring car shrieked as they yanked each other. A Mexican brunette, with the aid of a hatpin, pitched a blond competitor into the tan dirt as the horseless carriage chugged and belched its way south followed by a spiffy Oakland and a Stanley Steamer. Big Sam Jones understood all that. He knew who wound up with all the money in a gold camp.

None of it was as important as the hole in his belly. When the Goldfield-bound mob was only a plume of dust, Jones surveyed the area. Tonopah rose above him, as forlorn as a passed-over bridesmaid. Beyond the town he could see tailings and hoist works crawling up the slope of Mount Oddie.

The glare of the desert hurt his eyes: he had never seen country so godforsaken, naked, harsh, and cruel. Surely this stretch of Nevada, with nothing but creosote bush and rabbitbrush, glaring purple and orange mountains, and a golden haze of dust, was unfit for human habitation. Somewhere far to the west rose the Sierras, a source of water and timber. But except for a scatter of jackpines on top of a few rocky desert ranges he saw nothing that would support human life. It appalled him.

The thought of food galvanized him. He hefted his canvas warbag hoping he had the strength to climb the grade into Tonopah.

"Hey, Mïstah. Youse want a ride?"

Big Sam beheld an urchin who commanded a mangy burro connected by a homemade rope harness to a dilapidated wagon.

"Ten cents, I take ya to town."

Sam examined the boy, discovered a grimy face beneath a mop of unwashed brown hair. "Tell you what, pal. I'm in the promotion and advertising business. If you take me to town I'll supply an endorsement. I'll write it out. 'Big Sam Jones says that this is the best way to get to Tonopah.' How's that?"

The boy squinted up at him suspiciously. "You don't have the dime."

"Oh, I'm a man of means, sonny. Just let me say the word around town and I'll get you lots of business."

"Five cents? One plugged nickel?"

"Well now, for five cents I'll give you a hot tip. You can make money with a hot tip. How about it?"

"You ain't got a nickel."

"Why, sonny, I could buy and sell you a thousand times over. Now you just listen to Big Sam Jones. Invest your money in the Sandstorm Mine in Goldfield. She's a winner. If you knew the value of the tip I'm giving you free—gratis—you'd take me into Tonopah ten times and back."

"Smartass."

"Ah, lad, where's a good club? A place to wet my whistle? A place to chow down on red beef, pickles and beer?"

"Tonopah Club," the kid said. "Hey, three cents?"

"I'll walk, thanks." Big Sam hoisted his canvas warbag and began the painful ascent.

"Cheap lobster," the kid yelled. He turned his little burro around and headed toward town. "They wasn't no one to pick up," he muttered. The burro rotated a long ear and listened.

Jones took ten paces and halted dizzily. The kid waited.

"Kid, I'm temporarily flat. Tell you what. I'll trade you a shaving mug for a ride."

"Cheapskate. You think I got a beard?"

"No, but you can sell it for maybe two bits. Or you can put it on your shelf and call it an endowment."

"What's that?"

"Never mind. Is it a deal?"

"Aw . . ."

Sam took that for surrender and eased himself onto the wagonbed, his bum leg poking north like a compass needle. He loosened the drawstring of his warbag and extracted a chipped porcelain mug.

"Aw . . . ," said the kid, but he took it.

Seven minutes later the wagon deposited Big Sam at the

portal of the Tonopah Club. "I'll tell 'em about your cheerful fast service, kid."

"You're a lobster."

Jones pushed through some batwing doors into a huge
and gaudy saloon, where a single keep manned the long
bar and a single tinhorn sat beneath a skylight at the rear.
He decided to try the tinhorn. Gamblers were good marks.

The man sat idly at a green baize-covered poker table,
smoking a cigarillo and shuffling chips with one practiced
hand.

"Little game, pal?" the tinhorn asked.

"I play a bigger game than that, pard. I'm a promoter.
You want advertising, you call on Big Sam Jones. I can
sell anything. I can sell cactus in Tonopah. I'm going to
broker mining stocks only I ran into a little trouble getting
to Goldfield."

"You want a grubstake."

"Naw, a partner that enjoys money."

The tinhorn smiled lazily. He was a handsome devil with
a lean, square jaw, shifty blue protruding eyes, hair slicked
down from a center part, and an inscrutable manner.

"I'm Wingfield, George Wingfield," the tinhorn said.

"I'm hungry," Jones said.

Wingfield nodded. He studied Jones as if he were a carcass of beef. "What did you do before?" he asked.

"I was an equine locomotion broker."

"A horse trader," Winfield said. "You have a future."

"I knew you'd see the light," said Jones.

"I do favors. Maybe I'll ask you for one." He handed
Jones a stack of five silver dollars and smiled. "Remember
George Wingfield," he said.

CHAPTER 2

· ·

Goldfield squatted on burning sand under the dark volcanic brow of a mesa, a mile or so from Columbia Mountain and its treasures. Big Sam Jones surveyed the two built-up streets, Main and Columbia, with a keen eye and noted the tents and shacks to either side where the daily influx of gold-fevered pilgrims found shelter. He would bunk in one soon but business came first. He bucked a gritty gale as he surveyed the false-fronted buildings along Main looking for a place to employ his talents. Wingfield's silver wouldn't last long.

He paused before a board and batten shack and ciphered the gilded legend on the real glass window:

BORDEN DEVELOPMENT COMPANY
GOLD MINING PROPERTIES
BONANZA MINES GROUP

It sounded good so he propelled himself through the door into an emporium about the size of a horse stall. Behind the counter stood a bald gent who reminded him of soap.

"You've come to the right place," the gent said. "I'm Windlass Borden and I sell gilt-edged blue chips."

"Well, this is the right spot, all right," said Jones. "I'm in the advertising and promotion business and looking for a chance to make you rich."

"Ah . . . you're looking for a chance to make me rich? As it happens—"

"Windlass—say, that's a mighty fine name—Windlass, I'm the best promotion engineer and market locator this side of the Atlantic," Jones said. "If your company isn't cashing in the way it should, why, the thing for you to do is put me behind that counter there and go vacation in the

Sandwich Islands while Big Sam Jones ships you bales of greenbacks.''

Borden twitched. An eyelid drooped. ''Jones, I don't need anyone. I can do it myself. You're obviously a rascal. This is a respectable enterprise. We're developers of first-class, blue-ribbon mining properties. I underwrite the stock offerings of gilt-edged corporations endorsed by the government of the great state of Nevada. Why, we have claims so rich you wouldn't believe it. I have assay reports; I have actual samples of highgrade ore, two hundred dollars the ton—imagine it! I have the notarized statements of mining engineers and geologists, men with magnificent reputations.

''I have the stock certificates on file here, par value, yes just exactly par, one dollar a share for all—properties that would put you on easy street the rest of your life. Have you heard the name Vanderbilt? Carnegie? Maybe Roosevelt? Hmm, I see you haven't. You poor parsnip; I can see you need some blue sky, a handle on heaven above. What happened to your leg?''

''The bones parted company here and there, Windlass, the fault of gravity and a horse. Now you just show me the drill here and get me a stool to perch on and set your terms and conditions, and I'll fetch up folding green so fast you can retire. How'd you get that handsome name, Windlass?''

''Why, Mrs. Borden, my late mother, wanted a cub who'd go to the well. A name should be an inspiration, she thought. And so it is. I am a true Windlass. My friends call me Windy but I don't mind. Now, how about buying a hundred of Queen Cleopatra? That's the best prospect I've got.''

''Why stop at a hundred, Windy? You should sell me a thousand. I'm good for it. I am a recognized expert at word-of-mouth promotion. In twenty-four hours I can line up fifty customers for you. But you've got to give me your terms and show me the business.''

Jones noticed that Windlass never blinked. He fastened his gaze upon a fellow like a pair of handcuffs.

Windlass slid his fingertips over his shiny skull and considered. "I'm not saying I'll take you on, and if I do it'd be commissions only. No salary. What do you know about mining?"

"Hell's bells, there's this hole and you go in there and bring out the bacon, Windlass. It's the same as everything else. I've mined all my natural life."

Borden sighed. "In other words you don't know a thing. You're some smart-talking rustic from somewhere." Windlass stared a moment and then convulsed toward a decision. "All right. We'll see. Now lissen. The Borden Development Company represents some corporations seeking capital. Each company's authorized the sale of eight hundred thousand shares of development stock and is holding two hundred thousand shares of treasury stock. You follow me?"

"What's the difference?"

"The development stock is for sale to raise funds; the treasury stock represents the assets of the company."

"Well, who owns these here claims and corporations?"

"That's confidential, Jones. But I will say that I, myself, possess several splendid claims I'm developing. Let's say that I am the director of several corporations. Have you heard the names Crocker? Huntington? Harriman? I can see you haven't. And you want to sell my securities."

Jones privately allowed that he might have a bit to master but he wasn't going to confess it. He'd run into plenty of horse traders who'd took him. But he'd gotten smarter each time he got took. "I can sell this paper of yours faster than you can print it," he said. "If this Harriman's a prospect, I'll sell him a bushel."

Borden smiled knowingly. "We'll see. Now Jones, see these little pasteboard boxes? They're ore samples from each claim. They go into the safe at night. When some dude comes in here you find out what he's looking for and talk up the prospects. Let him heft that ore. Fingering gold's like caressing a mistress. See those fat folders? Those are assays and geologists' reports for each property, including estimated reserves. See those other folders? Corporate development plans, schedules, operations, cost estimates, purchases to date; ore sales to date; stuff like that. You show all that to the customers. They don't want to buy some pig in a poke, Jones. Let 'em feel the gold. Give 'em facts. You've got to read everything . . . you can read, can't you?''

"I never saw a word I couldn't cipher."

"That wasn't a reply to give me confidence in you, Jones. You should have said you have two degrees from Yale."

"Well, heck, Windlass. You just try me out. If I don't sell a hundred shares this afternoon, don't give me the draw I'm going to need to get myself settled in this fine little burg."

Borden eyed him thoughtfully. "I'm forming a plan, Jones. If you're the promoter you say you are, we'll work out a dandy arrangement. We should have one man here at all times and one man out in the saloons. There's more loose change in this camp than I've seen anywhere—and I've been everywhere. Ore's so rich around here the miners are highgrading it."

"What's highgrading?"

Borden sighed. "Thievery, Jones. The ore's too tempting. They commit larceny every shift, slipping thirty, forty pounds of highgrade—that's rich ore—into false-crowned hats, hollowed-out pick handles, pockets sewn into their jumpers, bags hung from the inside of their trousers. They waddle out of the pits right before the eyes of their bosses. Them miners, Jones, sell that stuff to assayers. Four-dollar miners are making a hundred a day. Whores and tinhorns are getting rich. There's cream here, Jones, and we're going to skim it, you and me."

Jones smiled happily. "Windlass, you're talking to a veteran horse broker."

Borden's smile turned beatific. "A horse trader, you say? A seller of quadrupeds?"

Jones's response was thwarted by the appearance of a

customer, a skinny drink of water with a carpetbag, who jangled the cowbell on the door.

"Let me," said Sam, limping around the counter.

Borden shrugged.

"You've come to the right place, my friend. I'm Sam Jones; what's your handle?"

"Well, I'm just here to—"

"That's all right, all right. Now our best property at the moment is the Queen Cleopatra. That little ol' glory hole is gonna turn me into a millionaire. It's down two hundred feet and into Christmas."

"Well, I'm not here to buy—"

"Of course you're not. You're just here for information. We've got it. Now you just look at this—it's ore from the Queen Cleopatra. Feel that stuff. It's smooth as a tit." He found the right pasteboard box and laid it on the counter. "Run your pinkies over that whiles I cook up the assay reports and all the Crockers and Vanderbilts and such."

The man's Adam's apple quivered. "Jones, I sell ads for the *Goldfield News*. If this outfit wants to make a profit it's got to advertise. Don't hide your light under a bushel, that's what the Bible says."

"The paper, eh? Well, you're a man after my own heart. Now, we'll run an ad in there for a few shares of this here stock. The Cleopatra's capitalized at one million shares and we'll just trade a few for an ad—isn't that right, Windlass?"

"Why—" Borden looked startled.

"Why, shoot, man, your little rag, it's gonna get rich. It pays to advertise, all right, and this Cleopatra mine, she's the hottest one in the district. Don't miss your chance. They're almost through development. Yesterday I saw a whole wagonload of winzes going in there."

The newsman looked pained. "A load of winzes, you say. A load of winzes . . . Good day, sir." The ad salesman banged out into a blistering sun.

"Jones, Jones," muttered Borden. "You'll never make it."

"What'd I do?"

"You know what a winze is?"

"It's mine stuff, like a pulley."

"It's a tunnel between one level of a mine and another."

"Well, that's all right. He'll go tell the boys at the paper about the winzes and they'll tell the story at every saloon in this burg—and pretty soon we'll have a mess of customers."

Jones patted the man's arm. "It's all right, Windlass. You just don't know the first thing about publicity. It don't matter what they say, good or bad, just so they talk about you. This here episode just sold us a mess of Cleopatra stock, don't you see? With all these Crockers, how can we go wrong?"

Borden pursed his lips, swiped his skull, and studied Jones. "All right, Sam. You're on. You get ten percent of the face value of your sales."

"How much are you getting?"

"That's confidential."

"I'm going to want a lot more than that, Windlass."

"That's all you get."

"Windlass, I'm going to move so much merchandise off your shelves that you'll be glad to pay me fifty percent. Meanwhile, pal, I need a ten-dollar stake."

"I don't know why I'm doing this," said Borden, reaching into his pocket.

CHAPTER 3

Professor Hannibal Dash stood immersed in frenzy in the middle of Main Street. Everywhere carpenters were hammering up stores, hotels, boardinghouses, restaurants, and livery barns. Wagons rattled, people shouted, saws scraped. Knots of miners hurried into saloons, Western Union messenger boys pedaled their bicycle through manure, news boys hollered the headlines.

He had never been to a mining camp and no description had prepared him for the gold fever that he breathed in, the seething excitement in the streets, the get-rich-quick hustle, the gaudy posters, the hurrying mobs.

Well, that's what he had come here for. He felt out of place. He wore a salt-and-pepper suit too thick for this fierce climate. His complexion had a pale northern look, except perhaps his hands, which were sun-stained and looked as if they could hold a hammer or pick. A close observer might also see the trace of tan around the wrinkled nape of his neck, but those were the only gold-camp qualifications he showed the world.

He still couldn't quite believe he had come here. Melanie had fought it fiercely from the start with alternating bouts of frost and pleading. She loved their big, rambling house on Langdon Street, with its huge veranda and its lovely view of Lake Mendota. She loved her busy rounds, her teas with faculty wives, her occasional sally into a classroom, and Madison itself, with its bright, scholarly vitality. She had bloomed there at the University of Wisconsin. Their children, Robert and Cecily, had matured into stable, affectionate youngsters now in high school.

When he had proposed giving up all that and moving to a wild desert place called Goldfield she had asked several questions with the intensity of a prosecuting attorney: What was this place like? A desert barrens. Were there civilized and educated people there? No. Were there good schools? None. Why in God's name did he want to go there?

That answer took some explaining while she stared dubiously, scarcely believing what she heard. It was the last frontier mining town, he said; the place of dreams where people flocked to transform their lives. The last gasp of the Wild West. When he was done she had looked at him as if he had dropped from another planet.

He couldn't quite explain what lured him. He just had to go. He had to put his geology to use. He had distinguished himself in the field of glaciation, not mineralogy or mining. But all the smooth years of college, then marriage, then the comfortable career at a great university, had deprived him of something he needed: a wild adventure. He couldn't use those words with Melanie, of course. He could only tell her that Goldfield was the place where he wanted to test his wits. If he made a fortune, fine; if not, it would fulfill something buried in him for years. He intended to try his luck. She stared, aghast.

"One year, Hannibal," she said, watching bitterly as he hefted his luggage. Cecily looked like a crushed flower and Robert refused to say good-bye. Melanie wouldn't hug him and stared hard-eyed, a flintiness in her face he had never seen. He wasn't at all sure she would wait for him or that he would be married when he returned—if he ever returned. It amazed him to think that way. Here was a self he had never imagined, and once he let it out of its mausoleum of the heart it dominated him. But leaving Melanie and his dear children had been the worst moment of his life.

The thought of his own erratic conduct never failed to astonish him but he put it out of mind. That was the past. Here he was in the middle of a dusty street, in the violent glare of the desert sun, listening to the cacophony of hammering and sawing, horses neighing, wagons rattling by, and teamsters shouting at him to step aside.

He needed a house. It was going to cost some of his carefully husbanded capital. He hoofed his way through the half-formed neighborhoods along Crook and Ramsey and Myers and then out Broadway and down Hall and Gold and Silver and Alloy streets, trudging past a score of canvas saloons, a tent beanery called the Waldorf Astoria, canvas-roofed stores, adobe houses, board and batten dwellings, false-front tarpapered stores, and giant wall tents serving as hotels. He saw stone, plank, adobe and canvas, but no brick or logs in this arid corner of Nevada.

He returned to a square cottage on Ramsey with a small shed off the rear.

"I don't suppose it's for sale," he asked a man on the roof.

The man stopped hammering down tarpaper long enough to laugh.

"Everything has a price, sir," Dash said.

The tradesman studied Dash, noting the wrinkled salt-and-pepper suit, the wilted white shirt, a pilgrim just off the stage, still leaking alkali dust. A certain cunning filtered into the man's face. "I suppose I could let it go, lot and house, for five thousand," the man said. "California lumber's five hundred for a thousand board feet—if ye can get it."

"I think you could let it go for two," Dash replied.

"Nah," the man said, returning to his hammering.

The erstwhile professor nodded courteously and made off, only to be halted by a yell.

"Three," the man said.

"Two," Dash replied calmly. "That's a hundred percent profit. You'll have a thousand to build another, and a thousand to buy mining shares."

"On the barrelhead?"

"Treasury notes," said Dash. "Let's go to the land office."

"If I do, you gotta finish this yourself."

"I'll manage."

Twenty minutes later Dash possessed a deed based on a federal townsite patent and owned a lot and house in fee simple. He spent the rest of the day nailing tarpaper and bruising his thumb. Late that afternoon he had his trunks and valise brought from the express office. That night he slept on the floor. The following day he built tables from scrap lumber for his assay office in the rear, and cobbled together a bedframe. Before dark he possessed a cotton-stuffed tick and a pillow from Miles and Company on Main Street.

The next day Dash began a tour of the mining district northeast of town, concentrating at first on the fabulous mines clustered south of Columbia Mountain. He needed work clothes, and bought some khaki cottons and a pith helmet against the glare. The clerks at the Miner's Cash

Store understood how to outfit a man for this uncompromising climate.

During the next weeks he poked and probed the slack piles of great mines that had aroused a national fever: the January, the Florence, the Combination, and others, cheek-by-jowl around the base of Columbia Mountain. No one bothered a scholarly-looking gent with silver at his temples who poked around the tailings, plucked up an occasional sample of dacite or andesite and dropped it into his canvas ore bag.

Once, at the Jumbo, an armed guard questioned him.

"I'm a geologist. This is my work," was all that Dash said, studying the igneous rock.

The man shrugged.

Most evenings, after a leisurely meal at the California Beer Hall or Ajax's La Parisienne, a fancy restaurant down in the sporting district—an utter novelty for Dash—he set to work in his assay laboratory. There, using his command of chemistry, crystallography, physics, geology, and smelting techniques, he pulverized, roasted, retorted and weighed, making small notes in a crabbed hand. Within a few weeks he knew the ores and country rock in each mine; the geologic history of each mine; the values in the discard piles; the values in the stockpiled ores that were too poor to send to the distant smelters; and an amazing amount of information that didn't fall into any pigeonhole, such as the predatory habits of miners at each site.

Even though mining geology hadn't been his field, he became an expert: if he was ever put to the test he felt confident he could exploit properties overlooked by others. He had assaulted the task feverishly and in the space of a month he knew much of what there was to know about the ores and mines and geologic structures of Goldfield.

Perhaps twenty million years earlier, huge effusions of magma had laid dacite and andesite over the earlier sediments. These had faulted in complex patterns and the percolation of hot water containing dissolved mineral salts had deposited gold along the faults, along with silver, copper, zinc, iron, bismuth, antimony, tellurium, and arsenic.

Much of the hard gray quartz was rich ore, although miners had never seen it before and often supposed it was worthless. The deposits were so irregular and hard to follow that the future of the whole district remained a question mark. It was nature's own shell game and he would try to find the pea.

He loved the labor and scarcely needed relief from it. But his loneliness drove him into the numerous saloons, especially those magnetic thirst parlors near the corner of Crook and Main, the Hermitage or the Mohawk or the National Club. There he sipped a brutal pilsener brewed south of town and simply listened inconspicuously. He listened to miners off shift, stock speculators, tinhorns, and an occasional manager or foreman. They all bellied democratically up to the long bars to wash away the grit of Goldfield.

He whiled away hours that way, utterly unnoticed, a medium sized man, bland-faced, vaguely scholarly, usually slightly rumpled. All about him he saw the gold fever and resisted it. Mad fools lost fortunes, plunged wildly on barren holes, succumbed to rumors, scrambled after frauds. He spent an hour listening to a glib, gifted scalawag named Jones, who barely knew quartz from limestone but had a long list of hot properties he was promoting. It all taught him something useful.

He tried hard not to think about the past and who he had left behind, and the secure, rewarding life he once possessed almost as a birthright in Madison. He agonized about Melanie. Some nights he could barely stand to be alone in his bed, so much did he yearn to talk with her as they always had, share the day, worry about the children, caress, and sometimes make gentle love in the deep peace of a midwestern night.

This new life, he thought, was a sort of infidelity but at least he hadn't deserted Melanie. He had left her with funds. Everything about this adventure had the aspect of a last chance. The mining frontier was dying except for this final efflorescence in the unexplored wastes of Nevada. He knew in his bones Goldfield would be the last of the great mining camps and when Goldfield died, so would an era.

Old Tinsley, his department chairman, had granted him an indefinite leave readily enough but with a strange shake of the head. Dash had said, simply, that he wanted to do some nonferrous mining research, a proposition which sounded cockeyed to the geology faculty in a state with few minerals and fewer mines.

Then, one evening, as he dawdled at the Hermitage bar, he watched a self-important oaf named Arbuckle trade his Golconda for a mug of beer, and Hannibal Dash knew his chance had arrived.

CHAPTER 4

························

The trouble with Maude was that she just didn't understand how hard Harry worked. It was a grievance that Harry Arbuckle brought to mind over and over, especially when he was in a sulky mood. She had no idea what it meant to carve a hole in living rock or how much the desert heat or cold sapped a man's strength. He needed rest, not nagging.

He liked it best when she headed for Goldfield to scrub clothes or cook at the Peerless Café because then he could do whatever he felt like doing. He liked it second-best when she put a packsaddle on Mother Dear and headed for the mountains for firewood. They couldn't afford to buy any from the Paiute Indians who sold it by the burro-load around town so she got it herself. He would watch her tall, skinny, work-worn figure vanish and know he would enjoy some peace.

He didn't know why he had ever gotten hitched. She was sort of pretty once, but not now. She had a narrow face that looked like it had been chopped from lake ice and hair the color of ashes.

Right now she was doing something or other in their tent-roofed dugout. The darned woman had the gold fever and not an ounce of sense in her skull. This claim wouldn't ever produce much but she had notions that it might. The ten-dollar-a-ton assay was a joke. It cost thirty a ton just to haul it to a smelter. You couldn't give this stuff away. You needed hundred-a-ton ore, not this worthless rusty quartz. But she got it in her head that they'd strike it rich if he just kept digging deeper.

The shaft had been sunk five feet, low enough so he could hide from her, yet peer over the lip to see what she was up to. She was always scrubbing and sweeping their canvas-roofed hut as if it mattered whether it was clean or not. Whenever she swooped in his direction he got busy and began hammering on his dulled steels, pretending to drill a hole that he could load with dynamite. Fortunately, the glory hole was just far enough from their shack so she couldn't hear whether or not he was hammering. That meant he could read his detective story magazines between furtive glances in her direction.

She emerged once in a while and beelined toward the hole, trying to catch him unawares. But she never did. This time, right in the middle of a triple-murder bloodbath, he spotted her black skirts clouding up his light and swiftly jammed his magazine under his jacket. When she arrived he was diligently banging on a steel that had penetrated about eleven inches.

"We'll never hit ore if you just read that detective magazine all day," she said, resignation in her words. "We've been here months and you've driven the shaft four dinky feet."

"Five feet."

"It should be twenty. That's where the gold is."

"How do you know?"

"Why, that's how it was at the Jumbo. There was gold right in the roots but when they got down fifty feet they'd already taken out two hundred thousand dollars."

"It wasn't that much and it wasn't the Jumbo," he retorted testily. The woman didn't know anything. "And this is still ten-dollar ore. We ought to sell this hole. There's plenty of pilgrims around. Let someone else pound his brains out for nothing."

She pushed a wisp of gray hair off her forehead. "Harry Arbuckle, you quit too easily. We're going to strike it rich—if you'd just get busy. We're a few rods from the Sandstorm and look what that's doing. If the ore's there, then it's here too."

Arbuckle laughed derisively.

"I have to get firewood. When I get back I want to see all the holes drilled. Some miner you are, taking weeks to drill one little hole."

"We don't have enough money to buy giant powder anyway, Maude. What's the rush?"

"You just drill, Harry."

"I work hard and you know it."

It was her turn to laugh. She had a cackle like a parrot. She didn't know what it was like to get old. He was over forty already and so stove up he doubted he could work another year. Arthuritis, he called it. Romantic arthuritis.

She glared down at him from above. "If you don't start digging, Harry Arbuckle, I'll dig it myself. You can rustle a living like I do. See how much fun it is to earn two dollars a week cooking."

Her threat paralyzed him. He discovered something new in her tone. "Don't get your back up, Maude. We'll sell it. Cash in."

She eyed him pensively. "Get out of that pit, Harry, and take that dirty detective magazine with you. I'm going to drill and you're going to take Mother Dear and cut firewood so we can eat. You're going to cook and keep house. You're going to wash dishes at the Peerless while I dig."

He stared at her aghast. She stood above him, putting him at a disadvantage. Marital spats should be conducted on level ground, he thought. She was being unfair to him. He peered up at a skinny bundle of wrath perched over him like a starving vulture.

"All right, try it," he jeered, gathering courage. "You'll see. It's a man's work."

"That's why you can't do it," she retorted. She motioned toward the homemade ladder. "Out."

Reluctantly he gathered his jumper and the magazine under it, and clambered up the pole ladder. The moment he stood in the desert sun, with familiar old Columbia Mountain off to the south, she descended the ladder and began hammering that steel, expertly rotating it between each blow.

Sinking a shaft was the hardest and most miserable task in mining but that didn't faze her. He watched her rhythmic swings and listened to the ring of hammer on steel. It made him testy that she was trying to shame him. She'd done this before and he was getting weary of it.

She'd be out of there in ten minutes. He grinned and meandered back to the shack, knowing he could read for a while without being nagged to death for it.

Crazy woman really thought she'd strike gold. He laughed cynically. Last he heard in town, around fifteen hundred claims had been filed in the district. And how many really produced? He figured maybe a dozen good ones and fifty poor ones. Besides, a small operator never had a chance. Let a claim show some real color and all those big mucketymucks would steal it. It wasn't any use. He should just pick up and head for Los Angeles. Start an orange grove. All you had to do was hire some bums to pick oranges for a few weeks every year.

That blamed woman. He wondered why he'd ever married her. It was the flesh, that's all. A young buck hankers for the flesh and he's trapped for life. He gets to sparking a girl and his thinking stops cold. She'd kept house for him all those years, and he had to admit she was good at it. There was always some chow or something, and his clothes were mended. But she sure was a nag.

The clang of steel on steel drifted gently through the cool autumnal day. He smiled. She'd wear out soon enough. The steels had dulled. He would have to take them into town and have the smith put a tempered edge on them. But how would he pay the smith?

She never quit. The rhythmic melody of her hammering continued without pause, a half hour and then an hour, making him itchy. He'd go to town for a beer. He hunted through the shack looking for some change she might have squirreled away. He poked in the Harvest Queen flour tin and the sugar jar. He probed under their canvas cots and dug through the ashes in the stove. Consarned woman. Somewhere she had some coin. She always had grocery money. She kept back a little whenever she was paid. But she kept shifting the hiding places.

He refused to go get wood. It meant walking for miles, cutting dead limbs and packing them on the burro. It wasn't a man's work but somebody had to do it or she would be serving him cold chow. Why didn't she tend to business, anyway? He was tired of her beans. The water jug was running low. Consarned woman.

Well, maybe he'd find a pal in town who'd buy him a Schlitz. He sure could use one. He could just see that cool foam dribbling down the side of a crockery mug and taste the good bitter flavor as it slid down his parched gullet. Give a man a couple of beers and a few chums to talk with and life was tolerable as long as there weren't any women around.

He wondered whether to hitch that starvation burro to the wagon or just walk. He eyed Mother Dear, whom Maude had picketed out in the greasewood as if the beast would eat it, and decided against the wagon. He figured he'd better hoof it even though it was an hour hike. If he took the wagon she'd expect him to return with something in it—like firewood. There was no satisfying her. Let him fetch some firewood and she'd be on his case for not bringing water. Let him spend fifty cents in a saloon and she'd complain that the money was intended for potatoes or Fels Naptha.

He wondered whether to scrape away the three-day stubble on his cheeks and decided against it. That'd use up the water and she'd make a legal case of it. Arbuckle scratched graybacks under his red union suit, hoisted his suspenders so his ragged britches wouldn't land on his toes, and set off for Goldfield where a man could find solace among men.

CHAPTER 5

....

Maude watched Harry shuffle toward Goldfield where he would try to bum a beer from men who despised him. He had ransacked the shack, as usual, looking for her hoard. He was right about one thing: she kept some cash socked away.

But her cache wasn't in the shack. It was out among the mining supplies where he would never look. For him, the picks and hammers and buckets and ropes were like a nest of rattlesnakes.

Her pa had been right. He'd told her those Arbuckles were a shiftless lot and she was fixing to marry the most shiftless of them all. He'd told her that she'd be supporting Harry all his life and it wouldn't win her any thanks. She hadn't listened. Harry made moon eyes that had her twittering on the veranda swing. She once thought she could reform Harry. A little lovin' and he'd come around. But he was as shiftless at lovin' as he was with everything else. She laughed whenever she thought of it. She didn't mind Harry so much and sometimes she could still summon up a big smile for him. He couldn't help being what he was; he'd gotten it from his folks. There was some good in him somewhere and she was going to ferret it out and nurture it like some hothouse orchid. That was her duty and what she committed herself to when he slipped the thin, gold-plated band onto her ring finger.

Maybe some day they would be rich. When she was a girl she thought she was the plainest thing in Jefferson

County. One day she asked Aunt Etta what good it was to be so homely. Aunt Etta replied that if you couldn't be beautiful you should try to be rich. That was an honest answer. She forgot it when Harry came along, sparking her all the time. He almost made her think she was pretty. But it wasn't long after her wedding that she remembered it and never forgot it again.

She pulled aside the old tarp that covered the mining gear and found the burlap sack full of good drilling steels. These she dragged to the pitiful dimple they had cut into a rhyolite outcrop that had some rust-colored quartz gleaming in it. She had saved her dimes, bought this second set of steels, and had never told Harry about them because he would take them to town and trade them for a few beers. She had waited a long time for this day: finally she had everything needful to begin shaft-work in earnest. There was gold down there. She had dowsed it. Her divining stick had tugged downward right there so she knew where to dig.

Exultantly she began singlejacking, rhythmically hammering as she turned the Blue Diamond bull steel in the hole. Now and then she paused to lift out the dust and chips with a little spoon on a wire. After she had driven six inches with the bull steel she switched to the second steel, a thirty-second of an inch smaller in diameter but longer. And thus she hammered, switching steels, spooning out dust, until she completed a thirty-inch hole.

She had toiled hard all her life. Her wiry body responded easily to the demand she put on it. She didn't pay any mind to the deepening November cold or the misery of sitting on native rock. She hammered until her arms tired, rested, and hammered some more, driving the steels deeper and deeper. Satisfied at last, she scooped the debris out with the tiny spoon until the hole seemed clean enough to swallow a stick of dynamite.

Sinking a shaft was the toughest part of mining but it had its advantages. She didn't have to hammer uphill or into a vertical face. It took her two hours to finish the hole. Then she threw her steels out of the pit and climbed the ladder. All the steels had dulled. She lacked a forge with which to temper them but she had bought a little grinding wheel that would hone an edge on them. She spent a half hour sharpening each set of steels. She wouldn't let herself rest. She wanted to do the whole thing before Harry returned. She smiled at the thought of what he would find. A mountain of rock to muck out. That shiftless old rascal would see the work he had to do but not the progress toward the gold. She set to work again, resisting the impulse to quit when her shoulder began to protest. Tough as she was, she wasn't used to driving steel with a six-pound hammer hour after hour. Except to suck on some water she'd hidden from him, she never paused until she had drilled the second hole. Debris clogged it and she had a bad time spooning it out. She wished she had a pressure hose to flush out the chips.

The autumnal sun arced far into the west but she sharpened her steels again and set to work on the third hole, the one Harry had started. She cast an occasional glance southward toward Goldfield, looking for a solitary, grimy, paunchy, stubble-cheeked old goose heading her way. But Harry had probably bummed a few drinks and was crowing like a rooster by now. He did it by becoming so annoying that those men bought him a mug just to shut him up. Mooching beers was the only industrious thing Harry had ever done.

She completed her third hole at dusk. Her arms tortured her and her back had stiffened so much she could barely stand but she paid no heed to the excruciating pain. Patiently she spooned and blew the rock dust out of the bore and then stood up, filled with an unfathomable joy. She was ready to fire a round. At a cache fifty yards away she gathered twelve waxy red sticks of Hercules dynamite she had bought from Exploration Mercantile Company, three copper-clad fulminate caps that looked like pencils, and a small coil of Bickford fuse.

Gingerly she toted these things back to the glory hole, her heart racing. She had never done this part before but she knew how. She had hung around prospectors for years in forgotten gulches that never produced. The dynamite was safe enough, she had been told, but the caps could be treacherous. Back at the pit she cut a three-foot length of Bickford fuse and eased the tarry cord into a cap. Then she crimped the fuse in place with pliers, all the while terrified of blowing herself up.

The fuses would have to be long enough for her to scurry up the ladder, pull the ladder up after her, and run. Bickford burned steadily at one foot each thirty seconds and she reckoned she needed a minute and a half. She cut one fuse three feet long; another three and a half feet; another four feet. She would light the longest one first with a spitter—a short length of notched fuse whose sparks would ignite the other fuses—and then light the other two fuses in order.

The next step was even trickier. Gently she sliced into a stick of dynamite until she could peel back the waxy paper that held the gelatinous explosive in the cylinder. She inserted the copper fuse in the opening and bound the stick together with friction tape. Then she spooned rubble from each of the three little holes again so the dynamite would slide in smoothly.

Patiently she pushed unfused sticks into the three holes, using a wooden rod. The dynamite resisted because her holes weren't clean. The tamping scared her but she pushed until the first sticks were all the way in. Then she slowly pushed the fused sticks into place above the bottom sticks using steady pressure, and followed with two more sticks in each hole beside the fuse. She didn't have any muck handy so she emptied some water on the desert to make mud. Then she plugged the remaining inch of hole with it, packing it tightly around the fuse. The little mud plug sealing each hole would contain the explosion momentarily and make it do more work.

Full dark had settled by the time she had loaded the third hole but she scarcely noticed. She worked without a candle, not wanting flame anywhere in the vicinity. The cold bit through her cotton shift but she ignored it. At last three long fuses snaked across the floor of the shaft. She felt around for her tools and hoisted them out of the pit.

She cut a length of fuse that, she hoped, was shorter than the shortest fuse and lit it with an abrasive fuse-starter that showered orange sparks over it. When the spitter was spewing white sparks, she touched it to the longest of her three fuses and waited until it spat sparks. It scared her witless. Her heart pounded so much that her body shook. Then she lit the second, resisting the urge to flee up the ladder. And then the third, which didn't want to catch at first.

She threw the spitter aside and raced up the ladder, missing a rung and clawing her way out. When she reached the top she jerked the ladder out and ran. Behind her the shaft erupted, three distinct thumps, throwing her to earth. She hadn't given herself enough time. A column of rock rose behind as she scrambled away. Chunks whumped around her and one piece stung her hip so much she cried.

She sprawled on the desert, awed by the force she had loosed. She smelled dust and acrid smoke. Rock debris still landed around her but most of it fell back into the shaft. Her ears rang. Something within her gave way and she trembled, too weak to pick herself up and walk to her shack. Night cold clawed her. She felt as if she had been punched in the stomach or thrown fifty feet by some giant hand. But she knew she was all right except for her ringing ears.

For a while she lay on her cot in the shack, too shaken even to peer into the pit. All she could think of was Harry, mooching drinks and trying to occupy the same world as real men. She thought of him in the Hermitage or the National or the Mohawk, wandering around, snatching the free pickles and pretzels, drinking the dregs from abandoned glasses, talking like a nabob, telling the world about his mining prowess while real men laughed behind his back. They knew Harry.

A thought froze her heart. This wasn't her claim; it was his. In the summer of aught-three she had hustled him to the tent town of Goldfield and had him file the claim. What if he sold it now? Or leased it? For a few dollars, a few beers? But of course he couldn't. Not ten-dollar ore. They would laugh at him. Or would they?

The fear drove her crazy. She scratched a lucifer and lit the kerosene lantern, turned the wick down, and replaced the chimney. Her entire body hurt. Then, her heart hammering as she trudged through night to that rank-smelling hole, she edged toward the pit and held the lamp over it. The dust had settled. She saw nothing but a jumble of loose rock, all of which she probably would end up mucking out. She slid the ladder down and descended. The pit reeked of exploded dynamite. She picked up rock at random, tucking the pieces into her lifted skirt, and then climbed out again.

Back in the shack, as she studied the rock in the buttery light of the lantern, she knew she had struck good ore. The rock wasn't just rusty quartz; it was yellow with tiny specks of native gold. Bonanza! She didn't have to scrub men's underwear anymore or clean chamberpots in hotels. She could retire! She should laugh and dance and whoop. But she didn't dare feel happy. She turned the pieces over and over, rubbing and licking the gold and wondering what to do about that danged Harry.

Chapter 6
••••••••••••••••••••

Olympus Prinz, editor, typesetter, and sole proprietor of the weekly *Goldfield Observer*, set down his typestick to accommodate the two gents at the counter.

"Mister Jones and Mister Borden, I believe?" He recognized Jones as the limping gorilla the color of a five-cent cigar; Borden the goose egg with the look of a dissolute monk. This was the pair who ran a bucket shop on Main.

"My friend Prinz, you've got an acute and exotic memory," said Jones. "You'd do well in the investment world with a brain like that. It'll make you rich some day."

"You flatter me, Mister Jones. What may I do for you?"

"We want to run an ad."

"I'm always ready to sell advertising space."

"Well, we're interested in a whole blooming page, maybe the rear one. How much a page?"

"A whole page?" Prinz was piqued.

"We wouldn't think of anything less."

"It's a lot of money. Ah, two hundred dollars. Cash in advance," said Prinz, improving his usual price.

"Only two? We've come to the right place. Now, Prinz, we want to talk turkey here."

Prinz knew the game. They wanted something. "Well, slice the bird and serve it up."

"Just a little thing or two, my friend. We'd like this issue to go out to papers across the Republic. You know, the *New York Herald*, the *San Francisco Examiner*. Do you have exchanges?"

"A few. I send the *Observer* to ten papers in Nevada and California." He waved toward a stack of papers still inside their mailing tubes.

"Well, in this issue we'd like you to think big. I mean *big*. How about a hundred copies to major papers across the country?"

"You want to publicize mining shares, I take it."

"Ah, Prinz, how your light does shine," said Jones. "Not just mining shares. Goldfield! We want to put our sublime little burg on the map. We want to perform a public service. The world needs to learn about Goldfield and its shining lights."

The newspaperman got the drift and nodded cheerfully.

"Now, Prinz," said Jones, brushing cigar ash off his lumpy black just-off-the-shelf gabardine. "Here's the way-bill. A full-page ad placed by the Borden Development Company with stuff on each of our mining corporations. Especially our hottest property, the Queen Cleopatra. And you, my friend, out of civic duty, will make sure this issue reaches major papers across the United States."

"I see. I've a circulation of 870, mostly street sales. Not

bad considering we're up against the daily *Goldfield News* and the town's mostly transients. You want a hundred copies shot out upon the ether. Especially the financial ether. Including Wall Street, no doubt. A little national advertising.''

''Well, yes, that's the general idea, my friend,'' said Jones, gnawing on the stub of a cigar. ''Especially Wall Street. And San Francisco. Now there's a little favor you could do us as well.''

''There usually is for a full-page ad.''

Jones smiled beatifically. ''You're an understanding man, Prinz. Good Teutonic intelligence. We'd like a story about the Goldfield mines. How the town is prospering. How bright the future looks. Nothing but blue sky. A simple matter. A few facts and figures. Why, in 1904, five millions of gold will depart these precincts.''

The figure startled Prinz. ''Where'd you get that? We've got only four big mines. Show me some figures.''

Sam Jones clamped his lips around his stogie and squinted. ''Look, Prinz. It's there. Lots of highgrade ore coming up by the hour, three hundred dollars the ton and better. So good they're only shipping the best, stockpiling the rest for the railroad. By the end of the year it'll top five million easily. This is no camp; this here's a metropolis, the Gotham of the West, the Rome, Paris, Athens and Sioux City of Southern Nevada. A thousand people a month flooding in.''

''Well, supply me with checkable figures from the mines and if they pan out I'll write it up.''

''Look, Prinz, we've all got to give Goldfield a push. The whole world pines for a new bonanza worse than the Second Coming. Have they heard of Goldfield in Davenport or Little Rock? Of course not. It's up to us to tell them the good news. We're the apostles of moolah. The Boodle Boys. We'd like the Borden Company to be mentioned, of course. We've been bringing in the bacon. Without our capital, Goldfield would hardly exist. We believe in the future.''

Prinz smiled. "I wouldn't be here if I didn't believe in Goldfield's future."

"Ah, you're talking sense. We'll slide you a few shares of the Queen Cleopatra."

"No, I don't accept gratuities for news stories. Now, you get your production figures together . . ."

Jones frowned. "Prinz, don't you want that ad?"

"Badly."

"Well?"

"I want my weekly to be believed. That's all I have going for me, Mister Jones. Truth, accuracy. With a weekly I have the time to sort things out. The dailies don't."

"Now, Prinz, you're reading something into this that just isn't there. No one's asking you to wax the woodwork. Just put the story of Goldfield in the most favorable light you can."

"I always do. I've never yet failed to. In the seventeen issues of the *Observer* you'll not find a story that puts Goldfield in a bad light."

"Well, then, take our word for it—based on confidential talks with several financiers. There'll be five millions of gold above-ground by year's end," Borden said.

"Whom shall I quote?"

"Why, quote me," said Borden. "I can't reveal my sources. You know that. Business is business."

"The most recent Carson Mint figures for refined gold from this district are well under two million," said Prinz implacably. He snatched at a Treasury report he had received only that week. "Here. It's in here."

"Of course. They can only report what they've received, not what's at the mine heads; not what's en route to the mills. Now, Prinz . . ."

"Two million. I'll be delighted to say that. In its first year of large-scale mining, the Goldfield district will produce over two million in gold, according to Mint figures. And more—I'll say the town has great promise."

The two wildcatters glanced at each other and seemed to come to a conclusion. "Yeah, well, Prinz, I guess we'll run the ad in the *News*," Jones said. "We prefer to work with men of vision; men who see the real future of Goldfield."

Prinz nodded and watched them leave. The odor of cigar lingered.

It had been a temptation.

He studied the letters he'd stuffed into the typestick, trying to recover his thread of thought. He hoped to buy a Mergenthaler Linotype soon. But he doubted he would be publishing a paper for long if he chased advertisers away.

It was his old stubbornness again. He didn't know where it came from. Maybe his father's Austrian honor. Maybe his mother's Greek courage. Maybe his Stanford schooling in philosophy. Maybe his own perversity. Whatever its source, it was bound to keep him poor. But he was young and he had a sardonic streak and an occasional comic insight. If Goldfield didn't want his wares, he could become a drunken poet, or a letter-writer for illiterates, or a Western Union messenger, or translator of German, Greek, French and Spanish, all languages he knew. His father was a professor of European history at Stanford. Olympus had grown up in Palo Alto amid words if not much money.

The scrupulous weekly wasn't much appreciated in a boomtown in which everyone was itching to make a buck. Most of his readers were miners, but he was going to scorch them sometime for stealing from the mines. Then he'd probably fold up, a victim of his own perverse nature. He sure wasn't in wicked Goldfield for the gold. He was in it because it was the crassest place on earth. Where better to publish a newspaper?

Still, he hadn't lacked for advertisements. The support had come from small businesses. He solicited ads from the assayers he knew were honest and rejected ads from the ones who were merely fences for stolen gold. He had acquired some regulars: merchants like Drabnick, Dunn and Co.; tailors like Franz Petz; the Esmeralda Shoe Store, Downer Brothers Assayers, Union Feed Stables, the Mohawk Saloon, Esmeralda Coffee and Tea Company, the Pearl Restaurant, the Main Street Grocery and Bar, and

Friedman's Ready to Wear. He'd rejected ads from certain saloons in the blossoming restricted district. Let them promote their vices in other ways.

And let the Borden Development Company swindle innocents by other means. Not with material reprinted from the *Observer*. He'd seen crooked promotions in papers all over the country, some of it exchange material reprinted from the papers in western bonanza towns, usually with the names of brokerages prominently displayed in the stories. Bait for suckers: widows seeking security, retired policemen hoping to stretch out a thin pension, and yes, even shrewd businessmen who lost their balance when they heard about gold mines.

He set to work on his front page again. He didn't try to compete with the daily paper when it came to breaking news. Instead, he examined one subject at a time on his pages. Last week he had discussed the need for a railroad. But unlike the town boomers at the *News*, he had explored at length the risk to the capitalists in bringing a railroad to Goldfield. No one really knew whether the gold would run out before a rail line earned a profit.

That's how he was: serious—when he wasn't being a humorist.

He liked it that way. He felt he was putting a good education to use. Since he couldn't escape his upbringing, maybe he could flaunt it a little. He believed in reason. He had a deep intuition that by approaching issues seriously, discussing all the pros and cons, he would do Goldfield—and the world—some good. And show all those Americans with names like Jones that a man with a funny foreign name might give something of value to the country he loved.

CHAPTER 7

·····················

Maude Arbuckle despaired. The claim belonged to Harry. He could do whatever he wanted.

She lay on her tick feverishly weighing options. But there weren't any. In the morning he'd wander over to the pit and discover a pile of shattered rock in its bottom—rock that glinted with yellow. Then what?

She wondered how much gold she had blown loose. Maybe even a hundred dollars' worth. It awed her. She was rich! They would have it assayed and find out just what they had. Maybe she could mine it herself. She was just as good as any man and she could drive that shaft down all by herself. But she knew Harry, and she knew that he would swiftly parade his ore samples from one end of Goldfield to the other, order beers for everyone, get a barber to shave him, and brag about his genius. She wished desperately she could hobble Harry like a horse for a few weeks; wished he would give her the mine; wished he would just listen to her for once.

Maybe he would change. Maybe the promise of abundance, comfort, the good life, would nudge him toward a better nature. Maybe he might even care about her a little or thank her for all she'd given him over the years. Maybe he'd be grateful. After all, she'd done it all: located the claim, dug the pit, found the rich ore. Maybe he'd remember her, hug her, tell her the words she had never heard . . . *I owe everything to you, sweet Maudie.*

She resolved at last upon the only course open to her: when he returned she was going to tell him everything, quietly and completely, and lay out the options and dangers. They were partners. Now they could start over because the world would be more generous and their life less desperate.

But to think it was to know the foolishness of it. Harry

Arbuckle had no senses to come to, and anyway, he was contrary. If she made a suggestion he would go out of his way to do the exact opposite. Oh, that miserable, lazy, shiftless bum! A despair thickened in her.

As she was suffering on her tick, Harry meandered in. She smelled beer on his breath.

"You've been drinking," she said.

Harry snorted.

She sat up, pulled on her wrapper and lit the kerosene lamp. Harry stared at her. He pulled off his shoes, releasing noxious fumes.

"Put your shoes back on," she said.

He grunted and began lowering his britches.

"Look at this, Harry," she said, holding out a chunk of rusty quartz with a distinctly yellow sheen.

He finished removing his britches, which she had mended again and again, and squinted at her in his red longhandles. Finally he took the rock, eyeing it with increasing interest. "Where'd you get that?"

"Harry, we're rich."

"On ten-dollar ore? You're up to something, Maude. You stole that from somewheres."

"It's not ten-dollar ore anymore."

"You been holding out on me, woman?"

"Harry. I drilled some holes and fired a round."

"You what?" He gaped at her. "You're cracked, Maude. You expect me to believe that? You aren't telling me true. What are you hiding from me?"

"I bought the steels and dynamite. I singlejacked all day. I ground new edges with a grinding wheel. My arms hurt so much they're ready to fall off."

She grabbed the lantern and headed into the night while he barefooted along behind.

"You was holding out on me. You was holding back. You wasn't fair and square. I never knew we had a grinding wheel."

She shrugged. "You didn't look. I've had it a month. All you did was read dirty detective stories."

"Don't you go making accusations. I ain't been sneaking around like you, holding back money I need."

She sighed. He would have drunk up every cent if he had known about it. They reached the pit and she held the lantern over it. Pinpoints of yellow glinted up from the shattered rock below.

"If you expect me to muck all that out you can guess again, Maude. You messed up my work real good. I had a hole mostly drilled."

She didn't reply. She watched him pick up rock debris that lay all about and study it in the lamplight, turning it this way and that to pick up the glints.

"By God, that's gold! I can see it. I'm rich. My claim, it's a corker," he bleated. "I allus knew it'd pay."

The truth was that he never believed it would pay anything. He'd told her so more times than she could remember. In town tomorrow he'd boast of how he'd clawed his way down to pay rock.

"Maybe *we* should get it assayed first," she said, fighting back tendrils of fear.

"Assayed! I got friends that can eye that ore, give it a lick of the tongue, and tell me what she runs better than any assayer in the district—and for free, too. Those assayers are just a bunch of crooks. I could sell this claim for five thousand dollars right now and I'd be on easy street."

It horrified her. "Sell it, Harry? Now?"

He glared at her. "Of course. Find some sucker and unload it fast before they figger out it's just a surface pocket."

"But Harry, you don't know if it's a big strike—"

"Don't you but me. I know how to play this game. I seen it day after day in town. I'll get five grand outa this, easy."

"But Harry, we could lease it. You know, like the other claim owners. That way, if it pans out we'll get a quarter of everything. That's how the big operators do it."

"I'm not letting anyone near the place. I'd just get cheated. Town's fulla sharpers, Maude. You know what they do to little guys."

"Harry, this could be worth millions, not five thousand dollars. For Lord's sake . . ."

He hefted a piece of ore and squinted at it wisely. "I know what I'm doing. This here's twenty-five, thirty-dollar-a-ton ore. Shows some promise—enough so I can get some of them orange groves."

Maude shuddered. "Harry . . . don't you dare sell out. We'll get this assayed tomorrow."

"This here's *my* mine, not yours. Now quit nagging."

Harry retreated to the shack and began dressing again. He hoisted his britches and tied his shoes while she watched in agony. He found an old burlap sack and retreated into the darkness. She watched him load ore.

"Don't wait up for me and don't you breathe a word of this. If I catch you sneakin' off to some assayer, givin' my game away, I'll—you'll be sorry."

"Harry, there's a good assayer, Alfred Held. An honest man. His shop is on Fifth Avenue. Most of the big outfits go to him."

"You stay outa it."

"Harry, promise me one thing: don't sell out tonight."

"I won't promise you a thing. If I get a good offer—"

"You don't even know what we've got!" she yelled.

He ignored her and pulled on his jumper against the sharp desert cold.

"This is the last time you'll ever nag me," he said, malice in his eyes. "I was a damn fool to marry you. I'd be a damn fool to keep you after all them years of suffering your bad mouth. You never had a kind word for Harry Arbuckle."

"Harry—we did this together," she pleaded. "Now we can live in comfort. There'll be enough money for both of us. We'll be happy. We'll enjoy life and nothing'll get us down. It'll be like we walked through the pearly gates. Harry, don't you see? It's not the mine, it's the happiness . . . it's the happiness."

She watched him trudge into the night toward the distant blur of golden light across the desert. It was probably ten o'clock. He'd be there by eleven, the shank of the evening in any of Goldfield's bustling saloons. Ten minutes after that half of Goldfield would know about Harry's strike.

Sorrow welled up in her, a sadness she couldn't fight. It had all been for nothing. Her body hurt and she lay upon her cot aching. She fought back tears. Self-pity never solved anything. Eventually she calmed herself and tried to think things through. She would need to act swiftly before Harry threw it all away. She resolved to get up at dawn, get some samples and have them assayed, all before Harry woke up. Then she would talk to some of the leasing companies. If the assay looked good she would have no trouble finding a lessee. She knew who to talk to: the men who were leasing the Jumbo or the Florence. If they weren't interested maybe they would give her some names. She could find lessees who had capital and experience and let them develop the strike—if Harry didn't throw it all away in town tonight.

CHAPTER 8

· · · · · · · · · · · · · · · · · · · ·

Harry Arbuckle turned into Myers Avenue in search of a certain assayer located on the corner of Second Street, not far from the sporting district. There were reputable assayers in Goldfield but the man Arbuckle wanted to see was not one of them. This one did business at any hour, obliging miners who wanted quick cash.

Most of these predators smelted the ore in their crude assay labs and paid the client half its worth the following day. But this particular one would pay cash immediately. Of course, it would only be a quarter of the estimated worth but where else could you get cash on the spot?

Arbuckle found the false-fronted place easily. Lamplight leaked from opaque window curtains. The barely visible sign above simply said ASSAY. He paused outside the door, plucked a few samples of the ore from the bag, slid them into the pockets of his ragged jumper, and entered. A cowbell jangled. A stubble-jawed bald man in gray longjohns and black britches materialized from a curtained area.

"Like this assayed confidentially. It's pretty fancy ore," said Arbuckle, with a knowing inflection.

"It usually is," the man rasped.

The man tumbled the ore onto a balance scale and added brass weights to the opposing pan until he had achieved balance while Harry watched suspiciously.

"You've nine pounds and three ounces here. I'll run it in the morning and pay half its worth tomorrow," the man said. "You want a receipt?"

"I want money now."

The man grunted. Lamplight slid off his gleaming skull. He pulled some wire spectacles over his ears and studied a rock, muttering. "I don't know. Never seen this before. Is it from around here?"

"I'm not saying. Lots more where it came from," Arbuckle boasted.

The assayer surveyed other pieces with a magnifying glass. "Some gold's visible—gives it that yellow cast. Have to assay it. That's rhyolite gangue. This isn't from any mine in the district that I know of. Unless it's from the Sandstorm. Maybe the Kendall."

"What'll you give me?" Arbuckle asked, impatiently.

The man peered into the darkness. "Oh, five dollars."

"A lousy five dollars?"

"Mister, that's fifty cents a pound. You figure it out."

Arbuckle did, stunned at the richness of the ore. The assayer was betting the ore would run two dollars of gold to the pound. Something swelled within him. "Lots more where that came from," he repeated. "Bet you wish you knew."

"What'd you say your name is?"

"Harry Arbuckle. And you'll be hearing more of me soon."

"Well, Harry, here's half an eagle. Bring me more." The

assayer dropped the tiny gold piece into Arbuckle's sweating hand. "We'll do business, yah?"

"Maybe, if you treat me special," Arbuckle said. He grinned toothily at the assayer and plunged into the night. A few doors south the red haze of the tenderloin beckoned but he turned toward Crook Street and headed for the Hermitage Saloon. Oh, this would be a night! Now they would know who Harry Arbuckle was. A man deserved a little blue sky after being stuck all his life with a woman about as cuddly as a spiked fence. Now they would talk about Harry Arbuckle.

He turned into the Hermitage and paused, savoring the oil lamps, crystal chandelier, brass spittoons, brass foot rail, lithographs of Thoroughbreds and boxing champions on the walls, and the long, polished bar with four mixologists serving up iced drinks or beer. Roulette, chuck-a-luck and faro layouts crowded the back, each presided over by a tinhorn in a tuxedo, the pretty serving girls in white blouses and black skirts. This here was a respectable place and Harry Arbuckle was a respectable man.

He slid between a pair of stiffs from the pits who were sucking draft beers and motioned to the nearest bartender.

"What'll it be, Harry," the man asked warily.

"A beer for the whole house—on Harry Arbuckle."

The man behind the dimpled cherrywood hesitated. "Well, Harry—"

"It's all right. I'm richer than Solomon. Here," Arbuckle said, thrusting the little coin at him. "That'll buy forty beers."

The mustachioed barkeep surveyed the crowd and nodded. "I guess you got lucky, Harry."

"I'm right up there with Al Myers and Taylor and Wingfield and all them," said Arbuckle. "A shrewd investment can pay off."

The two miners beside him watched. "Izzat Harry Arbuckle buyin' us one-bit beers?" asked one.

"You have to know what you're doing," Arbuckle replied. "Prospecting's tricky. Beers for the house."

That finally galvanized the bartender. He recruited two of his colleagues and began drawing mugs.

"Tell 'em it's on Harry Arbuckle," he directed. "Be sure to say it's on Harry."

They did and gradually the crowd collected around Arbuckle, men he'd bummed from for months.

"There's lots more where it came from," he announced. "Don't forget old Harry Arbuckle." He extracted two ore samples from his pockets and passed them to the nearest miners. "Have you ever seen ore like that? What do ya think she runs?"

One by one, the habitués of the Hermitage studied the ore, licked it, scratched it with fingernails, held it up to lamplight.

"That's some ore, Harry. It's not from any mine around here," said one.

"It'll run four thousand a ton," Arbuckle said.

"Baloney," someone shouted.

Arbuckle chuckled knowingly, letting them all know he was privy to certain facts. He certainly had excited them. For the first time in his anonymous life he was the cynosure of all eyes. Everywhere around him stood work-grimed stiffs with foaming beer mugs in hand, his largesse, eyeing him with wonder or skepticism.

A weathered man in a salt-and-pepper suit and wilted white shirt pushed through the crowd, one of the ore samples in hand. "Mister Arbuckle," he said, "where did this come from?"

"A certain claim," Arbuckle said coyly. It was the first time anyone had ever called him mister.

"I know the ore of every mine in this district but this is new to me. The closest thing to it is the Sandstorm. Is it local?"

"I didn't mine it in Peru," Arbuckle joked.

The man didn't laugh. "I'm a geologist. I'm interested in your claim, either buy or lease. Name's Dash. I'm looking for good properties."

"I'm not selling."

That didn't faze the man. "Well, I'm not buying—not without some assays. I'll need a good look at the property. After that—why, we might bargain. I'd like you to show it to me tomorrow."

Arbuckle gazed serenely upon a sea of faces, miners, workmen, gamblers, serving girls, bartenders, speculators, harnessmakers, blacksmiths . . . and the sight intoxicated him. They were seeing Harry Arbuckle doing big business instead of sitting around mooching drinks. He lifted his own mug and sipped happily, determined to enjoy it to the hilt.

"Well, I'm not sure I even want to tell you where she is. A man can't be too careful."

A flash of disgust crossed Dash's face. "I have references. You'll learn all you need to know. Here. Take my card. Do a Dun and Bradstreet."

Harry didn't have the faintest clue what that was but he nodded approvingly.

"You mind if I keep this ore? I'd like to run an assay."

"No, I'll do my own assays, thankee," Arbuckle said. He wasn't going to be outfoxed by some city slicker.

Something seemed to change in the geologist. He surveyed Harry with shrewd eyes. "If it's a claim you've located, I'll pay you a thousand cash for it right now, sight unseen."

"Why, you don't even know what claim," Arbuckle said, cunningly.

The man sighed. "It'll be registered. If you haven't claimed your ledge you probably should before half the people in this place beat you to it."

"Oh, it's filed, all right. Corners marked, assessment work done. You bet!"

"Well then, I'll visit you tomorrow . . . unless you want to sell it now. I'll write a contract and pay you right here. Would ten hundreds do?" The persistent geologist pulled a roll of bills from his pocket and peeled off ten of them, fanning them on the bar.

The crowd turned silent. A thousand dollars was a year's pay for most men.

Arbuckle looked around him fearfully. He'd never seen a thousand dollars before. For a lot less some of those watching him would knock him on the head when he walked home. "That's not enough," he said.

"Only a fool would buy a pig in a poke," the geologist said blandly. "Flashing some ore to sell a worthless claim is the oldest con in the mining camps. But I don't know this ore. You didn't get it from any mine in the district. That's the only reason I'm risking a lot of money."

"I know what you're up to. Trying to knock down the price. You can't pull a fast one on Harry Arbuckle."

The man smiled. "I tell you what, Mister Arbuckle. You agree to let me run those samples through my assay lab, and give me a one-year option to buy your claim for five thousand, and I'll give you that thousand tonight. We'll draft a little agreement right here on the bar."

Five thousand dollars. Harry Arbuckle could scarcely believe it. He blinked dizzily at the man. "An option?"

"To buy it. This is the first thousand. I'll be out there tomorrow." The man handed Arbuckle the ten bills. "I'll write it up on this pad and we'll sign the two copies and have it witnessed by a few people here. We certainly have witnesses, don't we?"

A few minutes later Arbuckle painfully scrawled his name, Dash added his, and three customers and a barkeep added theirs. Arbuckle tucked his copy of the handwritten contract into his coat. He could hardly believe it. Any time between now and December 1, 1905, Dash could pay the remaining four thousand and own the claim.

Arbuckle fingered the crisp greenery in his hand. One thousand simoleons and he'd get four grand more from that sucker. That sounded like orange groves. Meanwhile he had more money in hand than he had ever seen in his life.

"Set 'em up for the house," he yelled. "Set 'em up if you can break this hunnert. It's on Harry tonight."

CHAPTER 9

....

Harry stood, weaving slightly, in the golden light of the kerosene lamp, barely containing whatever news he possessed.

"I guess you think I don't know how to deal," he said.

"I never said that." A dread suffused her.

"Well, I'm rich. Lookit this!" He dug into his jumper and extracted a wad of bills. He fanned them out. She had scarcely seen a bill with two zeros before. There were nine of them. "One thousand simoleons," he purred. "One thousand shekels. I spent a little."

The dread deepened in her. He had sold a priceless mine for nothing. "Oh, Harry . . ."

"There you go. I knew it. I can't do anything right." He glared at her, set the century notes down, and slowly extracted a piece of note paper. "This here's an option. I don't suppose you know what that is."

She knew. She nodded dumbly, waiting for the rest of the nightmare to unfold.

"Some sucker offered me a year option to buy the claim for five grand. I got a thousand just for signing. I can go to Los Angeles and buy them orange groves."

"But Harry, what if it's worth—"

"There you go, nag, nag. I thought of that. What do you take me for, some idiot? I know what I'm doing. Lissen here. This sucker's gonna come out for a look-see tomorra. That's fancy ore, all right. He took one look and began peeling off the bills. But a little highgrade don't make a mine. I jist hope there's enough good stuff in the hole so's this sucker forks over. Otherwise, we've got to sell it again."

A bleakness settled on her. "Harry, you've thrown away our one chance. You . . ." She checked herself. She was going to say she had dug that hole herself. Her arms still ached and she had a bilious stomach.

"I'm rich, that's what."

"Who is this man?"

"Dash. He's some dude in a suit coat. He thought he could slicker me. He claimed he was some fancy geologist but that was just part of the line he was mouthing. He was just some slicker trying for an easy buck. I could see greenhorn written all over him. The whole camp's full of those suckers."

Maude could barely contain her nausea. "I want you to give him back the money and tell him the deal's off. I'm going to dig it deeper. We're going to get some assays. We're going to find out what we have. You just keep him off the place. I'll muck this out and drill another round and then we'll see. If it's just a little pocket then you can sell it."

He glared at her. "Five thousand dollars is more money than I ever seen in all my life. Five times more'n my pa's farm was worth. It fetches me a big, fancy orange grove. All I gotta do is hire some bums to pick the fruit. It buys me a nice climate, not this hellhole. You have no say in it. It's *my mine.* I'm going to get out of this cactus patch and go where it's nice. Anyway, the deal's done. You can't change it now."

She wasn't so sure about that. "When is he coming?"

"Tomorra."

"What's he going to do?"

"Look at the hole and decide whether to buy or not."

"He's not sure?" A ray of hope filled her.

"Don't worry, I'm not that dumb," he said. "It'll be cash on the barrelhead."

"But Harry . . ." She sank into her cot and pulled the ragged blanket around her. For almost a year she had toiled and scraped here, always with the hope of a bonanza. Gold would make up for life with Harry. She wondered why she had stayed with him. She had always known it would turn out like this. Harry would get his five thousand, not give her a dime of it, and squander it away buying drinks. There wouldn't be any orange groves.

She had supported him for years. When he wouldn't farm, she eked out a living with eggs and sewing and laundering. When they lost the mortgage she had traded the few things they had left for some camping gear and a few tools, and headed for Nevada where a patient prospector could still find a ledge or a bonanza. While they roamed the desert camps, she cooked and cut wood and waited tables to keep them alive. Without her he would have starved to death a hundred times.

It was the same here. He had not loosened two bushels of rock the whole time. She'd done all the rest—dishwashing and cooking in town, sewing, laundering, all for a few buffalo nickels. She could not think of a single time when he'd brought her some cash or relieved her toil or helped her.

She pushed aside bitterness. She had always supposed that bitterness was a useless emotion. Besides, she had always understood Harry's nature.

"Well, Harry, you're predictable," she said. She felt like saying a lot more.

"You should have seen them at the Hermitage," he said. "They gathered around me like flies on meat. I bought 'em a round, the whole place. Old Harry Arbuckle bought a round of beer and suddenly I wasn't—I mean, I never had so many people pump my hand and tell me what a fine fellow I am.

"And when this sucker comes up, why, they winked at me and let me know this greenhorn, he's just there for the plucking. You should've seen 'em grinning. Why, this fellow, he's itchy, the way all those greenhorns are when they see a little yellow in some ore, he's practically panting he wants the claim so bad, sight unseen, and I play him like a big trout. Oh, the boys liked that, the way I played this here pilgrim, always winking and elbowing because they knowed what I was up to."

He was recollecting that moment as if it were twenty-four carat, she thought.

"I reeled him in. I caught the sucker."

She left him there, admiring himself. She couldn't stand it inside the shack. She pushed through the door into the harsh black night, feeling the sting in the November air. It was cleaner than the air inside. She'd built that shack, like everything else, chopping out a slope, laying up walls of earth and rock, adding a wooden frame and canvas over it. All this was hers: that miserable pit, the shack, the supplies. She'd wrested it all from the unyielding desert. And she didn't own a particle of it.

She trudged barefoot down the familiar path to the shaft and peered into its mysterious blackness, wondering what riches lay there unfathomed. Maybe, under that mass of rock, there would be more gold than she could imagine. She could almost feel it there, waiting for her to pluck it out. This was no surface pocket, rich and unfaithful; this was an ore shoot that ran hundreds of feet deep. She didn't know how she knew that but she was sure of it.

For nine years they had drifted from camp to camp, always looking for the one magical ledge. She'd hacked along promising leads that only petered out. She knew gold. She could find it where no one else bothered to look. She could sense gold the way a compass needle sensed north. She had found it here and it could make Harry and her rich as Rockefeller.

She had never asked for much. But she was weary of cooking flapjacks and scrubbing clothes on a Howard washboard. All she wanted was to be free of that. By rights, everything should belong to her, not Harry. She knew in her soul that the rock down there was worth a hundred times five thousand dollars.

She let the hush of the night permeate her. There would be a wisdom out here under the cold black sky, a wisdom she couldn't reach in the rank confines of that shack. She peered anxiously into the bleak heavens seeking some guidance, perhaps from the God who remained a beautiful mystery to her. Whatever it was, maybe just the vastness of the dome of heaven above her, she felt its age-old calm and found herself slowly gaining heart. She needed only heart; no matter what happened, she could survive if she didn't lose heart.

There were things she wouldn't do; she wouldn't argue with Harry. There were things she could do. She could find this buyer and plead with him. She could find a lawyer. This very night she'd squirrel away enough ore to pay a lawyer. Maybe Harry had been drunk when he signed that agreement. There had to be ways to stop all this. The lawyer would know.

There was a lot more. She would get some real assays. She intended to fight this man who'd optioned the mine. She'd do what she could no matter that she was one poor woman and he might be a prince of finance.

Out there in the dark she knew she pitied Harry. He was like a big old lazy dog, his mind so cockeyed that a body could only take pity on him. He was just like his pa, figuring everything cockeyed and blaming the whole world. He wasn't all bad. There were moments, even now, when she saw some affection for her in his eyes; when they had finished a meal and he'd smiled at her. Maybe a little money would improve him.

Most people were pretty nice; she'd met a passel of 'em in the camps, all having the time of their life. If her old Harry could just see that, he'd be fine. He had only two notions between his ears. One was that nothing was ever his fault or responsibility. The other was that everything that happened was because someone was scheming or plotting against him. She'd known coon dogs smarter than that. Meanwhile, she'd look after her old mutt. Every dog deserved his bone and she'd give Harry his. She had gotten hitched for better or worse, richer or poorer, and it had been worse and poorer. But he was still her old Harry and she could still smile at him and mother him when he needed it.

For twenty minutes she shucked ore into the hillside

vault where she'd hidden the dynamite. Then she strolled
back to the shack. It was dark. Harry would be snoring and
exuding stale fumes. Tomorrow she would fight.

She slid into the blackness of the shack, feeling its faint
warmth. Harry wasn't snoring, so he was awake.

"We're going to keep the mine," she said to his back.
"We'll just get rid of that Dash fellow and I'll work it
myself. I'll talk Dash out of it. You don't have to do a
thing, Harry. I'll be glad to. We'll be happy. You'll have
everything you want, Harry."

He pretended not to hear her and she found that satisfying. Usually he got contrary.

Before going to sleep she made a vow to herself not to
lose heart. Once you lost heart they might as well plant you
in the cemetery over yonder, under Malpais Mesa.

CHAPTER 10

Hannibal Dash preferred to run his own assays. That
ensured that he got much more accurate results than if
he had employed any of several assayers in Goldfield. It
also ensured privacy, which was often worth as much as
the information in the assay report.

At the rear of Dash's modest cottage on Ramsey Street
stood his laboratory. Within it he could duplicate, in miniature, every known process of extracting metals, precious
or base, from rock. He could, if he wished, mill the stone
into powder to release free gold through the mercury amalgamation process; or employ the new cyanide process; or
simply smelt it, with or without fluxes. His modern crushing equipment saved him the task of pulverizing rock with
a sledgehammer—a task often relegated to an assayer's
devil, whose principal task was to pound on stone all day.

A great curiosity infused Dash this morning. This rusty
quartz was unique in the district and unknown to him. He

examined the fist-sized lump he had acquired from Arbuckle and weighed it carefully on scales as accurate and sensitive as a jeweler's. Three hours later he had his results; a button of pure gold too hot to touch. With tongs he lifted it from the crucible and set it on an extremely sensitive scale, balancing it with weights calibrated in troy ounces. Then he calculated the weight of the gold as a percentage of the weight of the 29.116-gram sample and stared at his own penciled figures, amazed. The ore ran better than 120 troy ounces to the ton. At $20.67 a troy ounce, the ore would yield about $2,500 a ton.

Dash sat back, pondering the situation. Quite probably he was not the only person in Goldfield who knew how rich the ore was. Arbuckle had traded some ore for spending money, no doubt with one of those quack assayers. He had boasted of his find from one end of the Hermitage Saloon to the other. There would be more than one hound chasing this fox. He had to hurry.

Dash swiftly donned a white shirt and strangled himself inside of a cravat. He slid on his salt-and-pepper suit coat and for good luck slid the cooled gold button into his pants pocket.

Sooner than he ever dreamed possible, he had his chance. But it would take consummate skill to bring it all to fruition. Soberly he considered his modest nestegg. He lacked the capital to develop a mine and would have to find partners. But he had other assets. His stocks in trade were two: his mastery of mining geology and his integrity.

There was yet another trait that had made Dash hopeful of success. He had always been an astute judge of people. Much of what now occupied Dash's mind was the unplumbed mystery of Harry Arbuckle's character. How could a man of such obvious degeneracy strike gold? Dash doubted that Arbuckle had ever done a lick of work he could get out of.

A quick hike took him to the offices of the Goldfield Town Lot Company, where the mining district records were stored along with copies at Hawthorne, the distant seat of

Esmeralda County. It took Dash only a moment to locate Arbuckle's claim on the great wall map of the district. It lay on the northern edge of what had been called the golden horseshoe of claims east of town. The nearest producing mines were the Sandstorm and Kendall, just as he had suspected. Harry Arbuckle's claim lay not far from a good mine and probably on the same ledge. Dash drew himself a small map on scratch paper and stuffed it in his vest pocket.

He observed the filing date with some interest: June 10, 1903. Arbuckle had been one of the early birds, relocating a claim abandoned by Goldfield's discoverers, Harry Stimler and William Marsh. That was promising. Cheerfully, Dash hiked to the livery barn and hired a one-horse rig. He could walk to the Arbuckle claim but it paid to show up in a buggy. He steered the lazy nag northward, using the whip unsparingly to achieve any motion at all, and forty minutes later halted at what he judged to be the boundary.

Nevada law required four-foot cairns on the corners and sidelines of the rectangular claims but Dash saw none. A closer look finally uncovered a small mound of rock, scarcely a cairn at all, at what was probably the southwest corner. The law required more than that: within ninety days of filing on the claim the cairns had to be completed along with other location work.

Dash studied the haphazard rock pile knowingly. Anyone could simply take this away from Arbuckle. The claim was almost certainly void. All one had to do was file on it. He whipped the surly nag into a shambling trot and rode along a faint trace toward the middle of the claim. Against a shallow ledge stood a tent-roofed dugout surrounded by mining junk. At first he saw no sign of any diggings.

As he approached, Arbuckle erupted from the shack, followed by a beaten-down woman. A certain sympathy filled Dash. Anyone hitched to a man like Arbuckle would have to struggle. Something about the pair suggested that they had been fighting.

"It's you," said Arbuckle. "I upped my price. It's seven

thousand now. I know your kind. You jist want to do me out of it.''

"Mister Arbuckle, would you introduce me to your lovely wife?''

"No. You can't git past me by flattering Maude. She ain't got a say anyway; it's mine, not hers.''

She studied him from a face of granite.

"I'm Hannibal Dash. I'm a geologist. I met your husband last night.''

She barely nodded.

"Mister Arbuckle, I have good news for you—if you'd like to hear it.''

Arbuckle scratched himself furiously and squinted up at Dash.

"I ran an assay on the ore you gave me. It's worth over two thousand a ton.''

"Why should I believe you, Dash?''

Dash fought back the disgust. He knew it would be like this. "If I were trying to cheat you I'd have kept that from you. Why don't you run samples with other assayers to confirm my work?''

"Two . . . thousand . . . ?'' said the woman. It was the first time she had spoken. "Oh, no . . .''

"Here are my figures,'' he said. He stepped down from the buggy and handed her his calculations. "You've found some highgrade ore. There's some silver in it, too.''

"What's your game, Dash?'' asked Harry. "Of course I'm rich. I knew that last night. You think I don't know good ore when I see it?''

Dash smiled. It didn't pay to do anything else. "Your claim is a public document. I've an option to buy it. We each have a signed copy. Would you show me the shaft?''

He could see it about fifty yards from the shack.

"No, I ain't gonna.''

"Mister Arbuckle, I have to see what you have here and do some more assays. That's in the agreement.''

"You get outa here. It's my gold. I'm in no hurry.

Maybe someone else'll give me a real deal, not this chicken feed offer.''

"I'm afraid it might not be your claim, Mister Arbuckle.''

That froze Arbuckle.

"I'll wager you didn't do your assessment work within ninety days of filing—and haven't done the additional hundred dollars' worth this year, either. You filed in the summer of 1903. Your shaft should have been sunk ten feet months ago to validate this claim. Your claim is most probably void. Anyone could file on it.''

"You fixing to take it away from me?''

"No, I'm not. I'm going to help you protect it. I hope—if it's not too late and no one else has discovered that it's void—that we can relocate it for you. I tell you what. We can make a deal: I'll lease this claim for the usual twenty-five percent royalty of the value of the shipping ore. Or I can go file on this claim myself. It doesn't belong to anyone.''

"Oh, Mister Dash . . .'' Maude whispered.

They gaped at him, frozen.

"How deep is that hole?'' Dash asked the woman.

"It was five feet. Now it might be eight, mucked out.'' She looked to be fighting back tears.

Dash grunted. "That won't do, will it? Does anyone else know? Where did you get that cash last night, Mister Arbuckle?''

"I ain't saying, Dash. I'm on to your game.''

"Suit yourself,'' Dash said gently. "The ground we're standing on can be taken from you. Maybe someone already has. Probably a hundred people learned about your strike last night. And some of them are going to try.''

The woman seemed to pass through some mental barrier. "Follow me, Mister Dash,'' said Maude. "We'll look at the pit. I dug it. I'll tell you what you need to know.''

"Maude!'' yelled Arbuckle.

But she ignored him. Dash followed her to the little hole bored into the ledge. She had answered one question. He knew now how Arbuckle had come up with valuable ore. She had dug it.

She stopped at the collar and he peered into a pathetic little dimple in the slope, but a dimple half full of shattered rusty quartz that glowed strangely in the morning light. There was plenty of country rock too. He had no inkling what sort of shoot or pocket she had opened but he sensed he was looking at several hundred dollars' worth of high-grade.

"Did you mean what you said about a fair lease?" she asked, her gaze searching him.

"Yes."

"Then I won't fight you. You got that purchase agreement out of a poor, pathetic drunk. I'd fight you tooth and nail in court if you take advantage of it."

He studied her closely, seeing a woman gaunted down to stringy muscle and grit. He liked the look in her eye. Determined, open, feisty, and courageous. She was everything Harry wasn't.

"I think I'm going to enjoy doing business with you, Mrs. Arbuckle."

"I hope I can say the same about you," she shot back with a hint of a smile.

CHAPTER 11

••••••••••••••••••••••••

Big Sam Jones sliced open another envelope with Borden's turk dagger and extracted a check for one thousand dollars.

"Look at this, Windlass. It's enchanting, how people throw money at us."

He opened the letter and read it for Borden's edification. "Dear Sir, I saw your advertisement in the Keokuk paper and I agree. We've got to prepare for old age. My wife and me, we're getting on and there's no one to farm for us.

Lost a boy in the Spanish war. A gold mine is the thing, all right. We put some by and I took it out and am sending it to you. Now, I want you to buy up the best mines in the district, spread it out so I don't have all our eggs in one basket. I heard they're going to pay off better than anything around here a man could sink money into. I know you'll do what's best for the Mrs. and me. Sincerely, Claude Crump, Rural Route One, Keokuk, Iowa."

"This sure beats working for a living," Borden said. "That's seven thousand in today's mail, twenty-six for the week."

"Send them some Molly Brown and a dab of all the rest," Jones said. "Like I told you, it pays to promote."

This boodle had come from ads in Keokuk and Oshkosh. They worked. Next time the Borden Development and Trust Company would place ads in a hundred papers, using the proceeds from this initial effort. "This here's better than a gold mine," Jones said. "Now Windlass, I'm not gonna do this for twenty percent anymore. From now on, she's fifty-fifty after expenses, or I'm going to be your competition."

Borden paused only a second and then nodded. Jones knew he would. In the space of this week alone the Borden Company had garnered more revenue than Borden's efforts to peddle wildcat stocks among Goldfield's denizens over the past year. He had operated too close to home.

"By God, this is the richest mine in Goldfield," Borden said. "When we get really cranked up we'll make ten thousand a day."

"More 'n that," said Jones. "Twenty a day. We've got to tinker some with the ads. We need two or three that really draw. I know how those farmers think. I didn't trade horses for nothing. Lot of 'em, it'll take three successive ads before the message worms through their thick skulls."

In only six weeks, Jones had catapulted from starvation to affluence, and it had barely begun. Goldfield would put him on easy street. Maybe busting a leg wasn't such a bad thing after all. It sure happened when he was least expecting it. A widow lady who said she needed cash to fix a hernia sold him a doped mare that rode as sweet as honey the first time. He gave her a hundred for it. But the next ride, that piebald mare peeled him off and stomped him, busting his knee and his leg in four places and his good humor in five places.

That had ended his life as a horse trader. The widow got her hernia fixed, but the episode had put him in a grouchy mood. He had always figured that only another trader, a sight smarter than he, could do him in. But he got snookered out of business by a specialist in mincemeat pies.

Jones had spent the first weeks trying to get Goldfield on the financial map by appealing to San Francisco and Wall Street capitalists. Men of means weren't biting, although they were sending their minions out to eyeball the mines and the town. Then Jones conceived of the idea of direct advertising in rural papers, avoiding the big-city skeptics altogether.

"An investment in the Molly Brown Gold Mine, of Goldfield, Nevada, is safer and more lucrative than money in a bank," his first ad read. After skimming quickly over the highgrade ore and the development plans of the company, he got right down to the heart of it: "Men and Women labor on farms, in offices and workshops, in mercantiles and factories, dreading the day when the infirmities of age put them out of work. What will happen then? A worker needs a solid retirement plan to see him through.

"The deep reserves and rich dividend potential of the Molly Brown Gold Mine offer security and comfort for those who face the time of retirement with anxiety. Invest in the famous Molly Brown—named after an intrepid and distinguished woman of the West—and secure your future forever.

"You've all heard of Goldfield, the richest bonanza town the West has ever known. The Molly Brown, according to certified geologists, bids fair to become the finest producer of gold the world has ever known, better even than the legendary Esperanza Mine of Mexico. This stock is now being offered at its dollar par value by the Borden Development Company, its underwriters—but hurry. The rich and powerful will soon bid up its price, and those who hesitate will be left standing at the station."

It worked. Before Jones rested a heap of checks and letters from Iowa and Wisconsin. "Windlass, my friend," he announced, "we have a trout on the line the size of a whale. We have a lollypop equal to the combined profits of the Combination, Jumbo, Sandstorm. We are, to say it modestly, rich."

The rest of that day Windlass Borden processed and mailed gilt-edged stock certificates, handsomely engraved with etchings of the unsinkable Molly Brown, crossed flags, the pyramid of Cheops, and a screaming American eagle. At the same time, Jones toted up the loot and prepared ads for papers in Ohio, Indiana, Illinois, Iowa, Kansas, Nebraska, Minnesota, and with some hesitation, Missouri, the Show Me State. He had cash enough for full-page ads in thirty-seven papers, as well as enough projected income to advertise steadily across the nation and pay himself and Borden a thousand dollars a day.

Some of the letters, from people who knew all about Goldfield, requested that the enclosed funds be invested in such successful mines as the Jumbo or the January. Jones resolved to do it—for a brokerage fee of course. Recently, curbside traders had been gathering each evening for some informal trading at the Northern Saloon, operated by the Alaska entrepreneur Tex Rickard. A rudimentary stock market had evolved in Goldfield.

"Windlass," Jones said, "I'll go dicker for stock tonight. We've got to plow some of this back in, like it or not."

"It's a pity," Borden said. "People are perverse."

That was Jones's outlook on the human race also. Long experience at the art of brokering horses had acquainted him with the perversity of human nature. Let a banker or a deacon or an undertaker try to sell him a nag, and half the time it had been galled or windbroke or the seller had failed to inform Jones that the nag couldn't be caught. Let a rube buy a horse and half the time he would pay with a rubber check or want his money back if the horse croaked anytime in the next three years.

All of which had rendered Jones into an alchemist. He had a way with horses and men. He could transmute a wild bronc into a gentle saddler, and turn a sluggard into a race horse, and turn a crippled horse into a prancer, and an old horse into a young one with a little application of file to tooth, soaps, oils, shoe polish, and hypodermic injections. Let a seller shave ten years off the age of a nag and Jones would treat him in kind. Let an oaf trust Jones to sell him a sound horse and Jones would provide a lesson in the art of living.

Jones figured that people got what they deserved: when it came to horse trading, he was the flaming sword of justice. That was a comforting thought: he dealt in justice, not horseflesh. He had seen the worst of human nature—bishops who would soberly tell him that the outlaw dray they were trying to unload on Jones was God's own gift to ladies with buggies. He sold gentle horses to old maids and widows, spirited horses to cowboys, fast trotters to young bucks wearing straw boaters, limping wrecks to butchers who advertised prime beef. Whatever they wanted he just happened to have in his string.

Goldfield was no different. The streets teemed with lustful mortals, willing to do anything, be anything, sell anything for gold. Every hour he passed miners laden with stolen ore, whores who'd mined the miners, tinhorns who had cleaned out everyone at their tables, freighters charging pirate prices to bring goods to the new camp, financiers buying stocks with money they didn't have, and yeggs getting rich in the night with knouts and revolvers.

It didn't occur to Jones that he was mulcting anyone. Caveat emptor, that was his motto. If some rube in Pocatello didn't have the brains to investigate a company, then he only deserved the wildcat stock he got. Certainly serious men, the ones with brains, didn't plunge on a stock without thoroughly examining the company. Jones didn't lose sleep at night about his new vocation as the most successful wildcatter in Nevada.

That afternoon, Jones stepped into the harsh light of Goldfield, blinked at the desert glare, and counted himself a worldly success. He would probably make more that week than he had in all his years of horse brokering. That required a celebration. He limped to the Miner's Cash Store and bought a ready-made suit, which fit except at the waist; new shirt, new underwear and new shoes. The clerk promised him the suit before dark. Then he rented a room for a hundred a month over the Hermitage Saloon and collected his warbag from the two-man wall tent he shared with three others in two shifts, each possessing a cot for twelve hours. After that he proceeded to the tonsorial parlor on Ramsey and had himself a hot-water bath in the back room, followed by a shave, a haircut, and a dose of witch hazel.

He smelled so pretty he could hardly recognize himself. Tonight he would buy several hundred shares of good mining stock from the curbside traders in the Northern. Not a one of them would touch his own wildcats, so it would be strictly a buying expedition. Still, it wasn't a bad idea to lay in a few thousand shares of this and that. Who knew what would happen next? And heck, the partners could afford the plunge. He also intended to sink his own boodle into every good mine in the district.

He had transmuted himself into a mining securities broker in a few weeks. He thought about it and had himself a good belly laugh.

CHAPTER 12

....

Olympus Prinz wasn't content to write the most pene-trating newspaper coverage in Nevada. He was also an entertainer at heart and believed a newspaper should sparkle with wit and a few chuckles. He had perfected a caustic literary style during his apprenticeship in San Francisco and then hunted around for an appropriate venue to enjoy him-self. Where better than Goldfield, where all the world's folly and vice had collected into a few square blocks?

Goldfield enchanted him. It was such a fevered, greedy little burg. Probe into anyone's head, like Sigmund Freud, and what would one discover? A dozen schemes to get rich quick. Since mortals were incurable and beyond redemp-tion, he laughed at those pious American reformers—God spare this rhinestone republic from its Horace Greeleys and Harriet Beecher Stowes and more recently the Eugene Debses—who actually thought they could improve life by fiddling with laws.

Olympus had traveled to exotic Goldfield in much the fashion of a big-game hunter in Kenya, to bag amazing species and hang them from his wall as journalistic taxi-dermy. How better to do that than with a small press? After a stint at the *San Francisco Chronicle* he invested a small legacy in a venerable flatbed press, type fonts, paper and ink, and headed southeast. The paper would either support him or he'd go under, a fact which added a certain paprika to his life since he was a born muckraker.

He avoided the vice of frivolity; his news reportage was uniformly serious and had both gravity and dignity. But his features and gossip columns were another case altogether. It was his proposition that the editor of a frontier journal ought to have a good time while causing trouble.

One fine January morning, while pondering ways to fill

his trenchant weekly, he recollected the Borden Development Company and its wildcat stocks. There was a story.

He untied his printer's smock, donned his bowler hat and chesterfield, and ventured into an icy gale. It was time to put wildcatters into his big-game collection. He knew of several. Borden and Jones for sure, and maybe one or two others, all of them capable of squeezing orange juice out of buckshot. The thinnest line separated the wildcatters from the rest of the brokers and security dealers. Prinz knew he would get around to the more or less legitimate brokerages in time, but for now he would see about the wildcatting.

He admitted to himself that he actually favored wildcatters. They functioned as admirably as scavengers in nature. The world needed its vultures to clean up carrion and eagles to rid the universe of rabbits. Anyone bilked by a wildcatter deserved it; and in his estimation ninety-nine percent of the money-grubbers in Goldfield either would end up bilked, or fully deserved to be.

It occurred to him, as he rounded the corner next to the Borden Development Company, that the premises had been upgraded. Main Street looked as rude as ever but the building sported a cobbled brown facade that extended along either wall far enough to conceal the board and batten siding from the casual eye, great plate glass windows, and most amusing of all, a polished brass plaque announcing The Borden and Jones Trust, Underwriters and Brokers, Mining Securities.

Delighted, Prinz scratched the exact wording into his notebook, stuffed it into his pocket, and entered. Borden himself emerged from a rear office with a long-lost-brother beam in his eyes. Prinz barely had time to absorb the new interior decor: a mahogany counter with brass furniture; varnished wainscotting, flocked fleur-de-lis wallpaper above it in whorehouse red; a crystal chandelier.

"My dear friend Prinz, what brings you to our establishment this windy morning?"

"It's this way, Borden. I'm looking for a safe haven to sink some publishing profits."

"Publishing profits." Borden eyed Prinz the way a coyote eyes a rabbit. "I have several; I can offer you stocks with varying degrees of risk and varying degrees of potential. On the absolutely safe end is Goldfield Coal and Water Company. It's developing some coal claims thirty miles from here. Its principal stockholder and developer is Dr. Frances Williams—you've heard of her, of course. She's one of Goldfield's leading lights . . . specializes in electrical therapy by galvanic methods. This company'll be shipping coal for the mine boilers any day now. It's rock-solid but not a bonanza opportunity, not the way to triple or quadruple your investment. Now at the other extreme is a stock I'm terribly excited about, the Gold Mountain Mining Company. It's a bit more speculative but I hear they're about to exploit the best ore in the district."

"Funny, I haven't heard of it."

"Oh, by design," Borden replied. Sunlight raked his skull, making it glow like a golden egg. "It's all hush-hush so local people can buy shares in it before the news breaks in the national press, driving prices up."

"I'd think you'd want to drive prices up."

"Oh, in time, in time. But not this first month when we can offer it at its par value of one dollar a share for our special friends in Goldfield. Lookee here." Borden reached for a little pasteboard container lined in black velvet like a jeweler's box. "Lookit this," he said reverently, lifting a goose egg of ore that scintillated in the white light. Yellow gold networked the dark quartz, sometimes beading into convoluted nuggets. "Did you ever see anything like it? Touch it. You can touch it if you want."

Prinz didn't. "It's impressive, Borden. But how do I know how much there is—and all that?"

"Read this. It's a report by that eminent geologist and mining engineer, Simon Bolivar, translated from the Peruvian. Let me say, confidentially, Prinz, that I expect this stock to increase a thousand percent—yes, from one dollar to ten, in a matter of weeks. I've bought a lot of it for my account.''

"And you're the underwriter?''

"Well, yes. It'll soon be listed on the San Francisco exchange. You may wish to buy it before that happens. Ah, how much did you say you wanted to invest? Perhaps we should spread it over several stocks.''

"I didn't say. Now let me see what else you have. Are you related to Lizzie Borden—you know, who gave her father forty whacks?''

"Uh, what?''

"You know, the axe-murderer in Fall River.''

"I don't think I've ever been asked a question like that.''

"I just thought I'd find out. I've always wanted to know whether you're one of the family.''

"Well, Prinz, your mind takes strange turns. I suppose that's what makes you an editor.''

Prinz shrugged. "They acquitted her. She's not the black sheep in your family.''

"Ah . . .'' Borden ran a pale hand over the oily yellow flesh of his skull.

"Never mind. Borden, I want to examine all of those ore samples you've got lined up there like whores in the windows of their cribs.''

"Oh, ho, ho, Prinz, I never suspected you of levity.'' He began unshelving the samples and setting them on the mahogany. He paused to put a match to a kerosene lamp while Prinz examined them one by one. They looked suspiciously alike, as if a single large lump of highgrade had been pulverized into several samples.

"How do I know how good this is? It all looks alike to me,'' Prinz said.

"From the labels—here, lookit this: this is from the Molly Brown. It runs seven hundred dollars the ton. Why, they fear the miners'll highgrade it unless they take special precautions. I shouldn't tell you this, but management'll have eyes and ears in the pits.''

"Who's the management?''

"It's all here in this brochure. The president and chairman of the board is the Reverend Willis M. Dalrymple. You know the bishop, I presume? He has pledged his entire share, eleven percent, to the diocese."

"Haven't met him. What's that one?"

Borden unrolled a parchment document depicting every claim in the Goldfield district, and pointed to a rectangle lying well to the south of the Golden Horseshoe, the fabled mines around Columbia Mountain. "There she is. When she starts producing—scheduled for June of aught five— she'll be the darling of the district. Why, I've two thousand in my own account and I expect to retire on it."

"Are outside investors buying?"

"Prinz, as a result of modest little ads in places like Akron and Tacoma, we're selling stock so fast I can scarcely record the transactions. Jones is a veritable cornucopia for Goldfield, a man who singlehandedly underwrites—"

"Is he around?"

"Ah, Prinz, he takes the mornings off."

"I see. I tell you what, Borden. I'm a careful investor. I'll want to study everything: the pamphlets, assay reports, geologists' reports—all that."

"Here, here, we've prepared the complete disclosure for each venture." He shoved several packets toward Prinz. "Now, Prinz, I'd love to see a kind word about any of these properties in your excellent little paper. I might even arrange to supply you with a few shares—"

Prinz laughed. "We'll see, my friend. How are you doing?"

"I can't begin to tell you, Prinz. I'm selling millions of shares."

"That's what I wanted to hear, Mr. Borden. I'll study these."

"Please do. I want everyone who walks through our portals to get rich. Now, wealth won't give you peace of mind, Prinz. In fact, great wealth might be a burden. I've always admired the saints. Lives spun out in deep poverty yet filled with riches unimaginable. Ah yes, there are finer things. I just want you to know that at Borden and Jones Trust we recognize that. We're here to help you make your dreams come true. If you're another Saint Francis I'd recommend that you not invest one cent. He found a finer gold than I can ever offer. But for lesser mortals, Prinz, ordinary flawed people with a need for comforts like ourselves, you just can't beat gold.''

"Well, I'm no saint," Prinz confessed. "I'm not even a believer, as you will see." He stepped into the biting wind. The next step was to visit each of the claims, a task that would consume time. He would have to work on this story over a couple of weeks. But it was going to be fun to publish when he got it all nailed down.

CHAPTER 13

·······················

Casey Pepper waited impatiently under the gallows frame of the Combination Number 1 Mine until the cage rattled up from the depths past the collar of the shaft. He stepped onto its battered iron floor along with other stiffs starting the shift. Moments later he felt his stomach churn as the cage plummeted downward and the little box of light above grew dimmer and smaller.

He stepped off at the fourth level into the murky world of the vestibule and followed the rest into a dark and cavernous stope braced by square-set timbering. The gold had collected in pockets along ore shoots and had to be mined from underground caverns rather like those in Virginia City. Pepper carried his round-nosed shovel and lunchbox toward the face he would muck out while his carbide lamp bobbed gray light into dim corners. A ten-hour day paid him three and a half dollars from the Combination Mines Company. Veteran powder men got four. He hadn't been around that long and he wasn't a Cornish Cousin Jack, either. But he knew mining; he'd grown up with it in Virginia City and then Silver City, where his pa had mined before him. He resented having to muck ore for a living when he was already an experienced powder man.

The job cost him twenty dollars a day. That's what he had to pay those straw bosses in the hiring hall to get it. Twenty dollars each and every day for a three-fifty-a-day job. It made sense only because this was a mine full of highgrade ore. A lot of the stiffs beside him were forking out twenty a day to come down here. But it depended on the mine. Some mines you could work just for wages, minus the union dues.

Pepper eyed the gray mountain of rubble that he would shovel into one-ton ore cars all day. By the end of his ten hours he would be so tired he could hardly stand up. His five-foot-eight body would ache from hair to toenails. He'd hardly have energy enough to haul his real wage, the highgrade tucked into his oversized clothing, out of here. The thought of that rich rock filled him with joy laced with hate.

Those mucketymuck owners, Hubbard and Brown and Winslow, could make thousands just sitting around trading shares or collecting wealth from the sweat of Pepper's brow. All those fancy men in the fancy offices, eating in fancy restaurants like the Palm Grill with fancy women beside them, were coining gold without lifting a pinky finger. But Casey Pepper had no fancy women or paneled offices and he slaved for those rats ten hours a day, pounding rock and shoveling it. This wasn't their gold; it was everyone's gold, stuck in the earth for everyone working it.

The acrid odor of giant powder lingered in the stope. The night shift's last act had been to detonate the Du Pont Hercules it had tamped in the face, leaving a heap of rock for the next shift. There was never enough air because the tightwads on the grass never piped enough down. Casey coughed. He'd get miner's lung from the eddying dust just as his pa had. His pa had coughed, wheezed, spat blood, sucked in air he couldn't absorb, and died young, used up by the big-time mine operators who bought and sold labor like beef.

Casey hated to start shoveling but the shifter would be along, ready to punch him or fire him if he wasn't mucking ore. This stuff was going to take some hammering. The chunks of gray quartz were too big to handle. He pulled off his oversized jumper even though the air felt chill. In a moment he would be too hot anyway.

"You ready for the day's sweat, Casey old boy?" asked Mugs Cahoon, a bearded Irish mucker.

"I'd like to trade places with those clerks that fill our little envelopes with nothing," Pepper replied.

Beside him the other mucker, Tim McMillin, laughed cynically. "They's those that get it easy and those that get it hard," he said.

Len Larson and Sax Fryer were already doublejacking on the new face. They were the elite, the drillers and powder men. They were still drilling by hand but soon the mine was going to shift to pneumatic drilling and they'd all go deaf. Soon, they said, electricity from Bishop, California, would bring plenty of juice. Right now the mines were hard put to fuel the boilers that drove the lifts and powered the pumps that sucked water out of the hole. There wasn't enough electricity in Nevada for that.

"There are times I could strangle 'em, the damned fat plutocrats," Pepper mumbled. He lifted his sledge feeling yesterday's hurts in his muscles and slammed it into a boulder, knocking off a small piece. This one rock would take him a half hour and the shifter would get mad.

The noise deafened him; he couldn't talk to the other muckers, not while they shoveled rock up from the iron turning sheet and threw it into the ore cars where it rattled and banged and pulverized his brain. He couldn't even think in all that racket.

Just before firing the round the previous shift had dragged heavy boilerplate to the face. It was easier for muckers to shovel rock off that iron floor than from the rough surface beneath it. Everywhere around him, the violent contact of rock and iron reverberated; he could only numb himself to the roar and clang and ignore the stink of his own sweat.

Casey hammered at his boulder, breaking it into move-able pieces. This was good ore; he could see that. Maybe worth pocketing. He glanced around for the shifter, didn't see him, and examined a small piece that glowed yellowly in the wobbling shadows of the carbide lamps. A dandy. He tapped it into half a dozen smaller pieces, keeping a sharp eye out, and slid them into the little pockets that lined the inside of his pants. That was three-hundred-dollar stuff. The Combination could keep the hundred-dollar-a-ton ore; no stiff wanted junk like that.

Casey Pepper felt a little better. He had ten dollars in his pants. He'd get five of it. The assayer who payed him half its worth would get the rest. Assayers were another set of pirates feasting upon his sweat. They would smelt a miner's ore in their assay labs and pay off the next day. Tonight, after he got back up to grass, he'd take his haul over to that little joint on Silver Street. The crook would weigh it and pay him for yesterday's bunch. Then he'd have a few beers and buck the tiger. After that he'd eat and maybe visit Minnie. That's who got Goldfield's gold, the tinhorns and the whores. Most of the stiffs hated the gold they stole and couldn't wait to get rid of it. He didn't know a one of them who saved money, including himself.

Pepper pounded on rock all morning but didn't find any little pebbles of gold like the ones he found at the start. He and Tim and Sax shoveled sixteen tons of ore into the cars in those morning hours. As fast as one car was loaded an empty appeared to replace it while the full cars were trun-dled off to the lift.

By the lunch break he was feeling morose. He'd have to stuff his britches with bum ore today. On a rare good day he took two or three hundred dollars' worth to daylight and netted a hundred or a hundred fifty, minus the twenty he paid for the job. But most days he was lucky to clear fifty.

A bell jangled. He set down his spoonbilled shovel and

reached for the lunchbucket. He bought a pastie each day from that Cornishwoman on Alloy Street and washed it down with hot tea he and the other stiffs brewed on the spot. He spread his denim jumper and sat on it beside his silent colleagues who were wolfing down their lunches. All of them had pasties, the meat-filled pies that could be eaten with the fingers while their tea boiled in a tin can set upon a carbide lamp.

"Lousy ore," said McMillin ruefully.

Casey smiled. They all shared a knowledge that remained unspoken.

"Company ore," said Cahoon.

"It's everybody's ore," Pepper replied angrily. "It didn't get put in the ground just so some bloated capitalists could get rich."

No one spoke. Not a man in the pits supposed it was stealing when you got right down to it. Just because a few fat cats put up the capital didn't mean it was their ore. Pepper wondered if they were all as angry as he was. He hated having to sneak out his pay each day under the flinty stare of his bosses, most of whom did their own highgrading. That shifter lived higher than them all and built a house in that part of town called Highgrade Heights. The carpenters, the blacksmiths, the hoist engineers, the men who worked up top, they all got their share.

That afternoon the muckers shoveled another fourteen tons. Each day Pepper's crew mucked thirty tons of rock. By the time the carbide was running low in their headlamps, Pepper had slid another twenty pounds of ore into his clothing, filling the space between the double crown of his felt hat, the numerous little pockets lining the inside of his jumper, the false bottom of his lunchbucket, and the hollowed heels of his boots.

He and the rest of the muckers left the area ahead of the powder men who stayed to load the round and run the cable to the battery-powered detonator in the vestibule. They did timber work and nailed down another length of tram rails while they waited.

But at the bell they gathered at the lift to board the cage.

"Fire in the hole," yelled a powder man. He was the last to show up in the vestibule. He waited for any possible laggards and then pushed the plunger on the detonator.

Pepper ignored the thumps and shocks of air that signified a blast off in the stope. He caught the cage up to grass and stepped onto the collar under the surly eyes of the bosses. Forty pounds of ore on his person affected his gait and when he lumbered by they studied him, knowing what he carried. He didn't care. It wasn't their ore.

They couldn't touch him; not without a warrant that would permit the search and seizure of his person. He waddled by, meeting their contempt with his own. The bloodsuckers! Getting rich off the sweat of cheap labor!

He waddled heavily toward Goldfield a mile away, hating the dead weight, hating the dead ore, hating his dead soul. It was time, he thought, for miners to make a better world for themselves. He wasn't getting ahead. He might save something from a good salary; he never saved a dime of the highgraded ore because it was something contemptible, to be gotten rid of in the tenderloin just as fast as he could smuggle it out.

He would unload the ore, collect for yesterday's take, and go have a beer. It wasn't much of a life. Pepper wanted more. He itched to form a real union, one big union, strong enough to fight the bloated capitalists. Stronger than the Western Federation of Miners which was organizing the Goldfield mines. Stronger than the American Federation of Labor's timid unions. He thought maybe Wild Bill Haywood had the right idea. He was trying to organize a new union, the Industrial Workers of the World, which would blow away bloodsucking capitalism forever.

CHAPTER 14

....

Hannibal Dash looked at the heap of shattered rock in the bottom of that little hole and wrestled with himself. He could take it all away from the Arbuckles. Harry deserved nothing better. The sight of all that magnificent ore made Dash dizzy. Gold fever was eating him alive. It drove sober men mad; it turned virtuous men into pirates. It excited lusts most people never knew they possessed. And now it was gnawing at his conscience like acid.

The Arbuckle claim was no claim at all. Nevada law required that the holder of an unpatented claim build a four-foot-high discovery cairn on the site of the mineralized outcrop along with a location notice; that the claim be defined by four corner cairns and two sideline cairns; that a total of 240 cubic feet of rock be excavated from the ore-bearing rock, making a hole at least four feet by six feet running ten feet deep dug in the first ninety days. Failure to do so voided the claim.

The Arbuckles had been puttering around on a void claim since 1903. Obviously, Dash realized, Harry Arbuckle's feckless reputation had protected them. No one bothered to check out a claim owned by a blowhard who begged beers—until last night, when Harry paraded rich ore from one end of the Hermitage Saloon to the other.

"Mrs. Arbuckle," he said urgently, "you've got to relocate this claim immediately. It was void ninety days after you located last year."

She sighed. "I know. He wouldn't do it and I didn't have time."

"You can relocate. If it's not too late. Half the people in the district know about it. I want you or Harry to go with me to the land office. We should post a location notice right here and then go to town and record it."

"How do we do that?"

"Have you the original location notice?"

"I guess so. It's in my trunk."

"Well, copy it with a new date. And make a copy of that to file in town. Then put it inside a can or something and we'll pile rock around it."

"Why are you helping us?"

He smiled sheepishly. "I suppose I'm a fool."

She glared. "You're not just going to take it away?"

"It's a temptation. Harry deserves to lose it. You don't."

Tears welled up. "I didn't know whether to trust you," she said. "I'm sorry I didn't. The world's too hard."

They ran to the shack, where Harry sulked. Patiently Dash explained it all to him while Maude rummaged around for some paper. "Do you know how to write a claim?" Dash asked. "Claiming fifteen hundred feet along the ledge? Three hundred to either side of the centerline? Naming directions?"

"I wrote the first one," Maude said. "I got it right here." She pulled a hand-lettered document from a battered trunk and began printing a new claim on a sheet of butcher paper.

"I'm on to your game, Dash," Arbuckle said. "You're just trying to take it away from me. What do ya think I am?"

Hannibal Dash didn't say what he thought Harry was. Instead he lowered his voice. "Just sign it, Mister Arbuckle, and put it out there. I hope it's not too late. Half the people you showed the gold to last night will be along to see whether you've a valid claim."

Even as he spoke he could see a distant body of men walking toward them. "You're going to have company. They're going to see that you never did the location work. Hurry!"

"They'll steal my gold," Arbuckle whined. "It's just sitting there."

"Sign this, Harry!" Maude cried. She slapped the notice in front of Arbuckle.

"Oh, all right," he muttered. "But you're not gonna get my mine, Dash." He scrawled his signature. Maude took the claim, shoved it into a butter crock, and hurried out to the glory hole, where she planted it in a pathetic little heap of rock that was supposed to be a location cairn. Back at the cabin she started work on the duplicate and induced Arbuckle to sign it just when a dozen tough-looking men reached the shack.

"Arbuckle," said the one on horseback. "Beat it."

"You can't do this to me, Bible," Arbuckle whined. "Old Harry bought you a drank last night. We're pals."

Someone laughed. "Vamoose, Harry. We're taking this one over."

Dash gathered his courage and stepped outside. This bunch had come equipped to muck ore. Some carried burlap sacks. Most had shovels. A few wore sidearms. They were young, lean, ill kempt, and grinning like wolves. He recognized several faces. They were habitués of the saloons at the corner of Crook and Main.

"I don't believe I know your name," Dash said to the one on horseback.

"Billy Bible, pilgrim. Now that you know, you can beat it too. Unless you want to get hurt."

"This isn't your claim, sir."

"It is now, pilgrim." The man's voice changed suddenly. "Get the hell out or we'll drag you out."

Maude bristled. "Over my dead body!"

Bible shrugged. "All right. Over your dead body. Where do you wanna be planted?"

"You would steal, would you? From a poor man?"

"He ain't poor now, lady. That stuff he was bragging all over town last night—he's a rich man. We only steal from rich men. Heck, just call me Robin Hood."

Several of them drifted off toward the glory hole and crawled into it. "Hey, Bible, lookit this stuff!" one yelled. "All nice and yeller. It looks like butter."

Bible hawked up a brown gob and spat at Arbuckle. He

rubbed his stubbled face, grinned, and slowly slid his six-gun from its sheath.

Dash grabbed Arbuckle by the arm and steered him away. "Come on quick, before you're hurt."

"They're stealing my gold!"

Maude glared bitterly at Bible. "You won't escape the justice of God. Grind a poor woman under your heel and you'll regret it for an eternity."

Dash was amazed by her courage. She stood there rebuking the claim-jumper, ignoring the huge bore of that carelessly handled revolver. "Let's go, Maude. This isn't over."

Bible laughed. "It's over, pilgrim. You lost. I'm an old, experienced heel-grinder."

Dash herded the Arbuckles toward his livery buggy.

"I know what you're up to, Dash. You're just putting on this show. You're one of 'em."

Dash sat down and took the reins, blinking back his anger. Maude settled grimly beside Harry, crowding the front seat. The claim-jumpers didn't wait to see them off. They poured into the pit and began mucking the rock.

"I coulda got rid of them," Arbuckle muttered. "They was just bluffin'. But you had to push me into this rig. I won't ever forget this."

"Harry, for once just be quiet," Maude snapped.

"It's not all bad," Dash said. "Let's get your claim recorded. I don't think it even occurred to that bunch that they could relocate your claim."

But the Arbuckles had slid into deep gloom and he drove silently back to town through a ticking noon. He pulled up at the Goldfield Town Lot Company office on Columbia. They were acting as agents for the county in the matter of mining claims.

"All right," Dash said. "If I'm understanding this right, you'll be able to record the new location."

Not even Arbuckle had any objections. Dash helped Maude out of the buggy and shepherded them into the small tarpaper and batten-covered office. A clerk looked up.

"We'd like to relocate a claim," Dash said.

"Not we—me. *I'm* relocating," snapped Arbuckle.

"Oh, Harry!" Maude sighed.

The clerk seemed to know the Arbuckles. "Didn't you do your location work, Arbuckle?" Then he answered his own question. "No, I guess you didn't. You got a copy of the new location notice?"

Maude silently handed him the duplicate.

"It's the same as the original one the Arbuckles recorded in nineteen three, but with a new date," Dash said. "This is the way to do it, isn't it?"

The clerk studied Dash. "I'm Deacon Wilbur. I heard about the option you got last night, half the town watching. You're the pilgrim."

"I'm Hannibal Dash. Geologist."

"He didn't get nothing," Arbuckle said.

Wilbur studied Arbuckle. "Look, Harry, I'll file this with the county. You've got ninety days to start over. If you spend your time in the saloons instead of doing the location work, you'll lose it. In fact, I'll file on it myself one minute after midnight, ninety days from now."

Harry looked subdued for a change. Maude stood there stiffbacked, her lips compressed while Wilbur studied the location notice.

"All right," he said. He stamped a date on it and added the time after consulting his Keystone pocket watch. They waited while Wilbur wrote something in a large gray ledger. "That's a dollar," he said.

"What do ya mean, a dollar?" Arbuckle bawled.

Maude's lips pinched even tighter. Dash pulled a bill from his pocket and paid.

"Mister Wilbur," he said, "how do the Arbuckles deal with claim-jumpers?"

Wilbur's eyebrows shot up. "You've been jumped? You know who?"

"A man named Billy Bible and a gang. They're bagging ore right now."

Wilbur whistled. "Bible, eh? Down from Tonopah. He's

a hairy dog. Tasker Oddie and some of the big operators there must've chased him out. He's caused a lot of grief."

Hannibal checked his impatience. "Is there law? Is there recourse? Where do we get help in Esmeralda County?"

Deacon Wilbur laughed cynically. "Not much law. Hawthorne's a long ways away. We've got a sheriff's deputy here, though; old fellow that's a bouncer at the National Club."

That didn't sound promising. "Is that where we'll find him? Is he a competent man?"

"Oh, Virgil's competent, I guess. Just not young is all."

"That's the only recourse the Arbuckles have, I'm afraid. What's his name?"

"Virgil Earp," said Wilbur. "Him and his brother Wyatt were the ones that Oddie hired to clean out the claim-jumpers up to Tonopah."

"They'll have to do," said Dash.

CHAPTER 15

* *

Finding the Esmeralda County deputy sheriff proved to be as easy as Wilbur had said. But Dash doubted it would do much good. An old time-server deputy with one good arm didn't sound very promising.

"I'd rather shoot them myself," Maude muttered. "If you'd lend me the money for a shotgun and some buckshot I'd drive them outa there. They're not likely to shoot a woman but I'm likely to perforate their hides with some double-aught."

"You keep outa this, Maude," Arbuckle said. "I'll handle it. As for you, Dash, I'm through with you. Vamoose."

Dash dropped a carriage weight in front of the National Club on Crook Street and snapped its line to the plug's bridle. He knew better than to suggest that Arbuckle stay

in the buggy, though he devoutly wished to deal with this
ancient deputy alone before Arbuckle ruined everything.
But Harry glued himself to Dash's side as they pushed
through double doors into a beer-sour, dark interior. Sur-
prisingly, Maude remained in the buggy, her lips a prim
streak of disapproval. No respectable lady would enter a
saloon.

It seemed hardly the place for the law of the land, Dash
thought as he pushed up to a long, dented bar.

"I'm looking for a fellow named Earp, the deputy—"

"There." The mixologist jerked a thumb toward the rear.

Dash pushed through rank air to the back, past some faro
and poker layouts, to a handful of old duffers sprawled in
wooden chairs around a rickety table like a herd of old
buffalo bulls. One indeed wore a steel circlet encasing a
star, but he was the sorriest specimen of law officer Dash
had ever seen, an obvious string-puller who'd gotten the
job by paying off someone.

"You the deputy?" Dash asked the man.

"Virgil Earp," the man replied. He sat up, letting his
useless left arm dangle. He looked about as healthy as a
throat-cut shoat, with puffy flesh bagging behind his mustache. "You've a little problem?"

"I'm Hannibal Dash, a geologist, and this is Harry—"

The weight of Earp's alert gaze fell upon Arbuckle. "I
know him," he said. The tone was carefully neutral.

It took Dash awhile to tell his story, in part because Arbuckle kept interrupting. Earp ignored the man and focused
steadily on Dash's story.

"You want me to run 'em off," Earp said. "I don't
usually get in the middle of that. Don't know what side's
right."

"Deacon Wilbur at the town lot office said for you to
check with him."

"I could do that. What did you say your interest in Arbuckle's claim is?"

"He hasn't got no interest," Arbuckle butted in.

"I have a signed and witnessed option. In all fairness

I've offered to convert it to a standard lease and Mrs. Arbuckle accepted.''

"I'm the man with the claim and you'll be dealing with me, not Dash,'' Arbuckle said to Earp.

Dash sighed, slid his copy of the agreement from the breast-pocket of his suit coat, and handed it to Earp. Deftly the one-armed deputy extracted some gold-rimmed spectacles and read it.

"Well, Harry?'' Earp asked.

"Dash stole it from me,'' said Arbuckle.

"This is my brother Wyatt,'' Earp said. "He's had some experience running off claim-jumpers. Just a few months ago he was cleaning up the country for Tasker Oddie up in Tonopah. I'd suggest you hire him. In fact, I'll deputize him for it.''

The other Earp stood up and extended a hand. At least this old boy had two good arms along with a bald head, jowls, and all the signs of advancing age. But he was lean and looked fit enough. Neither of the duffers excited much confidence in Dash, whose mind's eye was filled with images of tough and greedy young men bagging ore on the Arbuckles' claim.

"Look, deputy, we need serious help. Some of that bunch is armed. They're stealing hundreds of dollars of ore. There's a dozen tough men robbing that pit.''

A third duffer, this one a curb securities trader sitting beside a chalkboard full of stock quotations, laughed. "This pair's been around the ballpark a few times, Mister Dash. There's none better.''

"And who're you?''

"Richard Clark. Wyatt Earp, here, had an interest in a gaming concession I had in a saloon back in Tombstone. I've known this pair a long time.''

"That doesn't exactly reassure me.''

Something was tickling Clark and he looked amused.

"I imagine it's a ten-dollar job,'' Wyatt Earp said.

"The trouble with Wyatt,'' Virgil said, "is that he never learned how to hang on to money. He did right well in

Nome—and spent it. He's fiddling with some claims and finding pure sand.''

"I've never paid for the law before. It's like hiring a hurdygurdy girl,'' Dash said sourly.

Wyatt scowled. Virgil chuckled.

"You stay out of it, Dash,'' Arbuckle said. "It's my gold. I'm not gonna pay for these two croakers.''

But Hannibal Dash had concluded that the Earp brothers would be all the help he'd get. He fully expected to see both brothers shot to ribbons but his options were limited. Dash decided that the color of law was worth something and pulled an eagle from his pocket. "All right,'' he said. "The sooner, the better.''

Wyatt Earp peered at the gold piece with his penetrating blue eyes, took it, and smiled toothily. "I might do it for fun,'' he said. But he pocketed the eagle.

"That's what I mean,'' Deputy Earp said to Dash. "Wave money at Wyatt and he'll do anything.''

That pair of wintered potatoes wheezed through the National Club and into a cool afternoon with Dash and Arbuckle following. En route, Deputy Earp had plucked up a double-barreled sawed-off Remington with bores the size of a howitzer, and nestled it in the crook of his good arm.

Dash felt mildly sorry that he had condemned two old goats to pain and death, but not too sorry: some private amusement passed between the brothers. As they emerged into daylight a peculiar trick of light transformed them into something different, something Dash couldn't put his finger on. It seemed possible that these elderly coots might just rescue Harry and Maude—and himself.

Virgil Earp eyed the four-passenger buggy and Maude, who sat stiffly in the rear seat. "I think, ma'am, you'd better stay here. We'll return right smartly.''

"I'm going with you,'' she said in a tone that brooked no argument.

"I'm familiar with that livery horse,'' Virgil said. "It is offended by five passengers and rolls over.''

"Then I will personally kick it back up,'' she replied.

The deputy sighed. ''There might be fatal results,'' he said. ''You might be in the line of fire.''

''I've lived with Harry Arbuckle all my life so why should I be afraid of bullets?'' she retorted.

Thoroughly cowed, the four men slid into the seats.

''I'll thank you not to be so familiar,'' Maude said to Wyatt Earp, whose hip pressed into hers.

''The laws of physics dictate it,'' Dash said, whipping the horse. ''Two bodies cannot occupy the same space.''

The plug craned its neck around until it could see past its blinders, and beheld a carriage stuffed with people. The horse sighed, trumpeted some exhaust gases rudely into mixed company, and slowly folded into the dust, forelegs first, like a great accordion wheezing down.

Astonished, Dash whipped the collapsing beast and evoked only a yawn.

''I know the horse,'' said Virgil. ''It is from the Palace Livery. I must check my lethal impulses whenever I see it.''

Maude Arbuckle scrambled down from the quilted rear seat and Dash thought that she had surrendered. Now, the four-gentleman posse would come to grips with the claim-jumpers.

Instead, Maude Arbuckle attacked the horse. There really was no other word for it. She kicked the brute, hammered on its skull, slapped its soft muzzle, and finally leaned over, shoveled a battered ear into her grim mouth and bit it.

The dray recovered instantly. It rose up, a shamed quadruped, and shook off the manure of the street, eyeing the woman as a rabbit eyes an eagle. Maude Arbuckle climbed aboard, rocking the carriage and displacing Earps.

''All right, Mister Dash,'' she said.

The venerable horse broke into a smart trot north.

''I don't know why you hired us,'' said Wyatt Earp.

CHAPTER 16

• •

Maude Arbuckle marveled at the events of the past few hours as the creaking buggy conveyed her to the claim. She'd struck bonanza gold; Harry had stupidly optioned the mine to Dash; the geologist had helped Harry relocate in the nick of time; Dash was offering to switch to a fair lease; and now Dash had summoned the law, such as it was, to drive off claim-jumpers.

She squinted at Dash, in his salt-and-pepper coat, not knowing what to make of him. He seemed too good to be true. Something about him rose above most men. She knew she should be skeptical. Probably he'd try to take it all away. Even so, she brimmed with thanks which was more than Harry brimmed with. He was busy loathing the man who had rescued him from poverty.

Dash drove the burdened buggy out of town, choosing the most level route among the barren desert rock and brush. She eyed the crippled deputy in the front seat wondering how such a wreck could dislodge armed claim-jumpers, and then she sneaked a glance sideways at the deputy's brother who stared ahead, gnawing on a blond mustache. This pair didn't stand a chance. The desert would blot up blood this afternoon. The thought disheartened her.

"How far ahead, ma'am?" asked the brother, Wyatt, ignoring Harry.

"A mile."

"Is it hilly like this?"

"It's mostly level."

The sullen dray dragged them along the foot of a low ridge where the road ahead curved out of sight. Wyatt Earp tapped Dash on the shoulder.

"Would you mind stopping here, Dash?" He looked uncomfortable.

Dash shot a questioning look at Earp and reined up. Earp eased out of the buggy.

"It'll just be a moment," Earp said unhappily, eying Maude. He hastened around the bend and disappeared.

"Too much beer," said Dash.

Virgil turned. "No, my brother's suffering middle-aged complaints. He can't go an hour without relief."

Maude translated that. The men were phrasing things delicately for her benefit. Wyatt Earp's water was slowing up and the bouncing of the buggy had been hard on his kidneys. She pursed her lips and pretended not to hear.

"It happens," said Dash. "After fifty most men have problems. There's no help for it. I hope I'll be spared."

"Wyatt's fifty-six," Virgil said. "He's getting there."

The deputy's brother emerged from behind the slope and he settled silently into the seat looking embarrassed. Dash whipped the surly dray into locomotion once again.

"Are you also in law enforcement, Mister Earp?" Maude asked anxiously.

"Done a piece of it," Earp replied. "Not recently."

That didn't assure Maude.

"Been up in Nome; had the Northern there—ah, a saloon, ma'am. Started another one in Tonopah. Tex Rickard stole the name and got in here ahead of me. He gets the Yukon crowd. I'm poking around with a couple of worthless claims. There's more money to be had in Goldfield than the desert."

Maude had the impression of a taciturn man trying to be pleasant. The relief of an empty bladder lightened his tone.

"I heard of you," announced Harry.

"Oh?"

"Yeah, you're a friend of Bat Masterson. There was a piece in *True Detective Magazine* about him. Finest of the old-time lawmen. You were his deppity in some Kansas place. Guess he knew what he was doing. Guess you never thought I'd heard of you."

Earp nodded.

Dash whipped the dray up a slope and out upon a dreary

flat. "That's the southeast corner," he explained to Virgil. "Mister Arbuckle's just relocated. We'll be building up the cairns directly."

"I don't need your help, Dash," Harry announced.

"You wouldn't have the claim if he hadn't," Maude shot at him.

"You keep outa it."

Ahead, a dozen or so claim-jumpers busied themselves around the little pit and the shack a hundred yards off. A sudden tautness slid between Maude's shoulder blades. Maybe everyone in this creaking buggy would die.

"Rein up, Dash. I'd like you and the Arbuckles to stay out of harm's way," the deputy said.

Dash frowned. "Sir, if I may ask, how can a man with a . . . with an arm like yours evict them? You think that badge'll do it?"

Virgil Earp smiled. Maude confessed to herself she was smitten by that smile. The old deputy lit up the afternoon. He hefted the double-barreled shotgun easily and walked with his brother toward the trespassers.

Impulsively, she scrambled down from the buggy and followed them. Those confounded Earps weren't going to keep her from getting her two cents in.

"Mrs. Arbuckle!" Dash protested.

"Let her croak; she wants it," Harry said.

The Earps waved her back but she stomped forward, inflamed by the sight of those ruffians bagging up her gold. The pile of filled burlap bags had grown.

"You ain't bulletproof, ma'am," said Wyatt.

"I'm female." She stood very straight, unbudgeable, her worn shoes anchored in the hard desert caliche. A cold November breeze tucked tendrils of ice around her legs.

A faint crease built around Virgil's lips. "Suit yourself," he said. That Earp, at least, showed signs of civilization. The blond one, Wyatt, was grouchy.

Ahead, the trespassers stopped their looting and watched the progress of the law. Virgil walked with his heavy shotgun butt snugged easily into his right hip. She suddenly realized how a one-armed man could be deadly with such a weapon. The other brother pushed aside his suit coat and pulled out his big black revolver.

She eyed them both with wonderment. Something in those aging men had changed but she couldn't quite make out what it was. They didn't look old anymore.

"I hate to hide behind a woman's skirts, ma'am," said Virgil, amusement in his eyes.

Maude grunted. They wanted her to back off.

"If they get pesky, drop to the ground," Wyatt said. His gaze had turned bleak and hard.

The claim-jumpers spread out. A few were armed but none of them had a weapon in hand. They acted as if their sheer numbers would decide the matter.

"All right, beat it," yelled Virgil. "It's not your claim."

"You gonna make us, Tin Star?"

"I'm a deputy sheriff. Virgil Earp. This is my brother, Wyatt."

"Siding with Harry Arbuckle," one said. "How sweet." Several laughed.

"Siding with the county. If you have a quarrel with Arbuckle, take him to court."

One of them whispered to another, pointing at Wyatt. Several of them consulted, with frequent sharp glances toward the Earp brothers. Some of them seemed to know these brothers or know something about them.

"What'll ya do if we stay?" asked one.

"Try us," Wyatt said, softly. Maude marveled at how much menace lay in two velveted words.

"We're thirteen; you're two."

"Three," said Maude. "Get off my claim."

It was funny how those brothers just stood there on the brink of the chasm with the fumes of Hades in their nostrils. What happened next seemed even stranger to Maude. One of those ruffians, a big bearded fellow in jeans, shrugged and walked south. Four more followed. Then two more. The rest hesitated. One of two looked like they were mighty tempted to try something but their will melted away under the Earps' calm gaze. In the space of sixty seconds all thirteen claim-jumpers departed, one of them leading the horse.

"Hardly earned, my ten dollars," muttered Wyatt.

Virgil turned to Maude. "They'll leave you alone. I could put names to most of them. They know that I know who to go after if they give you trouble."

A shudder convulsed Maude. She needed to thank them. "Do you want some tea or something?"

Virgil shrugged.

Dash steered the buggy into camp. The mob of claim-jumpers grew smaller and smaller in the dusky south until their dust and the twilight merged.

"What a bunch of lily-livered sissies that bunch was. I coulda handled it myself," Harry said.

No one seemed embarrassed. Maude noticed that men treated Harry as if he didn't exist.

"I suppose you're gonna charge me for this," said Harry. "Everyone wants a piece of me."

Maude clasped Virgil's good hand scarcely knowing what to say. Then she clasped Wyatt's. "There's no way I can ever repay you," she said.

"I expect I earned a mug of beer," said Virgil. "You driving back, Dash?"

"I have to return the livery outfit, Deputy."

"We'll hitch a ride, then."

Dash turned to Maude. "I'll be out in the morning. We've cairns to build and location work to complete."

"I'm on to your game, Dash," said Harry.

"Please come," said Maude.

Dash paused somberly beside the buggy while the Earps settled themselves in it. "We'll write up a fair lease in the morning, Mister Arbuckle. Or, if you prefer I can exercise my option to buy the claim."

Harry ignored him.

Maude watched Dash and the Earps ride toward Goldfield, leaving a trail of dust.

Harry gloated. "Those tinhorns think they're something," he said.

Maude said, "Hannibal Dash is something, Harry. As long as I've lived I've never met a man like that. He's a man as good as his word."

CHAPTER 17

····················

Big Sam Jones scarcely knew how to spend all the cash that was rolling in. He and Borden were each clearing five thousand a week after expenses. He invested in rich gold mines such as the Jumbo and the January, and bought interests in leasing companies that were operating several mines. He treated himself to seven suits, one for each day, along with shirts and cravats. He bought a Desert Flyer touring car and explored the surrounding wastes.

Most evenings he repaired to Tex Rickard's Northern Saloon, where he bought or sold mining stocks from curbside traders. He sensed an invisible wall between himself and the others. They never bought his wildcats. He didn't mind; he was earning more than all of them put together. And he had his allies. He and Borden were pouring capital into Goldfield, spending in chophouses, saloons and dance halls, buying from mercantiles, purchasing shares in such volume that it kept their prices up. He ran a daily advertisement in the *Goldfield News* just for goodwill. Not many people in Goldfield purchased shares in his wildcat companies but plenty of them profited from his enterprise.

Life wasn't complete; he lacked a suitable lady and a fancy house, but he would have those things soon enough. He wasn't accepted among the town's elite but that didn't bother him. As a horse trader he had been driven out of more towns than he could name. He figured that all those lawyers and businessmen and parsons were pretty fine folks except when they bought gold stocks or traded horses. If he had become a banker he'd be a pretty fine fellow, too. Let them scorn him if they wanted to.

Still, there were moments when he peered across a subtle gulf, a real divide even in wild and treacherous Goldfield, and wondered about himself. The wondering never lasted long. It was not yet half a year from the moment he had stepped into Goldfield, broke and hungry, with only a few of Wingfield's silver dollars between him and starvation.

One bright day he meandered into the offices of the Borden and Jones Trust and beheld Windlass diligently cleaning a thirty-eight-caliber revolver. Six brass shells lay on the counter.

"We're ruint!" Windlass growled. "I'm gonna make that bum retract, or kill him." He waved Big Sam toward a fresh copy of the *Goldfield Observer*.

Olympus Prinz had made wildcatting his lead story and he had done a thorough job of it. Big Sam perused the lengthy article, discovering that Prinz had examined each of the companies being underwritten by Borden and Jones and found them all to be phantoms. The editor had personally visited each of the claims listed in the prospectuses and found that two didn't exist; four existed but showed no sign of development work; and none of the claims lay within the mineralized area around Columbia Mountain known as the Golden Horseshoe, although the prospectuses said they did. In fact, the location work had never been done on three claims and anyone could relocate them.

But that wasn't the end of it: Prinz had inquired into the directors of each company and discovered that some didn't exist and others had never been asked to serve on the board. Prinz had checked the assay reports and discovered they were the work of unknown assayers; the geological reports had been written by unknown geologists; the development reports had been drafted by unknown mining engineers. The engravings depicting various mines and works didn't depict anything in the vicinity of Goldfield. No incorporation papers had been filed with the Nevada secretary of state for any of the companies, including the Molly Brown, the Queen Cleopatra, and the Gold Hill.

In a separate editorial Prinz denounced the wildcatters, especially Borden and Jones, for perpetrating gross frauds upon the American people. He urged the law to clamp down. "Wary financiers know how to care for themselves but unwary working people don't," he concluded. "It's the humble people, least able to afford a loss, who are hurt the worst."

"That's a mighty good job he did, Windlass," Jones allowed.

"We're ruint. I'll drill him if he don't retract."

Big Sam eyed his partner, who was stuffing the shells back into the cylinder. "Ah, Windlass, you've never understood publicity. This is a bonanza for us."

Borden looked incredulous. "A what?"

Jones smiled. "It don't matter if it's good or bad; it all helps."

"This helps? Are you crazy?"

"Why, it'll help mightily."

"Jones, there're times I think you're nuts. Not one lobster that reads that rag'll ever buy a share from us."

"Windlass, you hold your horses. The worse something's attacked, the more folks rally to it. Why, think of all the greenbacks we're spending around here. It's not just mines making Goldfield rich; it's us. Do you think all them restaurants and saloons'll take sides with Prinz? He done us a favor."

Borden shook the paper. "You call this a favor? You think this'll make us some money? You're a fruitcake. I'm going to have a little talk with Prinz, and there'll be a loaded barrel between me and him."

Jones saw the frenzy in Borden's eye and knew trouble was blooming. "Tell you what, Windlass. Let's go put an ad in Prinz's paper. All that publicity, we should take advantage of it."

"Publicity!"

"Sure, we'll run that ad about retiring—how working folks gotta get set for old age."

"He'll reject it."

"Well, we'll just jaw with him a bit. Now you leave that popgun here. We don't want half of Borden and Jones to be charged with the perforation of that little German."

"By Gawd, Big Sam, you're either a Barnum or a nut." But Borden slid the revolver into his lower desk drawer.

Jones felt elated. He'd been hoping for a big publicity break in Goldfield. He wanted to unload a few hundred thousand shares locally. There were always plunger types, speculators, loonies, masochists, who'd gobble the stuff up. He found a proof sheet of his Retire in Peace ad, and limped through a sunny spring day toward the little shack that housed Prinz's rag.

"We're two against one, even if you walk three-legged," Borden observed.

"We're not going to brawl, my friend; we're going to transact some lucrative business." With that, Jones turned the corner onto Ramsey and headed west.

"You go in first," Borden said, eying the door.

Jones entered. His nose was greeted with the smell of molten typemetal and pungent ink. All print shops smelled like that. He'd been in them all his life, having posters printed.

Prinz looked up from his typesetting and scowled. "I knew you lobsters would come by," he said. "You're going to complain. You're going to bleed. You're going to tell me not a bit of it's true. You're going to threaten to ruin me. Maybe you'll threaten never to advertise in the *Observer*. Maybe you've come to pound me to a pulp."

A revolver lay within easy plucking and Jones was glad he had talked Windlass into leaving his firepower at the office.

"Why, Prinz, that was a mighty piece of reportage. We're not here to complain, man. We want to purchase a full-page ad."

Olympus Prinz chortled. "An ad and a retraction."

"Nope. We'll just run the ad and let you run the news."

"I don't know if I want your ad."

"Well, Prinz, my old friend, this establishment looks less than prosperous."

"What're the strings?"

"None. Just run the ad."

"Ah! The ad's a rebuttal."

"Nope. It's our standard ad. Ran it everywhere from Keokuk to Athens, Ohio."

"Perhaps you'll want me to refrain from comment if I run it."

"Nope. You can run her and say what you want about her."

"I suppose you'll want to pay me with that wildcat stock."

Jones pulled a roll of bills as fat as a doorknob from his pants. "Two hundred for a full page, ain't it?"

"Let me get this straight. You want to advertise your wildcat companies in the very newspaper that exposed your whole operation? That pleaded for a crackdown? Do you know that twenty, thirty people have stopped by to thank me?"

"Well, think of all those folks that'll thank us, too, for putting Goldfield on the map. Why, thanks to us, everyone profits that buys Goldfield stock. We build demand."

Prinz sighed. "I confess my brain runs along different rails than yours, Jones."

"Narrow-gauge track, Prinz."

The editor laughed in spite of himself. "Now let me get this straight. You'll pay me cash to run the ad. And if I choose to rip it to shreds in my columns, you won't mind?"

"Why, Olympus, my friend, we'd take it for a favor."

The editor sighed. He skimmed the proof copy and gently set it down on the counter. Big Sam peeled two hundred-dollar bills from his roll and laid them on the battered wood. Prinz lifted them gingerly, hardly believing it.

"All right," he said. "In Friday's issue. I'll use the ad as a little casebook for my readers."

"Mighty kind of you, Prinz," said Jones.

"Kindness had nothing to do with it."

They departed with the editor's gaze boring into their backs. "Now, Windlass," said Jones, "you get set up for a big old run on our stock."

CHAPTER 18

Olympus Prinz discovered that rocky is the road of a reformer. He ran the Borden and Jones ad and dutifully assailed every claim and assertion in it at great length on the page opposite the ad. It was the ultimate public service. He had rescued the citizens of Goldfield from fiends incarnate. He was rather proud of his subdued prose. The temptation had been to rant but he appealed to reason instead. Calm, sweet reason would always triumph. Let citizens know the truth and they would come to their own conclusions and exercise their native good judgment.

"Can anyone doubt," he concluded, "that Goldfield's wildcatters, and the Borden and Jones Trust Company in particular, prey on the poor, insensible and weak, robbing them of what little they have? Can anyone doubt that we have evil in our midst, a malign vice that requires ruthless extermination for the public good?"

For all his troubles he had received mostly abuse. In his mail were two subscription cancellations but also a dozen new subscribers. He received letters disapproving of his editorial view or accusing him of twisting the truth or inventing calumnies against an honest and valuable Goldfield concern. He received one note, slid under his door, threatening to tar and feather him. Three advertisers, all chophouses, withdrew their advertising. One widow stopped by and heartily thanked Prinz, saying that his exposé rescued her from the temptation of investing in wildcat stocks. But three other visitors popped in to remind him that all mining ventures have their skeptics and detractors; that even the best mines in the district, such as the January and the Combination, looked bad at one point. To no avail did Prinz persuade those blockheads that the Borden companies weren't mines at all; they were bunco operations.

But the most grievous thing of all was his discovery that Borden and Jones were prospering as a result of the *Observer's* assaults. On several occasions in the following weeks Prinz wandered up Columbia Street to the company's lair. The first thing he discovered was a new bronze plaque beside the door, sporting an even flossier name: BORDEN, JONES AND COMPANY TRUST; MINING SECURITIES, UNDERWRITERS, DEVELOPMENT CONSULTANTS, BROKERS.

Prinz sighed. The name was getting more highfalutin with every month. Within, he found both Jones and Borden actively huckstering to several customers, most of them pathetic women from the line on South Main Street.

"Why yes, ma'am," Jones was saying, "it's high risk. Who knows how it'll all come out? I'd recommend you buy five hundred and put it away to mature like a good annuity."

Before Prinz's very eyes over a thousand shares of bogus stock exchanged hands and over a thousand dollars in greenbacks and specie disappeared into the company's coffers.

"Why did you buy that bunco stuff?" he asked one pathetic woman.

"Because I always disagree with newspapers. The more they howl, the more they're hiding something. Lackeys, that's what they all are."

He stopped a shifty-eyed character as he emerged from the Borden company. "Lissen," the fellow said, "I'm no dummy. When they're all yelling about something, that's when they got something up their sleeve. This here newspaper, you can bet they want to scare off the public so they can have the whole pie to themselves."

"Well," Prinz replied, "I'm the editor of that paper and I was attempting to rid this community of predators."

The gent eyed him a long time. "Some foreigner," he muttered. "Get outa the way."

Prinz counted it a lesson in human nature. As far as he could tell, Borden, Jones and Company was exploiting the misfits, the twisted souls who found sinister design even in a newspaper's crusade. But he had to admit that something else was at work: gold fever. It was a madness in its own right, enflaming even the most reasonable people. Goldfield was chockablock with people hellbent to get rich, to grab the maddening metal or at least nab the wealth of those who had it.

The claim holders feasted on gold; the lessees and operators looted gold; company executives and straw bosses nipped their share of it; the miners pocketed it along with the fake assayers; the tinhorns and tarts extracted it from the miners; the saloons and mercantiles extracted it from whoever had it. And even he, an obscure editor, ultimately feasted on the gold. Each ad in his paper, each subscription, owed itself to the pernicious metal. No wonder a lot of people didn't like his exposé.

Prinz wasn't opposed to getting rich but he believed that those who made getting rich their sole occupation were fools. Other riches, of spirit and intellect, interested him more. A just civic body preoccupied him. A safe and comfortable city was one of his goals. Building a stable city that would survive beyond the failure of its mines was important. He had a lively sense of the moral and spiritual bricks that went into the art of living—and into the mortar of any worthwhile city. In the end, he consoled himself that for every fool or knave who had bought Borden wildcat stocks as a result of his crusading, he had warned away fifty sounder people.

Prinz forgot the matter until one day Big Sam Jones walked in, leaning heavily on his hickory stick. He certainly looked prosperous now. He sported a white linen suit, freshly brushed derby, a yellow silk cravat with a headlight diamond stickpin, a thick gold ring, stiffly starched white collars and cuffs, and oxfords so shiny you could see your

puss in them. Jones seemed to have his usual gleam in the
eye, a mask of affability waxed over his jowly face and
mustache. Prinz thought that Jones was trying to look like
a politician. Maybe he was running for governor.

"Ah, my friend Prinz, it's a glorious day, and I design
to enhance your coffers," Jones said.

"You want to buy an ad."

"Well, a series of twenty ads, actually. The full rear
page."

The vision of that much cash for his sorely hurting little
rag stabbed at Prinz momentarily but he resisted. Unlike
Jones, he possessed some principles and resisting fraud was
one of them. "Sorry, Jones. I ran that one ad only to attack
it. I'll pass."

Jones nodded, not at all dismayed. "I might simply print
our ad on flyers," he said. "Your ad got us about ten thousand dollars of sales."

"All of it wildcat stock, I suppose."

"Every bit. There's those that have independent minds,
Prinz. The more a newspaper howls, the more they get their
fur up."

Prinz set aside the roller with which he was inking a page
of type and wiped his grimy hands. "Jones, I'm going to
get personal. Doesn't it ever bother you that you bilk people?"

"I don't bilk them," Jones replied, unflappably.

"Of course you do. You sell shares in nonexistent companies, trading on people's greed and wild hopes of making
killings. You give them a gilt-edged piece of engraved
parchment that looks like money. And all those poor souls
who've put money aside, bit by bit through a hard life of
toil, end up penniless and hopeless. What have they got?
A scrap of wallpaper."

Jones beamed joyously and Prinz saw the affable salesman in the man. "Prinz, let me tell you something. I used
to trade horses but sometimes I was trading dreams. I'd
show a chap the sorriest old nag you ever did see, the faults
as plain as my mustache. I'd show a horse with cracked

hooves, or galled withers, or a mooneye, or a horse with half his teeth missing. I'd just bring it out and not say a word.

"Sometimes, Prinz, those people saw a different nag. That same horse filled a dream, somehow. They saw the handsome steed of their imagination. They saw themselves riding the range, or going hunting in the high country or trotting on a spirited charger past the admiring gals in town—especially that. And they paid out every cent I asked, even though I'd of taken half or a quarter, or even two dollars sometimes.

"They bought what they imagined. I didn't mislead 'em. I didn't say those nags were young and sound and had good manners and a smooth mouth. I didn't say a thing. Should I not have? Should I wreck a feller's dreams?"

Olympus Prinz listened intently, sensing that Jones's soul was on display this one time. "You might have pointed out the faults," he ventured.

"I used to, Prinz. But I learned that people are crabby and unpredictable. Most of those folks didn't thank me for opening their eyes. If I pointed out flaws they wondered what I was up to. If I just kept my mouth shut, I often sold the nag and they told me I was a splendid fellow."

"That's not true of the wildcat stocks," Prinz said quietly. "Everything in your ad is misleading."

"Sure it is. I'm selling dreams. Those people, they don't check nothing. The wilder their dreams, the wilder their judgment. I accommodate 'em."

"You do more than that, Jones. You send them fancy brochures about things that don't exist. Reports and assays you invented inside your devious brain. Claims, shafts, buildings that exist only in your imagination."

"Dreams, Prinz. I give 'em dreams. They read that stuff and get rich in their minds. They'll hit a bonanza and every share'll be worth five hundred dollars. They never think the outfit'll go bust. Or if they do, they think the odds are better that it'll make them rich. Why should I disillusion them?"

"Because you illusioned them. Why don't you steer them to good gold stocks—like the Combination—and take an ordinary broker's commission?"

Jones grinned. "When they ask, that's what I do."

Prinz didn't like the man's self-serving rationale. "Sorry, Jones. You're simply cheating people." He thought that would settle it and was surprised by Big Sam's response.

"People cheat themselves," he replied. "I learned that trading horses."

Prinz chortled. "They cheat themselves, do they? And all those brochures, those fake assays, those photos of non-existent works, those aren't fraudulent."

Jones gazed innocently. Prinz could not help but like the scoundrel. "I got repeat business trading nags and I get repeat business selling stock," he said. "Sorry you don't want to enrich your coffers. The *Observer's* a good rag. You're a good man, Prinz. Best paper in town, best editor. You got wit, too. Every issue jabs my funnybone. How about a hundred shares of Molly Brown?"

Prinz laughed. Jones laughed, his merry eyes unblinking.

Prinz could never figure out why he enjoyed that scoundrel, Big Sam Jones, who peddled dreams. He was worse than the opium peddlers in Hop Fiends Gulch. "No, Jones, I'm not going to run your ads," he said.

"Well, that's fine," said Jones. "You run the only rag in Goldfield I can trust. You wouldn't want my ads in there. They'd undermine your sterling character. Wipe the ink off your pinkies, pal, and Big Sam'll treat you to a salmon filet buried in creamed broccoli at the Montezuma Club. I had a time of it getting in there, but they finally let me in when I donated five grand toward their club rooms." He chortled. "They don't talk to me, though. You and me got a lot in common, I reckon. All those prominent men in there— that's what the *News* calls 'em—they'll give you the fish-eye. Your rag's too honest."

Prinz sighed and headed for the gritty soap.

CHAPTER 19

························

After a restless night in which Hannibal Dash worried his way through every possible calamity, he gulped some java and hastened out to the Arbuckle claim. He harbored a bad feeling; a sense that he was engaged in a great folly that would come to ruin. He found Maude and Harry at sword's point but he could only guess the cause.

"What're you doing here?" Arbuckle demanded truculently.

"I believe we have a contract, Mister Arbuckle."

"Beat it. I don't need you."

Dash had learned simply to ignore the man. "We've location work to do," he said. "Ninety days to build seven cairns and deepen that hole to ten feet. I'm here to help."

"Suit yourself, Dash. I'm taking this ore to town."

"You're not going to take it to one of those crooked assayers and get gypped," Maude said.

Dash got an inkling what the quarrel was about.

"I can help you get it to a smelter, Mister Arbuckle. We'll have to bag the rest and ship it. It'll go by wagon to Tonopah and by rail from there to the Selby Smelter in San Francisco. You'll get a check back in a short time. It'll come to a lot more than if you, uh, sell it locally."

"That's what I say!" Maude exclaimed. "But he won't listen."

"You both keep outa this. It's my ore. I'll do what I want."

"You already did. Twice." There was a pleading in her eyes. She turned to Dash. "Last night he went to town and flashed all that money around that you gave him. The hundreds. Trying to be a big man. He got rolled when he left the Mohawk." Tears rose in her eyes. "They took over eight hundred dollars from him. Now he wants to take this bagged ore to the crooks in town."

Arbuckle turned sullen and silent. Dash wondered whether it made any sense to have a business associate like Arbuckle.

"He asked for it, flashing those bills around," Maude added.

"Aw, shut up. You don't know anything," Arbuckle snapped.

Dash figured he had better tread carefully. "You've got a lot of ore in that hole and I'd better get busy bagging it," he said. "I'm sure you two'll work it out. Some might go to the smelter and Mister Arbuckle might reserve some for his own use. If you'd like, I'll arrange for a freight outfit to pick this up."

"You stay outa it, Dash."

Dash contained his withering answer, shrugged, and headed for the miserable little pit. He dropped to the rubble in its bottom and began mucking rock. It wouldn't be any fun. The claim-jumpers had mucked thirty-two bags and there was at least that much more to muck. Dash wondered why he bothered. He had, for a business partner, the most self-destructive mortal, the biggest fool, on earth.

He set to work in the chill morning and soon found both of the Arbuckles watching him contemplatively. He intuited that he had done the right thing not to take sides. He loaded a burlap bag, tied it shut with cord, and hoisted it up the rickety ladder. It took all his strength. He'd been in classrooms too long.

"I'm going to town," Arbuckle said, defying anyone to stop him. The man caught the emaciated burro, harnessed it to the rickety cart, and hoisted ten heavy bags into it. Dash had never seen Arbuckle work before and supposed he would never see Arbuckle work again. Harry whipped Mother Dear, who leaned into the ancient collar and then quit. He fought the burro while Dash continued to fill bags. Finally Harry removed four bags. The burro didn't budge. Only when Harry got down to two bags of ore would she move. Triumphantly Harry whipped her toward town.

"Don't you steal none of my ore," he yelled.

Dash continued to wrestle rock into the sacks and tie them while Maude stood above him wrestling emotions into some sack in her soul.

"Mrs. Arbuckle—Maude—would you like me to arrange a shipment for you? I can talk to a freight outfit in town. They'll pick it up. If you work at this the ore'll be ready when they arrive."

She nodded, and then smiled faintly. "Harry'll be very angry."

Dash paused, letting his heart slow down. Mucking was brutal work. "I think when he sees the check he'll have no objections."

"Why're you doing this?" she demanded.

"Not out of charity," he replied. "If we work together— and this ore shoot doesn't pinch out—we'll all prosper."

"He'll never go along."

Dash leaned into his round-billed shovel. "Mrs. Arbuckle, forgive me for saying this, but it doesn't seem to matter whether he goes along or not."

She nodded and then smiled suddenly, as if that insight had freed her from a thousand chains. "Go fetch the freight outfit. This'll be in bags by the time you get back."

"It may take awhile," he said.

"The sooner the better. Before Harry throws it all away."

It took Dash a couple of hours. The O'Keefe company, a stage and freight outfit that ran Celerity mud wagons to Tonopah and freighted with big Murphys, agreed to pick up the Arbuckle highgrade. Dash had to guarantee the payment himself. A twenty-mule tandem outfit was leaving shortly and would detour over there since the Arbuckle claim was north of town and close to the road. Dash bought some wire-on tags and some india ink to identify the sacks, and headed out to the claim again, hoping Arbuckle had settled into another bout of buying free drinks in the Hermitage or the Palace. If that was the way to make progress, then Harry's trading of licit gold to illicit buyers would be a small price. In any case, Dash reminded himself, he had no interest in the bagged gold. It was all Arbuckle's—and should have all been Maude's.

At the claim he helped Maude bag the rest of the ore—except for one sack she defiantly dragged to a cleft in the slope fifty yards away. She said nothing but he read the bitterness in her lips.

"Mrs. Arbuckle, I'd like enough to assay again. You'll get the gold and the results. I need to know if the values stayed constant. That rock's probably worth two dollars a pound."

She nodded. He selected a fist-sized chunk and put it in his duffel.

Arbuckle and the teamsters reached the claim about the same time. Harry wore a new derby and his beard had been scraped.

"What's this? You can't do this!" he bawled, as the O'Keefe teamsters halted at the stack of bags.

"Load them up," said Maude resolutely. The teamsters set to work while Arbuckle danced around them. "It's mine; you can't do that. I'll sue! I'll get even. What's your authority for this?"

Dash itched to intervene every time the O'Keefe men looked doubtful, but he knew better. The moment of truth arrived when the head man counted the bags, recorded their number on a waybill, and handed a clipboard to Harry.

"Sign here," he said.

Arbuckle stared, lifted the pencil, and scrawled a crude signature in the blank space. Dash felt a wave of amazement and pity. All of Arbuckle's howling came to nothing when the chips were down. The teamster handed Arbuckle a copy. "You got fifty-eight bags of highgrade. We'll get 'em to the railroad all right. These here boys are naught to trifle with."

Dash surveyed the teamsters, who were weathered nut brown and looked capable of withstanding armed robbery and any other threat. A few moments later, Harry Arbuckle's gold vanished around a hillside.

"I'll get even with youse for that," Arbuckle said to Dash.

Dash bit his thoughts back again. "I'll start working on the discovery cairn," he said. "Maybe I can finish it by tonight if Mrs. Arbuckle will feed me."

"Do what you want but it ain't yours and never will be," Arbuckle said. "I'm gonna sell this little deal before it pinches out. I want some orange groves."

"Fine, I've an option to buy it for five thousand. I thought perhaps you'd like to earn a lot more."

"I know what you're up to, Dash."

"Harry? For heaven's sake, Mister Dash has helped us from the beginning. He got that deputy. We wouldn't even be here—"

"Woman, just stay outa it."

Dash turned to work. Maude's shot had loosened plenty of country rock, so he began wrestling those chunks into a wide base that would ultimately form a four-foot pyramid and meet the law's requirements. It would take several days of grueling labor to build it and the six other ones; another few days to drill another round and deepen the shaft to the magic ten-foot depth that would satisfy Nevada and federal law. He couldn't count on Arbuckle for any of it but Maude would pitch in—if Harry didn't harass her.

"Harry, go help that man," Maude directed.

"Why? Do you think I'm that dumb? Let the sucker do what he wants."

"Harry, for heaven's sake, you've got to prove up the claim to sell it."

"Not for ninety days," Harry replied. "We got all the time in the world. I'll sell it before then." He obviously considered it the crushing rejoinder.

Maude muttered something under her breath.

Hannibal Dash didn't say a word. Instead, he sweated steadily, resting when he could lift no more or shatter no more with the sledge.

"I guess you figure you're getting on the good side o' me," Arbuckle said, watching Dash wrestle the shattered rock into place. "Guess you think you can cop a gold mine. You want to buy it? My price went up to twenty grand. Yeah, twenty."

Dash thought about the signed and witnessed contract in his suit coat and said nothing. If it came to the courts he'd win—if Arbuckle didn't give away the mine to his lawyers.

It occurred to Dash that a man so erratic and irrational would do anything. Arbuckle was impossible. All Dash could do was wait and see. Things might change when Arbuckle got a check for the full value of that highgrade ore from the Selby Smelting and Lead Company, payable through the Bank of California. It would run, Dash knew, well over the twenty thousand that Arbuckle was talking about—for better or worse. Dash confessed to himself that he couldn't even imagine what would happen when Harry got that check.

CHAPTER 20

．．．．．．．．．．．．．．．．．．．．．．．

Casey Pepper reached grass in a bad mood. He lumbered past the bosses, exchanged glares, and headed home. The Combination shifters had started picking up lunch-buckets and shaking them at random. If the pail rattled they opened it without so much as a by-your-leave, and if they found highgrade they pitched it onto an ore car. They'd pulled good ore out of Len Larson's bucket not a half hour ago.

There were rumors, too, that the operators were going to put in changing rooms, where miners would have to switch from street clothing into mining duds. That would stop the highgrading—at least the highgrading of the stiffs. The rest of them, the supers, the hoisters, the men working above grass, they'd all keep on pocketing ore. But the stiffs who drilled and blasted and mucked and sweat, the ones who did the work, they'd be shut down. But so would the mine. The W. F. of M. would strike.

"Want a beer?" asked Tim McMillin.

Pepper shook his head. He wasn't like most of the stiffs, heading for the nearest saloon after the shift. Pepper liked the company of his own thoughts. Half the time, when he did have a beer with the stiffs he got into a fight. They were all dumb as stumps and let themselves be pushed around like cattle.

Goldfield seemed quiet for a Saturday afternoon. A January wind lifted grit from the unpaved streets and lashed pedestrians. It wasn't cold yet but later in the night the desert chilled the bones. Pepper knew what he was going to do. He'd felt it coming on all day. But first he trudged toward Alloy Street and the crook he dealt with. The sign said ASSAY but Beaubein's business was fencing gold. He had a whole reduction works in his shack; a furnace, a cyanide tank, a little ore crusher.

Pepper entered and began unloading his pockets under Jacques Beaubein's cynical eye. Pepper didn't care. He pulled good ore out of the sturdy canvas pockets that lined the inside of his jumper; more ore out of his hat crown; still more from the pockets that lined the inside of his britches. Today's haul came to twenty-eight pounds on Beaubein's balance scale. They didn't exchange a word. The Frenchman grunted, poured the ore into a Three X Brand flour sack, marked it in some code known only to himself, and consulted a cryptic ledger. From a small safe with pink cherubs he extracted greenbacks and paid Pepper one hundred twenty-eight dollars for yesterday's haul.

Without a word, Pepper stuffed the greenbacks into his jumper and punched into the afternoon. He hated the man. He hated the greenbacks. He'd get rid of them by dawn.

His whole body hurt. He stopped briefly at his boarding-house on Hall and Second long enough to unload his lunch pail and lie down for five minutes on his cotton-stuffed mattress. He feared he would fall asleep if he stayed there longer so he forced himself to his feet again and headed for the tonsorial parlor on Hall and First where he would get a bath in the back room, a Saturday night shave and a coating of witchhazel.

Dinty Roderus, the barber, had some clawfoot tubs in the back room and employed a punk kid to fetch water from the public well and heat it. A bath cost two bits. The shave would cost a dime more. Tipping the punk would add a nickel to the tab. Pepper handed Roderus a bath ticket he had bought two weeks earlier. Water was so scarce in Goldfield you had to wait your turn. Roderus studied the number, 871, and nodded Pepper to the back room where he found a tub unoccupied, its water tepid and grimy. The punk would add a bucket of hot stuff. He drained the water every five or six baths or when some stiff blistered his ears about the typhoid.

Goldfield's meager water had turned bad, milky and polluted. There wasn't much from Rabbit Springs and the shallow wells stank. No one bothered to protect the wells from horse shit or keep outhouses away from them. Pepper knew the stiff in the other tub; a W. F. of M. firebrand over at the Red Top. Pepper smiled but didn't feel like jabbering so he stripped and lowered himself into the water. The punk sloshed some hot water in, bringing the heat up a bit, but not enough to cure the ache in his muscles. Pepper scrubbed himself with the bar of yellow Naptha soap and stuck his head into the grimy gray soup to rinse his hair out. He didn't feel like hanging around so he dabbed water off his rivering body with the used towel, and dressed.

After getting his face scraped, Pepper plunged into a gray twilight feeling no cleaner and a lot wetter. But what could a working stiff expect? Hot clean water?

He debated whether to attack some vittles first or hunt for something to do. There wasn't much to entertain a man in the winter. He played third base with the Goldbugs but spring was a long time away. So was the time when a man could hike out upon the desert for a pleasant evening, shaking the darkness and cold of the pit out of him. Some warm nights he had even walked out to Alkali Springs with a blanket and returned in the morning.

Oh, what to do? He could go to the Mint Theater for some variety acts, like Willard the Hypnotist or "a congress of beautiful women in artistic posing." He could stop at the Union Hall and sit around with other stiffs or get a bowl of free soup there. He didn't need free soup. He had cash in his britches and he was going to get a steak smothered in onions and feel like a king for once.

There was other stuff, too. The Elks always threw a dance on Saturday nights. He wasn't a member but they let people in and a stiff had a chance to whirl a decent gal in a burg where there weren't hardly any. He could join a whist club or go to a hall where the Veterans of the Spanish-American War refought their battles. Some bunch was putting on *The Mikado* at the Electric. He could shoot a few games of pool anywhere.

But he didn't feel like all that. It was all stuff to numb the pain of being alive. Instead, he headed for the Louvre, a place that could dish out miner-sized meals and wasn't too fussy about how a stiff dressed. He found a back-corner table and ordered a one-pound T-bone under a mountain of onions, some new red potatoes, and a Pink's ginger beer just to live it up. He polished it off along with half a dozen Parker House rolls stuffed with butter and a piece of apple pie.

He didn't know anyone there. Not many stiffs visited the place. It looked to be an outfit for fifty-a-month clerks who wished they could highgrade a little ore themselves. The steak was just fine. By God, one thing a stiff could do in Goldfield was eat. Next Saturday he'd go poke around one of those Mexican places and burn out his guts with beans and chilies.

The night was young and he still had over a hundred dollars of loot to blow. He never kept a cent of money he got from the assayer. It was a way of thumbing his nose at the rotten world. He drifted to the Monte Carlo, just off Crook in the heart of the saloon area.

He was feeling like a little roulette and that saloon had four wheels spinning on Saturday nights. They were operated by a gaudy tinhorn named Billy Ace of Spades along with the faro layout and chuck-a-luck, and a bevy of poker tables. You would always find Billy in a plug hat, pleated white shirt with cravat, black cutaway coat, and brocade vest. He said he had been a Mississippi riverboat dealer but no one believed him. That type usually dressed like a deacon and presented themselves as International Harvester Company salesmen.

Pepper pushed through the crowd to a wheel run by a tough-looking little cookie with black hair and a high-necked blouse, one of Billy's women. Pepper knew her and knew she would entertain her customers by blistering their ears with profanities. He bought a stack of blue five-dollar chips and began spreading them around the third twelve. She spun the ivory ball and cussed a dude who put a chip down too late. The ball caromed into the twenty-seven slot and he found himself a winner with half a chip on the number. She paid him seventeen and cleaned up the eight he had spread elsewhere.

Winning didn't mean anything to Pepper. It was the same as waddling off the shaft collar with a few pounds of ore. It was all fake. He wouldn't see anything better until the world's stiffs rose up and threw out the whole capitalist class and abolished money.

Twenty minutes and two mugs of draft beer later he had blown the hundred. Billy Ace of Spades nodded cheerfully from his station in the middle of the games and handed Pepper a free-beer ticket. Pepper hated Saturday nights and wondered how to blow the last few dollars so he could go to bed.

He pushed out into the sharply chill night and drifted south past the Esmeralda Hotel, and across Myers into the tenderloin. He wasn't looking for a woman although most of the stiffs did on Saturdays. Everything in the tenderloin was fake. Fake fun, fake friendship, imitation happiness, fake women faking the marital act. He didn't want them.

But he wanted a whirl or two. He found Jake's Dance Hall, a fairly decent hurdy-gurdy compared to some in that skunky area. The girls hustled drinks and dances like everywhere, but no one had ever been robbed there. The proprietor, Jake Goodfriend, was a respected man who ran some of the variety theaters around Goldfield.

Casey bought five dance tickets at the bar and waited for the current stomp to end. The place seemed noisy and the smoke hung so thick he wanted to suck in the cold outside air.

A gal approached him. "You vant Annamarie for a little drink, sveetheart?"

She was as good as any. He wondered what accent he detected. Eastern European, he thought. She was a short wide dishwater blonde in a demure gray blouse and full black skirt designed for stomps and turkey trots.

"Yeah, sure," he said. She smiled, signaled the barkeep and a moment later he held a glass of amber-colored stuff that tasted like turpentine. She held a glass of similar-looking stuff but it was tea. It cost him a dollar and she would get fifty cents from the transaction plus a tip.

"Where you from?" he asked.

"Romania." She smiled cheerfully but it all was lost in the bad light. "I am here in Vunderful Country three months." He didn't like her. She was faking friendship. Everything in the tenderloin was a fake.

When the "perfesser of the ivories" finished his drink and started hammering the piano, Pepper gave Annamarie a whirl at the two-step. He bought her more tea and himself more varnish and whirled her into a turkey trot. He didn't dance well and knew it. He had no rhythm. He hated fun. It was the opiate of all stiffs. Every time he stepped on her toes she smiled and called him honey. More fakery for money. Would she never get mad? Was that all there was in the whole universe? He wished she'd cuss him out for stomping on her toes. But she patted his arm, smiled and chirped.

He hated the laughter, hated her, hated Goldfield. He still

had three dance tickets but he wouldn't use them. When the music quit he left her abruptly, damned if he was going to thank her or tip her for her phony cheer.

"Hey, sveetheart—"

He tossed his remaining dance tickets onto a table and shoved out into the brisk night. The sultry tenderloin beckoned. Women sat in windows. Men hurried past. Pepper didn't have any money and didn't want another fake experience. Money. He hated money. Some day there would be a better world in which people didn't do everything for money and everyone took care of everyone else. He stared contemptuously at the tenderloin, the ultimate capitalism. He hiked to his boardinghouse and the room he shared with three other stiffs. Some day he and the world's working stiffs would overthrow the rotten world and hoist the red flag.

CHAPTER 21

....

Hannibal Dash slowly erected the cairns, shattering rock and hauling it in a wheelbarrow to the discovery site and the corners and sidelines of the claim. It was grueling work for which years as a geology professor had not fit him. He could not even imagine it in Goldfield's summer heat but the winter air seemed mild, even salubrious.

Maude helped when she could and by degrees the two toilers took the measure of each other and became friends. Arbuckle blustered, sputtered and joked, and fled at the sight of hard labor. Each afternoon, Harry chipped a few pounds of ore from the little shaft and vanished in town for another round of buying drinks. Those ten minutes each afternoon with a pickax were the closest thing to work that Harry had ever done, according to Maude.

When the seven cairns were complete, Dash turned to the shaft itself. It had to be widened before it could be deepened. It had been a glory hole. It had to be turned into a shaft capable of containing a lift. He began drilling into its sides, exhausting himself every few minutes. He marveled that the Cornish Cousin Jacks could doublejack or singlejack all day, pounding slender holes deep into native rock.

Still he persisted, and at last had four holes readied for a round. If he succeeded he would widen the shaft about three feet. Following Maude's instructions he carefully fused the dynamite, tamped in the sticks, and sealed the charge with muck. Late that afternoon, just as he was about to fire the round, Arbuckle emerged from the shack and ambled toward the shaft, pickax in hand.

"Harry, no! You might set off the round!" Dash cried.

"Don't you be telling me what to do," Arbuckle said, proceeding toward the pit.

"Harry—the percussion from your pickax could set off that fulminate of mercury. You'll kill yourself."

Arbuckle glared at Dash. "How'm I gonna get my ore?" he asked.

"It's too late to get your ore today," Dash said.

"Get off my claim."

Dash remembered his cardinal rule for dealing with Arbuckle and ignored him. He lit a spitter and one by one lit the long fuses dangling from the side of the shaft and then hopped out.

"Let's go, Harry," he yelled, pulling up the ladder.

They both reached safety in ample time. In fact, the pause was so long that Dash wondered if his fuses had quit on him.

But they hadn't. The blasts thumped hard, even back at the shack, and jarred the earth under their feet. Dash's heart raced. A tan column of rock and dust erupted a hundred feet up, and then clattered down into a ring of rock and debris yards away. When the breezes rolled the dust off, Dash and Arbuckle approached the pit and stared into the swirling haze and the mountain of shattered rock which had nearly filled the little hole.

"Dash—how'm I gonna go to town now? You buried my ore!"

Dash wished he had extracted a few pounds of good ore for Arbuckle, who was growing more and more petulant. It would take two or three days to muck out that rock.

"Well, Harry—"

"Don't you Harry me! Durn you, Dash, now you done it." Harry Arbuckle pulled a shiny new revolver from his new suit coat and pointed it at Dash, something feral and elated in his eyes. "Get out. Get out and don't never come back!"

Dash froze. "All right," he said. Arbuckle was so crazy it wasn't safe to argue with him. "I'll get my stuff and see you—" *See you in court.* Only Dash didn't say it. He'd learned not to say anything to Arbuckle.

That's when Maude returned from town, something wild in her face, breathless with her exertions. "Look! Look!" she cried, waving an envelope.

"I'm shoving this bloodsucker outa here," Arbuckle said.

She eyed the revolver, and Dash, and groaned. "But Harry, we're rich. The check. It's here. From the Selby Smelter."

"Yeah, well Dash just buried my gold. There's twenty tons of rock on top of my gold."

"But Harry . . ." She extracted the check. "This is made to you. It's for twenty-one thousand, four hundred and thirty dollars."

"Quit your lying, woman. I'm on to you."

"No, Harry. We're rich."

This time it penetrated Harry's thick skull. He studied the check, his lips moving. "I'm rich," he said.

"We have to get it into a bank, Harry."

"Oh no you don't! We'll never see it again."

"Harry, remember what happened to the thousand you got from Mister Dash?"

"None of your business." Harry reddened and fidgeted.

"You were robbed," she said relentlessly.

"None of your business."

"We'll put it in the bank."

"Yeah, I guess so," he said.

"Oh, Harry . . . this is what we've always dreamed of."

"I'm the richest man in Goldfield," he said. "Now I'll show those bums at the Hermitage a thing or two."

"Harry, we can have a real home, all paid up. We can lease the mine to Mister Dash and just move to town. It'll be like heaven."

"Lease it to Dash?" Arbuckle said. The man's gleaming revolver turned his way again.

"You vamoose."

Dash nodded. "All right. It looks like I'll be resorting to other measures. I'll exercise my option on the mine."

Arbuckle gloated. "I can buy and sell judges and lawyers, Dash."

Hannibal Dash persevered. "You have two choices. I'll exercise my option and you'll get four thousand more—or we can work together. I'll lease the mine and pay you the standard twenty-five percent of gross production."

"Vamoose!" Harry yelled. He fired the revolver into the sky, then paraded like a rooster, waving the revolver wildly, laughing and gloating.

"Harry!" Maude yelled.

Arbuckle waved his check and the revolver, danced a jig and laughed.

Hannibal Dash felt himself in the presence of a madman. He quietly eased back, picked up his baggy suit coat, and retreated. He was going to have to go to court. He had done his best to keep from stealing a bonanza mine only to have Arbuckle force him to it. For Maude's sake he would have gladly shared the bonanza. Oddly, it didn't elate him.

In town that evening he grew more philosophical. From the start he had dreaded doing business with a man who was so mean-spirited and perverse that he couldn't even grasp the idea that some people were honest. It would have been pure hell. The richer Arbuckle got the more he would employ lawyers to push Dash out. Now it would be clean:

he would force the sale in court and take over. It might all be for nothing. The ore might peter out. But not before the mine yielded *something*. He pitied Maude but he couldn't help her.

But it was not to be. That evening, Harry and Maude appeared at his door and he invited them in. Harry looked strangely subdued and let Maude do the talking.

"Is it too late?" she asked.

"For what?"

"For the lease?"

"Perhaps it is." He remembered all he'd done. Driving out the claim-jumpers. Helping Harry relocate. Days of brutal labor.

"Oh, Lord," she said. "I was afraid of that. Me and Harry, we've been talking. A real good talk. We've been married a long time. We know each other's thoughts. He agreed to pay you for the shipping. We owe it and we'll pay it. We're both happy. It's a lot of money and you helped us get it."

Dash listened, surprised.

"We got the check into the Nye and Ormsby Bank. It'll be safe enough. Mr. Modor, the cashier, let us in just when they were closing and we got a receipt. We'll pay you for the shipping. If you still want to lease it, we'll lease it to you."

"Lease it?" The offer dumbfounded Dash.

"I'm havin' a shyster look at your contract, Dash," Harry said. "Don't you mess with me."

"Messing with you was never my intention," Dash said. "If you don't grasp that about me now, you never will." He gazed past them into the winter night and agreed to accept a lease. "You're the owner, not me. It'll be your terms, Mr. Arbuckle. Will a one-year lease giving you a royalty of twenty-five percent of the milling and smelting proceeds do? If so, we'll execute it in the morning," he said. "I'll meet you at your bank at ten."

"All right," said Arbuckle. The man seemed subdued, almost amiable. Dash had never seen him like that. Maybe a little money, a little importance, was all it took to transform Arbuckle.

"Oh, Mister Dash," said Maude. "It's a dream come true. All I want is a nice cottage with a Home Comfort range, the kind with the hot water reservoir on top. It'll be so nice to wash my hair. So nice to cook for Harry. I want to get him a good rocking chair. Maybe I can have an Acme Queen parlor organ . . . Just a nice little cottage."

Hannibal Dash peered at the rawboned, work-roughened, half-starved woman who wouldn't surrender and knew why he had agreed to a lease. Something in her indomitable heart reached out to him.

CHAPTER 22

What Beth Fairchild-Ross feared most was discovery. Throughout the trip she had gone to radical lengths to conceal her identity. The day she left her Union Street home she bleached her soft brown hair a shade lighter. She chose a broad-rimmed picture hat with a half veil that largely hid her face. She disliked veils but this once she was glad to hide behind one.

Everything she took with her she carried in a small portmanteau, having mercilessly selected a half dozen necessary things from her vast wardrobe. She peered one last time at Tommy, Jimmy and Annette, her three darlings. She and Reggie still had the housekeeper, thank God. Mrs. Kennicott would arrive in a few minutes. Reggie had left for the bank at dawn, as usual. He was putting a brave face on it but she feared for his sanity.

She did not summon a hack because it might give her away. Instead, she trotted down the long slope to the cable car, took the ferry across the bay, and boarded the train in Oakland, keeping a sharp eye out. She saw no one she knew and her veil kept her from being recognized in spite of her social position.

The costliness of her gorgeously tailored woolen suit instantly revealed her class to the astute observer but she couldn't help that. She had no cheap clothing. Only when she had settled at last in a dreary coach in the Central Pacific train to Reno did she relax her guard. She was among strangers. Instantly anguish enveloped her and she wept for Reggie, for her dear children, for the shame of it, and finally for herself.

She and Reggie had no brakes. They had enjoyed the whirl, the parties, the yachting, the merry lunches, the balls, the Mumm's champagne, the bohemians. She had never thought about money. He had rocketed to his present position as director of the trust department at the Bank of San Francisco almost by magic, charming everyone around him with his ready wit, compliments, and endless ability to enjoy life.

Until now. The accusations had turned him gray and pinched his soul. His infectious cheer had vanished. They were only suspicions; no one had accused him of anything—yet. His trust accounts didn't balance and five thousand three hundred dollars were missing. They were waiting for him to find and remedy the error. Waiting, but for how long? No one had accused Reggie of anything—except Reggie. One night in their bedroom he had confessed it all to her—the borrowing, some of it for speculations in the gold markets to recoup the borrowing. He had never supposed he would *keep* the money. It had only been a little loan. He wasn't dishonest, just a little careless.

They had cried together. He faced financial ruin. They faced ostracism and poverty. Already there were whispers; John Pillsbury, the bank's president, had been gossiping at the Union League Club.

There was nothing they could convert to five thousand dollars of cash. They had spent it all on life's froth, on velvet suits for the little darlings, on a nanny and cook. Reggie had some worthless gold stocks he'd bought through advertisements. They had sounded so good he thought he could recoup everything in a few months. Instead, he couldn't even get replies to the letters he wrote to that Borden Company in Goldfield, Nevada. It had finally dawned on Reggie that he had only dumped an additional two thousand down the hole.

It was then that Beth began to entertain a plan so desperate that she put it out of mind again and again. But the more she thought of it, the more she knew it was the only way out. She could not tell Reggie about it. She had to do this thing alone, secretly, against the world and against all she believed in. Discovery would destroy her life.

As she sat in the Central Pacific coach, she reviewed her options once again, hoping for another way out. Her family had been wealthy once, until the Panic of 1893 and the death of her father a year later had destroyed their shipping fortune. Ever since then her mother had eked out a living selling the last of her jewelry. She could not ask her mother, or her brothers, for money. They didn't have any.

Neither could Reggie's family help. They weren't poor, but they didn't have money. Reggie had gone to Stanford on a full scholarship. She could not ask rich friends for money. There were rumors floating around about Reggie. To ask for money was tantamount to admitting Reggie's guilt. She could not borrow money without collateral. And the loan would instantly point the finger at Reggie. Every door was closed—except one, which she dreaded more than anything she had ever faced in her young life. It might win her some money, or it might demolish her.

Many hours later, when the California and Nevada train pulled into Tonopah, she knew she had made good her escape. Not a soul had recognized her. They would think she had deserted Reggie and her dears. Reggie would think so too in spite of the guarded note she had left him saying she would return soon. She would have a bad time putting herself back in his graces. He would never know where she had been. But she was prepared for that, if only she could bail him out and life could be happy again.

She stepped out of the crowded, rank-smelling coach into a mild April day. She still had twenty-some miles to go. The railroad hadn't yet reached Goldfield.

She had her choice of stagecoaches, assorted wagons, and automobile coaches. The horseless carriages had lined up in a row and their owners were loudly bidding for customers.

"A flat two hours to Goldfield," cried one. "Five dollars for a high-speed, safe ride."

She opted for that one, paid him with a five-dollar bill, and settled into the rear seat beside a portly drummer with a heavy Gladstone bag in his lap. When the driver had acquired four passengers, he cranked up the engine of his Stevens-Duryea, which sputtered to life and rocked the automobile. He leapt in, advanced the spark, adjusted the mixture, and jammed the car into low gear, jerking her back in her seat. She drew her linen duster around her and wished she had goggles like the driver. She had ridden in many horseless carriages and knew their discomforts.

The automobile pike ran well east of the stagecoach road so as not to panic horses and mules toiling between Tonopah and Goldfield. Her vehicle plummeted through the dust and grit in the wake of half a dozen other horseless carriages that had gotten off before her car. The naked countryside amazed her. Its desolation matched her own and magnified it. They were crossing a terrible valley where nothing grew except little balls of some sort of green shrub. Forbidding mountains of bare rock rose in every direction, as lifeless as the desert they crossed.

The horse road was heavily traveled; they passed countless wagons hauling ore north and succor for a city of seven thousand south. The dust drifted across her route, stinging her face with grit. How far removed she was from the soft, cool moist climate of San Francisco. She was plummeting through a desert hell. Goldfield would be no better; a dry, cold, stinging, lifeless camp in the remotest corner of Nevada, unfit for decent life.

But the town surprised her. It lay under the brooding

brow of a high mesa on one side and a conical peak on the
other. It had grown into a compact metropolis, with tents
and shacks crowding its outskirts, but solid-looking buildings lining its central streets. Beyond, around the feet of
the conical mountain, were the mines, ugly pimples of rock
and yellow tailings, dotted by dark wooden buildings.

Goldfield! She could scarcely believe that she had found
the courage to come here. She had completed the easier
part of her passage. The harder part, the passage into another life, still lay ahead like ice in her soul. The machine
chugged and popped toward some main thoroughfare lined
with board buildings as well as ribbed tarpaper structures
ready to blow away; advertisements and signs shouting at
her from every angle. Men held the bridles of horses as her
automobile chugged by. Horses bucked and skittered at the
sight or laid back their ears. They passed banks and chophouses and saloons, hotels and blacksmith shops, cobbler
shops and hardware stores, until at last the clattering machine pulled up before a board and batten building labeled
AUTOMOBILE GARAGE. The driver slid in beside a dozen
other horseless carriages and cut the ignition. The machine
backfired.

The men jumped out. The driver graciously lent her a
hand as she stepped into the dusty caliche street. The passengers scattered and in moments she was alone.

She peered about her upon a busy avenue. People hurried
everywhere; wagons and carriages dodged each other.
Goldfield exuded some sort of wild energy, a madness, a
fever that immediately caught and held her in its grip. She
felt almost dizzy with it and realized she was hungry and
thirsty. She searched for a restaurant, knowing that even at
four in the afternoon she would find them all crowded. She
discovered she was on Main Street, one of the two major
arteries. She passed the Louvre, the Mint, the Red Top, the
Monte Carlo, and settled finally on the Peerless Café, which
teemed with rough men.

It was a poor choice. She would have done better in any
saloon but she was an unescorted woman. The water looked

so filthy she feared it would sicken her so she chose wine.
Didn't Goldfield have clean water? It dawned on her that
mining camps were cesspools of lethal disease and that she,
a blooming twenty-eight, might succumb. She would be in
peril of her life from cholera or other diseases of filth. She
hadn't thought of that on the sweet slopes of San Francisco.

She downed her beans and stringy beef, tasting nothing,
and fled into the street, toting her small bag. A terrible
loneliness engulfed her and she ached to turn around and
go back. But to what? Poverty? Ruin? A life in slums? No.
She stood in the street, peering sharply about her for fear
of being recognized, and began to walk. She didn't know
where she was going but she would recognize it when she
saw it. Did Goldfield never slow its wild pace? Everywhere
mobs of men—she scarcely saw a woman—walked, drove,
gathered in knots, hammered up buildings, plunged in and
out of saloons.

She drifted southward on Main Street past the Esmeralda
Hotel. If she couldn't bear this passage would they let her
stay a night? She was a woman alone and aware of it. The
veil didn't protect her from the hungry stares of womanless
men.

The bustle petered out after she crossed Myers Street.
The saloons turned mean and low and dark and quiet. She
passed the Palace Dance Hall and knew she was close. Beyond, men strolled casually past a row of narrow identical
dwellings, sliced out of a single building. Her heart hammered. She got up her nerve and wandered farther south
on Main. She wasn't far from San Francisco but she was a
world away from Union Street.

"Hey, sweetie," said a man as she walked by.

Something froze within her and she hastened past.

"Two's company," he yelled.

Women sat in the lit windows of the cribs that bore labels
like SADIE and MINNIE on their doors. Most wore gauzy
dressing gowns that revealed the dark nubs of breasts
through them, and smiled at the men who paused to stare.
She had found the place. She turned back to the Palace

Dance Hall to inquire. She felt scared but also excited in her belly, like plunging downslope too fast. Her throat went dry. Here was the other side, the very thing all decent people railed against. She wondered if she could do it; lie with men for a price. Still, she thought, no one would ever know. She intended to get rich fast and leave the very day she had enough for Reggie. She gathered her nerve and pushed open the door of the Palace Dance Hall.

CHAPTER 23

. . . .

Beth Fairchild-Ross discovered two men in the silent, gloomy cavern of the hurdy-gurdy. One lounged behind the bar. An old man with hooded eyes smoked silently at a rear table. He eyed her as one would a side of beef.

"Yeah?"

"I—want to rent a place. Like those next door."

He studied her. "Why don't you go back where you came from?"

She hadn't known she was so obvious. "How much?" she said, steel in her voice.

"They're full."

"Where can I go?"

A faint amusement built under those thick eyelids. "One-dollar whores stay in tents over on First. Two-dollar whores, you go down to The Den. You get six feet with sheets for walls. Take your pick."

She winced. She wasn't one of those. No one would ever know. This was temporary. "Look, Mister—"

"Dollarhyde. That gorilla is Ned. I hire him because he's good with a baseball bat."

"Mr. Dollarhyde, what do you charge for one of those little apartments—if one becomes empty?"

"Seventy-five a week. Fifty for me, twenty-five for Ned. You'll need him."

"For Ned?" She couldn't imagine why.

"For protection. You get into a jam, you get Ned. And then there's twenty-five for the law. Constable or deputy comes around, city license and all that, but it really goes into their pockets. It's a hundred a week."

Beth's chest tightened. "Ah, how much do those women—Sadie, Minnie . . ."

"Whatever they can get. This here's the best. Some get five plus tips."

Beth calculated swiftly. She would have to lie with a man twenty times a week just to pay the rent.

"There's a lot of jack around, sweetheart. Some girls are doing nice. It's the highgrading. All this gold. You gotta worm it out of 'em. Sweet-talk 'em. Do tricks." He eyed her cynically. "Now you've done your slumming. You go on home to Daddy."

"Tricks?"

He shrugged. "Sadie's banking better than two hundred a week. She does tricks."

Two hundred a week. A thousand a month or something like that. "All right," she said, weakly. "I guess I better go."

"Hey, you want to stay? You pay me seventy-five right now, put your skinnies on the table, and you get a crib."

"I thought—"

"Yeah, well, I'm gonna boot one out. Gertie. She's behind. She's a hop fiend. You lay out the skinnies and you can move in. Ned'll toss her out."

"Just like that?"

He laughed nasally. "Just like that."

"Do you . . . have rules?"

"Start a fire and I'll break your knuckles."

"Do you set the . . . price?"

He laughed. "Sweetheart, you gouge them for whatever they'll cough up and if you empty their pockets while they don't notice, you'll get more."

"I see," she said, solemnly. The reality was worse than all her imaginings. She took a shaky breath and made her decision. She handed him four twenty-dollar bills. She had two left.

"What's your name?" he asked.

"I—I can't tell you."

"Come on, sweetheart. Gimme a name. For the sign on the door."

She stared at him, stricken. No one knew; no one would ever know.

"Daisy. You're Daisy," he said. "We'll put Daisy on your door." He nodded at Ned. "Throw Gertie out."

The big oaf with slicked-back hair vanished. Dollarhyde smiled.

"You owe me some change," she said.

He laughed. "Tell it to the constable. Remember, seventy-five every Saturday noon."

She sat, tautly, until Ned returned. A single gesture from the bartender told the story. Dollarhyde turned to her. "It's all yours, sweetheart. Maybe I'll sample your wares."

Fear flooded her again. "I—I'll need to get settled."

He grinned cynically. "Lie back and enjoy it, babe. That's all you can do."

A moment later she found herself the mistress of a ten-foot-wide slice of a cheap building. The tiny front parlor had a bay window and a chair. The clear electric bulb above cast harsh light upon the shabby chair and couch. The window had a roll-down shade. She knew she was to advertise herself there; pull the shade when she was occupied. Behind it was a narrow bedroom with a brass bed and dirty cotton pad with odd stains in its middle. She saw no sign of a sheet or blanket. Not even pillows. The rear room was a small kitchen with a tiny stove, cupboards, table and two chairs. At its rear a door led outside. She peered into the late afternoon gloom, noting a single outhouse. But a woman could run the back way to the dance hall if she had to.

A knock startled her. Fearfully, she admitted a buxom blonde with a wide mouth. "I'm Sadie. Dan—Dollarhyde, he sent me over to look after ya. He says you're a wifey fooling around.''

''I'm—''

''You're Daisy, hon. Lissen, you're gonna need advice, I can see that. You're new at this. Got some husband somewhere and it's gone bad. You got a blanket and stuff?''

Beth shook her head.

''Well gimme ten dollars and I'll get anything you need. You'll want some towels, pillows, blanket, washbasin, some kitchen stuff, some Naptha soap—''

''Uh . . .''

''Sweetie, this is no big deal. So you get laid. Now listen to old Sadie. You got to wash their pecker first. If you see pus dripping out, you just forget it, he's got clap. And after you do it, use a fountain syringe and some powders I'll give ya.''

Beth couldn't imagine that.

''Hey, you're white as a sheet. You wanna get out? You vamoose. Go home.''

''I have to stay.''

Sadie eyed her kindly. Beth couldn't tell her age; she knew that the life wore them out and eventually spat them out into an uncaring world. ''Hey, Daisy, it's fun. Mostly I have a great time. The fellows, they mostly like you. They want to have fun too, laugh a lot. Drink a lot. It's a big party sometimes. Did—you like it with your husband? I mean . . .''

Beth nodded. Reggie had introduced her to things she had never dreamed of in her maidenhood. He was a hedonist and he took her right with him. She almost had a double life and it used to bring on the giggles—polite society, all that company and all those nice people, and then at night, Reggie fooling with her, tantalizing her until they both went mad and groaned so loud they would wake up the children. She had liked it so much she often seduced him, pulled him away from the *Chronicle*, winked at him at a party.

"It's like that, mostly," Sadie said, reading whatever passed across Beth's face. "Not always. Sometimes they don't care, slam, bam, thank you, ma'am. But others, oh, Daisy, all you got to do is enjoy yourself. Quit worrying. They like it when a girl's having fun. They can tell. Have fun and make 'em happy and you'll squeeze some big fat tips outa 'em. You got a lot to learn. How to move 'em in and out. How to get rid of them." She peered out the window. "Gettin' time to open up my shop."

She darted out and returned moments later with some bedding, a syringe, some jars and powders, and a washbasin. "You owe me. I'll get it tomorrow," she said. "One more thing. Don't use that well on Main. You buy your water from the water truck. You boil it. I seen a lot of girls croak around here. They think they shouldn't pay for water and next thing, they got typhoid or cholera and they crap all over the bed and die. Wine's safe. Beer's safe. If you gotta have water, boil it good. But don't drink the well water or you'll be number thirty-seven. That's how many that's died around here." She patted Beth as if she were a puppy. "I gotta go. I got a regular john now."

Sadie vanished. Beth swallowed. Dusk was settling. A man peered right into her window. She pulled down her shade. She bustled around, stowing the washbowl and yellow soap, spreading the greasy blanket. She examined the syringe and knew intuitively what to do. Sadie had given her a jar of Vaseline and Beth understood that, too. She found a pail, fetched some tepid water from a barrel in the back, and washed the place. And then there was nothing more to do.

Something caught in the pit of her stomach. She had run out of excuses. But Sadie said it'd be fun. She'd have fun. Tonight, she'd find out what other men were like. Unconsciously, she rubbed her ring finger, empty now of the band that had wedded her forever. She had hocked it.

She had to get into something. She had to go sit in the window. She had to think about prices. Five dollars wasn't enough. Ten dollars. She'd charge ten. She was worth it.

She knew how to please men. Ten dollars. She would have to lie with men five hundred times to repay Reggie's embezzlements. And maybe another five hundred to pay her rent here and food and a ticket back to San Francisco.

Well, the sooner she started to earn money the sooner she could help Reggie and be back with her darlings. Slowly she slid open the buttons of her elegant suit coat. Carefully she hung it on a bedroom hook. Slowly she slid out of her skirt and petticoat and chemise. She opened her little bag and pulled out the frothy peignoir, a Parisian thing she had found in the Bon. She felt her flesh goosebump. It was cool and she had no firewood.

She entered her little parlor again and settled herself in the battered chair, resisting the final act. But she had come this far and she wouldn't retreat. It would all be fine. It would be a three- or four-month lark. She could see her breasts through the chiffon. The cold had puckered her nipples.

It was all for Reggie. It was all so she and her darlings could resume their life. No one would ever know. Even if some man who knew her walked in, her hair might fool him. That was the thing she feared the most. Not lying with one thousand men but being found out. She sighed, knowing that rowdy, wild Goldfield lay far away from San Francisco society, and she was safe.

Slowly she raised the shade and settled in her chair. Instantly two men paused, studied her, and said something. She refused to cringe. They would be fun. At the worst they would be interesting, something for her memories. She wondered who would be her first customer. The knock came and something quickened in the pit of her stomach, something very like desire. She opened the door slowly, and beheld both of them.

CHAPTER 24

∙∙∙∙∙∙∙∙∙∙∙∙∙∙∙∙∙∙∙∙∙∙

Maude Arbuckle knew just what she wanted out of all that wealth. It wasn't much; it couldn't possibly irritate Harry. She wanted a comfortable little cottage, some new clothes, a few dollars a week for luxuries, ribbons, restaurant meals, and fun. She wouldn't even ask for a cook or a housekeeper; she had toiled at those tasks all her life and they didn't bother her. Besides, she would hardly know what to do with herself if all those things were done for her. Laundry was another matter; she had seen more of a Howard washboard than she ever wanted and intended to hire a laundress just as soon as Harry gave her some money.

Life had brightened. Anything was possible. She was rich! Mr. Dash had wasted no time employing four men to muck out the rock and drill deeper. Once the proper location work was done he had gotten a lawyer busy proving up the claim for Harry. He'd formed a partnership with two men who had once leased the Florence Mine and now a crew was erecting a gigantic headframe over the little shaft, its great squared timbers poking into a cobalt sky.

The men had fired another round in the highgrade ore and the good news was that this ore was richer than the layer above. The bonanza wasn't petering out. They had bagged it and shipped it to the smelter just as before, but now Harry was grousing because Dash and his leasing company would get seventy-five percent.

"I'm being robbed," Harry complained from the doorway of the shack.

"You're not even lifting a finger, Harry. They're doing all the work and investing all the capital. They're paying those men, and buying those big timbers and pulleys."

"I coulda done it myself. It's my ore."

"Harry—Hannibal Dash showed us three other leasing

contracts. They're all like ours. He's not cheating us. If it wasn't for him we'd have nothing.''

"Like hell we wouldn't of. I was just on the brink of getting rich when you and him messed it all up.''

Maude said nothing. It was no use.

"I'm going to town,'' he said. She watched him crank his new Golden Flyer until it coughed, backfired, and hummed to life. He wore a pinstripe suit with a paisley cravat and a big headlight diamond. On his pinky finger he sported a huge gold ring. He would get his daily shave and then head for the brand-new Northern Saloon where he would hold court again. It was being said that a man could go to the Northern these days and drink all night for free because Harry Arbuckle was treating. The crowds had grown as word of Harry's largesse spread through Goldfield. The bills were running two hundred a night, so they said.

It alarmed her. Surely Harry wasn't going to squander a growing fortune on beer. But some awful instinct told her that he was going to do exactly that.

They were still living in the shack a month after he had gotten his big check. Every time she brought up the matter of buying the cottage he just snarled at her. "I'll get me a house when I get around to it. Quit your nagging. That's all you do.''

"Harry, I'm just asking for a little cottage. Not some big five-thousand-dollar mansion. I'll cook for you and keep it up for you, and we'll be happy.''

"You're just trying to git my money outa me. God-almighty, I've put up with you all my life and I don't know why. You're cramping my style. You keep away from me when I'm in town, you lookin' like trash. Just git away and leave me be.''

He had given her fifty dollars for groceries and firewood. She had bought fresh blankets and pillows for their cots and a cheap rug to throw on the dirt floor. He still complained a lot, but the tone seemed softer, and she thought that maybe things would get better as he grew richer.

Each day, the mountain of supplies around the mineshaft grew. Dash was going to build a hoist house with a twenty-horsepower gasoline engine to run the lift, and a pump to force air down to the miners. Each day, too, the shaft sank lower as the four men—all that could fit in the shaft without interfering with each other—mucked and drilled and blasted.

The shack was becoming impossible to live in. Her privacy vanished and the noise made life a trial.

"Mister Dash," she said one day, "could you help me?"

"I'd do anything I could for you, Maude."

"Harry won't buy a house. I've asked and asked but he just says I'm nagging. He can afford one. Just a little cottage, that's all I want. Could you persuade him?"

She thought she saw pity briefly in Hannibal Dash's face but it vanished. He eyed the shack and the advancing circle of gear. "I'll tell Harry we need this space for storage," he said. "That should get him off the dime."

"Couldn't you just give me part of his next royalty check? I'd buy a little house. Harry'd be mad for a week and then he'd forget it."

Dash shook his head. "I wish I could. I'm bound by my agreement with him."

"Is he—is he wasting our money?"

Dash looked uncomfortable, as if tempted to say things that needed saying. "He's a grown man, Maude. It's not for me to tell him how to spend his money."

"He could be buying orange groves. Investing in good mines. He could be buying property around Goldfield—it's appreciating like mad. He could be . . ." Suddenly she felt unfamiliar tears well up. She never cried but now she was crying.

Dash seemed to make up his mind. "I've ways to do it, Maude. You'll have your cottage."

"Oh, Hannibal," she said, through a blur.

Dash cornered Arbuckle the next morning. "Look, Harry. We're about to put on a second shift. We're down forty feet and starting a drift. We're timbering the shaft.

We're also putting in pneumatic drilling this week. Those big engines, those pumps . . . there'll be noise from six in the morning to two in the morning. I'd suggest you move. We'll need this area anyway.''

"Driving me outa my own home, are ya?''

Dash looked as if he wanted to reply to that but instead he ignored it. "I just wanted to let you know, Harry. You and Maude should be thinking about a nice little place in town. You can afford to pay cash.''

"No thanks to you,'' Arbuckle said. "You and her, you skinned me outa three quarters of my gold. That's all I get—one quarter, and you'd take that from me if you could.''

"Would you like to see a list of our capital expenditures, Harry? We've invested fifty thousand. You'd be investing as much if you had it.''

"That's what you say, not what I say,'' Arbuckle retorted.

"Harry,'' Dash continued. "You never named the mine. It's just the Arbuckle Claim in the records. You want to give it a name?''

"Whatever you want. I don't care.''

"How about the Maude?''

Harry cackled. "Call it the Nagging Maude,'' he said.

"I think you ought to try something else.''

"I can't even name a mine without you griping.''

"I'll call it the Free Lunch, okay?''

Arbuckle cackled again.

That afternoon Arbuckle shoveled his things into a burlap sack and addressed Maude. "I got a room in town,'' he said. "Over the Monte Carlo.''

"A room—for us? One room?''

"A room for me. You can do what you want.''

Fear lanced her. "But Harry . . .''

"I'm not forgetting how you and Dash took my mine from me. How you nagged and whined, year in, year out. You can fend for yourself.''

She stood stock still absorbing that. He was abandoning her. "Is this permanent?"

"It's whatever you want it to be. Just get outa my sight. I want no more truck with you."

It hit her like icewater. Harry was no prize but his mine was. Her mine.

"I know what you're thinkin'. You try to take it from me and I'll swarm over you with the highest-priced lawyers in Nevada."

"Are . . . you gonna file for divorce?"

He grinned. "Got you over the barrel, do I? Well, just hang around and wait."

He leered, walked into the spring sun, and headed for town. She knew he would never come around the mine again as long as the checks kept rolling in. She knew she would rarely see him again unless she sought him out in the saloons. She was on her own.

For a while there, after Harry got the big check, she thought he would soften up and they would be partners again. When they had prospected together out on the desert, far from people, he had been friendly. Once he had brought her some wildflowers. He had even thanked her one time for the humble meals she set before him. She had never forgotten those precious moments. But it hadn't lasted. He changed when he was around people. It had all come to nothing. She had been chasing rainbows.

She had the shack. No one would chase her off. But she wouldn't be sleeping much. She collapsed into her cot feeling her stomach cramp. She felt like she had been clubbed with a baseball bat. Three or four thousand a week—and not one cent for her.

She felt tired and old all of a sudden; discarded like an empty whiskey bottle. Maybe it wasn't all bad. She no longer had to cope with Harry. She could always make a living but it would be the kind of living that offered no hope. She closed her eyes tight and let this new reality wash over her.

Half an hour later an idea took her. She could prospect.

She could locate her own claim. She'd dug this mine; she could dig another. She had the burro and some gear. All she needed was a grubstake and she knew who to ask for that.

CHAPTER 25

· ·

Delia Favor had little time to spare. She stepped wearily to the caliche of Columbia Street, her entire body aching from the hammering of the Tonopah-Sodaville stagecoach that had borne her an endless distance from Bishop, through Coaldale and Candalaria. She pummeled dust off herself while she watched the Celerity wagon driver heft her steamer trunk to a waiting hack.

She eyed the young hack driver and decided he would do. She wasn't particular.

"Take me to the Brown Palace Hotel," she said as he handed her into his phaeton.

"Ma'am, if you don't have reservations—"

"They're holding a room."

The fellow bounded to his seat and hawed the plug to life.

"Do you know much about Goldfield?"

"Much as anyone, I guess."

"What's the best restaurant. I mean, the *best* of the best. Where the best people go."

"That'd be the Palm Grill, ma'am."

"Are you sure? Is there any other?"

"Well, there's the Parisienne—but that's . . ." his voice faded. He turned around and eyed her, apparently satisfied with what he saw. She dressed handsomely in a polished cotton suit that did not conceal her curvy figure. She met his gaze with a direct gaze of her own huge, glowing brown eyes.

"Who goes there?"

"Why, all the mucketymucks. This place, it just opened. But I'm always taking mining men, supervisors, financiers—"

"Do you know them by name?"

"Why sure. I'm always taking financiers. Mister Jones—he's the richest man in town, him and his partner Borden. They're brokers. They practically live there."

"Well, good. What's your name?" she asked.

"Drew."

"Well, Drew, I'm looking for an escort. I'd like to treat you to dinner at the Palm Grill. And I'll give you a dollar, too."

He gawked at her.

"A lady needs an escort. Don't suppose a thing," she said sharply. "I wish to have a gentleman with me while I dine. That's all there is to it. Have you some proper attire?"

"Well, I got my church suit that my Ma—"

"That's just fine. And a cravat. And shine your shoes. I'm Delia Favor and I'll be waiting at the Brown Palace. Pick me up at seven and do make a reservation, won't you, dear?"

"You mean you're going to pay me . . ."

"How old are you? Twenty?"

"Twenty-four."

"My age. But you lack experience. Very well, I'll teach you how to escort a lady."

He pulled up before a small hotel on the north edge of the business district. This Brown Palace was obviously nothing like the famous hostelry in Denver. But it would have to do.

He hoisted her steamer trunk into the lobby. "That's two bits, ma'am."

"Call me Delia, please. If you're going to be my escort, you mustn't act like a toady." She slipped a quarter into his hand. "Seven o'clock."

He nodded, looking half-alarmed.

"Don't stand me up," she said.

"Are you kidding?"

She smiled. She knew perfectly well she was probably the prettiest woman in Goldfield. She worked on it, too, keeping her chestnut hair lustrous, her flesh peachy, and her beestung lips faintly painted.

Minutes later she was ensconced in a tiny room that passed for luxury in Goldfield but was miserable compared to hotels she had seen in Los Angeles. She had paid the double rent for one month. Everything had to happen in one month. It just had to; she wouldn't have a dime to go back.

She wanted to rest but really there was no time. She had been battered all day in the rocking coaches from Bishop. They had driven through dry and forbidding country not fit for a bird, through sullen rock and jutting peaks that sent mean messages to living things. But she scarcely noticed all that; she was too busy flirting with the men in the crowded coach. But none fit the bill.

She found a lavatory at the end of the hall, complete with water closet. Gratefully she laved herself with a cool-water bath and returned to her room. She would wear an exquisite pleated dress of white cotton this warm night; the one with the high neck that would display her onyx choker. At least she had good clothing. She had insisted on that even though Lester objected. Of course he had objected to everything. He had the vision of a garter snake. He couldn't even imagine climbing up the ladder beyond being the head clerk for forty-seven fifty a fortnight.

She couldn't imagine what she ever saw in him. She'd married at eighteen, starry-eyed, thinking that wedlock would free her from her dowdy, amiable upbringing as a hardware merchant's elder daughter. Lester came from a good family—his father owned a factory that made headlamps for horseless carriages—but Lester turned out to be a wet firecracker.

They had no children because she was careful not to. She had intended to save money and buy a fine house in Holmby Hills but after six years married to Lester she knew it wouldn't happen. She took him to court, charging cruelty and all sorts of things her lawyer, F. Austin Bean, could contrive. Lester didn't dispute it as long as she didn't ask for alimony. Her case was so shaky Bean warned her that Lester would win unless she went along with his wishes. So she didn't resist.

It took a year but now she was free. She had hocked her chintzy little engagement ring, a third-carat yellowish diamond, to finance this trip. Now she would find a male who was really going places. She had plenty to offer. She was no Dumb Dora. She almost had a teaching degree. She played the pianoforte and listened well. She was completely at home with males and knew how to kid them. She was gorgeous, and oh, so sophisticated. She cocked an eyebrow when she thought it, making the word faintly lewd. But she had to act fast; at twenty-four she was practically an old maid and she'd lose her peachy, apricot dawn look before she knew it. Especially in this awful air. Well, all worthwhile things require some suffering.

Promptly at seven Drew showed up on foot, and she gathered that the Palm Grill would be only a few steps away. He looked serviceable enough except for his pomaded hair.

"All right, Drew. Now be sure and call me Delia. I want you to look like a man of affairs."

"Uh?" he replied.

"Well just sit and eat nicely. Hold your fork nicely."

"When do I get paid, ma'am?"

"Oh, after we eat. Remember, do as I say."

He steered her into the Palm Grill and a maître d' escorted them to a center table. The place would do. A violinist named Julius Goldsmith perambulated among the tables and banquettes, dispensing romantic Hungarian melodies. The customers were mostly men, she noted, and wore starched white collars and cravats.

A tuxedoed waiter approached. "Would the lady and gentleman care for spirits or an appetizer?" he asked.

"Uh . . ." said Drew.

"Why yes, Drew, I'd like a glass of claret. And I believe you said a scotch?"

While her escort absorbed that, she smiled gaily at the waiter. "We'll eat later," she said. "We've so much to talk about. Give us a while."

"Very good, madam." He hastened off.

She sighed. There was no point in coming here without spending as much time as possible at table. "I hope you like scotch," she said. "If you don't, pretend you do."

"I never tried her," he said.

"Now tell me who's here that you know."

He craned around, peering at one face and another. "I think that's Harry Ramsey—he owns a piece of the Combination," he said, pointing to a bewhiskered gray-haired man with bags under his eyes. "That's Patrick and Hubbard with him. They got a piece of everything around here. And over there, next to the wall, that's Jones—the one with the stiff leg pokin' out. He's that financier. He's so rich he gives out one-dollar tips. One dollar! I'm lucky to get a nickel. That's his partner Borden with him. Them two, they're the richest in town, I guess."

"How do you know?"

Drew shrugged.

"Is he—Jones—what's his first name? Married?"

"It's Big Sam. Naw, he just tomcats—roams around. He sure gets talked about. Everyone knows Big Sam Jones. He knows everyone, too. He just remembers who you are. He's building him a fancy palace up on Euclid Street, you know, with turrets on top. Like a fort. He's got a brand-new horseless carriage and likes to scare horses off the road. It's a big, shiny Winston. Man, I wisht I could drive it once."

"Well now, Drew, how rich is Sam Jones? I bet you don't really know."

"He's so rich he don't know what to do with his money, that's all I know. He gets it in the mail; it just rolls in from ads he puts in papers selling Goldfield mines. I heard tell he's a wildcatter."

"What's that?"

"I don't rightly know but it ain't good," Drew said.

"Don't say *ain't*."

"Yes, ma'am."

Big Sam Jones wasn't very old. He had all his hair and he was big but not fat. Those other gentlemen looked old. Once in a while Jones grinned in a way that lit up the whole place. She eyed him thoughtfully. She didn't know what a wildcatter was either but she'd find out.

The waiter returned with the drinks and she smiled at him. He looked dago and his return smile was definitely dago. It pleased her to be noticed by a worldly dago.

"Who else do you know?" she asked.

"That over there's Tex Rickard. He owns the Northern Saloon. He's a big-time operator, I'd say."

She decided against saloon men, no matter how big-time.

"And that dumpy feller in the corner, he's the town fool. He's Harry Arbuckle. Struck it rich, the Free Lunch Mine, and spends it as fast as it comes in buying drinks. That gal he's got with him, she's some, ah, fancy woman from, ah . . ."

Delia studied Arbuckle, noting a man lacking ordinary couth; a man who picked his nose, belched, cackled nasally, and seemed utterly unsuitable, not to mention too old. She had no desire to latch on to a man who blew everything he made on booze. Definitely not. She eyed him dismissively.

That left Jones. She studied the financier furtively—at least she thought she was being furtive until he met her gaze. Then she gathered up her courage and smiled. He smiled back, summoned a waiter, and said something.

A moment later the waiter appeared bearing another claret and a scotch. "The gentleman says to bring the little lady and her gentleman a drink," the waiter said.

Delia sighed. She didn't like being called "little lady" but that was all right when it came from someone dripping with gold.

CHAPTER 26

••••••••••••••••••••••

Hannibal Dash could scarcely believe his fortunes could bloom so swiftly. With his lease and assay reports and samples in hand he approached Stanley Rogers and Richard Underwood, two veteran mining engineers who were looking for a good claim to lease. These gents had some investment capital at their disposal and immediately set about to develop the Free Lunch Mine after forming a leasing company in which Dash, Rogers and Underwood each possessed a third.

The ore shoot reached virtually to the surface and grew richer as they sunk the shaft. Maude Arbuckle had bored into a feeder vein that got better and better. The ore that assayed a hundred dollars a ton or less they simply stockpiled against the day when a mill should be built in Goldfield. The rest they bagged and shipped to San Francisco under guard. Freight rates to San Francisco ran eight dollars a ton for ore under twenty-five dollars' value to twenty-two dollars for three-hundred-dollar ore, plus three to five percent of the value in excess of three hundred dollars. Smelting ran ten dollars a ton and up. It wasn't the most efficient way to transport ore but with values of two or three thousand a ton they could absorb the cost.

At the forty-foot level they drove drifts in two directions, which soon enabled them to use two face crews instead of one. Above-ground they completed a headframe and hoist works, a shed to house the carpenter shop, smithy, ventilation pumps and hoist machinery. They laid rails to a slack pile but rarely ran a car in that direction. Most of the rock that came up on the lift was either stockpiled for local milling or bagged for the smelter.

Within a month the rich, shallow mine was amortizing its investment while absorbing its operating costs and pay-

ing Arbuckle his royalty. If Dash had any regret, it was that
the company possessed the mine for just one year, of which
two months had already been consumed.

Faithfully, as each check came from the smelter, the
leaseholders prepared the one-quarter royalty check for Arbuckle and sent it to Arbuckle's bank. The Free Lunch was
yielding a hundred thousand a month even in its development stages. Harry Arbuckle was getting rich faster than
the lessees.

The miners were coining money too. They waddled out
of the hole at the end of each shift so burdened they could
barely walk. It angered Dash but he could do little about
it. A strike could devastate a leasing operation simply by
shutting it down. It was better for a lessee to mine night
and day, ignore the highgrading, and get as much ore
aboveground as possible before the lease expired.

From what he heard, Arbuckle was squandering his cash,
setting up drinks on an awesome scale at the Northern, at
which he was now a fixture. If the owner, Tex Rickard,
was getting rich, it was because Arbuckle's largesse was
attracting mobs of sports and tinhorns. Arbuckle had also
taken to peeling off big bills to anyone who wanted a grubstake. The grubstakes were a joke. Arbuckle's other vice
was faro. If he was winning the tinhorns easily goaded him
into bigger and bigger bets until he lost. All they had to do
was call Harry a piker and Harry would instantly prove that
he wasn't. As far as Dash could ascertain, Arbuckle wasn't
putting a dime into savings. He was trying to buy the things
that couldn't be bought, respect and friendship.

Maude simply hung on at the shack, enduring the mining
din and traffic, her face pinched and tired. Dash ached to
do something, divert Arbuckle's bonanza to the woman
who really deserved it. But he was obliged by contract to
pay Harry, whose mine it was.

Maude came to him one morning after what had probably
been a restless or desperate night. She settled into a wooden
bench opposite him in his shanty office. "Would you grubstake me, Mister Dash?"

That was all she said. She didn't need to explain.

"Of course, Maude. I hope I'm Hannibal to you and not Mister Dash. How much do you need?"

She eyed him gratefully. "Well, how about twenty? I got the old burro and the gear. All I need's some grub."

"Maude, here's a hundred. You'll want a rifle to protect yourself from varmints. You'll want trousers and a coat. Some boots and gloves and a good warm cap."

"I don't want charity, Mister Dash. I know it's charity because you're offering more'n I need." Her fierce gaze nailed him to his chair.

"Well, I confess, every time I think of Harry—"

"Forget Harry. He's no-account. I'll find my own bonanza. How about fifty-fifty?"

"Too much, Maude. I'll take a quarter, all right?"

She pondered it. "You've done so much . . ."

Dash slid a money clip from his pocket and handed her some tens. "I've been wanting to do something like this," he said. "Maude—I'd like to lend you something for a lawyer. You ought to divorce him. He's not supporting you. He's deserted you. A lawyer can get you a settlement."

Maude shook her head stubbornly. "Jist let him be," she said. "He got brought up the wrong way. It's not his fault."

"But Maude—if you find something, he might claim half on the ground of community property. You're still married."

"I'll shoo him away."

"I don't suppose you'll find anything. This district's been picked over. Fifteen hundred claims on record."

"I'm not poking around here. I'm going out where a person's got to carry water."

"Alone? That's not safe, Maude."

She laughed harshly. "I been doing that since I was half-grown. If I croak, I reckon that's my business."

"Well, at least would you tell me—confidentially—what direction you're heading? If I need to reach you?"

She pondered that. "I'm heading west. I'll poke around

near the California line. I'm gonna look around the Silver Peaks."

"That's been gone over. It's also the roughest desert of all."

She snorted. "That's what's kept 'em out. They don't have my eye. They can see good ore and not even know it. I got the eye."

"I hope you do. When'll you be back?"

"I'll carry enough vittles for a month."

"What about water? There's not a drop that way."

"Me and the burro, we can drink sand and do fine." She laughed at him. "I got ways."

"Maude—what ways?"

"Seeps in those mountains. Digging into dry arroyos. Cactus squeezins. Chasing butterflies and bees. Mother Dear leads me to water whenever she sniffs it."

That didn't please him. "Would you report to me when you return? I'll do your assays . . . in total confidence."

She smiled for the first time. "I'd take that right kindly, Hannibal Dash. You'n me, we're going to hit a ledge or two."

"Maude—I'll grubstake you again if you come back with nothing."

"I take that kindly too. But I'll come back with something. I got the touch. I can dowse it with a stick. I felt it right here. Wasn't much, you know. Just the slope and an outcrop of rusty stuff that didn't look like any quartz I ever saw."

"I hope you're right," he replied politely. He knew she didn't have the faintest chance of finding another bonanza. The age of the prospector had passed; the discovery of ores was now the realm of sophisticated mining geologists employing costly equipment.

She read his skepticism in his face and laughed. "Don't think a woman can do it, eh? Specially some old scarecrow like me. Here's a wager, Mister Hannibal Dash. A dollar says I can, within three months."

"Done!" he cried. She looked so determined and grim

that it gave him pause. ''Maude, why this? Why not something in town? They're crying for women . . .''

''That'd be like slavery. That's no-hope work. Lots of women do no-hope work for two dollars, three dollars a week. Lots of men, too. It's good, sort of. We all need to make ourselves do dreary tasks. Good for the soul, I say. I've done my share and then some. I believe work gives a person dignity. But it's still toil and monotony and aches for just enough to live on if you don't get sick. No, Mister Dash—''

''Hannibal.''

''—Hannibal Dash, I like hope-work. If I dream of making a killing, the hunting and hammering aren't so bad. Neither is the cold or thirst or being out of flapjack flour. I'm tough as nails. It's harder to claw up rock and climb slopes than it is to scrub but this skinny carcass of mine's made for it. I'll do any work with hope built into it. Women don't see much hope-work unless it's hope for their babies. If I strike it rich I don't know what I'd do with the stuff. Maybe I'd try it again. I've got about all I need except a good dose of hope. Once I get to digging I'll be plenty happy.

''Hope is what we live on, you know. You know why Harry blows all that money? Because he's got no hope in himself. He knows what he is and thinks others are like him. He doesn't see the goodness in people. He thinks the whole world's out to do him in, and now he's proving it. I don't hate him any. He's too slather-assed to hate at all. Me, I take kindly to folks.''

''Maude, you're a gem.''

''Well, you're the first person to call me that. I better get outa here before you start calling me worse.''

Later, he watched her return from town leading that scrawny burro burdened with supplies. She bustled around her shack and then departed late in the afternoon, plunging into a mild spring day. She seemed so alone, a spare vulnerable woman striding into a rocky desert without the grace of vegetation or water. He intuited suddenly that perhaps she would be happier prospecting out there, free from Harry, than she would be enjoying Harry's gold. For her, the gold was in the hoping. Maybe walking down the rainbow was better than finding the pot of gold at the end of it.

She vanished behind a ridge west of town and he felt a palpable hollowness affect the Free Lunch Mine. Her presence on the site had been a sort of benediction. She had been the mine's watchdog through the small hours when no shift labored; an owner's presence even if she hadn't been the actual owner.

He felt oddly buoyed by her feisty attack on life. She'd been the strong one all along; strong enough to carry a weak man on her shoulders. Now she was turning a cruelty beyond imagining into her own triumph. It wasn't necessary for her to find gold; it was only needful for her to keep on hunting and hoping. He vowed he'd grubstake her for twenty years if that was what would give her peace.

CHAPTER 27

· ·

Olympus Prinz always enjoyed a good joke, especially if it had a butt. One inspired evening he stuffed his notebook in his pocket and repaired to the Northern Saloon to interview the latest Goldfield bonanza king.

He found Harry Arbuckle in his usual throne at the rear, next to the roulette tables. Around him sat his cronies, enjoying his every word and the nectars he automatically paid for. Arbuckle sported a chalk-striped purple suit and a bowler these days, the bowler clamped at a rakish angle above his watery eyes. A fat yellow cigar, brown-slimed at one end, gravitated from lips to hand and back again every few seconds.

"Mister Arbuckle, I'm Prinz of the *Observer*. I'd like to interview you. You're the most successful man in Goldfield and I'd like to tell our readers how you did it."

Arbuckle beamed. "Why of course, sonny. Wet your whistle on old Harry. What'll it be? We got everything from busthead to Napoleon brandy."

Instantly a bartender appeared with a foaming mug of dark beer, which suited Prinz just fine. He set it on a table and extracted his notebook and stubby Venus pencil.

"Well, sir, how rich are you?"

"Why, Prinz, I'm so rich I can't even count it. And it keeps growing so fast I'm desperate to spend it. You're not really rich until you don't even count it. I lost twenty-eight grand bucking the tiger last night and don't even feel it."

That evoked chuckles from the motley mob.

"To what do you ascribe your good fortune, sir?" This was what Prinz was really after.

"Prinz, I got a nose for gold. I knew right where she was, like a basset hound clawing up a skunk. The dad-blamed woman, she didn't believe me, but I allus knew. I sez Maude, this here ledge is it. I staked the claim and there she was, a million dollars popping outa the ledge. I'd be making ten times more iffen the lessees hadn't euchred me."

"You have deep experience prospecting, I take it."

"Sonny, I was rooting hog before you was born. I got started by prospecting for aggies in the schoolyard." Arbuckle tapped ashes to the floor. Some filtered into his lap.

"Well," Prinz said, "it takes some strength of character to do what you did. Tell me what strengths you drew upon."

Arbuckle pondered that a moment. "Prinz, I allus knowed I'd find it. See this here nose? It's a gold smeller."

"Yes, but what did you do?"

"Do! I took it to an assayer."

"Did you work? Dig? Did you suspect there was gold in that white rhyolite out there?"

"Sonny, I never gave up. I dug like a gravedigger." He chortled.

"I see. Did you have help?"

"Not a lick. That confounded woman never thought I'd find it. If it weren't for her I'd be rich."

That evoked an appreciative chuckle.

"Where's she now?"

"I haven't the faintest idee. She just taken off. I don't miss her none. She cut me a bad deal and the lessees are getting rich on old Harry. Not that it matters. There's gold enough to buy and sell Santa Claus."

"That's a good one, buy and sell Santa Claus. I'll quote you." Prinz thought it was the most quotable item he'd heard in years of newspapering.

Arbuckle beamed.

"What'll you do with your wealth if it's piling up so fast you can't spend it?"

"Sonny, I'm giving it to the world. Grubstaking pore old souls. I been there, rooting hog. Have some more suds, sonny."

"You've no plans to buy other mines, invest in other deals, put the money into a trust?"

Arbuckle turned crafty. "I can't rightly tell you; it's something my trusters are working out."

And so it went. Twenty minutes later Prinz trotted to his offices and set to work on the story, composing as he slid the letters into his typestick. By the time he was done he had created a formidable American hero.

That week the *Goldfield Observer* featured a long front-page feature about the new bonanza king.

"Mr. Harry Arbuckle, who believes himself to be the richest man in Goldfield and perhaps the United States, sits upon an inexhaustible bonanza known as the Free Lunch Mine. He reported to the *Observer* that he's making money so fast he doesn't know how to spend it.

"His generosity, however, has become a legend in Goldfield, where people down on their luck need only ask to receive a hundred-dollar bill he peels off of a fat roll tucked in his purple trousers.

" 'I've been there, rooting hog,' he said, explaining why he shares his incredible fortune with those around him. He grubstakes anyone who asks, even those who have no intention of repaying. 'I could buy and sell Santa Claus,' he said.

"Arbuckle ascribes his incredible good fortune to a mastery of geology and an encyclopaedic knowledge of minerals and ores. He confesses, diffidently, that he can virtually smell the gold in the ground and once he is certain of it no amount of skepticism or scoffing will deter him from digging. As for the rest, he cites his industry and diligence, perseverance and moral courage as the building blocks of his success. His greatest asset, he believes, is his virtue, which gave him the resources with which to weather hard times, perfidy, and domestic strife.

"Mr. Arbuckle is a man of keen philosophical insight, with a mind that rivals Kant and Spinoza, if not Aristotle. He is self-educated, but possesses a shrewdness that exceeds the best minds in the state.

"He is estranged from his wife who, he confesses, seriously hampered his single-minded quest. 'But I always was patient,' he went on. 'The thing to do is endure.'

"Asked what he intended to do with a major American fortune, Mr. Arbuckle turned chary, saying only that his trustees were working on it. He admitted he didn't know what to do with a fortune so vast. He is considering founding a morticians' college.

"Mr. Hannibal Dash, of the leasing firm of Dash, Rogers and Underwood, reported to the *Observer* that the mine is producing highgrade ore, running anywhere from $3,000 to $6,000 a ton, and that the mine, expanding drifts at the eighty-foot level, has yet to reach the perimeter of this massive body of quartz ore. He estimates that by year's end, if present values continue, the Free Lunch may yield two millions.

"The lessees are now operating the mine twenty-four hours a day and employing over forty men. He declined, however, to say what his leasing arrangements are with Mr. Arbuckle or to respond to Mr. Arbuckle's sharp criticism.

"Mr. Arbuckle is eager to assume management of the

mine when the lease expires. 'I could operate that mine blindfolded,' he said, 'and pull a lot more highgrade out of it than those lobsters.' It is known that Mr. Arbuckle is dissatisfied with the present lease.

"The likelihood is that Mr. Arbuckle may soon become a millionaire, maybe even become a multimillionaire. He is unusual for his kind because his life is devoted to philanthropy, the theater arts, the sciences, higher education, moral philosophy, and cultural improvement."

Prinz's feature continued in that vein for thirty column-inches and instantly was the sensation of Goldfield. It had just the effect he hoped: The whole lusty camp celebrated Arbuckle with a horselaugh, although Arbuckle, when the article was read to him, beamed happily and pronounced it a corker. He sent Prinz a magnum of Dom Pérignon.

Within two weeks several of the *Observer*'s exchange papers reprinted it, as Prinz knew they would. Americans doted on bonanza kings. Give them a new Morgan or Rockefeller or Hearst, and they converted a ruthless money-grubber into a fairy story prince; proof that this great and bountiful nation could bless those who employed the right strengths of character. Within a month the article had been reprinted across the country.

Then the mail filtered in, some of it addressed directly to Arbuckle, but most of it sent to the *Observer* to be forwarded to the great man. Each day, Prinz gathered a sheaf of perfumed letters written in a feminine hand and handed them to Arbuckle on his throne at the Northern. And each day, Arbuckle professed to have forgotten his spectacles and asked Prinz to read them.

Thus it was that this new bonanza king, American hero, philanthropist, and semisingle prince of Nevada, received a stream of breathtaking proposals and propositions.

"Dear Mr. Arbuckle," wrote one lady from Norfolk, Virginia. "I saw the article about you and I want to express my utmost admiration for the selfless life you live after years of hardship. I think we have a lot in common and I would love to meet you. I adore older men and think I could make one very happy. I've carefully guarded my virtue though I am said to be very beautiful, tall and willowy, with tender lips and a Gibson girl figure. I think you would enjoy my company. Of course I ask nothing but your companionship. I'm awaiting your response breathlessly. Love, Dora.''

"She sounds like a dilly, Prinz," said Arbuckle. "Ah, my fingers are so arthritic I can hardly scribble. Tell her I'd enjoy meeting her. I enjoy the company of sweet young ladies. Send her two hundred for fare. Here''—he peeled off some bills—"you take care of it."

Prinz figured he wasn't Arbuckle's amanuensis but the fun was irresistible. He wrote about twenty such responses over the next few weeks, addressed to virtuous maidens, ladies who professed to have not a shred of virtue, good cooks, good housekeepers, good mothers, good lovers, women who proposed marriage, women who proposed to help Harry in his charitable endeavors, women who offered Harry undying love, and so on.

But Arbuckle drew the line at vegetarian reformers, orphans, monasteries, poor widows and others who begged for cash for this charity or that ministry.

"Bloodsuckers!" he snapped at Prinz. "Don't even read them letters to me. They're worse than them leasers, bleeding me dry. A man gets ahead with hard work and strong turpitude, and every leech in the universe bores into his skin like ticks."

That made a good quote for Prinz's numerous follow-up articles. To the enchantment of all of Goldfield, Prinz kept Arbuckle in the limelight in every issue. Each front page offered nuggets of Arbuckle's wisdom. It reached the point where people were subscribing solely to keep up with the reportage on that American legend, Mr. Harry Arbuckle.

Olympus Prinz was enjoying the wildest horselaugh of his young life.

Meanwhile, Arbuckle's suitors arrived in town one by one by one—and left almost as fast. And the ones who stayed set their sights elsewhere. Olympus Prinz's little weekly bloomed and subscriptions grew. The young editor added a printer's devil, Uriah Horn, bought a new type font, and celebrated his triumph of journalism. The *Observer* was the best-read paper in Nevada. He was still in his early twenties and his whole life glistened before him. He lacked only a loving wife to be complete.

CHAPTER 28
....

Big Sam Jones laughed at the stuff in the paper about Harry Arbuckle. If anyone was the richest man in the bonanza camp, it was Jones himself. He and Borden were coining anywhere from ten thousand to twenty-five thousand a week, peddling gilt-edged, engraved gold mine shares to hog butchers in Davenport and schoolmasters in Ponca City. They both processed mail during the mornings. Afternoons Jones devoted to perfecting his advertisements, which now appeared across the nation in scores of papers each week. He didn't mine an ounce of gold but he had the biggest and best mine of all.

He hardly knew what to do with all that boodle he and Borden split fifty-fifty after expenses. They had taken to investing in Goldfield's operating mines, or publicly traded leasing companies, and actually held a fine portfolio of glittering gold stocks.

The only thing that was holding him back was general ignorance about Goldfield. Some day, somehow, he would put Goldfield on the map. When anyone in Philadelphia or Atlanta could tell you that Goldfield was the Golconda of the republic, he would triple his sales. It wasn't gold he was selling; it was Goldfield.

Spending all that cash was no easy thing even for a man as dedicated to it as Jones. He bought Thoroughbred race horses, San Francisco real estate, Goldfield lots, railroad stocks, ranch land, the fourteen-room stone palace that was

abuilding on Euclid Avenue, half of the Goldfield State
Bank, the Palace Livery Barn, a faro layout in the Monte
Carlo Saloon, and an interest in the Mohawk Saloon. He
brought a dozen shiny silk suits in pastel colors, ordered a
gross of Stetson hats, had giant gold cuff links made from
Mexican fifty-peso pieces, and organized a new Goldfield
water company. He bought matched trotters, a surrey, a
barouche, and a victoria.

"Windlass, I've run outa things to buy in this burg," he
complained. "I can't even find a reliable rathole to pour
my money down. Whenever I buy stock in some spavined
mine, it starts running like a filly. You gotta help me spread
it."

Borden sighed. "A woman is what you need, Big Sam.
It takes a woman to help a man enjoy money. I've got three
now and between 'em they're keeping my money problems
in hand."

That struck Jones as a great and famous idea. He stared
at the cherubic Borden and marveled that he hadn't thought
of it. The trouble with being an itinerant horse trader is that
you don't think much about women—at least not the sort
of women you'd consort with in public. It occurred to him
that he might dicker in women; it'd be more fun than horses
and mules.

The vision of that curvy little brownhaired beauty he'd
seen a few times at the Palm Grill rose to mind. He had
sent her a drink that first time he'd seen her but nothing
had come of it. She always had an escort, but each time
he'd run into her the young buck was different. She was
probably available. He had no notion where she lived or
what she did; he only knew that the sight of her set his
pulse running. She had everything a man wanted in the
right places, along with big brown eyes that gazed innocently about the restaurant, her gaze alighting softly on this
or that—and on Big Sam Jones himself, more than once.

A sweetheart indeed. It was time to fall in love, share
his delightful life, escort a comely lady around town, find
someone who'd care for him when he was blue, find

someone to hug. Why hadn't he thought of it? Was it because there was scarcely one woman for every twenty men in the camp and even fewer of the variety he could squire to a restaurant? That evening he settled into his familiar seat at the Palm Grill, listened to Julius play Hungarian rhapsodies, ordered a duckling dinner, a magnum of Beaujolais, and waited.

A little after seven she appeared with yet another young gent, this dude a blond buckaroo with a cowlick and a lazy eye. From his usual seat, a table against the wall where he could park his stiff leg, he surveyed her. She was younger than he'd imagined, mid-twenties or even less, and dressed primly right up to her chin. That disappointed him. He was sort of looking for someone less inhibited.

Moments later morose Reuben, his usual waiter, appeared at her table, opened a bottle of white wine, poured it, and explained that it had been sent with the compliments of Samuel P. Jones. Big Sam watched intently and this time when she glanced his way he met her gaze and smiled. She said something to Reuben, who nodded solemnly.

"The lady expressed her gratitude and said they would join you for an after-dinner drink," Reuben said. That seemed like a long ways down the racetrack to Jones, but he nodded, smiled incandescently in her direction, watched her bat her big eyelashes, and settled into his duckling a l'orange, which he had purchased because it was the most expensive item on the menu.

Once Jones got his nose into the feedbag he tackled his meal with professional skill. He regarded himself as a professional trencherman. He could reduce a platter of vittles in one hundred twenty seconds without spilling a bean. But she was far behind, twiddling her fork, mooning around that acned young lobster as if he was the only man on earth. He recognized the fellow: he drove a hack around Goldfield. Surely a woman so delicious could do better than that.

But at last, after she had spooned the last mousse into her dainty mouth he hoisted himself onto his bum leg and lumbered over to her table.

"Please join us, Mister Jones. I'm Delia Favor and my friend is Willard Petrie. Did I pronounce that right, Willard?"

The hack driver nodded dumbly, his Adam's apple bobbing up and down as he put away a forkload of sherbet.

"Why, Delia, I'm plumb tickled to know you. I'm a horse trader by profession and you remind me of a little brown filly I once owned."

Something shadowed crossed her face. "Oh, is that what you do? I thought—"

"I horse-trade mining stocks and securities," he said. "Got a little old money machine up the street. It keeps body and soul together."

"I know," she said.

"You do?"

"Certainly. I'm going to buy some stock soon. You're the Jones in Borden and Jones. Perhaps you'll recommend some shares to me. I know nothing about high finance."

"Oh, I can do that, all right. I've got the inside scoop about a lot of 'em, Miss Favor—it's Miss, isn't it?"

She sighed. "No, it's not. I know it's almost a scandal but I'm divorced. I can't bear to talk about it."

"Well then, we won't," Jones replied cheerfully.

"It wasn't anything very bad. I mean, nonsupport isn't really bad. Lester was very virtuous and I'm fond of him. But the poor man wasn't very capable. I mean, a man should make a living, shouldn't he? I never wanted much. Just an itty-bitty cottage and a big old wonderful hubby. But it didn't turn out that way. Most of the time he didn't work and we starved. I don't mean literally. I sold some securities my parents gave me. But it wasn't long before I went through those, and we had nothing. That's when I knew that Lester, well, that it'd been a mistake. Fortunately we didn't have children." She smiled. "I don't know what I'd have done with a little baby and nothing in the house to feed it. Sometimes things are blessings even when we don't know it and all we see is the suffering and hopelessness."

Jones understood. "I've bought horses like that, Mrs. Favor. Doped-up critters that step fancy when I'm buyin', and then turn into a bag o'bones about an hour after some cocky farmer's gone down the road with my cash."

"Oh, Lester wasn't like that. He's a very decent person. It's just that . . . life became a trial. I summoned all the bravery I had, but . . . the day came when I had to go to a lawyer and risk the scandal. You know what people think about divorces—that something immoral happened. And about divorcées. That we're . . . well, you know, eager." She averted her gaze, delicately.

"I don't know's I ever thought about it," Jones said.

She eyed him gravely and pursed her beestung lips. "I couldn't even ask for alimony because the poor man didn't earn anything."

As far as Jones was concerned a divorced woman was nice and saddle-broke. He liked her voice, which was velvet and peppy. She spoke well and he liked that. But most of all he liked her friendliness. This one was no skittish little filly a fellow could hardly get a hand on. "What brings you to Goldfield, Mrs. Favor?"

"Why, I'm looking for respectable employment. I'm afraid that I didn't receive much in the settlement . . ." She stared resolutely at the linen tablecloth. "I thought maybe secretarial work. I have a Spencerian hand and I can keep books as well as any man. So far, though, I've just been looking."

"Well, look no further, Mrs. Favor. I'll hire you. Borden and Jones could use a dozen clerks."

She hesitated. "Thank you, Mister Jones. I'll think about it. I'm not sure it's suitable. A woman shouldn't be out in the world very much. A woman really should be tending the hearth and finding ways to make her man happy. That's all I ever wanted, just to give myself to a worthy loving man. But the Good Lord wouldn't give it to me. I suppose He's testing me. Trials build character, you know. I tried— oh, my, why am I spilling all of my troubles out upon you?" She smiled bravely. "It's so good of you to join us.

Willard is the nicest young man and here we are.''

"Here we all are," Jones said, reaching for a fat cigar.

Later, when Jones looked back upon it, he realized that Willard had been nothing but a prop. They were all props, those hack drivers who had come and gone at the Palm Grill never to be seen within its confines again.

He corraled Willard on Columbia Street the next day, handed him two bits, and began asking questions. Delia, it turned out, had paid him two dollars to escort her to the Palm Grill. She had paid one or two dollars to other boys too, some hack drivers, some Western Union messengers, pumping each one about the town's eligible rich men, especially Mr. Sam Jones, the financier.

"Thanks, pal," Jones said, flipping Willard another quarter.

Delia was in town to do some gold digging. He didn't mind. He mined gold; everyone mined gold in Goldfield. He'd mine Delia. She was an age-old species of female who knew a man's needs and met them for her own price beneath the veneer of respectability. The more he thought about it, the better it seemed. Jones could not do better than Delia, especially in a camp where women were scarce. In fact, he liked her ambition. A gold-digging grass widow was just the lady for Big Sam Jones. Beneath that prim exterior was a woman with unbanked fires, ruthless ambition, and the will to reach for her goal. Maybe he might even fall in love. That little gal did something to him, made him happy from muzzle to hock.

He figured it was just as nice a trade as an old horse trader could ever make. His rock pile would be done in a couple of months and he would park Delia in it and give her an allowance and let her rip. At last Jones had found his mate. He understood mares. Geldings baffled him, but never a mare.

"Windlass," he bellowed when he reached the office, "I'm gonna waltz my way to heaven. I've fallen in love with a lady who'll spend it faster than I make it."

Borden stared. "That's not possible," he said.

"Believe me, it's possible. I have a hunch that Delia'll outspend the United States Congress. I'd hate to fall in love with some old gal who cooks pig knuckles to save on the butcher bill."

"Are you gonna marry her, Big Sam?"

"I reckon so, Borden. I figure I've met my match."

CHAPTER 29

. . . .

Beth Fairchild-Ross eyed the two men at the door, a certain thrill of anxiety coursing through her body. Both seemed to be miners. They wore denim jumpers and looked none too clean.

"You selling it?" the taller and darker one asked.

She winced but then gathered her courage. "Yes."

They barged in as if they had every right. "What's your name. It ain't on the door," said the other.

"Daisy. I just got here."

"Yeah, well, Daisy, what do ya want?"

"Ten dollars."

"Each or for both of us?"

"Each."

"That's nothing," the taller one said. "I'm Ansel; he's Turk. We'll do it all at once, okay?"

"You mean together?"

He grinned. "Yeah."

Anguish tore at her. She didn't want that. "No, one at a time. One can wait here."

He leered at her. "You new at this or something?"

"I don't talk about myself."

"You're acting like a blushing bride, sweetheart."

"You can pay me now."

Ansel extracted two fives from a pocket purse. "There's ten. That'll buy anything you can give me, Daisy dear. You got lots of cheaper competition."

She hesitated. "All right," she said. "You first. You can wait here," she said to Turk. She took the two fives, folded them into a tiny knot of paper. Her hands were clammy.

"Well, hurry up," Turk said slyly. "You're driving me nuts."

"How come you charge so much? Greedy, eh?" asked Ansel.

She summoned a smile. "Maybe I'm worth it."

"We'll see," he said. "Maybe you're worth fifty cents."

She felt insulted. She and Reggie made dreamy love all the time, soft and voluptuous. She didn't reply. Abruptly she turned into the narrow little room where the bed of sin lay forlornly deep in the shadow of the parlor lamp. She slid the damp money into a slot in the dresser. It vanished into a sheetmetal lock box inside the top drawer.

He followed into the gloom. "Light the light," he said.

"Why? It's nice in the dark."

"Because I want to see you. You new at this or something?"

She lifted the glass chimney of the kerosene lantern, lit the wick with a kitchen match, turned down the wick so it didn't smoke, and replaced the chimney.

"That's better, Daisy," he said. He was studying her, amused. "This is your trick. Playing virgin. Okay, okay," he muttered, tugging at his shirt. She stared, transfixed, at his trousers and then at his nakedness and desire. He had a long scar on his thigh. His body looked hard and lean and abused.

"Jesus, Daisy, whatsa matter with you?"

That galvanized her. She slid off her gauzy peignoir, feeling his gaze pummel her with a force almost physical. The sight of his manhood stirred something deep within her and she sighed.

She washed him, discovering her lust. It came unbidden, rolling through her body like a tidal wave, consuming her. Moments later she ceased to think about what she was doing. She surrendered to it, engulfed in flame. This was the forbidden thing. She was violating the contract she made

with herself but she couldn't help it. She groaned and her
groaning whetted his ferocity. She sobbed, utterly out of
control, catapulted to a frenzied pain that seemed leagues
away from anything she'd known with Reggie. She
screamed and slowly subsided while he lay inert over her,
a stranger whose name she barely knew.

Delirium enfolded her. Not this, she thought through a
gauzy peace. It ran against her rules. She had intended to
keep herself distant; live on another planet of the soul while
men used her. That was the moral thing. They might use
her body but she would never enjoy it; she belonged to
Reggie. She belonged to her children. She had intended to
return to San Francisco with that justifying knowledge;
none of the men she would lie with would ever touch her
passions. She would return to Reggie inviolate, a woman
who'd merely lent her body to rescue her poor husband.

But that hadn't happened.

Ansel rolled slowly off her. "You're a good actress," he
said. "That's why you charge like a bandit. You almost
made me believe it."

"Yes, an actress," she said. Then she wished she hadn't
said that. She wanted repeat customers. "Maybe it wasn't
acting, sweetie. Maybe I just like you. Now you go wait in
the parlor."

He didn't move. She climbed out of bed, turned her back
to him, poured water from the pitcher into the porcelain
bowl and washed her loins. He still didn't move.

"Look," she said testily. "I have to make a living. Either you pay me again or go."

"Ten dollars buys an hour."

"No it doesn't." She wondered if she would have to get
help her very first time.

"All right," he said. He reached into the britches which
lay atumble on the gritty floor and found some more bills.
"Here's nine," he said.

"All right," she replied, hating herself again. She took
the worn bills without counting and stuffed them through
the slot.

Her body betrayed her again. She cried and groaned and finally screamed. She slowly returned through the haze of sensations and discovered Turk at the door, watching and grinning, hunger licking his face.

"Had to see that," he said. "Daisy, you're some broad."

"Go away, go away," she cried, and then thought better of it. "That's ten dollars. If you look, you pay."

Turk didn't even quibble. He laughed, dug into his pants, and tossed her an eagle. It landed beside her on the bed. They both were enjoying her. She swung out of the bed and dropped the gold coin into the slot. Her heart hammered. The sheer forbiddenness of all this had excited her, irritated her flesh, like some itch that couldn't be satiated. Here she was, Mrs. Reginald Fairchild-Ross, of San Francisco, the best society, naked with two men, one of whom had just enjoyed her while the other watched. That was terrible enough. Worse, she had been transported to realms of passion she hadn't even imagined; realms where Reggie had never taken her.

Awhile later she saw them out the door. She was forty-nine dollars richer. She was already so tired she only wanted to pull down the shade and turn down the wicks. But she knew she couldn't. The faster she made money, the sooner she could escape.

By midnight she had taken thirteen men into her bed. It astonished her how different they all were: lustful, angry, joking, frightening, simpering, weary. Some said nothing. Others tried to be friends. Some snarled at her price. Others paid it and added a huge tip. She did whatever they wanted, plastering her smile over her face. She had washed them, washed herself, studied them for signs of disease, taken them into her, one by one, amazed by it all. A few expended themselves in moments. Others were lovers, swiftly building a fine madness within her, even more painful and wild than Ansel's lovemaking.

The lovers troubled her most. Each reminded her of her broken contract with herself. Each showed her that Beth Fairchild-Ross wasn't even remotely the woman she had imagined herself to be. The old Beth had soft and voluptuous moments; this Beth had pain and lava in her belly. By midnight she felt sore and used and terribly depressed. There were wanderers strolling the tenderloin still; in fact, it was the shank of the evening in that district. But she saw her last customer out and didn't lift the dark green shade again.

She fled to the bed, the very bed of her shame and self-discovery, and furiously shook the grimy sheet and the grubby blanket. She poured fresh water into the bowl and scrubbed herself until it hurt, scrubbed until the flesh of her thighs felt chafed. She unlocked her box and counted one hundred and eighty-nine dollars. It stunned her. Some had tipped her with large bills. They liked her. They said they would come again. Half of them told her she was the best fake they'd ever had. Even paying for the awful rent and protection she wouldn't have to stay long. Tomorrow she would open an account in a bank.

She didn't feel clean. Not even a hot bath would sweat from her pores the sin of this night. She donned a soft, white cotton nightdress she had brought and collapsed in the bed, smelling the faint odor of men and lust about her. Her lust and theirs. She didn't feel good. Sorrow filtered through her, and she felt like crying. This wasn't what she thought it would be. She wasn't able to abstract herself from the sordidness as she had planned. She had enjoyed some of the men.

Some wanted to talk, be friends. One showed her a gold button on his lapel. It had an AB stamped in it. He said that stood for Arctic Brotherhood and it was a sourdough button worn by those who came back from the Klondike and the button was the shape of a gold pan. She liked that one. He had seen Daisy as a person and a friend, not just flesh. Another with an accent said he was Yugoslav and belonged to the Vijonac Fraternal Order. Another was Irish and said he belonged to the Gratton Club and the Goldfield Brass Band. Much to her astonishment he sobbed after he had emptied himself. Another, a Greek or something, said he owned the Need More Dance Hall down the street and wondered if she would like to work there; the corkage was good. He had bad breath.

She consoled herself with the knowledge that they all were strangers she would never see again. They didn't know her except as a pretty woman named Daisy. They would never learn where she came from, who she was, what class she had been born into. That comforted her. When she had earned enough, she would leave Goldfield behind, leave Daisy here and become Beth again. Only she knew she couldn't ever do that. Daisy and her white-hot heat would reside in Beth's body ever more.

She wondered if she could ever approach the communion rail at the Episcopal cathedral on Nob Hill with her husband and children again. Whether she could ever present herself to God as a contrite woman; whether she could ever confess this even through a wall of fabric; whether the Daisy in her had separated her forever from the life she had known.

She didn't sleep well that night and when she dozed the demons plagued her. She awakened time and time again, resolved to gather her courage. She didn't know if she could endure it. But she knew she could be brave. Beth, or Daisy, or whoever she now was, would be a woman of indomitable courage if only she could stem her tears.

CHAPTER 30

Hannibal Dash had never felt so alive. Instead of teaching acned students in fusty old amphitheaters and laboratories for a predictable little salary, he was engaged in a great enterprise, as unpredictable as roulette. He swore he was growing younger each hour. The spiritual numbness had lifted. Like countless others before him he had ventured into the West to remake his life. The fabulous frontier hadn't passed him by: He had caught the tail end of it in this forbidding corner of Nevada. Oh, it made his blood sing!

He could not say whether he had reached for this new life, or had been driven to it by private demons. He had enjoyed his life in Madison and he loved Melanie. His fine children filled him with joy. Robert was reaching manhood and Cecily had become a vivacious girl with lots of beaux. But here he was. They wouldn't follow him and he couldn't return. He missed Melanie so acutely he was tempted just to sell out and go back to her loving arms. Something about his pillow talk with Melanie had always buoyed him and strengthened him for the next day.

But now she was two thousand miles away. He had no idea what the future would bring but he thought Melanie might soften and join him in Goldfield. Until then, he would subdue the mountains and leap over stars.

The soft yellow metal fascinated him. Around him were men who had devoted a lifetime to pursuing gold yet he had done better. But that wasn't it, really. He had few competitive instincts and measured his worth by achievement. He had tried to plumb himself, to find out just what had lured him here, but he couldn't. He was rather a mystery to himself. He knew only that the quest for gold required the utmost concentration of mind, learning, wits, muscle, and character, and without all those assets, plus a natural daring and a taste for risk, he would never have succeeded.

He enjoyed his waxing bank account and investment portfolio which he took as the measure of his success. He had done the impossible. His monthly letters describing his triumphs had no doubt astounded Melanie. She had not seen this Hannibal in her quiet, professorial husband. He chuckled. He had not seen this Hannibal in himself. Only here in naked Goldfield had he an inkling of what had lain dormant in him.

He was blessed by his selection of partners. Stanley Rogers proved to be a feisty mine administrator, keeping supplies coming, ore on its way to the smelter, labor hired and paid, and the major construction projects on schedule in spite of railroad traffic delays. Richard Underwood turned out to be a solid man with the books: amortizing debt, filling the brown payroll envelopes with cash, arranging the best rates for construction loans. Dash himself turned to the geology of the enterprise, spending hours in the several stopes collecting samples for assay, attempting to grasp the complex structural geology of the mine, and overseeing underground operations even though he lacked the training of a mining engineer.

The Free Lunch was a typical mine of that district, with gold concentrated in pockets of hard, flinty quartz along shoots. Percolation had deposited the gold and other metals along giant faults radiating from Mount Columbia, forming pockets of rich ore that could be mined in large stopes timbered layer upon layer. The country rock here was a white rhyolite, markedly different from the dacite and andesite of the richer mines to the south.

That was Dash's bailiwick. He steered the face crews to the richest ore and tried to project the ways the partnership could mine the highgrade and ignore the ore with lower values during the shrinking term of the lease. Every hour the clock ticked was an hour forever lost to the leaseholders.

They still faced formidable difficulties. The Goldfield Railroad would not reach town until late summer. Every stick of California wood going into the mines still arrived by ox-team or mule-drawn freight wagon. Every pump, compressor, electric motor, boiler, pulley, cable, or hoist arrived by the muscle of draft animals while every pound of highgrade ore leaving the district still went by wagon to Tonopah for rail shipment to the smelter. It was up to Dash to sort the ore, sending the richest to the Selby Smelter in San Francisco and stockpiling the lesser grades, known as milling ore, at the mine head against the time that a local mill began operating.

The partners wouldn't reap a golden harvest until the railroad arrived and a local mill was built. They heard rumors that the Consolidated Mines would build one soon but so far that was only rumor. The one person profiting handsomely from the Free Lunch was Harry Arbuckle. Faithfully, Underwood deposited one quarter of each check received from the smelter into Arbuckle's account and sent along the supporting documents, copied and notarized. Harry Arbuckle, the king of the saloon corner, was receiving awesome amounts of cash. Dash didn't really mind: the partners would profit as long as the ore held out. He wasn't very sure that it would. Pocket mines could be treacherous.

But what Dash did mind was Harry Arbuckle's constant slanders upon the partnership. Word constantly filtered back to him of Arbuckle's accusations: he said he was being bilked and swindled; that he had been pressured into a bad deal; that if it weren't for his crooked lessees he'd be earning ten times more; that they had never done a thing for him except pick his pocket.

It angered Dash that his reputation was daily being blackened and that his work proving up the mine, rescuing it from claim-jumpers, and putting the Free Lunch into operation was being ignored or buried under a mountain of Arbuckle's self-serving myths. According to the official Arbuckle version, widely circulated in Goldfield after riding a tide of beer foam, Harry had scented out the bonanza, dug the glory hole, patented the claim, driven off claim-jumpers, only to be bamboozled by his faithless woman and Dash into surrendering it just when he was ready to mine it himself. Worse, in recent weeks Arbuckle had been boasting that he would employ some high-powered shyster to take it away from the leaseholders.

Some of this arrived secondhand as his miners and foremen and friends reported Arbuckle's boasts to him. Other pieces of it arrived in print, boldly front-paged in the *Observer*, the rag that had turned Arbuckle into a local hero. That was more than Dash could endure. Prinz, the editor, needed a horsewhipping. One May afternoon, at a moment when Dash had had his fill, he pulled on his suit coat even though the temperature had reached ninety, and stormed into town intending to have it out with Prinz.

He did not pause at the door of the print shop but bulled back to the press, where Prinz was overseeing the printing of his next weekly edition.

"Prinz, stop that thing and talk with me. I'm Hannibal Dash, and I'm one of the leasers of the Free Lunch. I'm sick of your damned lies—"

Prinz grinned and let the noisy flatbed press run.

"Stop that thing. You're in for a thrashing." Dash knew he was twenty years older than the young punk, and vulnerable, but he didn't care. "You're in for a libel suit. You've slandered us issue after issue."

This time Prinz stopped the press and wiped his inky hands on a grimy towel.

Dash didn't wait for a response. In ten blistering minutes he laid out the reality to Prinz, showed him the canceled checks, production figures, and told him about what he had done to rescue the claim and prove it up. He ended up telling Prinz about his original purchase agreement and how he had offered a lease, a fairer arrangement for Maude's sake.

Prinz grinned like an ape. "I know all that," he said.

Dash gaped at him. "Then why do you print that garbage?"

"Not a soul in Goldfield believes it, Dash. It's the biggest joke in town."

"Well, the joke's on me. People do believe it. I'm libeled. So are Rogers and Underwood, good men and honorable. By God, you're going to quit quoting Arbuckle or we'll meet in court."

There was something about that smirky, cunning young punk of an editor that Dash loathed. He'd seen enough of that type in college.

"Tell you what, Dash. I'll go talk to Arbuckle. You come along."

The offer made Dash's flesh crawl. The editor of the *Observer* was going to squeeze another story out of Dash's wounded reputation. But it wasn't an offer he felt like refusing.

"All right," he said, against his better judgment.

"He's in the Northern," Prinz said, cheerfully.

Dash felt he had been somehow bested in a game of publicity and promotion he knew little about.

They found Arbuckle at his usual stand, surrounded by beersucking sycophants. The man's chalk-striped turquoise suit looked stained. Arbuckle's face had thickened and reddened with capillaries. His derby lay askew over wisps of hair. He wore three gold rings and a headlight diamond on his cravat. But what had changed most of all was the look of insolence in Arbuckle's lidded eyes; a cockiness rising from that heady wealth; the cronies; the things that could be done with a wave of his soft hand.

He eyed Dash malevolently and turned to Prinz. "You come to say stuff about me again, Prinz?" Without waiting for a response he turned to his cronies. "Pretty smart for a printer, wouldn't you say?"

They laughed. Prinz smiled patiently.

"What's that peckerwood doing with you, Prinz?" Arbuckle asked.

"Oh, he's just along. I'd like to get your story straight, Harry. I can call you Harry, can't I?"

"Call me anything, only spell it in Latin."

It amazed Dash that such feeble attempts at humor could elicit such a guffaw from the mob surrounding the throne.

"Well, all right. I want to get the history of the Free Lunch right, okay? Now, who dug that first glory hole, you or Maude? Who found the highgrade?"

This time Arbuckle studied Dash. "He filling you with crap, is that it?"

"No, I just want to hear it from you, Harry."

"I done it all," Harry said. "I dug 'er, drilled 'er, located 'er; you name it, I done it."

"Well, Mister Dash here has a different recollection, sir. He says that Maude—"

"Horseapples. What're ya talking with that crook for? He's bleeding me white."

"Well, I don't know. Lots of people saw you do a contract. You gave Dash an option to buy that glory hole for five thousand dollars. He was pretty nice, offering you a lease instead of taking it from you for peanuts.''

Arbuckle's face tightened into a squint. "Horseapples. I never signed nothing.''

"And who helped you relocate, do your assessment work, fight off claim-jumpers? I just want the facts, Harry.''

Arbuckle pursed his lips. "This here's spoiling my afternoon. You bring this bloodsucker in here, he's bleeding me white with all them lies.''

"Well, Harry, you're not answering. What'll I put in the *Observer*?''

Dash was utterly unprepared for what happened next. Arbuckle growled something to a pair of plug-uglies next to him. Two monsters in double-breasted green suits arose. They had been built of slabs of muscle which strained their suit coats. Each of their coats bulged where a shoulder holster would be. Each wore a peculiar thick ring on each finger—the equivalent of brass knuckles.

One collared Dash; the other collared Prinz. Dash stumbled toward the doors, being driven by an irresistible force. A final shove catapulted him into the manure-filth of Crook Street while Prinz tumbled beside him.

"Don't come back. Don't ever pester Harry again,'' said one, amiably dusting off his suit.

Hannibal Dash lifted himself out of the mire knowing that Harry Arbuckle was being Harry Arbuckle and that spelled trouble for the partners.

"It's a great story,'' said Prinz, picking himself up. The editor started laughing like a lunatic while Dash glowered.

CHAPTER 31

· ·

Maude Arbuckle didn't mind being alone in the wilderness. She had Mother Dear and that was enough. She had always felt closer to Mother Dear than Harry anyway. She and the burro understood each other and had their own language. If Mother Dear needed water or rest, or if her load had shifted, she made herself perfectly clear. If Mother Dear sensed danger or worried about a desert storm, Maude swiftly understood. They were both female and tough. That's how Maude looked at it.

Maude wandered south and west through trackless barrens, broken by brazen blue mountains to the west and yellow ridges closer by. She had never been in country so vast and it made her feel like an ant. Thanks to Hannibal Dash's grubstake she had a small water cask, a frying pan, tin cup and plate, sheath knife, .22 caliber rifle, a bag of flour, pinto beans, and sidepork. A bedroll consisting of an old blanket and a tarpaulin kept her warm. She also had a complete prospector's kit containing stoppered flasks of reagents, magnifying glass, charcoal block, candle, blowpipe, moil, prospect pan, hornspoon, matrass, and knife gauge. She carried a shovel, a pick, geologist's hammer, four-pound hammer, and some sacks. It was all Mother Dear would carry. Load her too heavily and she'd stop in her tracks and never budge until the load suited her. Maude didn't mind. She and the burro were kindred spirits.

The soles of her ancient boots had worn through and she wished she had new ones cobbled to them before she left. But she made do. She looked a sight in her bib overalls and faded flannel shirt. Her unraveling straw hat gave her shade but not enough to keep her face from weathering like driftwood or help ease the perpetual squint from slits of eyes.

She could walk fifteen miles a day if she had to, but rarely did. There was too much to look at. She traversed a vast rocky waste uninhabited by humans or large animals. She saw only small creatures: giant skipper moths, a few woodpeckers and hawks, ground squirrels, geckos, a pack rat or two. Such vegetation that managed to survive the harsh climate and sun was thorned and rarely edible. She found some yucca and prickly pear which Mother Dear would eat if the needles were burnt off.

The vast playas and slopes leading nowhere made her feel small and feeble. Her explorations were severely limited by water and feed for Mother Dear although the cask permitted one dry camp. It was dangerous country, a murderer of the ill-equipped and foolish. Prospectors ran out of water, went raving mad, and died. Sometimes the sands sucked at her feet and slowed her travel; other times she lumbered up rocky slopes, feeling her heart thump and her throat parch. The only good thing about all this was that it hadn't been prospected much; its sheer ferocity, roasting in summer and numbing in winter, walled off solitary prospectors.

She always looked for the telltale tree or line of brush following an underground watercourse. Usually, when she dug a pit at such a site she found nothing but dry sand. Once in a while she would hit a seep and that would become her base to prospect a new area. Mother Dear wasn't particular about what she devoured and seemed to thrive on creosote bush and rabbitbrush and the smooth bark of an occasional cottonwood. She would drink gyp water, rotten-egg water, almost any kind of water. Mother Dear tended to roam like all burros, but Maude kept her around camp with a single handful of barley each morning.

Maude found little firewood on the barren floors but plenty upslope, usually dry cedar or stunted piñon pine. Often she paused to gather a bundle of it for Mother Dear to tote back to water. Fire made coffee and flapjacks and good cheer.

Finding gold in such a sea of rock was a daunting task

even for Maude, who took to it. She hunted for unusual color. A streak of red might indicate iron oxide, commonly associated with a mineralized area. She knew enough to steer clear of sedimentary rock except where it butted against igneous areas. Likewise she steered clear of basalt. She hunted for faults, complex structures, broken country, rock that didn't belong, or clays that lay beside igneous rock. She was looking for certain igneous rock: granite and quartz, rhyolite or andesite, porphyry dikes, or the black, yellow, orange and red of mineralized zones.

Glistening rock could be a good sign. The glint of light-colored quartz might signal success but the shine of fool's gold or mica would not. She had a sourdough's knowledge of geology and mineralization but no formal training in it. Hannibal Dash had expanded her horizons with an hour-long talk about the chemistry and structural geology of mineral deposits. Thus she had started her venture better equipped to spot the gold or silver tellurides that eluded sourdoughs.

She had the notion that bottoms would not yield gold even though the bottoms around Columbia Mountain had done exactly that in the Goldfield district. If she found a ledge it would be high up, hard to get to, a place not visited by others if they could help it. It would require a mountain goat's agility, patience, and a willingness to climb daunting slopes in the vast silence of a lifeless land.

She had nothing by way of a map and couldn't say whether she was in Nevada or California, but she knew she was somewhere west of the abandoned town of Montezuma and well south of Silverpeak. She would get back out the way she came in, following a familiar passage. Her vittles were running low but she thought to explore one additional ridge, brooding and black, that seemed to suck in light and drown it. Instinct sweetened the task: she had been eying that ridge for twenty miles. It beckoned her like the songs of the three sirens.

That spring morning of 1905 she set off with Mother Dear from a base camp in which she had dug out a seep that had nursed a single live oak. The ridge lay five miles northwest, gauzed by desert haze, blotting up the glare of the morning like some black hole that ate light.

She had thought some about dying. The land evoked such morbid thoughts. She was never far from disaster. The slightest trouble—something as small as a sprained ankle or as large as a leak in her water cask—could lead to a terrible death. A fall, a miscalculation, a spell of sickness could ramify into trouble, the way the tiny bite of the malarial mosquito could ravage a whole body.

She had no intention of croaking. She wanted to live for several reasons. She wanted that little yellow cottage with a picket fence and rambling roses which had eluded her as long as she had been married. If Harry would never provide then she intended to provide for herself. She had come to love prospecting and itched to show Harry what a woman could do. She had begun it in desperation years ago when it became plain that Harry would never earn a living.

"Well, Mother Dear, we're going to climb that ridge," she said. Mother Dear yawned. They were a pair, all right, gaunted down to nothing, ratty-looking, half used up and tough.

She trudged quietly across a burning playa, wrestling with the sucking sand, and then through miles of sloping talus that threatened to sprain her, and arrived at the base of a vaulting bluff too steep to climb. Although it was hot she felt the gloomy chill of the mountain and knew it was repelling her. The land spoke and she listened. She cocked her head, hearing its warnings. She checked for sidewinders, lizards, vultures, and found nothing except creosote bush. The rock lay faulted in all directions like an ancient sea of lava that had crumbled into blocks over eons of time. Mother Dear watched her alertly.

"I'm coming," she told the mountain. "You can't stop me. I'll dig gold outa your gut. I'm gonna carry some gold-wired quartz back there that'll drive 'em all mad and not tell 'em where I found it. They'll come chasing after me but I'll give 'em the slip. They're no match for Mother Dear and me.''

But the practical problem of finding a way up soon dampened her feistiness. She could probably climb the slope but Mother Dear would have trouble. Its blackness proved to be a cover of juniper growing out of deep brown igneous rock. Some trick of the winds had watered this ridge enough to cover it with the scrub. The Sierras, brooding far to the west, hadn't quite wrung all the moisture out of the air that flowed here.

She saw not a sign of mineralization; not a glint of quartz seaming the dull rock; no flash of bright colors that might spell silver or gold, copper, lead or antimony, or even iron. And yet the ridge raised her hackles, mocked her, challenged her to find riches in the midst of a ten-mile-long waste of worthless rock.

She squinted upward finding little hope in a direct assault and ended up trudging south, where the ridge rose higher but vaulted on a gentler grade. She stopped at each dry watercourse, looking for float, bits of lode that had traveled far from their source. She picked up piece after piece, seeing nothing. Not a glint lightened the fine-grained dull rock.

This was another wild goose chase; she knew that. But prospecting itself was a giant wild goose chase sustained by foolish dreams of the bonanza that always lay just over the hill. If life consisted of the pursuit of things, then prospecting was life intensified, narrowed down to the elemental hunt. It was amazing how time flew when her mind was so concentrated.

She began to sweat in the fierce spring heat, poured a cup of tepid, sour-tasting water from her cask. Mother Dear eyed her indignantly. Then she hiked another two or three miles until she topped a shoulder and beheld, below her, a vast arroyo that dropped out of the ridge and extended eastward as far as she could see. It had been formed by a fault. The side nearest her lay fifty feet below the far side. An occasional cottonwood survived along its dry watercourse, hugging the far cliff.

Mother Dear licked her lips and sighed, and Maude knew she scented water. She might camp here if she could dig into wet sands. She eased down a tough grade filled with gigantic boulders cast off the shoulders above, and skidded into the arroyo. Maude eyed the cobalt sky nervously. This was the sort of arroyo that could produce a flash flood, a deadly wall of water from a storm too distant to know about.

She began to work up the arroyo, passing likely camping sites because the day was still young, all the while looking for float. Mostly she found the fine-grained brown country rock that formed the ridge. But here and there, lighter-colored stones caught her eye and some of them had streaks of milky quartz running through them. She licked the stones, tasting nothing. A good prospector could taste gold and silver. The arroyo wasn't promising.

A half mile farther up she found three cottonwoods in a line. It looked like a place to dig for water. She was running low on chow but she could manage a spare day. Mother Dear was savaging the bark of cottonwood saplings. Maude unloaded her shovel and began digging at a point close to the rock wall that hemmed the arroyo. She reached three feet without finding a sign. At four feet she knew she wasn't going to find water there. The cottonwoods had their taproots into an aquifer ten or fifteen feet under. But the ridge beckoned. Maybe she could manage a day and hang on. She peered into her cask, finding it half full.

"Mother Dear, we're going to tackle that ridge," she said. "There's something up there."

CHAPTER 32

. . . .

Delia Favor had come to a painful crossroads. Time was running out. Her money bled away. She would have to land Big Sam fast or cut loose and find someone else worthy of her attentions. There seemed to be a few eligible ones around, though their numbers were smaller than she had imagined when she first read about fabulous Goldfield in the *Los Angeles Times*.

Jones puzzled her. The mocking in his eyes made her doubt that he cared for her, though he professed to, and even showered little gifts on her almost every night at the Palm Grill. She had made an impression on him; she knew that. Sometimes he seemed on the brink of telling her he loved her. He had a way of peering at her intently from that battle-scarred face—my goodness, imagine getting involved with an itinerant horse trader!—as if to read everything within her until she felt flustered. Yes, that was the very word. He flustered her.

But nothing had happened. She had talked demurely of a new life. She hadn't fallen into the trap of berating Lester. Once, when he asked about Lester, she had described him in flattering terms and expressed a great sadness about the way that youthful marriage had failed. She hadn't missed a trick; he knew she was a virtuous and sweet woman, forgiving and kind; he knew she sought only a modest little bungalow and the chance to make a good man happy. He knew she was nicely schooled, comfortable in his company, gracious with others, and she had a sweet singing voice. What more could a man want?

But the inoculation hadn't taken. If it didn't work soon, she'd be broke. She couldn't bear the thought of being trapped in this raw, wild place with its epidemic disease, whirlpools of dust, tent shanties and makeshift life. There wasn't even an opera house in Goldfield and her hotel barely passed muster. The water wasn't fit to drink and she stayed healthy only by mixing wine with it.

She eyed herself nervously before the mirror in the hotel's lavatory and liked what she saw: she certainly was curvy, with peachy flesh, shiny brown hair, and full lips she painted slightly just for emphasis. She couldn't fault her lovely dresses either, crisp cottony things, freshly pressed, exactly what should be fashionable in this hot place.

The mirror reflected a demure young woman with bright eyes and she could see why Sam had fallen for her. She was a catch and she knew it. She could be witty, too, and knew how to make him laugh. Her descriptions of the many prospectors wandering around town always evoked a wheeze of joy from him. But nothing more. Sam was bashful. As she eyed herself restlessly, she knew it was time to play the ace of hearts. She had never played that card before but she knew exactly how. She slipped back to her room and pulled off her high-necked blouse and chemise.

Moments later, when Jones limped into the lobby, she greeted him in a getup he had never seen before. The neckline of her black silk blouse plunged deep, revealing the peachy sides of her bosom; and the gray suit she wore this evening wrapped tightly around her figure, pinching in at her waist, blooming over her bust and hips.

He eyed her slowly, missing nothing, and offered her his arm. "You're sweet as sugar. A lollipop. We could try Ajax's Parisienne tonight, sweetheart," he said, easily.

Her heart skipped. That place was in the heart of the tenderloin district. "I hear it's just divine," she said.

He summoned a hack. "I could've driven us in my new Winston Space Annihilator," he said. "Twelve horses under the hood and a walnut locker for the Mumm's Extra Dry." But he handed her up and eased into the carriage, letting his leg poke out as she settled beside him. They descended Main Street into an area that shouted its wares. She watched fascinated as men strolled past Jake's Dance

Hall, the Den, the Need More, the Goldbug, and houses of shame where half-naked women sat in lamplit windows with light spilling through their gauzy shifts and beckoned men in.

The elegant restaurant, La Parisienne, stood in the midst of a line of cribs and Delia eyed them nervously as the carriage pulled to a halt. But once they had entered the gilded cage, with its flocked red fleur-de-lis wallpaper, quilted leather with brass trim, and crystal chandeliers fitted for electric lights, she could almost shut out the district and its whores. But not quite. The clientele seemed to be sports, flashy tinhorns escorting ladies of easy virtue, drummers with gold watch fobs across their portly middles, and half a dozen women whose occupations weren't hard to guess. They made her blush and draw her black silk blouse closer together. He sat across from her, obviously enjoying her introduction to the sporting life.

"Well, it's rather fast," she said.

"You're semisafe, sweetheart."

"You're a gentleman, Sam. That's what I like about you. Some men think that just because a woman's been married she's willing to . . . do anything. You wouldn't take advantage of a woman. That's what's so dear about you."

"Oh, I could pass for a deacon, Delia. No doubt about it." He grinned that grin again that belied what he had said. It unsettled her. "I loved to trade horseflesh. It wasn't just the nags, it was the folks I traded with. Sometimes they outsmarted me. Now, I reckon the times I traded with women, they were more fun than trading with men. They used their wiles. They'd get me all flummoxed and I'd forget my cautions, and end up buying some old plug they called a Thoroughbred that I couldn't peddle for glue."

What was he saying? She couldn't imagine. "I've never been in a district like this before," she said primly. "Imagine those poor pathetic women, diseased and vulnerable, without any reputation left."

"Oh, I reckon they don't see it that way. Some are here for the fun. Most are here to get rich. They're about as

good at prospecting as anyone in town. They got a commodity and they sell it for all they can get. Some dudes,
they put a fancy price on it. Those women got it all figured
out, down to the penny."

His candor embarrassed her. "I can't imagine it. Why,
some things are sacred, Sam."

"Money, for one," he replied, his eyes mocking her
again. "Lots of 'em are pretty cute. Hardly a one's past
thirty. They can earn enough here in one year to retire for
life, they say. Any gal that's got something a man wants,
she don't need to go poor if she don't want to."

"Big Sam, you're awful."

"Well, I'm just laying it all out."

Something about him tonight made her indignant. Maybe
it was the mockery in his eyes. She demolished the glass
of claret he ordered for her, and another, while they talked
about the Jumbo and Red Top and the Goldfield Electric
Light and Power Company and the Goldbug baseball team.
She had a third and fourth claret during their prime rib
dinner, and he kept pace. She relaxed and let her slinky
black blouse gap open. He peered at her peachy flesh cheerfully. There was nothing furtive about Sam.

"You're real pretty this evening, Delia," he said, patting
away juices with a snowy linen napkin. "Seems like I hardly took a gander at you before. I think you should own a
few tons of my stock so I'm giving you a hundred shares
of the Molly Brown, one of our best prospects."

"A hundred shares?" He amazed her.

"Sure. Little old gift from Big Sam." He extracted a
beautiful certificate from his breast pocket. Engraved on
gilt-edged parchment was a naked nymph holding what she
took to be an ingot of gold, with elaborate hundreds in each
corner.

"Oh, Sam, I'm going to cry," she said, dabbing her eyes
furiously. "You'll make me cry all night. You're so good
to me. I—I can't thank you enough."

"Think nothing of it," he said, as he summoned the
serving girl. "We'll get a hack and go for a little ride."

Big Sam told the hack man to drive up two dollars of fare, and the man took them down Main Street, past Hop Fiends Gulch, and out to Rabbit Springs near Malpais Mesa where the city got some of its awful water. She enjoyed the naked night air, and starlight, and the closeness of Big Sam beside her, and the steady clop and yawning of the old dray horse, and the glint of moonlight off the nickel-trimmed hames. Then he drove east toward the brewery and back up Franklin Street where they could see the giant headframes and works of so many of Goldfield's great mines, the January and February, the Combination Number 1 and Number 2, the Florence and Red King and Combination Fraction.

At the corner of Euclid and Miners, he waved at a half-built house. "That's my rock pile," he said. "I'm waiting for the railroad to ship the interior stuff. Two, three months more and it'll be done. Then by God, I'll have fourteen rooms, a dining room so long I'll have to shout at the cook, two water closets upstairs, a ballroom, and a wing for the help."

"Oh, Sam, that's so grand. I'm thrilled that you're so successful."

"Successful, heck. I'm so rich I could light cigars with hundred-dollar bills like Arbuckle—but I'm not that dumb."

"Hundred-dollar bills! Oh, what a waste. A pure waste. I'm so Scotch I cringe at the thought," Delia whispered. "I'm a girl who loves an itty-bitty cottage with honeysuckle climbing it. I'd love to have a parlor organ and sing old hymns for someone each evening."

"That's how you cast a spell," he said, and whickered in the moonlight, disconcerting her again. He aimed the driver toward an address on Miners Street, and shortly the hack stopped at a two-story frame building.

"Got a flat here. Thought you'd like to see it," he said, paying off the driver.

Delia realized the moment of decision had come. If she weren't careful she might make a fatal mistake. "Why,

Sam, I really shouldn't,'' she whispered, leaning into him.

"You shouldn't but you will," he said, helping her out. She stood in the moonlight adjusting her skirts.

"Well, just for a minute, Sam. I've always been curious. That's what killed the cat."

"You got nine lives, kiddo."

She watched the hack retreat, stranding her. She smiled brightly at Sam. "Maybe just a nightcap and then I'll be off," she said, sliding her arm into his. "I'm a proper girl, you know."

"Of course you are, Delia," he said, steering her up a long dark stair that smelled of varnish.

"I always care about true commitment," she whispered. "I mean, things of the spirit. Things that last forever, like gravestones and love. Sacred bonds. You know, respect and goodness." Something quivery was happening to her flesh.

"You're the sweetest gal I've ever known, Delia," he said, his voice husky. "You make me very happy."

He steered her into a fancy parlor and lit the lamps. He took her duster and steered her down a gloomy hall while she shivered.

"Is this the way to the nightcap?"

"Sure is, Delia," he said, leading her into a big room. He lit the lamp, revealing a quilted four-poster in the soft light.

"Oh Sam," she whispered, "you'd never respect me again. I'm a very proper person . . . Sam? My goodness gracious."

But he paid no attention at all and she knew she had won.

CHAPTER 33

· ·

The dark mountain tugged at Maude Arbuckle, enticing her up its brooding slopes. She felt its voice within her, a siren luring her onward.

She knew she was running out of water. She was making the fatal mistake that experienced prospectors understood and resisted; letting the bonanza dream draw her beyond her water supply. She had never felt a tug so powerful, something magnetic.

She toiled up the silent arroyo keeping a shrewd eye on the afternoon sun, clinging to the cliff for shade, stopping every few feet to examine float. She found several more with the thin streaks of milky quartz but that was all. It didn't discourage her. Gravity and flood didn't transport heavy metals as far as lighter rock. She might find gold closer to its source.

She penetrated a half mile, plunging into steep foothills where the arroyo cut a deeper notch, all the while ignoring the clamorous warnings that she needed to return to her base camp fifteen miles away. Mother Dear eyed her dolefully, often stopping until Maude bullied her on.

Where a tributary canyon dropped into the main one she found a different rock, whiter with lustrous quartz which lay ribbed between silky gray stone. It looked mineralized. But with what, she didn't know. Her prospecting had been largely confined to the quest for native gold which might be seen with the naked eye in wires or lumps winding through quartz of many colors. Her brief instruction from Hannibal Dash had awakened her to all the things she was missing: rock that held gold in flecks too tiny to see; rock in which gold was alloyed; rock with no visible indication of its riches. She confessed to herself that she knew even less about silver. This piece of milky gray rock mixed with quartz looked more like a silver ore than gold.

Plainly it was time to test all those newfangled chemicals that Dash had shown her how to use. She led Mother Dear to shade and extracted the wooden case that contained her mineral kit, trying to remember just what he had said about silver. She used her magnifying glass first, hunting for specks of gold she didn't see. A lick of her tongue didn't tell her anything either. Slowly she pulverized the float in her castiron frying pan, using her four-pound hammer and a lot of patience. With her gold pan she dry-panned the lighter material off until only the heavier dark granules remained. When she had reduced her specimen as nearly to granules as she could, she poured it into her matrass, or test tube. Dash's instructions hovered just out of mind but she remembered that nitric acid would be next. She found the acid bottle, unstoppered it, poured a dab into the matrass and then heated the tube over her candle.

Dash had explained that any metal other than gold would react with the nitric acid to produce nitrates or chlorides. She couldn't remember much else, though; especially how to tell one from another. But she remembered that she was to add some brine and if there were silver present it would turn into silver chloride, which would precipitate as a milky white cloud that would swiftly turn purplish black in sunlight.

So she added the salt, which created a milky cloud that turned vaguely darker as she watched. Surely she had found silver! Hastily she repacked her kit and started uphill again looking for more silver float. Within an hour she had found a dozen more pieces in the immediate area, which she carefully packed into a sample bag.

She knew she should return to water but the hot heady joy of tracking down the silver float drove her upward. She found no float above the junction with the tributary so she retreated a half mile back, turning up the secondary canyon stretching, she guessed, southwest. There she discovered float again, a steady parade of it as she ascended the steeply inclined dark gulch. Somewhere below, Mother Dear had quit her but she kept on, sample bag over her shoulder, geologist's pick in hand. The canyon narrowed and shot upward until she struggled for breath with every step. But the trail of float led her on, heedless of the deepening dusk and the absence of her burro.

She studied each specimen and was pleased to discover more of the lustrous dark ore. Surely she was heading toward a fabulous ledge. As darkness settled along with a brutal desert chill that rivered down the gulch, she realized suddenly she was alone, parched, unprepared for icy cold, and that Mother Dear had vanished along with the little remaining water in the cask. She had done the very thing all veteran prospectors guarded against. They had a saying intended to guard them against just this fix: Tomorrow will do.

She hastened downslope, the heavy sack of float bouncing against her hip and bruising her. She felt the race of pulse that told her she had become seriously dehydrated. She felt her knees go weak and her legs refuse to brake her downhill plunge. She knew she had to stop and orient herself, return by stages, and deal with the ghastly dryness building in her body and baking her soul. She might make that water hole without Mother Dear—if it hadn't filled up with sand and if she hadn't turned mad.

She forced herself to rest but now her thirst worked on her like a ticking clock. The faster she walked, the sooner she would arrive at water or find Mother Dear. She descended for what she thought was an hour, pacing herself, keeping a sharp eye for the ghostly shape of her burro. She struck the main gulch and continued descending, her deliberate pace as much the result of exhaustion as it was from the need not to overdo. Night fell and with it the last hope of spotting Mother Dear. She lacked a moon and starlight didn't let her choose her footing. She tried to call to Mother Dear but her parched throat refused to resonate.

Where had she last seen Mother Dear? In truth, she couldn't remember. She hoped it had been below the junction of the arroyos. She stumbled into a jagged piece of table rock and settled on it to catch her breath. But her wildly pulsing heart refused to slow. She was close to thirst-madness.

In that deep silence, with only the thunder of blood in her ears, she heard a snuffle and a snort. Mother Dear emerged out of the night, her muzzle so close that Maude could feel the burro's hot, moist breath.

"Oh, Lord, it's you!" Relief engulfed her. But she lacked the tears to cry.

Mother Dear lowered her muzzle to Maude's arm and clamped yellow teeth around it. "We'll share it!" Maude cried.

She struggled around the side of the burro, found the pack askew, felt for her water cask, and found her gold pan. She dribbled a cupful into the pan and drank it greedily; then she poured a quart and let the burro lap it up. She had enough to give the burro another pint and herself one more cup later on.

It was enough to stall trouble an hour or two. She felt her pulse slow. She needed another quart. She would have to rediscover her base camp before the furnace heat of the next day caught her. She would have to find the miserable little hole she had dug two days ago in caliche beside a stray tree next to an anonymous cliff in the middle of a vast wilderness and a black night. It was all downhill and harder to negotiate than level passage.

She headed downslope into the tunnel of the night, her senses keen, her mind filled with foreboding. In country that defied backtracking even by day, how would she arrive at her salvation by night? She banished such morbid thinking from her mind; no sense borrowing trouble, she told herself. She was no Harry Arbuckle. She had steel in her spine.

Thus nourished by her own courage she trudged steadily into the gloom, with Mother Dear behind, heading toward the last water out there somewhere. It didn't take long for Maude's water-famished body to protest again. She had gone dry even in the icy night. She stopped, rummaged for a sweater and put it on, comforted by its warmth. Then she doled out the last of her water to Mother Dear and herself. It didn't stop her raging thirst.

Two hours later, by her reckoning, she had reached the place where the giant arroyo had. leveled out, where the occasional cottonwood stood, and where she had dug a dry hole that morning. The doubts began again, flitting through her mind like bats. Where should she cut north and how far should she go? From that base camp water hole she had traveled west to the foothills, then south across several arroyos until she reached this one. She had no more chance of finding her way back than if she had been blindfolded, spun around a dozen times, and told to pin the tail on the donkey.

She continued down the giant arroyo, past some trees whose leaves rustled in the eddying air. Cottonwoods, no doubt. Which trees were these and when should she abandon the arroyo and start north across drainages? She spotted a soft glow on the eastern horizon and sat down to wait for her lantern to light the way. She desperately needed the rest anyway. Some while later, with the gold of a gibbous moon partly above the horizon, she started walking again. She knew she could find the turnoff now. There had been a line of single cottonwoods pressed against the cliff wall. She could see forever in the bright air.

She passed the place where she had dug the dry hole and reached the place where she should turn but Mother Dear kept trotting straight down the arroyo.

"Come back, you durned thing," she yelled in a voice that cracked. "Here's where we head for water."

But Mother Dear perversely trotted straight east, down the giant gulch which widened into a broad dip in the dry hills. The burro was notional but not this notional.

Maude faced a choice. She could doom herself by chasing that burro through the night or she could head for water without Mother Dear. She chose to stick with the little four-footed beast and panted along behind as the animal broke into a trot, bouncing its packload.

Maude saw that her critter was heading straight for a tree nowhere near the cliff-walls of the arroyo, and wondered about it. In all Maude's experience she had never found water in the very middle of a dry watercourse.

The burro stopped in a depression at the roots of the tree and began licking the sand there. Maude could see no water but she could smell it and the smell made her dizzy. A mat of dried vegetation lay in the bottom of the depression. Even in white moonlight she could see animal tracks at the place, including the cloven hooves of deer. She walked into the low spot, stirring up skipper moths that had been sitting on the earth. She knelt and felt the earth, finding coolness and the faintest trace of water. Mother Dear pawed away sand.

Maude untied her shovel from the gear hanging from her packframe and began shoveling. The very first spadeful yielded wet sand. A few more brought her down to water, which seeped into the tiny hole. Mother Dear didn't wait; she poked her velvet muzzle into the pit and slurped up the muddy water. Maude let her. She dug another pit a few feet away, lifting off the matted vegetation and a foot of soggy sand, and drank.

Gold and silver, she thought later, murdered people.

CHAPTER 34

....

Maude sat patiently in Hannibal Dash's laboratory at the Free Lunch Mine while Dash assayed her samples. His lab was nothing but a miniature mill and smelter; a rock crusher capable of pulverizing an ore sample to dust and a furnace to reduce the ore.

His was like a dozen others she had seen. He had a double-deck assay furnace made of iron-banded fire clay, work-tables laden with crucibles and other glassware, and a costly brass balance with finely calibrated weights and measures.

Dash labored in the adjacent room where he had a small rock crusher, a pair of iron plates that were driven by an eccentric. This reduced the rock to pea size. These fragments he poured into a mechanical mortar and cranked it to turn the rock to dust or sand. Then he ran the grainy rock through a hundred-mesh sieve. He took the oversize—the grains that would not pass through the sieve—and ran a heavy castiron muller over it until this rock was further reduced and Maude's samples had been turned to dust.

Dash weighed the dust on his fine balance, removing bits until he had exactly 29.116 grams, or just over two ounces, the standard assayer's sample. He poured the measured dust into a glazed china crucible and added lead oxide, borax, argol, some wheat flour, and a needle of pure silver of known weight. After stirring these into the powdered rock he put the crucible into the lower deck of the furnace where it would be heated to 1,500 degrees centigrade. The carbon monoxide in the furnace would draw the oxygen from the lead oxide, releasing the lead, which would drip through the rock powder, collecting, fluxing and smelting the metal in the rock.

"It'll take about a half hour," he said to her, relaxing at last. "We'll know soon."

"I reckon it's mighty fine ore," she said. "I could feel it in my bones. I should've dowsed it. I can dowse gold and silver like you never did see."

He smiled and she knew the scientific skeptic doubted her. It didn't matter. She knew what she knew and new-fangled scientific methods didn't add or subtract a thing.

"You found the ledge, Maude?"

"Nope, just the float. Ran outa water and had a close scrape. But I can find that ledge next time. . . ." She let it hang. She needed to be grubstaked again. If she had found a good lode he surely would do it. He would get half. But she knew she couldn't depend on him for grubstakes forever. She'd been out for weeks without much luck.

After her encounter with the dark ridge she had made it back to Goldfield without further difficulty, finding the town larger than when she had left it. It amazed her. New mercantiles and saloons stood where nothing but desert had been. The streets bustled with teams, buggies, and horseless carriages, as well as mobs of people. She saw well-dressed women strolling along, who eyed her with distaste.

"You've been out, what? Six weeks or so?" he asked. She nodded. "Then you probably haven't heard that Harry is talking about suing us."

"Sue you? For what?"

"We don't know yet. He's been interviewing lawyers. Maybe it's more of his talk. But we're taking it seriously."

"That darned Harry. I'll tell the judge what happened."

Dash sighed. "The courts don't put much credence on the testimony of spouses for or against one another. Especially estranged spouses."

"But it'll be a pack of lies, Hannibal!"

"We're working on it. We've got witnesses lined up. The Earps, although Virgil, the deputy that came out here— he's in bad health. But the other, Wyatt, he's around, working for Tex Rickard at the Northern. Maude, if this came down to facts—the leasing contract signed and sealed, location work, claims filed, and all, we'd be able to deal with it. But we worry that Harry's money might influence justice."

"Well, I'll do what I can. That bum. It's my mine. I found it. I dug it. I found the good stuff."

"Maude—it'd help if you filed for divorce," Dash said. "And ask for the mine. Your allegations would help our case."

"Now how'm I gonna go prospecting and file a lawsuit? How'm I going to pay for some fancy-pants lawyer?"

"Well, Maude . . . I could arrange that."

"I'm into you deep enough."

"The divorce action—and your claim to the mine— could only help us, Maude. Once you're divorced, your testimony would be valuable."

"Well, Lord's sake, it's not very proper, getting a divorce. It makes me look like some hussy."

Dash disagreed.

"That Harry—he wouldn't stop at nothing. I mean, he'd say anything to a judge. I'd have to sit there and take it."

"Maude, there's another reason. Do it for your own sake. As long as he's married to you he can claim whatever you discover. Community property. Don't you think you'd better protect yourself?"

She didn't cotton to it. She'd as soon cut the rattles off a live sidewinder as get into a lawsuit. "How about me doing this when I get back. I wanna find that ledge and stake it."

"That's what I'm worrying about. If you find something and file a claim when you're still married, he'll go after it."

"He'll never find out," she said stubbornly.

"He has resources, Maude."

Hannibal had trapped her and she felt like a cornered kangaroo rat. "Well, let's see how that assay looks and then I'll decide," she mumbled.

He turned to his furnace, which leaked a dominating heat into the laboratory. She felt bad. Fighting Harry would cost the partners a ton of money. This is how Harry planned to repay Dash's decency. She felt ashamed that her name was Arbuckle; ashamed to ever have known Harry. But not surprised. She had learned all about Harry's bullyboys and his raving threats.

With a long rod, Dash opened the D-shaped furnace door. The withering heat smacked her. Within, in the blinding white light was the crucible that held her fate and her dreams.

Using a fork-shaped iron crutch, Dash lifted the conical crucible and poured the white-hot seething broth into the cup of a castiron mold and waited again.

"We have to wait for it to cool," he said. "Then we'll knock away the slag and get rid of the lead. Then it goes into the oxidizing furnace." He grinned apologetically. "Measuring the amount of metal in rock takes some doing."

But her mind labored over the wound Harry might inflict upon the man who had rescued him from ignominy. "Maybe I can help. I'll go talk to him," she said. "Lord, I'll talk to your lawyers. I'll tell 'em how it was."

A thought seemed to pass behind his eyes. He looked troubled momentarily. "Maude," he said at last. "Do you know how Harry's changed?"

"No, I haven't seen him since he walked out of the shack."

"I don't think it'd be wise for you to talk with Harry. There might be some danger in it." Dash let it hang.

"Danger! You think he's going to pick on his wife? Harry's so soft I could twist him into a pretzel."

"Harry may be soft but his bullyboys aren't. His money wins him a whole saloon full of people who do his bidding. He's over in the Texas now. They'll find ways to mortify you, hurt you. Maude, I think you'd better not."

She cackled. "There wasn't a day in twenty years that Harry Arbuckle ever scared me," she said.

He wasn't happy with that but he didn't resist. "Maude, you're a grand and strong woman," he said. "But you're made of flesh like all the rest of us."

"Not so's I know it," she retorted. "I'm made of post oak and whang leather. They'd only bruise their knuckles." She laughed. He eyed her affectionately and laughed too. But there was something in his eyes she couldn't put a name to.

Dash knocked the conical biscuit out of its mold and hammered away the glassy slag while a dish-shaped cupel of moist bone ash was heating in the upper deck of his furnace to drive out the moisture in the ash. He pounded the conical biscuit into a little cube and placed it on the hot cupel with tongs.

"Cooler this time," he said. "About nine hundred degrees. I have to watch it through an open door." He slid smoked glasses on to protect his eyes and face. "There's nothing like bone ash in this process. After the lead in this little cube combines with oxygen it'll drip into the bone

ash and leave the precious metal. But I can't let it get too
hot.''

She watched Hannibal Dash at work. He was the consummate technician, absorbed in his work, measuring carefully, making sure everything was exact. She could see how
easily some assay results could be distorted by carelessness.

They didn't talk much during the next half hour; they
were getting close to a result now. She sat stolidly, knowing
that fidgeting wouldn't make time pass faster or the result
better. At last Dash raked the cupel out of the furnace with
a little iron hoe and let the tiny button of red-hot metal
within it cool. She couldn't read his mind, but she saw the
frown when he looked at it. While it cooled, it blicked, or
surrendered its heat in flashes of light like a tiny thunder-
cloud.

With tongs he put the bead on a scale and weighed it
with great care.

"I'm sorry, Maude," he said. "The amount of metal
here is scarcely over the amount of the inquart needle I
used. There's not enough silver or gold in that rock to
amount to anything. I can run another batch if you want."

She had started to feel bad a moment before when she
saw his frown. Now she felt angry and defeated.

"If the bead were larger, I'd put it in nitric acid and heat
it to separate the gold and silver and find out what you
have. But . . ." the words trailed off. "Do you want an
assayer's certificate?"

"No," she muttered. She stared out the window upon a
desert of burning sand, wondering what she would do. She
couldn't ask him for another grubstake.

"Maude," he said.

She turned and found him holding some ten-dollar bills
in his hand. "Try again."

"Oh, lordy, Hannibal, I just can't . . ."

"I'll grubstake you for as long as you want to tromp the
desert, Maude," he said. "Let's dare to succeed together."

. . . .

PART II

Devil Catch the Hindmost

There is thy gold; worse poison to men's
    souls,
Doing more murther in this loathsome
    world,
Than those poor compounds that thou mayst
    not sell:

> —William Shakespeare

Gold has worked down from Alexander's
time. . . . When something holds good for
two thousand years I do not believe it can
be so because of prejudice or mistaken theory.

> —Bernard M. Baruch

Again I saw that under the sun the race is
not to the swift, nor the battle to the strong,
nor bread to the wise, nor riches to the intelligent, nor favor to the men of skill; but
time and chance happen to them all.

> —Ecclesiastes 9:11

CHAPTER 35

· · · · · · · · · · · · · · ·

In September of 1905, Hannibal Dash watched Goldfield explode. That's when the first railroad arrived. Instantly, mobs of gold-seekers boarded the Tonopah Railroad to Tonopah, the Goldfield Railroad the last twenty-eight miles, and spread into the town of eight thousand, jamming every accommodation. From coast to coast, people had heard of the fabulous wealth of Goldfield.

The leading men of town created a tent hotel on the outskirts to handle the mob. They charged a dollar for a night in the canvas dormitory and limited the newcomers to three nights. Goldfield was mushrooming, with boardinghouses and hotels and homes being completed each day to absorb the swelling crowds. Nearly every room in Goldfield was either double-rented, twelve hours to the occupant, or triple-rented, eight hours to the occupant.

Something in the goldbug fever affected Dash. He loved it. In all his quiet years as a don he had never experienced this pulsating, throbbing life that spilled into the streets night and day, that made everyone cheerful, that gilded every business, that made cobblers, clerks, accountants, drummers, auctioneers and supervisors rich. He couldn't remember seeing such visible happiness in Madison. Often he roamed the streets, simply amazed at the get-rich schemes and enterprises of unfettered human nature which sprang up through the business district and spread down all the alleys. Goldfield was magic for anyone with a dream.

He swore that Goldfield's population was the healthiest he had ever seen in spite of bad water, and supposed it was simply because some radiant optimism pervaded the soul and body of all. Where else in all the world did people laugh so much? Even the losers at the faro tables shrugged, accepted a stogie from the tinhorns, and marched off to make another fortune the next day. Goldfield was *fun*.

The new Consolidated Mill had opened in April, enabling the partners to mill their lower-grade ore locally. At once, Stanley Rogers had shipped his ore over to the plant near Columbia Mountain for custom milling and gradually reduced his stockpiled ore while sending his best ore to the Selby Smelter. The new mill started operations with ten stamps and amalgamation plates which enabled it to extract over sixty percent of the gold from ore. The remaining concentrate could then be bagged and shipped to a smelter. But the situation improved when the mill installed concentrating tables and cyanide tanks, and now could extract ninety-five percent of the gold.

Dash had marveled that the coal for those boilers was being hauled by the muscle power of mule and ox teams. Not long after that a transmission line from California brought ample electricity and the mill switched to electric motors. With the local mill reducing the stockpiled ore, he and his partners were suddenly making more money than they thought possible. They scrupulously sent Arbuckle's share to him, along with notarized receipts and assay reports to keep the owner of the Free Lunch well informed. It was reported to Dash that Arbuckle used the notarized reports to light his cigars, thus amusing his cabal.

Tex Rickard had grown weary of Harry Arbuckle's abuses of customers and staff and thrown him out of the Northern. Arbuckle had breathed threats of arson and retaliation but nothing had come of it. Arbuckle now held court in the Texas Saloon, which was getting rich from the crowd of moochers soaking up suds at Harry's expense.

Dash had never forgotten that rough eviction from the Northern by Arbuckle's goons. It had turned into comedy in Hannibal's mind. Goldfield's alchemy did that to its citizens, transmuting sin and darkness into vaudeville.

Meanwhile, each week added awesome amounts of cash to Dash's accounts. It seemed perfectly ridiculous to make five-figure deposits every few days. He kept some in bullion and invested much of the profit in the best local mines, whose ore he assayed and studied as carefully as he had earlier.

One reckless night, at least by professional standards, he bought a cheroot and lit it with a dollar bill just to experience Harry Arbuckle's little conceit. Dash sighed, watched the innocent bill dwindle to ash, and decided Harry's voluptuary pleasures weren't anything a midwestern geology professor would ever envy.

The Free Lunch seemed inexhaustible. They had tunneled down to the hundred-foot level and were still finding rich ore along the central faultline, fading off to lower values to the north and ending abruptly fifty yards to the south when they hit country rock. They had not yet reached the lateral limits of the claim, either. Data from other mines in the Goldfield district indicated that the ore ran as deep as the four-hundred-foot level; no mine had, as yet, sunk a shaft lower than that. But Dash considered himself a realist: the Free Lunch lay farther out from the golden crescent of rich mines than any other major producer. He couldn't count on anything and took pains to let his partners know of his doubts.

Goldfield's fame had reached the calculating men of Wall Street and the great entrepreneurs in the East. An emissary of Charles Schwab, once president of Carnegie Steel and then United States Steel and now Bethlehem Steel, had quietly approached Dash and his partners, offering two hundred thousand for the remaining six months of the lease. The financier Bernard Baruch had put out feelers too. Dash and his colleagues had examined each proposal, totted up the prospects, and turned it down.

Would Goldfield ever stop booming? The only thing holding back progress now was the new Tonopah and Goldfield Railroad itself, which was so overburdened that freight had to wait weeks for its turn for delivery. It maddened the mine operators that even with a new railroad they still had to wait weeks for their new hoists and electric motors and cables to arrive. Rogers and Underwood finally resorted to costly ox teams to get the pumps they needed to push air into the hundred-foot level and suck up the water that accumulated even in that desert milieu.

Magical Goldfield was attracting a darker species of mankind too. Thieves, footpads and muggers got off of every train. Floozies and ladies of easy virtue did too, knowing they would get rich in weeks when the gold was flowing. Town Constable Claude Inman kept a wary eye on them but he didn't get much support. People were too busy getting theirs to worry about the muggers and tarts getting theirs.

Trainload after trainload of miners arrived; word had spread through the Western Federation of Miners that a stiff could pocket a hundred dollars a day of highgrade in Goldfield. They drifted in from Cripple Creek and Telluride, nursing the wounds of labor strife. They filtered down from the Yukon, where the great bonanza was fading fast. There weren't very many poor miners in town. They might grumble about four-dollar-a-day wages in the Miners Union Building but it was nothing more than the haranguing of fiery socialists attacking the corrupt capitalist system and the heartless rich. The stiffs stood around and cheered and continued to highgrade shamelessly.

Dash and his colleagues tolerated it. The nimble-minded Underwood calculated the tonnage going up the shaft, the value of the gold in it, the receipts from the mill, and concluded that the lessees were losing from two thousand to five thousand dollars a day, depending on what sort of ore they were mucking.

But they were in exactly the same position as all the leasing outfits in Goldfield. Time ran against them. They couldn't afford a strike or a slowdown. They couldn't afford pickets, strife, or trouble. Each tick of the clock pushed them further toward the end of the bonanza. All Dash could do was glare at the grinning, smirky Cousin Jacks and the rest who waddled off to Goldfield so burdened they could hardly walk.

He and other leaseholders did resort to other means. They hired private detectives to track down the fake assaying outfits, gather evidence, and turn the matter over to the authorities. Now and then a successful raid yielded a few tons of highgraded ore, which any geologist could easily track to the mines it came from. But in spite of vigorous prosecution and lawsuits, the robbery continued almost unabated.

Goldfield's tenderloin bloomed into the largest den of sin in the West with some five hundred denizens cheerfully mulcting miners of their boodle and tossing them into the alleys to sober up. There wasn't much violence in Goldfield because people were too busy getting their share of the spoils. Dash couldn't imagine why the stiffs didn't save their loot and move on to a better life somewhere else. But they didn't. It was all easy come, easy go. Or perhaps the stiffs felt guilty about the ore they pocketed after all and needed to get rid of the proceeds. Or maybe they were simply living for today because they could replenish tomorrow.

Dash lived in the same frame cottage he had purchased when he arrived. Some day he would find a handsome place, but as long as he had his small comforts he was content to stay where he was. He could have bought a mansion like the one that scoundrel Big Sam Jones was erecting. He could have retired to Tahiti or moved to San Francisco. But all of that was no account. What he needed now was another mine, another strike, another way to outfox all those veteran goldbugs, assayers, mining engineers, geologists who were every bit as eager as he to discover new Golcondas that would catapult them to the next layer in the stratosphere.

Another way, he admitted in his reflective moments, to dull the pain of being alone.

CHAPTER 36

· ·

Turner P. Reilly, Esquire, knew exactly who got rich in bonanza towns. It wasn't mine owners; it was lawyers. All it took was a familiar brew: greed, envy, and gold, and pretty soon the lawyers would pocket the highgrade.

Thus it delighted him to represent the abominable Harry Arbuckle in certain delicate matters. He had intuited exactly what to say to win Arbuckle's custom. The king of the Texas Saloon had simply invited one lawyer after another into his lair to pay court, and one by one the barristers of Goldfield had bowed and scraped. Reilly had gotten wind of it long before his turn came and had instantly perceived how to drill a little mole hole into Arbuckle's awesome vault. Reilly remembered the interview perfectly because it had been a flawless performance on his part.

When he had approached the throne a few weeks before, some lout stuck a mug of beer in his hand and the interview with the King of Goldfield commenced.

"I'm looking for the sharpest lawyer in town," said the famous man. "I got took bad and I want it all back and then some. What do ya say to that?"

"Mister Arbuckle, you probably can't afford me," Reilly said suavely. "I don't think I want your business."

That affronted the bulbous-nosed Lord of the Texas. "I can afford anyone I want. I could import a dozen better'n you," he retorted. "I could buy a dozen Montgomery Street lawyers and make 'em dance for supper."

"I'm sure you can, sir. I charge five thousand a month as a retainer, plus expenses, which will be large because I do a lot of preparation. It pays to know everything. That's all I have to say. I never lose. If it's worth it to you, engage me." Turner P. Reilly turned to leave.

"You. Just a minute. How come you charge like that?

That's ten times more'n the rest of these shysters want.''

"It should be obvious, shouldn't it?''

Arbuckle grinned. "Yeah, I get the idea.''

A few hours later a bank officer arrived with a cashier's check for five grand and Turner P. Reilly knew he had struck a vein of pure gold.

After that he had listened patiently to Arbuckle's meandering tale of betrayal. It was perfectly absurd on its face but Reilly didn't mind. The trick was not necessarily to win, although that was always an amusing possibility, but to keep the retainer rolling in for as long as possible. He was an expert at that. The court system offered endless opportunities for delays, postponements, and motions. With any sort of luck he could keep this little mine going for years.

"A complex matter, but I haven't the slightest doubt that I can make you whole,'' he told Arbuckle. "Watch for the results.''

There really was nothing to prepare and nothing to investigate. He brushed dandruff from his dapper suit, adjusted his polka-dot bowtie and set off merrily for the Free Lunch Mine, aptly named, he thought.

By great good fortune he discovered all the partners were present. He withdrew a business card, placed it before Dash, and announced himself the attorney for Mr. Harry Arbuckle.

A vast silence filled the office.

"Mister Arbuckle is aggrieved by your treatment of him and has asked me to pursue the matter,'' he began. "I'm instructed to tell you he wants fifty percent of the gross proceeds or he'll begin litigation.''

That occasioned another long silence.

"Of course we can escalate from there: injunctions, writs, you name it.''

It was Dash who responded. "That sounds like Harry, all right. He's been threatening it for months. The answer's no. We have a valid, signed, witnessed lease and another five months to operate.''

"Well, of course, that's open to debate," Reilly said. "One could argue it was coerced from Mister Arbuckle in a desperate moment."

"It's a standard lease, Reilly. He gets twenty-five percent of gross production. We pay all development cost, operating expense, and labor out of our three-quarter share. You know the economics perfectly well."

Reilly did. He had read Arbuckle's crude scrawl on his copy of the lease, duly witnessed by three bank people. As leases went this one was normal and fair. He smiled. "That's subject to debate, of course, Dash."

Rogers spoke up: "I'm sure your bread is buttered by the money Arbuckle receives out of every smelting check, Mister Reilly. Those payments to Arbuckle could go into escrow while the matter is litigated."

"Why, Mister Rogers, I'm quite sure Harry Arbuckle could easily weather a shutdown, even one lasting to the end of your lease."

"We'll reply to this . . . coercion, I assure you. Mister Arbuckle might find himself in distress," Rogers said, his voice very hard and very quiet.

Reilly knew that tone, knew it would be all-out war, and the first thing to suffer would be Harry Arbuckle's bank account. "Why, it needn't come to that, gents. We're here to come up with a reasonable adjustment."

Dash dug into his file cabinet, pulled out a handwritten document and passed it to Reilly. "As you can see, Mister Reilly, I have a one-year option to buy the property from Harry Arbuckle at five thousand. This acknowledges that I paid him a thousand for the option and owe four thousand more to exercise it. As you see, his signature was witnessed by three people." Dash paused to let that sink in.

Turner P. Reilly read the document, astonished. Arbuckle had never mentioned it.

"The reason I didn't exercise it was because I wanted to be fair to Arbuckle," Dash continued. "It was really Maude—his wife—who dug that pit and found the rich ore. It assayed two thousand dollars a ton. The decent thing to do was offer Arbuckle a standard lease instead of taking the bonanza away from him as—I assure you—most people would have done. Arbuckle's lucky to get his twenty-five percent. It was by my sufferance.

"That's not all. Arbuckle never did his location work. I helped him relocate in the nick of time, helped him get rid of claimjumpers, and helped him do the location work and patent the mine. It's all on the record. The relocation's filed in Hawthorne. The mineral claim patent is there and in the federal offices. I have receipts from the attorney I paid to patent his claim for him. I think that settles the matter."

Turner P. Reilly knew that was no doubt the case. "Why, all that's debatable, Dash. One might discover the five-thousand-dollar purchase was coerced, mightn't one? And maybe you hired the claim-jumpers? It's just speculation, of course."

Dash looked apoplectic. He reddened, sweat, clenched his fists, and gritted his teeth. Reilly considered it all good form. He counted it a day lost when he didn't enrage someone or reduce someone to blubbering.

Underwood, meanwhile, was pawing through file folders, pulling out smelting company receipts and canceled checks. "Here, Reilly. This accounts for every penny. Arbuckle got his exact share."

Reilly grinned. "Why, I'm sure it's perfectly accurate, Mister Underwood. That's not what I'm here about. It's to modify that coerced contract to be more generous to my client."

Underwood stared and stuffed his displayed records back into their folders. Reilly enjoyed it. It was easier to win concessions from people full of righteous wrath than from cunning, shrewd operators as ruthless as himself.

But Dash surprised him. "That's it, Reilly. Out. We'll see you in court."

"But I'm far from done. We've matters to discuss."

Dash had rounded the desk and began herding the dapper attorney toward the door. Reilly remembered that Dash was a geologist with plenty of muscle from hard outdoor work.

A firm hand gripped Reilly's elbow and steered him effortlessly down a corridor and into sunlight.

"I'll write you a letter with our terms, Dash," Reilly said amiably. "Thanks for the hospitality."

"There's the property line, Reilly. Head that way." Dash was pointing at a gate in a barbed wire fence.

Turner P. Reilly didn't mind. He'd been steered out of more doors than he could remember. It was all for a good cause, a monthly retainer worth as much as the annual wage of five laborers.

He hoofed it back to his chambers on Silver Street, analyzing what he had found out. The most obvious was that Arbuckle was not telling him the entire story. So Maude had found the gold. So Dash had rescued Harry. So Dash held a valid option to buy the mine for five thousand dollars but decently offered Arbuckle the lease instead. Dash was a fool. Anyone who'd offer any kindness to Harry Arbuckle was seven kinds of fool. The world always had a few decent fellows like Dash, touching in their rectitude. Turner P. Reilly didn't mind running fools through a meat grinder.

Still . . . it seemed plain that Dash and his colleagues would be formidable opponents and might get the whole thing thrown out of court. Not that it mattered. Whether Arbuckle won or lost was of no consequence. Dash's lease had five more months to go. At a retainer of five thousand a month he could see twenty-five grand on the horizon plus some expense boodle. He could go through the motions for five months. Good enough, thought Turner P. Reilly, Esq.

CHAPTER 37

•••••••••••••••••••••••••

Delia Favor sat on her double bed debating whether to invite her parents and sister to the wedding. Her folksy parents just wouldn't understand how to behave among rich and important people and her sister would probably spill the champagne punch all over her dress.

But in the end she relented. She wrote Horace and Violet Biddle about her forthcoming wedding to a fine, outstanding investment banker, Samuel Jones, and invited them to Goldfield. She added, however, that she was doing the wedding in whites and lavenders and navy blues, and therefore she would ask her father to buy a good double-breasted navy blue suit from that clothier at Figueroa and Wilshire. Delia could survive her mother's plebeian taste, but not her father's. Her sister, Letitia, could do what she wanted. She would embarrass Delia no matter what. The bill, she assured them, would be taken care of.

Fortunately, the only rail route to Goldfield was so roundabout that it turned a modest distance into a formidable one. She knew that the Biddles wouldn't resort to a stagecoach. When her mother wrote, wishing Delia happiness but declining because Horace was suffering gout and edema and wasn't up to it, Delia was delighted. She had been estranged from them since the age of fifteen when she discovered they didn't act or think like successful, worldly people. In due course Delia received a wedding gift, a sadiron, which Delia carefully hid from Sam.

If they had come they would have found her ensconced in a luxurious flat with no visible means of support. Not that she cared what the Biddles thought of her. She'd left behind their pettiness and fussy morals long ago, and freed herself to live as she chose. When Sam moved her into the flat she had feared for her reputation. But Sam said it was only temporary; they'd get hitched as soon as they could move into his fourteen-room mansion.

"I'm your fiancée, aren't I, Sam?" she'd asked as he picked her up and limped into the shiny bedroom with the canopied walnut four-poster in it.

"Why—I forgot to ask. Will you marry me, Delia?" he asked, undoing her buttons.

"Oh, Sam, darling! I'd love to! I'd love nothing more!"

"Good, now we're engaged," he said, taking liberties. She'd sighed and let him, enjoying this moment of triumph.

He'd laughed and kissed her ear, and she worried about whether he really meant it. She decided he did. He always seemed a little amused about things she took seriously. "I love you, my darling," she'd breathed.

"I love you too, Delia," he said, sliding his hand along her thighs.

She didn't mind making love very much, even to a man with a deformed leg. But a lover ought to look like Adonis, she thought. She'd seen a figleafed statue of Adonis in a museum once and thought that all rich men looked like that—or should.

"Sam," she whispered while he was caressing her peachy flesh, "I'd like a formal wedding, very traditional. With lots of lilies. We can be married by a judge if you want. You don't have to find a minister."

"Anything you want, Delia," he whispered. She was letting him take everything he wanted and they weren't even married yet. She had no cards left to play. She couldn't really say no to a man who wanted her and slipped her a hundred dollars anytime she asked. She decided it was simply a risk she had to take, even if it might ruin her. But oh! If he let her down, she'd go after him! She would hire a fancy lawyer if he didn't keep his promises after seducing her.

"Oh, Sam, you're a dear," she said. "We'll have the biggest one in Goldfield."

Sam had laughed wickedly, and she knew it was time to pleasure him. She couldn't expect to mesmerize a man without knowing the arts of love. So she obliged Sam and wished she knew every little thing that would make her unique. She sighed, and groaned, although she didn't feel much of anything, and at the right moment she squealed and bubbled and moaned long and soulfully. She didn't know what was so exciting about making love but she enjoyed his embraces and his warmth and the pool of joy she found within herself. She hugged him happily while they melted into each other again. This was better than Lester, she thought. Sam was someone she could hug.

"Sam," she said softly a moment later, "would you let me pick my wedding ring?"

"Anything you want, Babe," he replied, flat on his back.

"Just an itty-bitty diamond," she whispered.

"Itty-bitty heck," he said.

A day later he slid a three-carat blue sparkler over her finger. "Oh, Sam," she breathed, "is it all mine?"

He laughed. "It's a token of my undying love and everlasting devotion," he replied. She detected that mockery again, and fretted. Why couldn't he be serious about it?

Norris Timmons, Esquire, Nevada Supreme Court justice, married them forever and ever, Amen, before man and God, in the flossy parquet-floored ballroom of Jones's new palace before ranked banks of lilies shipped from California, and an assemblage of Goldfield's sports in tuxedos and evening gowns. The bride, according to local newspapers, wore ermine and silk, a gown sewn in Paris and rushed westward by steam packet and train. Windlass Borden was best man. The reception for selected guests—all of them from the demimonde—was the most lavish in Goldfield's brief history, and the nuptial dinner that followed had fourteen courses. The *Goldfield News* reported that the bride was deliriously happy, while the *Observer* reported that when it came to the part where they pledged to stick together for better, for worse, for richer, for poorer, the bride had stumbled while the groom had a Cheshire cat look about him.

While the violinists still scraped in the ballroom and the

dancers still whirled, the joyous couple bid their guests adieu, and climbed the mighty bannistered stairs to their little bit of heaven.

"Did you see who Windlass brought to my wedding?" she hissed in the safety of their suite. "That slut. Everybody knows what she does. She runs a *house*."

"Effie. He's been taken with Effie a long time, Babe."

"Well, Effie wouldn't be welcome in Los Angeles society."

"This isn't Los Angeles," he said. "In Goldfield, anyone does anything for money, and especially on their backs. I know half a dozen mine owners and stockbrokers whose wives came out of the tenderloin. We're not snobs here. You'll fit right in."

"Oh!"

Big Sam wasn't sounding very romantic. She hoped he was just joking. It was time to change that vector. "Sam, dear, look what I got for you. It's my wedding present to you." She handed him a slim envelope.

He pulled blue ribbon off it and withdrew two rail tickets. "What's this?" he asked.

"Two tickets to Los Angeles."

He looked puzzled. "What'll we do there?"

"Why—meet nice people. We could go to Venice. We could go to . . . I had the dressmaker do a whole trousseau . . ."

He was laughing. "Thanks, Delia. We'll do that."

She felt vaguely offended. She thought he'd leap at the chance to mingle with good California society. But of course, it would take some adjusting for a former horse trader. "You know, it's like horses. You want to see blooded horses, don't you?"

He laughed again in that strange way, and she could see lust building in his face.

"How about a drinky-poo?" she asked. A bottle of Dom Pérignon lay cooling in an ice-filled silver bucket. "Pop the cork?"

"That's not all that's going to pop tonight," he retorted.

But he pulled wires loose, covered the bottle with a linen towel, and twisted the cork free. It popped and the champagne fizzed upward, spilling over his hands. He poured two full glasses and handed her one.

"Here's to a pair of wildcats, Delia dear."

She decided he wasn't very couth. And not a bit tender. She wanted tenderness on her wedding night and felt vaguely cheated. Maybe she should have waited longer before letting him climb on top of her. She decided to laugh and did it heartily. She was Mrs. Samuel Jones now, the richest woman in Goldfield. She could laugh if she felt like it.

"It's nice," she said, sipping the tickly stuff.

"What would you like for a wedding present? Alaska?" he asked.

"Alaska?"

He shrugged. "Well, I could buy you Tiffany's instead. Or maybe the Southern Pacific Railroad. Would you like the Pacific and Orient Line?"

"Oh, Sam, you're such a tease!" she giggled.

"Oh, no, I'm serious. I want you to lay out that green paper. No fun in having money if you just stuff it all in a closet."

"Oh, Sam, dear," she said, fondling him, "all I want is an itty-bitty cottage and a chance to make my big old Sam-daddy happy."

He laughed, disconcerting her all the more. "What the heck," he said. "I shoulda married a washerwoman."

"But Sam," she said, trying to discern what lay within him.

"Delia, I ain't given you your wedding present yet. What do ya want?"

"Why, Sam . . . why . . . I don't need anything. I'm just your cuddly little girl, is all. I don't need anything."

"How about a Winston Space Annihilator like mine?"

"Oh, that'd be grand, Sam."

He snorted. "Delia, sweetheart, honeypot, don't limit your horizons. Think big. I'm the chief rooster in Goldfield.

Now you tell me what you'd like for a wedding present from me.''

"Just a little old hug from my Sam-daddy.''

"And what else, sweetheart?''

She was treading ground that quaked under her. But he was entirely attentive, awaiting some response while he undid the studs in his shirt. She blinked at him, read his mocking grin, and took the plunge.

"Big Sam,'' she said, "I want an itty-bitty twenty-room cottage at Newport Beach, a steam yacht, and a trip to Peru.''

"By God, I'll keep you,'' Sam said.

She giggled, half in terror. Sam opened a pigskin valise and extracted green Treasury notes bearing hundreds in the corners, each packet wrapped by a strip of paper. He kept pulling them out, packet by packet, making a great heap of them on the white nuptial bed. "There's five thousand,'' he said. "When you run through it, come back to the well. I love you.''

She recovered slowly but steadily. "Sam,'' she said huskily. "Tell your itty-bitty baby what you want to do now.''

CHAPTER 38
....

The devil got into Olympus Prinz one night after he had put his weekly *Observer* to bed. The next issue would deal with Harry Arbuckle again but no longer as a joke. The man and his bullyboys were a menace, and Prinz said so. This issue wasn't going to thrill Harry, who was capable of anything and inclined to cause trouble.

Why do I do this? Prinz asked himself. He had an answer and it amused him: because he was young and reckless, and his newspaper was a sword. He could be a masochist as well as anyone. And it beat getting rich.

His weekly was earning a profit and in a modest way even Olympus Prinz was becoming affluent. The paper became known for its candor and controversy. No matter whether people agreed with Prinz or hated him, they read it. Advertisers flocked to the paper that commanded so much attention, keeping Uriah Horn busy composing the ads.

Tonight Prinz felt itchy and knew what bothered him. His bachelor juices were percolating. He had not met an acceptable young lady and probably would have insulted her if he had. He was at once a graduate of an elite university and an outsider with a funny name, which usually demolished his chances when it came to the fair sex. In any case, in Goldfield he would never meet the sort of intelligent, bright girl he might fall for. His sole recourse was Vice. He always capitalized it because of its importance. Vice, for Olympus Prinz, was almost religion.

Being a veteran bachelor had its conveniences, he thought as he untied his printer's apron and scrubbed his ink-stained hands with gritty soap. He did whatever he felt like, without censure or objection. He never had to account to anyone.

Wrapped in the friendly cloak of darkness he strolled toward the tenderloin—an apt name, he thought—and surveyed the dens of sin one by one. He passed hurdy-gurdies where a fellow could buy a two-step and some watered varnish and a woman—and maybe get rolled, too. He passed saloons and brothels pretending to be saloons. He passed semiclad ladies in windows who smiled and beckoned. He started along a row of identical narrow cribs, each with a bay window where the tart could invite men like himself, men with a need, to sample their wares. Sophie, Goldie, Daisy, the signs said.

He surveyed Daisy in her window and found her comely, a striking lady with a proud lift of the chin and assessing eyes. She smiled. He could see her breasts through the gauze of her peignoir. She wasn't well endowed. He felt a tightening across his belly, and knocked.

"May I come in?" he asked when she opened. He beheld a tall, slender, attractive woman who radiated a sultry heat.

"Yes, you may," she said.

Something about her piqued him though he couldn't say what. He liked her voice. He entered and surveyed the bleak, miserable parlor, which whispered nothing of carnality. It had been cheaply furnished with things not intended to last. The whole room looked like it was about to fold up and vanish. He discovered her gazing at him.

"I'm Daisy," she said.

"Your nom de guerre," he replied.

"I have no other name."

"You were someone else."

A coldness stole through her. "I charge a lot and I don't waste my time talking."

"You're no doubt worth it, Daisy."

"It's ten dollars and I'm worth more than that. I'll make you very happy."

"Where'd you learn French, Daisy?"

"Ten dollars—or I'll have to ask you to leave."

"What does that buy me?"

She smiled dazzlingly. "I'll show you." She began to untie her peignoir until it sagged away from her taut breasts. "Pay me ten dollars, honey, and you'll have all the rest." Her voice had turned husky, filling Olympus with urgent need.

"How much time does ten dollars buy me?"

"Twenty minutes."

"You make thirty bucks an hour?"

"Sometimes a lot more. I have my regulars. Some men like me and give me tips. Now, are we going to . . . or not?"

He caught a hesitation, a delicacy that avoided certain words and phrases. He suddenly wished to know her rather than copulate with a stranger.

He pulled out his billfold and extracted three tens. "Does this buy me an hour?"

She stared at the Treasury notes and sighed. "I guess."

She didn't sound happy about it but she wasn't refusing either.

"Daisy, I just want to talk."

"You what?"

"Talk."

"You don't want to . . . you know?"

That delicacy again. He had discerned something about her. She hadn't done this long; she had never belonged to this class; and she sounded like a young debutante.

"Of course I want to. But it's more pleasing when you know someone."

She shrugged. "As long as you pay," she said. She took the bills, drew the shade on the street window, vanished into the bedroom, and emerged a moment later in a prim wrapper.

"I'll have tea in a few minutes," she said, settling herself into one of the two chairs. She eyed him expectantly. It would be up to him to fill the time he had purchased.

"I'm Olympus," he said.

"I knew you were something," she replied. She perched on the edge of her chair, not accustomed to this sort of purchase of her time.

He translated that to mean that she knew he had blood she didn't share.

"I'm Austrian and Greek. I'm a graduate of Stanford, magna cum laude in philosophy. I edit a weekly paper here. Perhaps you've seen it. The *Observer*."

She withdrew into herself, studying him distrustfully. "I don't have anything to talk about," she said.

"I'm not here for a story. I'm not collecting news. I'm here because I feel like it. Because I'm young. Because there's something about you that's familiar."

"I will never talk about me. Don't ask."

"Daisy, all I said was that you seem familiar."

She met his gaze, her lips tightly compressed.

"I love Goldfield," he said. "It entertains me. I try to catch that in my paper. I poke and probe around. Probably get my nose bloodied sometime. Worst that ever happened to me was getting bounced from the Northern by a pair of bruisers who lifted me by the seat of my pants and tossed me into the manure.''

She laughed.

"Do you know much about the town?'' he asked.

A sudden wariness masked her face again. "No,'' she said slowly, as if even that violated her privacy.

"Well, it's a town where you have to be an idiot not to get rich,'' he said. "The gold turns everything golden. You know what I mean?''

She smiled again.

"You're not starving, I'll wager,'' he said.

"No . . .''

"It's deliciously greedy. Everyone's trying to figure an angle, and the devil takes the hindmost. I'm making money even though I actively resist it. I came here to start ruckuses, cause trouble, make an ass of myself—which I succeed in doing with each issue—but all I do is make money. You ever read my rag?''

She shook her head.

"It'd be beneath you anyway. I'm Goldfield's *Police Gazette* and *New York World* rolled into one.''

She drew a shaky breath. "You're going to write about me. You're doing some big exposé. You're going to close us down. I'd better ask you to leave.''

"Daisy, I'll bring the next two issues to you. There won't be a word about you or the tenderloin. That'll persuade you if nothing else.''

"Olympus, I don't mind talking but keep off the subject of me—please?''

He shrugged. "All right. I'll talk about Olympus Prinz, the would-be womanizer with a name that scares 'em off.''

She smiled again. "Why do you say that?''

"You ever heard of some nicely bred young maiden taking up with a treacherous foreigner?''

"But Olympus—I think you're simply imagining things. I know some women who'd enjoy you even if their daddies might get mad.''

Olympus eyed her amiably. Daisy wasn't very good at concealing her past. She had been bred for a better life than one in a Goldfield crib, on her back every night.

He talked about anything that came to mind. She listened, nodded, laughed—he had a way of making women laugh—and sipped the tea. Once he won her trust—to a degree—she seemed starved for just this; for companionship, for shared thoughts, for something other than the transactions she made with strangers several times every day. He didn't know what to talk about, so he talked of his undergraduate years at Stanford, the restlessness he always felt as an outsider among people with Yankee names. He talked of American history, which he semi-approved of. He loved the young Republic, even while mocking it.

He talked about being a cub reporter in San Francisco and learning the trade from cynical drunks and poseurs. He talked about the stories the *Chronicle* didn't run, and the scoops he had gotten, and the time he had published some great gossip about William Randolph Hearst even before the *Examiner* got wind of it. He talked about an old deskman with a green eyeshade, Dale McCord, who'd taught him how to write by brutally marking up his copy to show him how wordy he had been. McCord had showed him how to lead off with the most important thing in the story, how to be concrete and plainspoken, how to put facts before the reader.

She listened raptly as she sipped tea. Her eyes shone.

And then the hour had passed. She eyed the cheap Westclox ticking away on a battered table.

"I have to go now," she said.

"You mean, *I* have to go now," he translated. More evidence of her cultivation—somewhere, someplace far from here.

"I . . . enjoyed this more than I can tell you," she said earnestly. "I . . . need this once in a while. It . . . reminded me . . ."

He desired her madly and thought to empty his purse of his last two tens and engage her in a wild, furious bout of lust. For an instant she read that raging need in him. Her eyes betrayed the same terrible need.

"Here, Daisy, this is a tip," Prinz said, jabbing his last two tens at her.

"A tip?" She looked bewildered, took the tens, and began to laugh. "I usually don't get a tip for nothing."

"It wasn't nothing—it was being a friend," he said.

He struggled to the door, fighting the impulse to whirl to her and clutch her to him.

She opened it. "Please, please come back, Olympus. And don't write about me," she whispered.

"Trust me," he said. "I want to come back."

CHAPTER 39

Harry Arbuckle could scarcely believe the apparition that was materializing before him in the Texas Saloon. Maude, in bib overalls, brogans, faded flannel shirt, and battered straw hat, pushed through crowds of sports—still guzzling for free, courtesy of Arbuckle—and paused before him, surveying him with a gaze that missed nothing.

He hated that calm gaze. All his life he'd dreaded it. Whenever she studied him like that it turned him into jelly.

"What do you want?" he asked, unhappily. He turned to Cyrus and Mick, his enforcers. "You got any idea what it is?"

They laughed. Arbuckle knew he had a keen wit.

"Well, Harry. I've heard a lot about you. I wanted to see how you are. Who your friends are. What you're doing with your one and only life. Are you happy?"

"Couldn't be better, Maude."

"Perhaps you could introduce me to your friends." She turned to all the sports. "I'm Maude Arbuckle. I'm pleased to meet you."

No one responded.

"I suppose you're all Harry's friends," she said. "Or maybe you're here to enjoy some free drinks. My husband's a generous man with our gold."

That elicited some laughter. "Aw, Maude, lay off," Arbuckle bawled.

"Of course friends aren't the same as leeches," she said. "Some people pretend to be a friend if there's some advantage in it. I suppose you're all fond of Harry. You bring him gifts and treat him to drinks, just as he treats you."

Some of the sports looked pretty edgy.

"Maude, you lay off. You come in here dressed like a man and rile up all my friends. You always were a nag."

That steady gaze of hers pinioned him. "I'm sure you enjoy treating all these nice people, Harry. And I'm sure they enjoy your company, too. I suppose when you run out of money they'll gather around and help you, remembering your kindness."

"I know what you're up to, Maude, and cut it out."

"What am I up to, Harry?"

"Don't pull that stuff on me. You just wanted to push me around again."

Maude didn't reply. Instead she addressed a knot of sports, most of them tinhorns who ran some of the keno layouts. "If you're Harry's friends, buy him a drink. You've had a lot on him, so return the favor."

"I wouldn't want to keep Harry from his pleasures," a suave one replied.

"Then buy him a drink. You owe him a few."

"Hell, I owe him five hundred."

The sports laughed.

"Set up a round, it's on me, gents," Arbuckle yelled.

"Friendship isn't something you can buy, Harry," she said.

"They're my pals and you're wrecking the party, Maude."

She turned to that knot of them again. "Some party. You're just taking advantage of a pathetic man. He doesn't know any better. Harry is just like the rest of us. He wants friends. He wants to walk tall. But he never knew how to win those things. No one ever taught him. He's trying to buy all those things from you. It'd be nice if you'd give back to Harry what he's tried in his own way to give to you. If you don't esteem him and enjoy his generosity, what does that make you?''

"Button your lip," Arbuckle snarled.

"He thinks you like him," she continued relentlessly.

"Why, ma'am, there's none better than Harry Arbuckle," said a tinhorn. "Looks like you just don't appreciate his talents."

She ignored that, and addressed them all. "Why don't you pity this poor man? You all know what he's like. He can't help it. Maybe you don't know how to be friends. Maybe you never heard of charity."

"Oh, Harry's the biggest charity in town," said one. They laughed.

Arbuckle laughed too, knowing that Maude's moment had passed.

She turned to him. "If you can buy drinks for all of Goldfield, you can buy your wife a cottage."

"I'll buy you a drink," Arbuckle said, knowing she never touched the stuff. "If ya don't want it, vamoose."

"All right, Harry. I'll go."

"You prospecting?"

"What else can I do, since you haven't shared a dime with me?"

"Had any luck?"

"It's none of your business, Harry."

"The hell it ain't. You're my wife."

"I didn't know that," she said. "You're full of surprises. Lord, I thought you'd ditched me."

"Lissen here, Maude, if you hold out I'll have Reilly—he's my pet wolf—eat you alive."

She didn't flinch. "I'm glad you're a loving husband, Harry."

That evoked laughter. Harry spotted several sports chortling. He turned to Mick. "Throw her out. I'm tired of this."

Maude stood her ground. "Throwing me out, Harry? I guess you're planning to divorce me after all. I was just wondering."

"Who said anything about that?" he yelled.

"I did."

She waited for the gorillas, refusing to retreat on her own. They lifted her bodily and hauled her out to Main Street.

"I never did like no woman in pants," he said. "Have a drink on old Harry."

The crowd wasn't inclined to laugh with Arbuckle staring them down. He'd show them all who was the chief rooster in the Texas Saloon, daring anyone to smart off at his expense.

Mick and Cyrus returned amid a profound silence.

"Laugh," Arbuckle yelled.

But no one did.

Harry slid into a foul mood and retreated into himself. He was afraid of a divorce. It'd get a big play in all the rags, him being the richest man in Goldfield and all. It'd stink, that's what. She'd fill the judge full of lies, too, about all she done for him. She'd try for a few million and sit on the witness stand shedding crocodile tears. If she started a divorce then he couldn't get a piece of her new bonanza. By God, he'd tell Mick to bust her knuckles if she tried.

"Get that damned Reilly," he said.

Cyrus pushed through the saloon and out. Reilly always came when summoned. For what Arbuckle was paying him, Reilly would crawl through a pit full of rattlers. Arbuckle sucked Old Crow and sulked.

"Get them idiots outa here," he said. "This ain't for publication."

Mick herded the mob. "Party's over. Go pay for your booze somewhere," he yelled.

Mick had a way about him. He bulged out of his suit like a sumo wrestler in a corset. His fingers were as thick as ladder rungs. The last thing several men in Goldfield remembered before seeing stars was an acre of Mick's fist coming at them.

The Texas cleared.

"You wrecked my trade," the proprietor and mixologist, Duck Drake, grumbled.

"Tough luck, Drake. You're getting rich off of me."

That damned Maude. Coming in there dressed like a man in boots and overalls. Arbuckle couldn't help but remember younger times when Maude was nice, too skinny but smart. He liked to show her off then, let all them snot-nosed punks see what Harry Arbuckle catched for a woman. There'd been some good times, too, before she began whining and complaining every time he took ten minutes off.

They'd even talked and dreamed a little before she took to making him feel bad. She wanted to keep on farming but he was darned if he'd spend his life grubbing dirt and looking at the ass-end of a mule. He always knew she had bad blood; her pa had it and passed it along. Her ma, too. Both sides of Maude were bad, turning her into a shrew. Maude's folks had that nice big place but the old man wouldn't even share it with Harry. He thought Harry was beneath him. Harry laughed. Now he was the richest man in the United States and by God he'd show them the elephant.

Turner P. Reilly, Esquire, hurried through the empty saloon to Arbuckle's customary chair. "Money speaks and I answer," he said.

"Maude asked me if I was gonna divorce her."

"What's the problem? Divorce her and be done with it."

Arbuckle stared, distrusting the wavy-haired shyster. "No, she's staying hitched. She's maybe got a new ledge and I want a piece of it. I'm her old man and she owes it to me."

"All right," Reilly said, nimbly reversing himself. "If she starts a divorce proceeding I'll handle it. Quit worrying, Harry. This is easy. We'll just keep her tied up in knots."

"Maude ain't easy."

Reilly smiled patiently. "Look, where's she been? Where'd she come from? It's been a long time. Who's supporting her? Why didn't she come around sooner?"

"She didn't say. But I know who's supporting her. Dash, that's who. Him and her, they're thick as fleas. She's holding out a new ledge on me. She ain't even a woman now. You should see her in bib overalls, shameless as can be."

"How long ago was this?"

"Just now."

Reilly nodded. "Then she's still around. I'll find out. I'll put an investigator on it. If she's found a ledge she'll go back to it. We'll find out where it is and whether she's filed a claim. I'll get my associates in Hawthorne to check the records. She's tied up with Dash, eh? He's grubstaking her? That's all to the good. Dash took your mine and your wife. This gets better and better. We'll get it all back for you, Harry. Just be patient. This is a big, complex suit."

Arbuckle smiled. Good old Reilly. "Have a wash on me," he said.

"Oh, no, I've got to dig into this a little."

"How's it coming? I mean, are you ready to file the mining suit?"

"Just capital. We've got it nailed down. I should have some pretty good news for you soon. It'll take a little cash, though. Your monthly retainer's due, Harry. I have a statement here for expenses. It'll be six thousand seven hundred."

Arbuckle sulked. "I'll pay you when I feel like it. You just get me my gold mine back from them pikers."

"It'll be like swiping candy from a babe, Harry. But it takes research. I have to look up all the precedents."

"By God, if you don't, Reilly, you'll sweat."

For an instant Reilly's composure deserted him but only for an instant. Arbuckle saw it and enjoyed it. He had discovered the power, and pleasure, in making threats. Having a pair of well-paid gents at his side had done wonders for his life. They'd pounded on smart alecs and critics, cut up a few doxies for him, and pulverized a couple of bartenders.

"Quit worrying, Harry. I'll get someone on this. She's still in town and I'll find her." Reilly screwed his homburg down and departed in haste.

"Mick," Arbuckle said. "Go find me a good desert rat real fast. I got plans for that old nag."

CHAPTER 40
....

Big Sam Jones spotted the customer from his opened office door. A middle-aged man stood at the counter, so skinny you could use him for a pipe cleaner. He looked so fragile he probably could fly; with a razor nose, an Adam's apple that bobbed up and down a neck smaller than a fire hose. He wore a black suit, a cravat so wide it looked like a spaghetti bib, and gold-rimmed spectacles. But what amazed Jones was the man's black umbrella. He swore it was the first umbrella he'd seen in Goldfield.

Borden was off diddling his current mistress, Aggie Sopworth, so Jones hastened to the counter.

"Are you Borden or Jones?" the man asked in shrill voice.

"Sure am, pard. I'm Sam Jones. What can I do for you?"

"Are you sure you're Samuel Jones?"

An odd question, Jones thought. "None other."

"Then your time has come!" the man cried. He yanked a nasty-looking piece from his bosom and shot, just as Sam jerked himself sideways. A shower of plaster cascaded from the ceiling.

"Hey!" Jones roared, leaping straight over the counter and toppling the skinny rooster. After a brief scramble, Big Sam sat on the chest of the rooster and the revolver lay five yards across the waxed wooden floor.

"That ain't friendly," Jones growled. Slowly he eased off the quivering fellow, wary of the umbrella. He used the counter to lever himself to his feet and retrieved the revolver. He broke it open and jacked out every shell from the cylinder. Only then did his racing pulse settle down.

"I suppose you're going to arrest me," the man said.

Jones thought about the publicity and grunted.

"I hope you do. I have plenty to say. I'm going to tell the world you're a crook. When they put the noose around my neck, my last words will denounce you as a fraud and a charlatan and a swindler and a despoiler of decent mortals."

That settled it. Jones had no intention of pressing charges. "Look here, Mister—"

"My name is unimportant," the man said. "You wouldn't know the name of an obscure schoolmaster you bilked out of his life savings. You wouldn't care if I told you."

"Well, get up and we'll gab about it," Jones said. "I'm a friendly feller and we'll just make things right."

The wrenlike gent slowly arose and dusted himself, eying Jones and the disarmed revolver. Sam waved the chap to his office and the man primly walked that way.

"You know my monicker but I don't know yours," Jones said, holding out a meaty hand.

"Of course you don't. You wouldn't care if you did. You haven't conscience enough to care. For your reference, it is Hiram P. Bonesett."

"Hiram, mighty glad to meet you."

"It offends me that you address me familiarly. It is bad enough that you bilked an obscure Indiana headmaster with very little money to his name because he chose a life dedicated to larger purposes than lucre. It is worse that you call me by my Christian name. Men who call me by my first name but don't know me are invariably crooks and cons. False friendship in order to sell their goods. I include all insurance salesmen, horse dealers, automobile salesmen, lightning rod salesmen, and investment brokers in that category."

"Mister Bonesett, maybe we can just work this out, eh?

What'd we sell you that's making you unhappy?''

"You sold me a thousand shares of a fictitious mine called the Molly Brown,'' the man cried, his voice shrilling like a steamboat whistle. "I have visited the site, sir. It is barren sand. It contains no mine; no works, such as you showed in your brochure; I've received not a nickel in dividends. I've received not one report detailing earnings and operations. In short, sir, you have stolen my life savings and for that you should be drawn and quartered, put to the rack, tied to a stake, and burned, until your foul soul departs your roasting flesh and sinks into hell.''

Big Sam sighed. He'd been suffering more and more of these episodes. "Mister Bonesett, I just float securities; I hardly keep up with all them companies.''

Bonesett pulled off his gold-rimmed glasses and glared. "There's an appropriate word for that, but it is foul—I cane students I catch saying it—but it is nonetheless the exact and appropriate word, involving the excrement of a bull.''

Jones laughed. Years of horse trading had taught him the value of a belly laugh. "How'd you cotton to this?'' he asked.

"Laughter is inappropriate, sir. I came to Goldfield to check the facts, and if necessary, dispatch your vile soul to its natural abode. Here!'' He exhumed a clipping from the mortuary of his breast pocket and handed it to Jones. A glance told Big Sam exactly what it was.

Olympus Prinz's handiwork. The editor had quit storming and ranting about wildcat stocks and wildcat brokers. The wildcatters had brought so much boodle to Goldfield that no one dreamed of shutting them down. Instead, Prinz had done something far more shrewd. For months he had run a list of Goldfield mining stocks in each issue. He grouped these in several categories: operating, profitable mines; mines under bona fide development; and wildcat mines, paper without substance. An explanation of the selections followed. The list changed from time to time, especially when Borden and Jones floated a new wildcat issue.

It had been effective. Jones's operation scarcely saw any street traffic. But Prinz's column had also been picked up by exchange papers around the West, and even back east in a few cases. Jones could lay this brush with the tomb upon Prinz's rag.

The column was beginning to bleed the company, too. Sales had flattened in spite of aggressive nationwide advertising and a small but ominous trickle of people were threatening lawsuits and demanding to be paid off. Some had even filed suit. Windlass Borden had retained a counselor, a slick shyster named Turner P. Reilly, to settle each case without litigation or publicity. The payoffs were getting expensive and Reilly didn't come cheap.

"Mister Bonesett, this is a simple matter. I'll convert your shares of Molly Brown into any Goldfield shares you want."

"Do you think I'd trust you? Ha!"

"I guess you nosed around town, looking at the mines, eh?"

"I did."

"Then you name the one you want. I've a portfolio that includes stock from each one."

Bonesett squinted suspiciously. "I'll take the Combination. It has a future, a past, and proven reserves. It's quoted at four dollars and an eighth asked, and four dollars bid today. I want a thousand dollars' worth, plus five percent representing lost income, plus my train fare, plus a hundred dollars' worth as a rebuke to your slumbering conscience." He bristled with his demand, daring Jones to object.

Big Sam laughed happily. "Hiram, I'll fix you up."

"Hiram, is it? I am a perfect stranger and you presume to address me familiarly. Give me the certificates. I shall march forthwith to the general offices of the Combination to register myself as a shareholder. If I do not receive full satisfaction, the last you'll see of me is behind the smoking muzzle of that revolver there, or something just as deadly. They can hang me from the nearest Joshua tree but I shall have done justice."

Jones swiftly completed the transaction and without a quibble. Bonesett studied the certificates as if they were about to disintegrate, and stood.

"I can't say it was a pleasure. Give me my Smith and Wesson."

Jones hesitated, and then complied. The .38 caliber shells, one expended, lay on his desk. The smell of burnt powder permeated the brokerage. He was alone. The two clerks wouldn't come in until after the mail arrived.

Bonesett expertly snapped the cylinder back and entombed the revolver in its shoulder holster. "I practiced; I'm a fair shot," he said, and walked out.

Jones slumped in his chair, shaken. He'd been run out of town by rubes a dozen times but never shot at. Horse traders never were shot; in fact, anyone wanting to deal livestock regarded it as a great game, full of knee-slapping fun. Like the time he'd sold a farmer in North Platte a galled nag he had doctored with some oxblood shoe polish. That night he'd stopped at the local tavern for some pilsner and there the rube was, laughing about it. They all thought it was a slick trade. They even bought Big Sam a mess of beers and asked him how to snooker their neighbors. But danged if people took to gold mines with the humor they took to horses.

Fixing up Bonesett hadn't cost him much. As each Goldfield mine floated its shares to capitalize itself, he and Borden had bought thousands of shares at par value and stuffed them into the company portfolio. Who could tell which of the magical Goldfield mines might turn into a bonanza? The Combination stock was trading at around four dollars and Bonesett had walked out with three hundred and fifty shares. But this had been going on for weeks as Reilly settled one suit after another. Those fat portfolios were shrinking fast.

Worse, the shyster was warning he was going to have to settle some suits for big money; he wanted fifty thousand set aside to quiet the thunder that was growling and rumbling just over the horizon. Reilly had compiled a long list

of potential suits and the cost of quieting each one. It was
enough to make Big Sam nervous, an estate he had never
experienced in his long, slippery life. He didn't turn over
the fifty grand, though. He intended to sign all the checks.
Somewhere in that pile of litigation, he suspected, lay some
of Reilly's own jokers. Borden and Jones would deal with
the claims one by one, using their portfolio as much as
possible.

The yellow stuff made a difference. Nowadays, a little
skinning could put a bullet into a man. Now, his world was
full of shysters and lawsuits and serious-looking fellows.
He always figured he was as honest as the next man but
that was back when doping an outlaw horse was a mighty
fine trick of the trade. He had to change. Maybe he could
become a regular broker; slide out of this before the next
bullet got him or he ended up marking days on a jailhouse
wall.

Big Sam Jones knew he was not the person he had been
an hour earlier. He wondered how many men had been
reformed by a near miss.

CHAPTER 41

Time dragged for Delia. She amused herself by buying
everything she could, but Goldfield didn't offer much.
She bought wicker chairs, kept a dressmaker busy making
summery things, and wandered through hardware stores
looking for stuff to grace her home. Sam's mansion. She
despised it.

She wondered how long she could endure Goldfield. It
was so ghastly. It lacked an opera house or hippodrome
although there was a variety theater. But she wouldn't go
to a variety theater because it was too pedestrian. She didn't
meet anyone worth knowing, either. She didn't feel much
like joining the Goldfield Women's Club or the Ladies' Aid

Society. Goldfield women weren't up to her standards. She liked Sam and wanted to spend her time with him. But Sam spent his time at that new Montezuma Club above the Palace Saloon.

She dreaded the very thought of children but was pretty sure that the great infusions of pennyroyal tea she drank at certain times would keep that from happening. She sometimes thought that her curvy flesh was the only thing that kept Big Sam around the house. She tried to be a good lover but it wasn't her favorite occupation. She quit seducing him, too. Before, it had amused her to arouse him with her wandering hands while he read the *Goldfield Observer*. But now that she was safely married she never bothered. He was always grinning in her bedroom, as if he could read her thoughts.

Recently he had started calling her his Firecracker, but it was mockery. Then he called her his Love Bug and then his Cigar Store Princess. She sensed that he was disappointed but she couldn't help it. He wanted more love and affection from her but it was so hard to give it. She knew she wasn't making him very happy.

Someone had told her that Sam was a wildcatter and at first she supposed the word had something to do with their intimate life because he'd called her a wildcat. But then she found it meant that he sold worthless stock; he was a sort of con man. It dismayed her. She had always thought he was a fine securities broker. It was bad enough that he had been an itinerant horse trader, a vagabond going from town to town with livestock, like some icebox hawker or sewing machine peddler or lightning rod drummer.

The outdoor life had stained and weathered his flesh so badly that she would be embarrassed to introduce him to good society. And yet . . . he made oodles of money and that was in his favor. And if she ever divorced him, she'd get tons and tons of it, and she would tell bank clerks in stiff white collars to guard it for her. But she would have to wait awhile. She wouldn't get much if she divorced him so soon. Maybe in 1907, after two years, she could unload him and get piles of alimony. But she hardly knew how to wait that long, especially in hot, ugly Goldfield.

She had intended to move him to Los Angeles right away; he didn't need to be here. His partner, that awful Borden, could run the firm. She'd dreamt of introducing him to good society on the coast, nice people who played lots of golf in knickerbockers and ran the Southern Pacific and owned steamship companies. They had all gone to Stanford or Southern Cal or places like that. What she really wanted was for Big Sam to be a good golfer and play some friendly poker at the country club while she played whist.

But he had been a *horse trader*. It was written all over him. And he used uncouth grammar, too. People in good society had manners and knew what was acceptable. But he didn't. She simply had to reform him or give up that idea: they wouldn't look twice at Big Sam and it would mortify her if they ever found out what he had done all his life.

"Sam," she ventured one rare evening when he loitered at the dinner table. "There's nothing to do here. You promised me a steam yacht and a little cottage at Newport Beach."

He eyed her somberly. "You've got a fourteen-room house. All the cash you need. A carriage and a butler and a maid. Three automobiles, dusters, goggles, and spare tires. The best pair of trotters in Nevada, and a fine sulky. Unlimited credit at any joint in town."

"I'm lonely. I don't know anyone."

"Well, I'll introduce you to people."

"They're not worth knowing. I'm not interested in trash."

He laughed. "I'm trash, Delia. I'm never gonna make the social register. You married a horse trader. You tied the knot with a wildcatter. I guess you don't want to associate with me."

It wasn't far from the truth, and she bridled. "But there's nothing to do. There's no golf course. There's no club."

"All we got is gold, sweetheart. And each other. You're a honey. I love to squire you around town and watch 'em envy us. I don't know about you, Delia, but I'm happy and you're good to me."

His compliments heartened her. "Sam, would you rent me an itty-bitty cottage at Newport Beach? And an itty-bitty yacht for a few months? There's such nice people there. You know, very nice. Manners. Just the kind I grew up with. I just want to be with the nice people I grew up with."

"Like who—the Huntingtons, the Crockers?"

"Yes, like that. I don't know them personally but of course they're sort of, you know, part of our group."

Sam guffawed. She could barely stand it when he hoorawed like that. "I guess I don't add up," he said. "I'm just a wildcatter. You know what I did all my life? I skinned suckers. I'm giving it up, though. Maybe I'll retire. I'll be a retired pirate."

"I wish you wouldn't talk like that."

"You want someone better?"

"Well, you could mind your manners a little, Sam. I mean, no one in Los Angeles says *ain't*, and no one laughs like that, and no one uses a dirty handkerchief. I mean, you could try to polish yourself a little. For me . . ."

"You don't like to be seen with a big old stiff-legged horse trader. You had other dreams, I guess."

She paled. "I never said that. Sam—let's not fight. Let's—you know." She smiled at him. Then she nodded ever so slightly toward the stairwell that would take them up to her spacious room.

"Delia, if you don't like being hitched to someone who ain't up to snuff, just say the word. We've been in double harness about three months. I reckon that'd fetch you a nice little annulment. Don't have to bother with no divorce and all that arm wrestling." He spoke seriously and yet she detected that humor in him. It was as if this whole scene were a comedy for him. She shrank from the implications.

"Oh, Sam, I never said that." She couldn't cry, but she

could look like she might. "Don't you love me?"

"Delia, sweetheart, I love you heart and soul. I love you until the grass grows over my tomb. I love you as long as the sun shines. I love you from here to Tonopah and back. I love you more than Joshua trees and gray quartz. You're as pretty as a highgrade ledge."

"Oh, Sam. If you love me, take me away from here."

He considered that gently. "When it all dies down, we'll go, Delia. Right now, this is the most important place on earth. You just wait a few years and we'll go get you a beach house and stuff."

He disappointed her. "I'm going to my room," she said crossly, hoping he wouldn't follow her.

"I'll be at the Montezuma Club."

She retreated to the dark stairwell, mounted the oriental runner held in place with brass rods, whirled into an upstairs foyer, and entered her suite, a sunny bedroom with walk-in closets and her own water closet and clawfoot tub. The last of the summer sun lit the gauzy curtains, dazzled off the beeswaxed furniture, intensified the blue and gold dyes in the carpet. She lived in pampered luxury.

She closed the door behind her and locked it. She wouldn't let him near her, not after this. It had been their first tiff and maybe it would be their last. She sat on her bed, feeling the costly mattress surrender to her weight, and tried to think. She'd never been so rattled in her life.

Her every instinct led her to one thing. He didn't care enough about her to heed her wishes. Another thing she knew: she wasn't going to bring Sam to Los Angeles. She could never make her way into the social set with that oaf.

She studied herself. The sole feeling in her was annoyance. She'd picked the wrong bonanza king. She needed another. She had lost many months seducing him, becoming his lover and then his wife. But she consoled herself with the understanding that it hadn't all been wasted. She could begin looking for a suitable husband—and do it in comfort and perfect security. Of course she wouldn't cheat; she wouldn't get alimony if she did. She would just look.

There were lots of gold kings in town and some of them would be perfectly presentable men who would help her reach her goal. Someday, all of Los Angeles would envy Delia.

She felt the house close in around her. Mercedes would have cleared off the table, and Armando had probably retired to his quarters in the rear. The night was young, scarcely nine o'clock.

The Palm Grill. That was the only place to meet suitable men. But she would be unescorted. She puzzled it out and then decided on a course of action.

Swiftly she changed into a seductive white dress, gauzy and clingy for a hot Goldfield night. She added a gold necklace. She plucked up her little evening purse and raced out the door. It took too much effort to crank up the Winston so she walked the four blocks, letting the dry desert air cool away the beads of moisture at her brow.

She entered the Palm Grill and heard Julius scraping rhapsodies as he wandered among the linen-clad tables.

"Why, it's Mrs. Jones," said Coffin, tapping tasseled menus in his palm. "You're expecting Mister Jones, I imagine?"

"He'll be along in a while. I thought I'd just have a toddy while I wait."

He slid past hesitation in an instant. "Of course. Shall I seat you at a table?"

"No, I'll have a toddy in the saloon, please."

He smiled one of those smiles that conceal a thousand thoughts, and led her into the glowing saloon. She chose an over-stuffed banquette in the corner.

"Thank you, dear. I'll have a glass of Sherry while I wait."

The maître d' vanished in the direction of the bar and Delia settled back to wait. Before her were a dozen or so men she would enjoy meeting. She knew who some of them were, and she knew that they might enjoy her charms. She was the sort of gal men loved to be around, and that was her key to a better life.

CHAPTER 42

·······················

The Goldfield newspapers liked to say that most of Gold-field's business was done at the Montezuma Club on the second floor of the Palace Building. That is where men of means, financiers, mine superintendents, merchants, bankers, as well as mining engineers, doctors, and vice presidents, all gathered to guide Goldfield toward its manifest destiny.

Which always occasioned a horselaugh from Big Sam Jones. If they'd take membership dues from a rogue like him, they'd take dues from anyone. What talked loud at the Montezuma Club was gold and greenbacks. He enjoyed that corner of Goldfield more than any other. There, amidst solid comforts—stuffed ebony leather chairs, brass spittoons, cut-glass chandeliers that shed dazzling electric light, and a huge walnut bar presided over by Emil Beerbohm—he found a home.

Beerbohm, a walrus-mustached zealot behind a bib apron, would never let a clubman go dry. He knew the tastes and capacities of all one hundred and twenty-five members. Jones had only to park himself in one of those commodious armchairs, his stiff leg propped out before him, and Beerbohm would settle a foaming mug of ice-cold lager beside him. After Delia's perpetual pleading, the Montezuma Club seemed like a piece of real estate on the outskirts of heaven.

In truth, most members wouldn't speak to him, and passed him by as if to shake hands would contaminate them. Some owners and operators of profitable mines were among them. He had seen bug-eyed George Wingfield in here too, and wondered if the Tonopah tinhorn, who had acquired a major interest in several Goldfield mines, even remembered staking Big Sam.

The Montezuma not only stooped to admit Jones, it also admitted Windlass Borden, who showed up now and then when he wearied of his latest doxie, Mrs. Bettendorff. It even admitted George Graham Rice, whose Sullivan Trust Company made Borden and Jones look like church deacons.

But even though he was welcome in the Montezuma, he knew he was considered a rogue. He had never supposed he could pass in good company anyway. No vagabond could. At times, he had settled himself in some wing chair where Goldfield's prominent men were talking, and always the conversation turned away from business to jovial quips and slightly condescending small talk. Once it had amused him. He had enjoyed his reputation. But now it didn't.

Ever since that bullet almost found its mark, Jones had found himself entertaining long thoughts about his past, his present life, and what he wanted in the future. Everything in the past had been the occasion for cynicism. Skinning suckers was his life's entertainment. But nothing seemed funny anymore. There were men conversing in chairs over there whose opinions he would esteem, whose wisdom he would treasure. They were separated from him by an invisible wall even though they shared the same club, the same room.

It had to do with the very thing he'd laughed at most of all, their rectitude. Some of them were pious pirates but most of them had won their wealth by honorable means, investing shrewdly, or using great entrepreneurial skills, or employing professional skill, like that geologist Dash, over there. That was the difference. Most of them hadn't hurt anyone and most of them adhered to conduct that won trust from others. It gave Jones a pang to know that the big bills stuffed in his pockets were the hopes and savings of widows, retiring clerks, and the legacies of unwitting children. It was the first attack of conscience he had ever had, and he turned it over in his mind, not quite admitting that those whom he'd skinned didn't deserve the skinning.

That was his mood as he sipped lager. One moment he

yearned for acceptance; the next he called himself seven kinds of fool. But he couldn't shut the door now that he'd admitted he wanted something better from his life.

"How does it feel to be a rich man, Windlass?" he asked Borden later that evening.

"As long as it flows in, who cares?"

"I came close to being a rich dead man," Jones said, broaching the topic he had been worrying for weeks. "I don't know how I ever got into the securities business. I come limpin' into town thinking I'll be a promoter. Anyone that traded nags for a living knows how to sell sand to Arabs."

"Well, Sam, that's what did it. I owe you that. Those ads, they put the company on the map."

"Well, that's the trouble. This gold, it's not like dickering on a horse. It ain't fun and it's plumb dangerous. I'm thinking of getting out. You want to buy my half?"

This time Borden paused amid-sip and slowly set his rye down. "You're thinking of selling out?"

"Yup, I'm thinking on it."

"You planning to start up your own outfit?"

"Nope. I'll guarantee I won't."

"You thinking of taking those advertisements you worked up with you?"

"Nope. All yours. Every ad and all the data about how each ad performed. All you got to do is keep putting them in papers in Maine and New Jersey and raking in the moolah."

Borden frowned, trying to find the joker in that deck. "How come?" he asked.

"Gold's too serious," Jones said. "I sort of look at life as something that should be fun."

"Ah, Sam, it's that potshooter Bonesett. You'd sell out because of an occasional Bonesett? We've got the armed clerk out front now."

"Oh, that's part of it. Wildcat gold mines are too tribulationary. When people get around gold, they ain't themselves."

Windlass Borden wiped his oily scalp and puzzled through all that. "I always thought you had a fondness for gold," he said. "This certainly is a surprise. I suppose it has to do with Delia. She doesn't take kindly to Goldfield and you probably want to go live in Santa Monica."

"No, it has to do with thirty-eight-caliber holes and unexpected funerals. It has to do with who I am. I'm not liking this racket anymore. I'm gonna change my ways. Delia's not the trouble. She's unhappy, all right, but she'll come around. I'm not selling out because of her. I'm calling it quits because I don't like it anymore. Bonesett's bullet didn't hit flesh but it hit me even so."

Something steeled in Borden's eyes. "All right, what're the terms?"

"One hundred thousand. You get everything, including earnings on ads now in place and the chandeliers."

"Everything? So . . ." Borden checked himself. "That's reasonable. And this would include a noncompetition agreement?"

"I'd buy and sell shares for my own account."

Borden pondered that. "But you wouldn't float securities?"

"Nope."

"I don't know why. Sam, is there something you ain't divulging? You figure Reilly's settling too many claims? That's it?"

"Like I said, it ain't good for my health, Windlass. That's my main reason. If you don't want to buy me out, I might sell my half to someone else."

"It's not my business, Sam, but what're you gonna do?"

"Oh, I'll be a capitalist. I'll buy companies that look promising. Now, is it a deal?"

Windlass Borden sucked in cigar smoke. "Done," he said. "I'll draw up a little agreement. See what you think of it."

"You'll have to accept assets and liabilities, Windlass. You get my half but you'll have to take over all the claims that Reilly's settling, too."

"They ain't but one bumblebee in a square mile of flowers," Borden said. "And if you're pulling out, that just doubles the garden."

"Borden, old friend, I knew you'd see it my way," Jones said.

CHAPTER 43
....

Beth Fairchild-Ross endured, though she scarcely knew how. The men came to her door and left, one after another, and she somehow greeted each one with a smile, subjected herself to each one's lust, and took each one's money. She had been robbed once, cheated several times, and beaten once. She had dealt with drunks and fools as well as amiable fellows who wanted a female friend.

She had had a dozen proposals of marriage and even more propositions to become someone's mistress. She had numbly acquiesced to men whose tastes were repulsive. But none of those things troubled her as much as her utter loneliness.

Her life became a succession of visitors, a parade of males ranging from timorous romeos to brutes. She tried to numb her loneliness with rotgut and once with morphine, but she came to her senses the next daylight and didn't spend another penny.

Her savings swelled almost magically as she deposited her previous night's earnings in the Nye and Ormsby Bank. She began her day by dressing in the most severe suit she had, topped by a veiled wide-brimmed hat, and carried her bills to the safety of the bank. She hoped it was safe. Banks sometimes weren't. If she lost what she had gained she could never do it again and never escape this corner of hell.

She rejoiced when she had accumulated one thousand, but five seemed far away. Then came the second, third, and fourth. She was close to her goal and could see ahead to the time when she would abandon Goldfield forever and fall into the arms of her dear ones. She counted the hours and days, projected her income, schemed to earn more, learned ways to get tips, turned herself into a plausible liar as she muttered endearments to each of the males who grunted themselves limp over her.

She took a bitter pride in selling sex at a higher price than any of her sisters in the district. No one matched her ten dollars. Her very high price brought its own business as men came to try out the most expensive whore in Goldfield. She tried to pleasure them all; it meant shortening the time she had to endure this shame. She learned that a laughing, good-humored tart won more than a sour or depressed one, so she made a great show of joy, letting her eyes light up with delight when her regulars returned.

And yet, in the hours before dawn after she had pulled the shade, locked her door—there were occasional knocks and poundings all hours of the day—and retreated to her bed, the very bed where many men had lain that night—a great grief swept her that she couldn't resist and didn't try to resist because she found she needed it. The grief was what separated her from the professional whores at every side of her.

She could scarcely remember Reggie. She could remember her little dumplings much more easily and she feared they would forget their mama or resent her sudden departure so much she could never win them back. Worst of all, she questioned over and over the sense of what she was doing. Maybe all this was for nothing. Maybe it was utterly stupid. It might have been better to let go of Reggie. She would have divorced him, yes, a scandal, but in these modern times once in a while a man might marry a divorced woman. Maybe that would be better than this.

The initial lust she had experienced in the midst of sleeping with strange men had dried up. There had been something erotic about it at first, the fruit of its very forbiddenness. But that had passed and now she felt nothing. It was all business.

She ceased worrying about being discovered. San Francisco society didn't come here. She would carry this secret to the grave. Her lips would never reveal to Reggie the source of her money; even a deathbed confession to her Episcopal priest would not cover this ground. If God forgave, surely he would forgive a woman using the only means open to her to salvage her husband's honor.

But even though she rarely worried about discovery anymore, the other dangers haunted her. The price of her services had not gone unnoticed in the district. Not a few of the pimps wanted a cut. Any one of them was capable of maiming or kidnapping her. Once one had held a knife to her throat and told her he wanted half or she would die. She had fled to the dance hall for help, and got it from Ned.

She was never more than an inch from white slavery and for that reason she kept her protectors in the Palace Dance Hall as happy as she could. It was costing more and more, as if a giant noose was tightening around her as word of her success filtered through the rat-infested corners of the red-light district. If Dollarhyde didn't protect her—she might never see San Francisco again.

She thought at times she would go mad but for the quiet attentions of Olympus Prinz. She welcomed him so eagerly she almost leapt when he knocked, always late in an afternoon before the night's trade began. Whenever she opened the door to him her heart melted. He entered with a cocky smile, tossed his bowler in a corner, and they hugged. But even though they had both felt the terrible tug of their bodies—he alone aroused her desire and she ached to enfold him within her arms—it hadn't happened. She ritually poured tea; they talked for forty minutes as if at a church social. Then he paid her twenty dollars plus a five-dollar tip for her time and walked out into the twilight. She had begged him to stay on just five minutes more, but he never did. It wasn't what they talked about—she could scarcely remember it all—but simply that he came and went as a friend that drew her to him.

He talked about his newspaper mostly. The *Observer*

flourished in spite of the three dailies in town, mostly because of Olympus Prinz's humor, his unique ability to write a story that other papers didn't touch, and above all his exposés of scandalous conditions in Goldfield.

He came to her three times a week, three joyous moments out of so many, but they were the most important episodes of her life on the Line. She wormed out of him a terrible truth: the money he was spending out of the earnings of that little paper should have been going toward a Mergenthaler Linotype machine, which would allow him to set type in hours instead of days and to reduce the complex business of breaking down the pages to minutes as the slugs of type metal were all thrown into the pot to be melted down again.

But he had chosen to spend those precious dollars on her; indeed, not upon her body, but upon a simple friendship. As much as she loved him for that she gladly took his money. Something was happening to them both as weeks lengthened to months and his steady calling turned into social intimacy. He cared for her. That was obvious from the looks in his eyes and from his lingering hugs. But it was most obvious from his mounting pressure upon her to talk about herself. No one else had tempted her to do so but she had to resist violently whenever he approached the forbidden ground.

"Who are you, Daisy?" he asked intensely one night. "You know all about me. I know nothing about you. Whoever you are, your secret is safe with me."

"Olympus, I'm Daisy," she said, making a little moue.

That's when he came closest to exasperation and she feared he would stop coming and leave her entirely inside her dark and brutal world.

"I can't tell you, I just can't!" she cried. "Don't ever ask me, Olympus."

He sighed. "Daisy—God, how I wish it might be Genevieve or Susan or Andrea—Daisy, I know more about you than you realize. You weren't born to this and you don't have to be here. Your talk, your choice of words, well,

I've heard these figures of speech in . . . society?'' His eyes were question marks.

She smiled and turned away, for once wanting him to leave. ''Tell me, Olympus, how is the Combination doing? I hear two of the mines are bonanzas.''

''Daisy, for God's sake, have pity on me. I love you. Maybe I'm crazy, but I love you. You're the woman I've always dreamed of. Nothing that happens here touches your soul. That's your miracle. You're filled with grace. I love you. We'll leave here and go somewhere fresh and good. I can't give you a luxurious life but I've some skill at making a paper pay. I'll give you—Daisy, I'll give you everything, including respect and love. There's more to life than money.''

He stared at her hotly, his need and hope and fever palpable to her.

''I like the money,'' she said flatly.

''You don't spend a dime! Look at you. I haven't seen a new robe on you since I met you. I don't see a new thing here. You don't buy clothes or books. You don't buy booze or visit the hop fiends or smoke cigarettes. You earn tons of money but where does it go? Every cent goes somewhere, for some purpose you never tell me about. I'm here to help you. I love you, Daisy or whoever you are. I want you just as you are. You don't have to justify yourself to me. Whatever you're doing, I know you're reaching toward something. You've a desperate need for money.''

He stopped, staring at her wistfully. ''I guess you don't care. I'm just another trick.''

''Olympus, that's not true!'' she cried.

''Then share your life. Try trusting me for a change. Try me and see. Dare to share yourself with me. To the best of my ability, I'm an honorable man.''

She could see the desperation in his face. He loved her so. She could read it upon his face. She loved him too but it rose as a red pain inside of her, a love-pain she couldn't endure. He had given her his heart, his wit, his wry opinions, his philosophy, his exasperating experience as an

American with a funny name. She ached to cry out, My name is Beth! I love you, Olympus! But she swallowed hard, feeling the constriction of her throat, and clamped her lips into a bitter line.

"You're the most precious thing in my life, Olympus," she managed to say.

It didn't help. He rose, earlier than usual, scarcely twenty minutes into this bought visit. She read the somber defeat in his face.

She reached to him. She threw her arms around him and drew him tight to her. He responded with a groan, his hands clamping her to him, his hug desperate and impassioned. They clung fiercely. She felt his desire building and thrust her loins to meet it, the ache in them so fierce and terrible that nothing could stay the flood.

But then he wrestled free, his mouth a gash of agony.

"Oh, Olympus," she cried, feeling tears well up. "Don't leave me. Don't, don't, don't . . ."

He dug into his pants for his purse and extracted two tens and a five as he always did. For a split instant she thought he would toss them to the grubby floor, let her stoop for her money. But his face softened and he handed them to her. "You are a vision of grace," he said softly. "I guess I will never win you."

He looked like a man who had been electrocuted and lived to take another jolt. He wiped tears out of his face.

"All right, Daisy," he said, with such resignation that it sounded like the tolling of a funeral bell.

He opened her door and vanished into the dusk. She watched him go, wondering whether she would ever see him again and whether she had compounded her mistakes beyond help. She was only four hundred dollars from freedom—and debating whether to return to Reggie at all. Dapper Reggie, the Stanford grad and man about town and casual crook, didn't begin to measure up to Olympus. It was a truth she couldn't bear.

CHAPTER 44

....

Maude Arbuckle knew she was a natural-born desert rat. She liked the big bleak barrens almost as much as civilization. They offered her peace and safety as long as she was careful about water.

Something about Goldfield had stirred her up. Maybe it was Harry, sitting there in pomp and glory, surrounded by leeches and sports without an honorable instinct in them. She had tried to help him see what he couldn't see. It hadn't done any good but she had tried. Her visit to the Texas Saloon had shown her his pathos, and her deepest feeling about Harry Arbuckle was a simple pity.

She wended her way westward again, drawn once more to the black mountain for reasons beyond fathoming. Mother Dear trailed behind, leaving a trail of elongated burro prints in the occasional soft dust.

Maude had added one thing to her outfit, a two-quart canteen, suspended by a shoulder strap. She intended never to get into such a desperate thirst again. If she were separated from the burro she would have at least a little water with her at all times, no matter that the canteen weighed heavily on her shoulder and was an annoying presence.

She would find gold this time. And she would share half of it with that quiet man who had grubstaked her over and over and would again if she asked. Hannibal Dash was a gentleman, a rare enough breed. She didn't suppose gentlemen lacked their own vices. But their instincts led them to be civil toward others, honorable in all things, and generous to all.

She had found that out about Dash from the beginning. She had never known such a gallant act as to rescue Harry's claim for him—and her—instead of simply taking it away as he had every right to do. She still couldn't quite believe it rose from some innate decency in Dash and not from some crass motive. He probably had clay feet like the rest of mankind but so far she hadn't discovered his weaknesses.

He had warned her that her way of prospecting was coming to an end. "The day of the prospector, hunting for outcrops, is about gone, Maude. I hope you'll find something but I doubt that you will," he had told her. "The future belongs to science; drilling for samples, mineral sciences, geology. You can't hope to compete with trained scientists."

She didn't like that. "You do it your way and I'll find the stuff my way," she had retorted, an edge in her voice. He didn't know a thing about her prospecting. She didn't really hunt down ledges or outcrops; she felt the metals in her bones, some canny intuition telling her to focus on some ridge or another. And she had done right smartly that way, too. Darned scientists!

Even Mother Dear seemed happier away from Goldfield. The town had mushroomed and Maude didn't like the people she saw there, so many of them toughs and tinhorns. The types who rushed to a gold camp were a greedy lot: people who wanted easy wealth; people who hated to work and grub; people who wanted to snooker good workers out of their rewards. People who'd skin their own grandmothers if it meant an easy buck.

Lordalmighty, a real prospector hiked and sweated and dug and packed and unpacked. A prospector pitted his wits against a wilderness. A prospector lived in constant misery from heat, cold, dryness, chafing wind, sunburn, landslides, rattlers, lack of company, too much company, a diet of moths, lizards, kangaroo rats and yucca pulp; from starvation, mirages of the saints, visitations from God, deals with Beelzebub, rotting memories, deeds relived, and alkali water. That made every darned cent of a bonanza legitimate. And that was the one thing she had against Hannibal Dash. He hadn't grubbed for five or ten years. Maude spat, punctuating her thoughts. Lordalmighty, no sonofagun ought to find a bonanza until he'd served an apprenticeship!

She paced westward through a fierce heat, scarcely bothering to grumble about it. No sense griping about something you couldn't change. Mother Dear didn't like it and lagged behind until Maude caught her long cylindrical ear, whispered to Mother Dear that she'd get her butt whipped, and then bit the ear. The burro was plainly offended and bit Maude's hip.

"I'll slit your throat," Maude retorted.

Mother Dear decided to perform her duty, yawned, muttered, and trotted along, equaling Maude's determined stride.

She made a dry camp in the lee of a bluff that night; refilled at a seep mid-morning the next day after chasing off a cloud of bees, skipper moths, a banded gecko, a pair of ladder-backed woodpeckers, and a desert tortoise; dug for water near the familiar cottonwoods that night and reached the black ridge the next day, well watered and in fine fettle.

She spent half a day raising the black mountain; that's what she called getting closer to it, until it loomed above her like some sinister wall intended to keep her out. The dense juniper on its upper reaches was the source of its gloom, not the rock itself, which ranged from gray to brown.

She stood listening to it, hearing its soft growl as it defied the furnace air. Listening to it sigh, expel gases, and mock her efforts to penetrate it. She spotted a long ledge that lay crosswise of the watercourses and gulches and knew it for a good sign.

She felt scornful of her patron, Hannibal Dash, with all his geology, mineralogy, bottles of reagents, beakers, tubes, and delicate scales. He couldn't feel the mountain or hear it the way she could. That was the trouble with all those scientists. They measured the world the way blind men measured an elephant.

"We're goin' up, you ornery beast," she snarled at

Mother Dear. The burro worried a yucca leaf, her pink tongue dealing delicately with its spiky edge.

That day Maude tromped the highest ridge listening to the mountain, scorning her usual cautions about water. She would go for water when she was driven to it and not a moment before. The last trip she had struck southward; this time she hiked north, feeling the furnace heat burn through the soles of her brogans, feeling the blast radiating from the flaming rock cook the juices out of her. She felt like Moses walking around the top of Mount Sinai, waiting for the tablets.

She heard the gold, smelled it, felt the gold in her fingertips, but she didn't see it. No ledge showed any sign of quartz. No yellow glint caught her eye; no bead or thread or wire; no nugget lying coyly in a crack. As the sun plummeted she felt angry, hating the mountain and its treacherous lode. She would have to retreat soon. She had even tapped her emergency water that bounced at her bony hip.

But before she did she would show that scientist Dash a thing or two. She cut a forked juniper branch with her hatchet and skinned the handles clean until she had a wooden dowsing rod. She gripped the forked ends and leveled the stem. It tugged downward gently. She walked a circle, feeling the dowsing rod surrender and then yank. She headed northwest, over the top of the ridge and halfway down the far side when the stem plunged so violently she lost her balance. She was standing on another transverse ledge cut by drainage here and there. But she saw no quartz of any color.

Her dowsing rod was acting berserk. Every time she crossed the gray ledge it yanked her arms down. Whenever she distanced herself from it the rod became as lifeless as a corpse. But she could see nothing that resembled ore in its cracked igneous formations. Maybe the treacherous rod was divining water, or lead, or zinc, or copper, or fairy castles. Why should she suppose it was revealing the most precious of metals?

The low sun blasted her as she hunkered over the ledge

on the western slope. She plucked up rock, looking for float. She studied a lustrous gray rock, almost pearly. The ledge was solidly gray and fine-grained, and it had spilled float downslope for eons.

If this was gold-bearing rock she couldn't tell it but she knew she was at the source of the float below. It had all turned into a mind-numbing mystery and she cussed the dowsing stick that had led her to this time-wasting hunt. Whatever this was, it wasn't anything she understood: it wasn't quartz or quartzite; not granite or diorite or gabbro; not rhyolite either.

Irritably she collected samples of the pearly gray rock and resigned herself to what few tests she could manage. It was growing gloomy. Mother Dear was restless and eager to reach lower reaches and the thin grasses that grew among the junipers. Maude jammed several pounds of rock into her sample bag and retreated after sharply orienting herself. Too many bonanzas had been lost by prospectors who couldn't remember where they had been.

She walked straight up to the ridgeline and threw together a small cairn around her dowsing rod so that its forks poked the sky. She felt a blessed temperateness in the swift air as she labored. Satisfied at last, she studied her locale once more in the gloom, imprinting it on her soul, and then descended down the west facade to a rincon she thought might have water at its rear, and some grass for Mother Dear.

It was a long way down, some of it in darkness that made her footing treacherous. But at last she reached a sandy corner marked by a single cottonwood and dug there, hearing the night breeze waltz its leaves. She found moisture a foot down and water in another six inches. It tasted alkaline but she could live with the trots if she had to. She dug a large shallow well three feet deep. She unloaded Mother Dear, watered herself and the burro, and set to work at a small fire of cedar limbs.

She didn't intend to eat until she had run that lustrous gray rock through the two or three simple tests. There wasn't a hint of gold shining in it, and no quartz either, but she sensed it was ore.

While her fire burned hot and settled into glowing orange coals she pulverized a rock sample in her skillet and screened out enough of the grainy dust to run a charcoal test. From her kit she extracted a charcoal block with a hollow in it, her blowpipe and a candle. She poured the dust into the hollow and with her blowpipe slowly smelted the little sample, turning the candle's flame into a tiny blast furnace that scorched away any sulphur, chlorine or carbonate.

If the rock held iron it would not reduce at those low temperatures and she would have only a brown powder. But if it was copper it would reduce to a smelted bead; if silver, there might be a dull white bead that could be rolled in dampened salt and exposed to the sun to see if it would turn black—a sure sign of it. If lead, the button could be easily remelted. If gold, it would probably reduce to the familiar yellow pellet.

She blew patiently, feeling smoke and heat and common minerals swirl away until a curious-looking lump of silvery gold metal remained, glowing like a cat's eye in the firelight. She stared at it exultant. When it had cooled she ran her fingers over it, feeling the gold under them. And finally she pocketed it.

The ledge was black gold, or telluride, and she had found what had no doubt eluded dozens of prospectors before her. She had never seen this kind of ore before. She thought it might be calaverite. Oh, Lordy, land sakes, hallelujah, and God Bless America!

"Mother Dear," she bawled. "I'll keep you on grain all your days."

She stared into the blackness feeling she wasn't alone although she had heard and seen nothing. Maybe it was the silence. She shrugged it off as nothing but her natural suspicion now that she had hit her bonanza. But the night didn't feel right.

That wasn't a small button; it was amazingly large. She

was rich. She had done it. Tomorrow she would run more tests, post her claim and measure boundaries, and head for Goldfield and the assay offices of her dear friend and grubstaker, Hannibal Dash, the self-same feller who hooted at dowsing. Oh, that would be a laugh!

CHAPTER 45

••••••••••••••••••••••

The next morning Maude ran her blowpipe test on a second sample of pulverized ore with identical results. An impressive gold button lay cooling in the hollow of the charcoal block. Elated, she packed Mother Dear and sprang up the mountain slope, finding her discovery ledge easily. She studied the lay of the ledge, trying to find its strike, and decided to run her fifteen hundred by six-hundred-foot claim east and west.

That required a cairn and a location marker. She set to work on the cairn, wrestling rocks one by one into place until she had a two-or three-foot mound of them. Much of the rock was float off the ledge and she reckoned it was just about the most valuable cairn a prospector had ever laid up.

Halfway through her arduous task she spotted movement below. A man with a burro was ascending the slope over a mile away. She eyed him warily. Why had he shown up at the exact moment when she'd made a discovery? She watched distrustfully and then decided to finish writing her claim. She emptied a screwtop cannister she always kept for the purpose, sat down, and scratched out her claim with a pencil: "I, the undersigned, hereby claim the gold-bearing lode outcropping here, along with all its dips, spurs and angles, variations, and sinuosities, for a distance of three hundred feet north and south of this site, and seven hundred fifty feet east and west of this site." She signed her name and dated it, August 7, 1905. Then she wrote out a duplicate to file in the Esmeralda County Courthouse at Hawthorne. The original she rolled up and tucked in the cannister and screwed its top back on. The cannister she wedged into the cairn and added rock to pin it in place against all the forces of nature.

All the while the lone man toiled upward. She saw he wore a sidearm and was bearded. She noted that his outfit lacked the tools and picks hanging from the pack that marked a prospector. Her pulse lifted. After weeks of her seeing no one at all, this bum appeared just when she discovered gold. He had probably been observing her all the while with a glass. It would be all too easy for him to murder her, leave her body on a distant peak for the vultures, and steal the claim.

She made a decision. Swiftly she loaded Mother Dear and raced up the ridge and over the top. He was at least ten minutes off. She raced down a few feet and then cut north. He would expect her to continue east toward Goldfield, not the way she headed. She hurried Mother Dear toward a swell in the ridge a half mile distant where she might observe the man from an unexpected quarter.

She found a cup of naked tan rock that would conceal the burro from eyes below and extracted her .22 caliber carbine, a pathetic little weapon but all she had. She clambered to the lip of the hollow on the ridge in time to spot him down at her cairn. He was pawing away rock to get to the cannister. When he found it he opened it and pulled out her claim. He studied it, extracted a pad from his pack, and wrote his own. This he inserted in the cannister and returned it to the cairn. Then he collected some rock samples and stowed them.

Maude could scarcely contain her rage. The lobster had been following her. His theft could get him hanged in any mining district but it didn't seem to bother him any. He worked easily, pausing to study the country around him and now and then, especially the ridge above. She made herself calm down. She couldn't think when she got too angry. Sometimes in the old days, when Harry drove her to such rage, she had clenched her fists and counted slowly until she could bring the flood of feeling under control. She counted now, but it didn't help much. She knew she was mad because she was cussing. She never cussed. Whatever else she was in life, a desert rat in bib overalls, she intended to remain a lady.

It struck her that he might hunt her down and kill her. Either that or outrun her to Goldfield and file first. In either case, her troubles had barely begun. If she had been mad before, now her temper turned volcanic. Angrily she collected Mother Dear and headed his direction but staying well below the ridge and out of sight. Her carbine wasn't good for more than thirty or forty yards. That was better than his revolver and she intended to do what she could.

She padded swiftly toward him, keeping an eye on the ridge. She would shoot him the instant he topped it. But he was dawdling at the site, acting as if he knew he could best her. At a point immediately above her location site she edged up to the ridge and peered down, finding him drawing a map. His burro stood close by. She leveled her carbine, sighted on the base of the water cask on the burro, and squeezed. He scarcely noticed the pop but when he saw water gushing from it he whirled. She reloaded just below his vision and then slid up again. This time he was watching and spotted her.

"Hey!" he yelled, drawing his revolver.

"Drop it," she yelled.

He didn't. He fired three quick rounds which spat by angrily as she ducked. She didn't dare poke her head up so she scrambled north a few yards and waited behind a slab of tan rock, ready to fire.

She trembled at her audacity. He was no doubt reloading and would have six quick shots to her one. But she didn't see him for a while and realized he was probably trying to plug the cask. She edged up, peered over, and discovered him lifting the cask off and setting it on its side with the hole skyward.

She shot another hole in the staves and water gurgled out again.

He turned slowly and emptied his revolver at her, the lead spanging off rock and whipping above her. She counted six. She was trembling so badly she couldn't control her fingers as she reloaded. All she had done was turn him into a stalker now that his water was gone and hers was all he might have.

She peeked and saw him scrambling straight at her.

She rose, her carbine ready. "Stop," she yelled.

He didn't. Cursing under his breath, he clawed his way upslope. She sighted down the barrel, hating to shoot. She had never shot anyone. The barrel wavered and she couldn't control it or aim. She shot. His right forearm bloomed red. He screamed and dropped the empty revolver. She screamed too. He crumpled into the slope, clasping his bloody arm, howling like a wolf. She groaned but some hard thing within her urged her to rearm, and swiftly. Somehow she pulled the bolt, plucked out the empty little shell, and reloaded, all to the howling and sobbing of the man.

She edged out carefully, her body wilting under her but her terror lessened.

"That's a hanging offense, stealing a claim," she said. "It won't be popular with a miner's jury."

He grunted. "I'm bleeding to death," he cried.

He was at that. But she didn't feel like helping him. She edged toward his revolver, snatched it, and threw it down the cliff. It tumbled fifty or sixty yards.

"You were going to murder me," she said more calmly than she felt.

Blood gouted from a long wound along his right forearm. "Dammit, help me," he snarled.

"Use your belt for a tourniquet."

He did, singlehandedly yanking it from his britches and tugging it tight above the elbow, howling with every move. The bleeding slowed. "Get it tighter," he said.

She pulled off her bandana and plucked her geologist's

hammer from its loop on her overalls. "On your stomach," she said. "Try anything and I'll shoot."

Slowly he obeyed, groaning with the slightest movement. She stepped over him, wary, one finger on the trigger. She didn't know how to help him one-handed so she set down her carbine a yard from him in the direction he couldn't see and made a proper tourniquet of the bandana, twisting it tight with the handle of her hammer. The bleeding stopped, more or less. It was hard to tell.

He didn't move. She realized he was in shock, aware but passive, his eyes glazed.

Carrying her carbine with her she poked around in his gear for a shirt, tore it up, and bandaged him, knotting the strips of cloth tightly. She retrieved her bandana and hammer, and made a tourniquet of his things, one he could twist tight and release with his good hand, all the while wondering what to do with the rat. Anger had permeated her terror and she was cussing again. That was a good sign that she had herself in hand.

"What am I gonna do now?" she demanded.

He didn't reply. It was still early. In a few hours the ridge would be a furnace. His burro stood unmoving. Mother Dear eyed the strange critter amiably. Warily Maude examined his water cask. Almost everything had gurgled into the ground. Two miles below was that rincon. She thought she would take him there and leave him.

"I'm taking you down to a rincon. Water and shade. I knew something was out there last night. You were watching an old woman, weren't you."

He was listening but not responding.

"You can get well or not, get off this ridge or not. I don't care."

Actually she did care. She didn't want death upon her soul.

She realized suddenly that she was dealing with a crime and the man was a criminal. She poked around his gear, looking for a name and finding none. He had chow enough and a bedroll. He might make it. She extracted his partly empty pasteboard box of .44 caliber bullets and slid them into her pockets.

She found her own claim in his warbag and scrambled down to the cairn and moved rock until she could lift out the cannister. Now she would have a name, a criminal, a piece of evidence. She unscrewed it and extracted the paper. Her own words had been copied in a crude hand on blue-lined school paper. The new claim was signed, *Harry Arbuckle*.

Maude's knees buckled. Harry had hired a man to steal it from her. She gripped the cannister a long time, registering this terrible thing. Then she tucked the fraudulent claim into her pocket, inserted hers into the cannister, and returned it to the cairn.

"Harry hired you," she said.

He didn't respond, but he was listening, alert, the delirium gone from his gaze.

"Down there where I stayed last night there's water and wood. You can work your tourniquet. You got grub. If you go back to Goldfield, I'm gonna come after you with the law. I don't know your name but I'm reporting this and I don't forget faces. If you got brains, you'll get out of Nevada."

This time the man nodded. He stood slowly, staggered to his burro, clung to it and headed down the long hard slope. She watched until she was satisfied he would make it.

CHAPTER 46
....

Hannibal Dash read another of Melanie's letters and set it aside. They were messages from another world, as distant as the arctic. She had written them once a month, upon the turn of the calendar page. Quietly, in her rounded hand, she detailed her life in Madison, the school progress of Robert and Cecily, the campus gossip she gleaned from faculty wives, along with her favorable opinion of Governor La Follette and his multitudinous reforms. Some of the envelopes bore brief, brittle notes from his children—duty letters imposed upon them by their mother. Their bitterness at his dereliction radiated through.

Melanie didn't speak of the future, didn't demand tokens of his love, and didn't let any bitterness seep into her letters, which were simple and neutral. But Hannibal knew that the one-year ultimatum stood: return or face the dissolution of a family. He had replied in kind once a month, knowing intuitively that the end of all this would be misery. He dutifully sent her a five-hundred-dollar cashier's check each month, which made her the most affluent of Wisconsin faculty wives. But the checks would not do. She saw him as a deserter.

Time was rolling by and soon the year she had given him would expire. That would be October 1905. His lease with Arbuckle would expire that December. If it came to divorce, it would be a scandal. One or the other of them would be judged a deserter. He didn't doubt that it would be the ruin of his academic career. Serious scholars just didn't kick over the traces and head for the wilds.

He dreaded the day when he would have to decide: return to Madison, Melanie, Robert and Cecily, or stay in Goldfield and ride the tiger. Return to his generous office in North Hall on Bascom Hill, with a view of Lake Mendota filtered through the trees; return to his quiet quest to enrich the world's knowledge of glaciation, especially the most recent Wisconsin glaciation which had won him his reputation, those papers lauding and elaborating his work, geological society dinners in tuxedos—and a future studying the movement of mile-high sheets of ice across a land.

Odd how little his academic reputation meant to him. From the moment he stepped out of the stagecoach into this mad, dry place filled with the worst and craziest dregs of humanity, he had felt his heart lift. He was simply doing something exciting that drew upon strengths he never knew he had.

He had never dreamed, amid his peaceful study of moraines and kettles and his lectures to acned boys in that yellow-varnished amphitheater in Bascom Hall, that another Hannibal lurked just under the surface, waiting to chop gold ore out of a barren desert and rub shoulders with schemers and crooks.

But anguish had furtively crept into his Goldfield life. He had never stopped loving Melanie or delighting in his children. He felt pierced by loneliness, and some nights he sank into gloom. Could he surrender his own beloved family, the children of his heart, a wife who was a constant comfort and companion? He didn't know and didn't even want to think about it. In moments like this, when bewilderment crept over him, the only thing he could do was push it savagely back. He had no solutions. He could not give up his new life and he could not be torn from dear ones far away.

He had become moderately rich. His net worth had passed two hundred thousand and was mounting every day. The Free Lunch showed no sign of petering out. Reilly's legal threats had fizzled. The shyster knew full well that Dash held not only a valid lease, but an option to buy the mine which could be exercised at any time. Let him sue on Harry's account and Harry's royalties would go into escrow, and Turner P. Reilly would find himself unpaid when the dust settled.

But it never had been wealth that had drawn Hannibal to this restless corner of Nevada. He scarcely knew what to do with all that money. He began to buy shares in the nation's railroads, electric utilities, and streetcar companies. Surely railroads would be the hallmark of the new century and the source of the nation's wealth, the streetcars would take people anywhere in cities, and electricity would power everything. He selected not gold, passive, inert, a mere store of value, but those dynamic industries that gave something valuable to the human race. He could think of several other stocks to buy: gas companies and the little concerns that were even now turning the horseless carriage into a reliable means of travel.

That was one side of him. The other was, he supposed, the paradox that ruled him. What had brought him to Gold-field was simply that it was the last bloom of an era. He didn't really want to march bravely into the twentieth century; he wanted the old frontier to linger on, one wild camp after another, populated by brawny, reckless, laughing rogues who would walk into the Pacific Ocean before they would settle down. He was one of them himself.

The frontier west tickled him. He had absorbed the story of Virginia City, Nevada, and its silver kings. He had read about the wild rush to California's gold, and the fabulous story of Horace Tabor, the silver king of Leadville. He knew all about the mines of Santa Rita and Silver City in New Mexico, and the great placer bonanza of Virginia City, Montana, where men panned gravel and grew rich in days. All of these lit the fires of his imagination and he saw himself, in the secret corner of his heart, chasing his own golden dreams.

He was wallowing in his bewilderment when Maude walked into his laboratory one September day, her wily burro tagging along behind. She looked as weathered as an old stump and had been roasted by the sun to the color of a chestnut. But there amidst that ruin of flesh those bold blue eyes took him in.

"You look like you just wrestled the devil," she said.

"Well, that's quite a way to greet someone. How are you, Maude?"

"Fighting off catamounts, shooting claim-jumpers sent by Harry, and striking a bonanza. I swear, it's worse than the pox. I haven't been out but a week or so, but it was some week."

"I'll want to hear about all this one at a time or I'll never get it straight."

"Well, you just run this stuff and I'll give you a few earloads while you do," she said with peculiar cheer. She dropped a gunny sack of rock on his battered desk. "This time, you and me, Hannibal Dash, have gone and jumped over the moon.''

She extracted some gray rock shot with lustrous seams and laid it in his palm. ''This here's what you danged professors call telluride gold, and I've got a claim on a ledge so thick and long you'd faint dead away. I reckon you got half of it with me and if you're halfway smart you'd better get out and stake the rest of the outcrop.''

He eyed the rock doubtfully. Some of it showed little sign of mineralization but those seams gave off a milky metallic luster faintly silver. It might be calaverite. ''How'd you find this?'' he asked, studying it.

She whooped. ''I cut me a dowsing stick and I dowsed it. I walked over this ledge and that stick almost pulled me down the slope. It made my hands hurt. I walked back and forth over that ledge and that stick went crazy. So I dug up some and did that little blowpipe test, and here's what I got.'' She plucked two buttons of porous gold out of her pocket and pressed them into his other hand. He studied them, his pulse lifting. He ran a thumbnail across one and left a mark.

''You dowsed this?'' he said stupidly.

''You scientists think you know everything. Tell me how dowsing works.''

''It doesn't, Maude.''

She hooted at him. ''Run that stuff. I'll make a believer out of ya.''

Swiftly he did just that. While his furnace heated, he smashed the generous samples into grainy sand, filtered it through meshes, reduced it further until he had a powder. Carefully he measured the standard assayer's sample into the crucible and smelted it. While he waited for the little furnace to do its work, he listened closely as she described her encounter with the assailant. He read the fraudulent claim notice left by Harry's paid thug, and listened, amazed, to her account of holding the man at bay with a little .22 carbine.

"You've got to report this to the sheriff, Maude," he said at last.

She considered it. "I will, but it's gonna take a few days. You and me and a surveyor, we're going out there and stake some claims. I don't know where it is. It's nowhere on any map. It's never been surveyed. It's just out there. Just to make sure, we've got to get some kind of description filed, because it'll start a rush and I have no intention of getting shouldered out of what's mine. What's yours and mine."

"I can do that, Maude. Any geologist can figure coordinates if he has to. You won't need the surveyor for now." He was skeptical. "Maude, what happens if we find a body? If the man didn't make it?"

She glared a moment and then the fires dimmed. "He'll be all right. He was coming around. I got him in the arm, not the carcass, and put a tourniquet on. If he's still at that rincon beside the seep-water hole I dug, we can bring the rat back and file charges."

Dash shook his head. "I've scarcely handled a firearm in my life, Maude. I could no more shoot someone than I could jump over the moon."

She bristled. "Well I'll do it, then."

He laughed suddenly. Harry Arbuckle hadn't an inkling about Maude. The woman was as tough and independent as a Missouri mule and would not be defeated.

He opened the furnace door and extracted the crucible with a V-shaped fork. There was the button of gold, all right, blinking faint orange light as it cooled. But he wasn't done. He would find out whether there was silver in it too, or any base metals. In short order he placed the crucible, with added fluxes, in the cooler level of the furnace and fired it again.

"Maude, you're in danger. I don't even want you to be seen in Goldfield. Harry's changed, you know. He's gotten harder. He's mean. He wanted your claim no matter what happened to you, that's plain."

"That idiot doesn't scare me."

"Maude, he can claim half of this. You're married, you know."

She grunted guiltily. "I guess I better get shucked of the man. I suppose I'll get a divorce but I hardly have time to hang around Goldfield to do it."

"Maude—listen. You've got to start a legal action today. *Now*. Don't worry about funds. File. I'll come with you. I've a fine attorney, Porter Crecelius. You're in a corner. If you file your claim, he'll get wind of it fast."

She smiled. "Maybe I'll do it. But I know Harry a sight better'n you, Hannibal. I'm just gonna go over there to the Texas and give him what-for. Oh, quit worrying. I won't say a thing about that claim. I'll just tell him that if he sends another bum after me I'll cut his tonsils out."

Maude's resolve didn't please Dash, who could see holes in it and doom stalking that amazing woman.

He opened the furnace door and once again extracted the crucible with the tong. The contents took almost forever to cool, but at last he measured the results on his fine scales and was astonished by the result.

"Maude, that's about two percent silver. The rest is gold. The ore's worth about nine hundred dollars a ton. Once you dig lower, where there's less oxidation, the tenors should drop. But it's a big strike."

She grinned, her blue eyes sparking light. "Well, don't you scoff at my dowsing, now, Hannibal."

He felt nonplussed, reddened, and then grinned.

She pulled him into her arms, bussed him on his cheek, and laughed. "You got half, you old lobster," she said.

Chapter 47

．．．．．．．．．．．．．．．．．．．．．．

George Wingfield sat at his green baize table at Tom Kendall's Tonopah Club, studying Nixon's letter. "Cut out the cards," the senator had written from Washington. Go on down to Goldfield and start trading those mining stocks because "you can do better than any of those lobsters."

Wingfield sighed. He hated to give up his half interest in the gambling concession at the club. He had to think about this. Goldfield never struck him as much of a camp and he had always supposed that it would dry up and blow away at any moment like all the rest. But the fact of it was, Goldfield was outshining even Tonopah and attracting stiffs by the thousands. The jam was so bad that pilgrims laid over in Tonopah for days because they couldn't buy a ticket that would take them the last few miles. Not the railroad, not the stagecoaches, not the twenty autos of the Nevada-Utah Automobile Transportation Company rattling down the newly scraped road, not the freighters and their twenty-mule teams, could move the mob to Goldfield as fast as it flowed in.

Wingfield had gone down there a few times himself just to look around. He never quite believed what he saw: the streets jammed with fortune-seekers, so thick at times that you had to dodge bodies to get from one joint to another. Hotel beds rented for six hours a crack, four dudes a day, and no sheets. A motley crowd including Bohunks, Greeks, Portuguese and Swedes fresh from Ellis Island had landed in Goldfield. There were militant stiffs sporting the red flags of the Western Federation of Miners, licking their wounds from Coeur d'Alene and Cripple Creek and itching for revenge; whores and tinhorns doing a land-office business, and stock brokers of all breeds, making and breaking prices, cleaning out hopeful fools, exploiting dreams.

He didn't want to go down there. The town perched on barren desert flats while Tonopah enjoyed the cooler comforts of its silver-bearing Mount Oddie, and its partner, Mount Brougher. George Nixon had always been more sanguine about Goldfield than Wingfield and now Wingfield had to choose. He knew that letter was almost a command and what it didn't say was just as important as what it said: go, or the senator would find another business associate.

Wingfield pondered it, while his hand idly shuffled the twenty poker chips on the table, cutting them into piles of five, shuffling the fives, shuffling all twenty singlehanded, and starting the whole ritual over again. He couldn't think if his hand had nothing to do, so his hand worked while his mind worked.

He had known George Nixon for a long time, dating back to the days when Nixon ran a bank in Winnemucca and Wingfield was a drifting cowboy. The story Nixon loved to tell about how they met always embarrassed Wingfield and he never mentioned it even though it followed him around. He'd walked into Nixon's office, demanded a loan of twenty-five dollars and dropped a diamond ring into Nixon's hand. "There's the rock. Loan or not. It's up to you," he'd supposedly said. The banker, taken by a feisty cowboy who didn't know the difference between a bank and a pawn shop, was amused, gave him the loan, and became his friend.

It was true. He'd grown up on an Oregon ranch, the son of stern Methodists who intended to ship him to college. Thomas and Martha Wingfield neither smoked nor drank and his mother supported the Woman's Christian Temperance Union. But young George preferred easy company, cowboying, fast horses, and good booze. He had an eye for a skirt now and then. He left in 1896, tired of ranch chores, poverty and boredom, and spent his life as a tinhorn or part-time cowboy, mostly in dead-end camps. They had called him the Peely Kid because his fair skin never tanned; it just burned and peeled.

Poker turned out to be his best resource. He learned to win a square game and knew how to lose graciously. He didn't cheat because he didn't need to. He was probably the best poker player in Nevada, a state with a lot of tinhorns in it. And after that he never had much trouble keeping himself fed. But he had a bad habit of picking short-lived boomtowns, like Golconda, to set up shop. Maybe that was why he'd stuck with Tonopah. He didn't want to buck another dying burg and watch his winnings drain away.

He shuffled the chips again, eying the empty club. Soon it would fill up and another good evening would begin. Prospectors and would-be gold tycoons would try their luck and he would beat them. Someone had once told him his secret, which he hadn't even known about himself. He always looked like he was bluffing when he wasn't and the others misread his slightly embarrassed face and lost.

He only knew he'd never lacked for cash, but he'd never made a real pile either. Mostly he studied the prospectors as they sat in and figured out ways to bust them good. With a little luck, he'd pick up a claim or two, or a piece of a claim for a gambling debt. He had a pile of claims, some worthless, most unproven, a few showing signs of life. He was the sole owner of the Burnt Hill, the Bull Con, the Silver Cup, and the Gold Coin down in Goldfield, and he had a piece of others. Not that it had done him any good.

The truth of it was that he could have picked up some great mines down there for pocket change. He could have bought the Sandstorm for a few dollars, or a dozen others he had laughed at, and now regretted it. Like the Florence, now worth millions. He could have gotten it for twenty dollars in 1902. He had seen too much of dead-end camps and it had blinded him. He had even tried to sell Jack Hennessy, his gambling partner, a half interest in his Goldfield claims but Hennessy was having no part of them either.

A couple of sports sat down at his table and Wingfield smiled. He always smiled. He wasn't one to drive away sports. He could be affable, but mostly he was silent and amiable, always listening to the talk around the table, trying to sort out the guff from the occasional sterling silver item he could use. He never talked much. It kept him from making mistakes.

"Evening, gents," he said, and started the deal but his mind wasn't on it. He would play by rote this night and probably lose. It didn't matter. Cut out the cards, the senator had said. There was more to it than that. Cut out the sporting life; a senator can't be associated with a tinhorn. Nixon never lacked for cash, and ever since the legislature had packed him off to the Senate in 1904 he'd had even more of it.

Without quite saying so, the senator was inviting him to turn himself into a trader and get in on the bonanza down there. It wouldn't be much different from being a tinhorn and the odds were better. Half the bonanza kings down there had sat at this table. He knew most of them and knew their weaknesses too. Like Charlie Taylor, that Nova Scotia practitioner of phrenology who owned the Jumbo and the Florence—who had lost piles of cash at Wingfield's table. Wingfield had once watched Taylor lose thirty-four thousand dollars in twelve hours playing faro right there at the Tonopah Club. Maybe a couple of great mines might lie on the green baize some day if the cards fell right.

Wingfield won that night, scarcely knowing how because his mind was calculating odds and bluffs and jackpots on the Goldfield hand. Four men whose faces he never noticed played steadily and then cashed in. He quit about two, when the last pilgrim went bust, and walked to his apartment.

May was still up. They had a simple relationship. She kept house for him and kept him comforted in bed. He gave her a little cash and freed her from life on the Line. They had never married, didn't talk much, and had little to talk about anyway. He had met her in a Tonopah hurdy-gurdy, suggested she live with him, and she did. She called herself Mrs. Wingfield and he didn't mind. May Baric always wanted something decent from a life that never gave it to her.

"I'm thinking we'll go to Goldfield," he said.

"It'll be more fun than here," she said.

Ten minutes later he spent himself upon her. He never called it love. He was too much of a Methodist to pretend.

The next morning he got up early so he could catch the train. It would be standing room again but a few dollars would cure that. He scraped away the fuzz from his face. He had turned thirty-four in August. May always said he looked pale and told him to get some sun. He hated daylight. Nothing good ever happened while the sun shone. He admitted, though, that he looked about the color of a Ku Klux Klan sheet, and if he wanted to switch from tinhorn to stock broker he should take the air down there. He figured he wasn't much of a looker, with slightly bulgy eyes and a face devoid of features. He stood five feet nine and weighed a hundred sixty-five, and could lose himself in a crowd. But some day, he figured, they would know George Wingfield.

"I'll get us rigged up," he told her. "Then I'll buy you a ticket."

She rolled over, nodded, and went back to sleep.

An extra two dollars got him a comfortable perch in the caboose of the Tonopah and Goldfield mixed passenger and freight train that chuffed south, loaded with everything the Consolidation two-eight freight engine could pull. He pulled out twenty chips and began working them again because he needed to think. A brakeman watched silently as he divided the stack into fives, shuffled them, reshuffled, and started over.

It was a good time. They had a new exchange in Goldfield, over eighty stocks being traded in a Main Street basement by a mob of cutthroats. And when the regular afternoon and evening sessions closed the mob simply moved out to the curb and kept right on. Eastern money was flowing in, too. Half the brokers in that place had arrived in Goldfield from Philly or places like that. Wingfield smiled. He had been slow to grasp Goldfield's potential but he would make up for it.

Most of them were dummies, laying money on stocks they thought had value, ignoring the stocks that didn't. But that wasn't the way to get rich. Who wanted to buy successful mines at inflated prices? He'd make more pushing a few duds, like the ones in his portfolio. He had a lot of handsome, engraved, gilt-edged shares sporting eagles and waving flags in his portmanteau. He'd need to set up an account at John S. Cook's bank, which was lending anyone cash to buy any stock on margin. He would need to contact Nixon and ask for directions. The man scooped up more valuable knowledge back there in Washington, lunching with Charles Schwab or Bernard Baruch, than Wingfield ever could on the curbs of Goldfield.

He felt oddly elated as the train rolled into the T. & G. station on Grand Avenue. He eased down the iron steps of the caboose into a harsh desert sun, blinked, and peered astonished at the skyline of a town that had doubled and redoubled itself since he had last been there. He rarely felt emotions and distrusted them when they pounced on him. But this one he trusted. Some day soon he would be the king of Goldfield, Nevada.

CHAPTER 48

. . . .

Delia felt trapped. The marriage was a mistake. She was sure of it even though they had spent only a few months together. She had been so dazzled by Samuel Jones's money that she had scarcely paid attention to the man himself. And now that she knew his real nature she recoiled from him.

She knew herself to be a refined and gracious young woman, cultivated and mannered. She had inherited these things from her mother and father, although she could only grudgingly admit it because she could hardly stand them. Horace and Violet Biddle had given her high standards. She always used good English and had social graces. It simply embarrassed her to be around Sam. It wasn't just his professions—horse trader and charlatan; it was his rough, uncouth manners, his hard, cynical approach to life, and his base nature.

At first, in the honeymoon weeks, she had scarcely noticed his coarseness. She had snared a wealthy man, and that intoxicated her. He had poured money upon her, and she spent those early weeks buying everything there was to buy. But there came a day when she didn't want anything more. Nothing caught her fancy. And Goldfield didn't offer much.

When the fun of spending faded, she began examining Sam in a new light. He embarrassed her. She could barely endure being seen in public with him. Every vice he possessed magnified itself in her mind. His cigars became loathsome; his horse-trading profession vile; his manners atrocious; his wealth ill gotten and shameful. Worse, he seemed to be enjoying himself, and lacked even a rudimentary conscience.

She knew, within three months of their wedding, that the marriage would never last. She had made a terrible mistake. She knew also she would have to stay married awhile if she hoped to get anything out of it. And she would have to behave herself, too.

That night she had decided to meet some other rich men at the Palm Grill had ended in ignominy. The maître d'hôtel, Coffin, had swooped over to her every time some male showed any interest. "Mrs. Jones is awaiting her husband," he said to them, tapping tasseled menus in his palm. After an hour she told him that she supposed Sam wasn't coming, and left. She tried again the next few nights and each time she was about to meet some interesting man, that awful Coffin materialized at her banquette to inform the gentleman that Mrs. Jones was awaiting her husband. It dawned on her that Sam was playing some shadowy role in all that.

She could have anything money would buy, but she was

miserable. What had riches gotten her? Embarrassment every time she was seen in public with him. She was a Biddle, and she came from a respectable family. Her father and mother wouldn't even associate with a man like Samuel Jones.

As bad as her public embarrassments were, the private ones were worse. She couldn't bear his touch. He always seemed to be amused by love. A gentleman would have been tender and sensitive, but not Sam. She was simply some filly to him, not a treasured and respected wife. His weathered flesh and crass nature repelled her so much that she could scarcely endure the marital act, and she found excuses to avoid it.

But money governed her life now. She would have to endure until she could get some. Shrewdly, she opened a savings account in the John S. Cook Bank, and another in the Figueroa Bank in Los Angeles, and squirreled money into them as fast as she could. If she couldn't get anything from a divorce, at least she would have a few thousand dollars stashed away for emergencies.

She dreamed of meeting another man, this time a handsome, gracious gentleman with the best manners and lofty ideals. Rich of course. Delia knew that she deserved a very wealthy husband. Whenever she studied herself in the oval mirror, or listened to herself talk, she knew she was entitled to the best of men.

She took to her bed because there was nothing else to do. At least in bed she could dream of better times. She let her mind meander through the groves of good society in California, where men in knickers played golf and beautiful women played whist and occasionally they all got into a white yacht and sailed down the Mexican coast under a cloudless sky. That was where she belonged.

She sighed. Things had gone from awful to terrible. She wept, letting her tears slide down her cheeks and into her monogrammed percale sheets. She wished she could die. She wished lightning would strike Samuel Jones and she would inherit his money. She wished something, anything, would come along to free her.

Then one November day she gathered her resolve and decided to confront him. She had nothing to lose. She left her bed of tears at dawn, descended the stairs into the somber house, and found him reading the *Observer* in the dining room.

"All right, Sam," she said. "We're going to talk. This marriage isn't working. I want a divorce and I want a nice settlement. That's the least you could do."

The amusement in his face enraged her. It had become his mask and she itched to rip it off.

"What's the trouble, sweetheart?"

"Trouble? You've done all you can to make me miserable."

He laughed and she couldn't bear it.

"Samuel Jones, you're not fit for decent company. You're nothing but a swindler."

At last the humor dissolved from his face. He didn't say anything for a long while and she was tempted to rake him over the coals.

"Well, let's see," he said slowly. "I remember once I traded for the prettiest little filly you ever did see. She was put together just right, a bay with gentle eyes, perked-up ears, good deep chest, and plenty of stifle for power. She looked like she'd go all day, ride like velvet, handle so lightly that you hardly had to tell her anything, and enjoy herself all the while, too. Well, she wasn't like that. Looks aren't the whole story. She'd been spoiled by some fool, and she'd balk. She pitched now and then, didn't take a bit, and walked so slow a feller wanted to get off and push her."

"Don't tell your horse stories in polite society, Sam."

He laughed, but not meanly. "Once upon a time this old horse trader spotted a pretty gal hanging out where she could be seen, with some poor messenger kid as a paid escort. It took this old horse broker about ten seconds to figure what this was all about: this little lady was looking for a rich husband, making goo-goo eyes at any likely-looking prospect in the Palm Grill.

"Well, this old horse trader don't know much about women. I mean about nice women. I was always on the road and I didn't meet any. The only women I ever knew were the other kind, the ones that didn't mind having some old crooked horse trader around for a short spell. Not the kind that wanted love and family and going to church on Sundays. They sort of scare me, you know? But you didn't scare me."

She somehow knew where this story would end.

"Well, this little gal, she was making mooneyes at me while eating with a gawky hack driver, and sure enough, we managed to meet. Now the thing I happened to have a lot of was money and she thought that was a mighty fine asset in an old wildcatter."

"Stop!" she yelled.

"I guess she was a little old gold digger only it turned out she was the queen of all gold diggers, willing to donate her curvy little body to charity if she could just latch on to all of that money. I thought, This is a pretty nice filly, and she's good company, kidding with a man, not shy, just nice to be around. Oh, I got hold of one of the hack boys I'd seen you with and asked him, and he told me you were paying the freight and asking who's rich and who isn't and where do the rich ones eat. So I knew what you were right from the start.

"But I didn't mind. This is Goldfield, and half the schemers in the country are right here. But once we got into double harness all them wiles sort of disappeared and you had a mess of migraines I'd never heard talk of before. It's pretty plain, isn't it? You married me for my money and I married you for your good company. I confess I was taken with you. Laugh if you want, but I was in love."

"You beast!" she shrieked. "All you thought of was lust!"

He shrugged. "No, I reckoned I was in love with a lady sort of like me. Well, we're a pair. You're a gold digger

and I'm a wildcatter. Only I got to thinking it ain't wise.
I'm a capitalist now. I kind of wonder which of us is the
worst, gold digger or wildcatter. How do you add it up,
eh?''

"I won't dignify that with a reply." She turned to flee
but he caught her hand.

"The truth be known, Delia, there's not a man with deep
pockets in Goldfield that doesn't have you pegged. Heck,
I've told a few dozen the story myself—about the messenger boys you paid to escort you to the classiest chophouse
in town.''

"I can't believe you're saying this to me. I kept telling
you all I wanted was an itty-bitty cottage but you didn't
believe me." Tears welled up.

"Tell you what, Delia. Let's go out to the coast for a
couple of weeks and you can introduce me to all them
socialite friends of yours.''

"What?" It stunned her. He sounded as if he meant it.

"I'll behave myself. You just let 'em know we're in
town and we'll throw a little soiree. I'll swing a mashie
with the gents while you have a little hen party with them
nice ladies at the country club.''

"But Sam—"

"That's what you've been wanting, isn't it?"

"I'd be embarrassed to introduce you to them," she
snapped.

He laughed amiably. "Delia, you and me are a pair."

"I refuse to listen. I've got a headache.''

Sam chuckled. "I sort of thought we had an understanding. Not anything we talked about, just something we figured out. We'd be a pair of sports together. I thought it'd
be pretty much fun. The truth of it was, I enjoyed your
spending. You couldn't keep up with me, no matter how
hard you tried. You even got your silk drawers monogrammed. Best entertainment I had.''

"Oh, God, Sam . . ." She didn't know whether to rage
at him or flee to her room.

"Truth is, we could head out there to Newport Beach

and meet up with all those California rich folks, and they'd have themselves a good horselaugh. Not because of me but because of you. Chickadee. You can't pretend. You're not one of them and you weren't raised up that way. The one thing they can't stomach is someone pretending.''

She felt incredibly tired. "Sam, I'd just like to go away. Let me have enough to go to Los Angeles. Just give me a nice settlement and we'll go our own ways. I can't stand this—''

He grinned again but there wasn't any unkindness in it. She saw nothing but affection in his face. "Let's have breakfast at the Brown Palace, Delia. It's time for a pair of wildcats to get to know each other.''

"You're on,'' she said, surprised at herself.

CHAPTER 49

····················

Delia could not say why, but she had the sense of great portent as Big Sam steered her into the dining room of the Brown Palace Hotel on an ordinary Sunday morning.

"Ah, Mister Jones,'' said the headwaiter, "and madam. This way, please.'' He led them toward a corner table partly obscured by potted palms. Sam eased into a chair where he could stretch his stiff leg.

Delia always enjoyed the attention lackeys paid to Sam. Everyone in Goldfield knew him and treated him like a prince.

Big Sam didn't bother with ordering. "Bring a load of stuff,'' he said, waving the waiter away.

"All right, Delia,'' he announced, "we're gonna pow-wow.''

She nodded hesitantly, a hundred dreads welling up in her.

"I have the notion you like money,'' he said, and hastened on before she could reply. "I bet if I filled your

bathtub fulla dollar bills, you'd swim in it and flop around
like a seal. I bet if I held a hundred-dollar bill over your
head and told you to bark, you'd yap like a coon dog. I
know the feeling. I take the notion to spread it around and
roll in it like a horse in the dust. I got buckets full. I got a
mountain of it. I got it in gold and silver and Treasury notes
stacked in little bundles, floor to ceiling. But it's not
enough. I want so much money that I could light a bonfire
of the stuff and never miss it.

"I like the smell of it. I sorta like going around town
smelling like money. Smell of money's better on a woman
than perfume."

"Oh, Sam!"

"Well, you smell better rich than poor, Delia."

She felt miffed. "Sam, you're so offensive."

He cocked an eyebrow. "I am at that. I came by all that
filthy lucre the easy way. I noodled it out of thousands of
rubes that didn't have brains enough to check me out. Don't
call me respectable, I always say. It'd be an insult."

"Sam, you're embarrassing me. I'm not like that."

"You aren't, eh? Now listen here. There's no sense in
having a ton of money if you don't flaunt it. I mean, show
it, wear it, burn it, eat it, wallpaper it. You got the idea?
It's no fun just to have a heap of it stuffed away in some
mattress. That's why I got into double harness with you.
Here, I sez, is a lady that knows how to make proper use
of a mighty fine and rare commodity. You got to have
imagination to flaunt money. You got to have class. You
got to be a sport. What good is it to hang fancy drapes in
a parlor where no one'll see 'em anyway? If I may say so,
Delia, you're trying too hard to be proper.

"Now, this is a gold town. They understand gold around
here. They're all out there, scurrying around, looking for
some way to get some or noodle someone out of it."

Three waiters arrived, hefting pewter salvers filled with
scrambled eggs, mashed potatoes, bacon, sausage, ham,
sliced beef, sliced lamb, pork chops, sliced canteloupe, rolls,
croissants, pastries, toast, bottles of jams and jellies, mar-

malade, a dish of thick butter, pitchers of coffee and tea, oranges, apples, steaming oatmeal, Cream of Wheat, a stack of snowy linen napkins, finger bowls with mint leaves floating in them, a toothpick jar, and two Cub cigars. Swiftly the impresarios dished out dabs of everything until the table before Delia was a sea of plates, cups, bowls, platters, and glasses.

"It's enough for twenty," Delia whispered.

"There now, that's what I mean," Big Sam said. "You got to flaunt it to enjoy it. The dogs get ninety-nine percent of this and you get to be a legend. Those fellers, they'll go home and tell their wives about serving Big Sam and Delia everything in the kitchen."

The fragrance of that sumptuous feast dizzied Delia and she plunged in with gusto. "You're right, Sam," she said between chomps. "If you got it, use it."

"You're seeing the light," he said, grabbing a Parker House roll. His lecture was slowing down under the assault of viands but Delia knew he'd be raring to go as soon as he put it all away.

When Sam finally came up for air, he eyed her speculatively and he employed a solemn tone. "Now the whole fix, as I see it, is this social-climbing business you got rattling around behind them pretty eyes. You got this notion that if we go out there to California and put on white flannel pants and knock a few golf balls and go to a few teas and take them folks out on our old yacht, we'll just be swimming in it the rest of our natural lives. Well, sweetheart, it don't work like that. They ain't gonna pay you no account. You're a true blue nickel-plated gold digger and I'm a crook, and they ain't dumb by a long shot."

"Sam, stop that! I don't like being called such things."

He picked his teeth and chuckled. "You just don't like looking at yourself, that's what's bothering you. Now, Goldfield's more generous. You want to be the Queen of Goldfield, you can buy it. I can buy it. They don't lock the door and keep you out just because you're a gold digger. Heck, we're all gold diggers. Why, half the rich cusses in town are married to whores, at least they used to be whores. It's too bad you weren't one; it'd sort of gotten your notions out of the way. You ought to sort of think of yourself as one.''

"Sam! Stop that! I'm a respectable woman. I'd never do that, not ever, ever ever . . .''

But he was laughing and finally he made her laugh too, although she hated herself for it. Just a few hours ago she would have gone into a rage and thrown something at him.

"You sure got a fancy notion of yourself, Delia Biddle Favor. You came tooting out here to latch on to some gold and claw your way to the top and you didn't mind using that curvy little body to do it.''

She didn't reply but her cheeks were burning. This time he had wounded her to the quick. She felt tears welling up, and her composure dissolved. She dabbed at her eyes with the linen. "You're the cruelest, crudest man I know. Are you done now? I want to go home. I want to leave you. Just let me go, let me have a divorce. You don't even respect me. I just want to go, oh, God, please, Sam. I don't care if you give me nothing. I'm a good girl and you've cheapened me.''

He lit a Cub and sucked it, saying nothing. She wept bitterly at his gross accusations, his insults, his vile insinuations. She felt ashamed and glanced furtively around to see if they had been observed. But this table stood in isolation, screened from the rest.

"Delia, sweetheart, I happen to love you. I have it in mind that we might enjoy Goldfield. You want society? You'll be the queen. You want to be on top? We'll just be on top.''

"Queen of tarts, is that what you're talking about?''

"Nope. Goldfield's the biggest burg in Nevada. Last I heard, over fifteen thousand and still busting out. It's a big enough place to have fun—if you want fun. Big enough to give you anything you want—if you're willing to try it.

"Here's my deal. Since I'm a crooked old lobster you'd better listen. I want you to stick in Goldfield for a year. To the beginning of aught-seven. If you want to go then, I'll run a divorce through the courts and give you something generous. If you stick around here I want you to take a whack at having a high time. Parties. I'm thinking of throwing the biggest parties Nevada's ever seen. I'm thinking of inviting the whole sweet lovin' town, serving up more chow than most of 'em ever laid eyes on, more good hooch than they ever thought was in the kegs. Nice dance orchestras, put that parquet ballroom floor to use over in the manse. Flowers, bouquets, corsages like you never seen. You want to be Queen of Goldfield? I'll buy it and dish it up all for you. We'll call it the first annual Gold Diggers Ball. You send out the monogrammed invites. And if you get tired of it after a year of that, why, you can dump old Sam and I'll keep it friendly." He gazed directly at her.

She gaped at him, so amazed she could hardly process what he had suggested.

"Now," he cautioned, tapping ash off his cheroot, "some of them over at the Montezuma Club, they won't come. They won't rub shoulders with an old pirate and his little gold digger. So, maybe you won't have what you'd call a social triumph, the hostess they all want the invites from. Maybe not. But I reckon you could have a time of it just trying. Let 'em sniff, let 'em condemn. You don't care. We'll rake in the miners and managers, the saloon keepers and the sports. We'll open the door to tinhorns and librarians."

Delia giggled. The idea sounded perfectly comic. "Are we going to let in the madams, Sam?"

"Only if they're in uniform," he replied. "We're semi-respectable."

They laughed.

"You gonna be a balky filly?" he asked, and she saw lights in his eyes that glinted of other things.

"Oh, Sam, sign me up," she said somewhere between laughter and tears.

CHAPTER 50

· ·

Harry Arbuckle grew more and more fond of money. He had hardly thought about money until he had gotten rich by putting one over on those dumb yokels who leased his mine. He loved to flash his greenery, big fat century notes in a roll so thick it'd choke a moose. It gave him power he never knew he wanted. He had everything and was bent on getting more.

He was getting smarter, too. He had paid snitches all over town. He had a snitch in the Montezuma Club serving booze to those dumb suckers in there. He picked up a lot of tips that way and kept an eye on all those clowns. He gave the snitch ten clams for every hot tip he came up with and there was hardly a day when the snitch didn't get fifty or a hundred bucks out of Arbuckle. Because of the snitch, Harry knew who the power was in Goldfield. It was George Wingfield, a tinhorn gambler with a lot of boodle he got from Senator Nixon. The pair of them were swiftly buying up every good mine in town. Arbuckle thought about selling the Free Lunch too, for maybe a million clams or something like that. He'd talk to Wingfield when the time came, but not now.

Arbuckle had a dozen snitches around and two muscle boys that he paid just to make sure he got what he wanted. That's what money did. You could get anything you want. That was quite a payroll but who cared? The stuff just rolled in like thick gravy. He had some dames, too, but they annoyed him and he kept booting them out and getting more. One of his muscle boys found them for him and he put them up in a little flat and kept them happy until he got tired of them. Then, boom! That was the fun of having some loot. Boom! He could turn people into a grease spot.

He had the best shyster around, too. Turner P. Reilly charged two or three times what anyone else did but he was worth it. He really had the goods on those lessees, Dash and them. Man, if it ever came to lowering the boom, old Reilly could turn them into dust. Reilly didn't come cheap and he kept asking for more. He needed cash for some research and Harry figured it'd be worth it. Research was Reilly's word for dirt. The way to get what you wanted in a gold town was to know the dirt. Reilly had come to him just the other day and wanted another grand so he could find out the dirt about Dash, the Wisconsin professor with a wife and brats back up there somewhere. Man, could Reilly come up with stuff. Like finding out that punk editor, Prinz, practically lived down in the sporting district.

It cost bucks to keep Reilly around, just like it cost plenty for his payroll, but it didn't matter. The shyster was like a hired sharpshooter.

He had bought the Texas from Duck Drake. The idiot had tried to boot him out, saying he was bad for business and no one came in anymore. So Arbuckle just applied a little muscle. "Duck," he had said, "you losing money? I'll fix you up. You're gonna sell this old Texas Saloon to me for a grand, right?"

Arbuckle laughed every time he thought about the way Drake turned white. "But I got eleven in it, Arbuckle," Drake said.

The king of Goldfield summoned some of that beef he kept in his employ. Duck watched the brass knuckles slide over the fingers and figured one grand was a mighty fine price after all and sold out the joint, along with all the stock, furniture, and goodwill, too. That little deal alone had paid for all his hired meatballs and there had been a few others. No one ever saw Duck Drake again and they said he'd hopped the next train outa Goldfield. God, how Arbuckle loved that yarn.

He still had a few scores to settle and the biggest of those was Maude. He'd fix her good. That Les Weed he'd sent out to keep an eye on her, he hadn't come back yet. He

could hardly wait for Weed to come in and tell him a good
yarn. But his snitches over at the Free Lunch had seen her
go in and out again. That dumb sucker Dash was obviously
grubstaking her. Arbuckle laughed. That pair deserved each
other.

Meanwhile, it paid to keep an eye on her just in case
that old nag found another ledge.

Arbuckle couldn't have been happier. He arrived in the
Texas after lunch each day, wearing one of his purple
chalk-striped suits and a derby, and smoking the best Havana he could find. He had him a fancy quilted leather seat
in there where he could shoot the bull with the boys. No
sooner did he walk in than the joint leaped to life. A cold
mug of pilsener would arrive and the Paiute boy would
shine his shoes until he could see his brown puss in them
and his snitches would come in, one by one, with the day's
load of horseapples. He always got a good laugh out of
deciding whether some item was worth a few bucks or not.

A couple of times he had spent loot faster than the bank
got it but they carried him, of course. He told them he'd
shoot them if they didn't. They had laughed politely and
waited for the next check from the lessees. Dumb bankers.

This November day one of his lackeys brought him another deposit slip from the bank. More moolah. He looked
at it casually and looked again. Those crooks had put only
fourteen grand into his account this month. Fourteen lousy
grand! Usually it was forty. What the devil. He found another document, the usual notarized copy of the Combination Smelter check. Fifty-six grand for October. Harry's
share was fourteen. The smelter was in on it. Those pirates
were all in cahoots, out to skin old Arbuckle. But he was
on to them. It was time to act before they bled him white.
He thought about corraling Reilly but Reilly would only
find reasons not to do something.

Instead, he turned to his meatballs. "We're goin' out to
the Free Lunch and settle a score or two," he said.

Moments later Arbuckle, and two bruisers, Mick and Cyrus, climbed into his spiffy Desert Flyer and roared north

for a surprise visit. Arbuckle drove it himself, laughing up-
roariously as he terrorized horses and dogs by rattling
through Goldfield at fifteen miles an hour. By Gawd this
was going to be fun. If them dummies thought they could
get through the last month of the lease without grief from
old Arbuckle, they would soon be sucking pickles. He had
never gone out to the Free Lunch so this little foray was
going to make their jaws drop. He could hardly wait to see
old Dash's face when Arbuckle and his meatballs walked
in. Mick and Cyrus packed iron that bulged from their
striped suits.

Arbuckle throttled down his Desert Flyer at the mine,
surprised by what he beheld. The gallows frame rose
straight out of the desert with no shelter over it. Some
roughly built shops and an office hulked nearby. Next to
the mine collar stood the hoist works, while tram rails led
from the collar to a trestle that extended into a gulch where
they were dumping the slack. Soon it would all be his. That
was the thing about leasers: you let them do all the hard
development work and when their lease ran out you walked
off with all of it. He chuckled. Leasing had been a pretty
shrewd deal.

He cut the engine, which backfired and rocked the touring machine, and admired his mine. He was a genuine gold-
plated mining king, like all them silver barons up in
Tonopah or George Wingfield, the tinhorn.

"Ain't it cute?" he said to Mick.

Mick cackled appreciatively. Arbuckle had always
known he could be funny but Maude never appreciated it.

They corraled a green-eyeshade clerk in the office.

"Where's Dash and them?" Arbuckle asked.

"Mister Dash's out in the assay lab, sir. Shall I get him?
Who shall I say—"

"Nah, we'll just drop in." He wheeled toward the shack
housing the lab and barged in. There was old Dash, firing
up his furnace in his canvas work smock, his salt-and-
pepper suit coat hanging on a coatrack. He closed the door
on a crucible and discovered Harry.

"Well, Mister Arbuckle," he said neutrally.

"Yeah, it's old Harry, just in case you forgot. Lissen here, Dash, this crap's gonna stop and right now. I'm on to you."

Dash looked mildly bewildered. "Sir?" he asked.

"This crap. I got that check for October and I'm on to you."

Dash said nothing, awaiting what would come.

"That check for fourteen grand. I know what you're up to. Your lease's running out and you just want to squeeze the last drop of blood outa old Harry."

"Maybe I ought to get Richard Underwood," Dash said. "He does our books."

"Naw, you stay right here. You lissen or my friends'll pulp you good. I want the rest. Them checks, they've never been under thirty, thirty-five and seems like the last five or six were around forty thousand."

"Oh, that, Harry. If you'd read the assay reports you'd know that—"

"Don't you Harry me, Dash. You call me Mister Arbuckle. Nobody calls me Harry without an invite."

Dash smiled faintly. "The tenors are down sharply. If you'd kept up with the assays—copies to you every month—you'd know that."

"Yeah, and who does the assaying? You do. You can't pull a fast one on me, Dash."

Dash sighed. "All right. You drive over to the Consolidated Mill and look at the records—the weight of milling ore we ship over there, the values, the payments. It's all there in the records. All you have to do is talk to them."

Arbuckle snorted. "I know how your crowd works, Dash. I want a check for twenty thousand simoleons and these gents'll see that it gets written."

"We're running sixty-, seventy-dollar ore, Mister Arbuckle, and down three levels. That's how it is. The high-grade's mined out, unless we find more, and I don't think we will."

"That's horseapples, Dash. I know what you're up to.

That mine's richer than ever and there's enough highgrade
down there to swamp the Carson City Mint.''

Dash stood resolutely. ''Hire an independent assayer,
Mister Arbuckle. We'll take one down to the stopes anytime.''

''Oh no you don't. I know what'll happen. You'll slide
him some moolah and that'll be that.''

Dash looked disgusted. ''You go with him, Mister Arbuckle. Why don't you come with me? I'll take you down.
You need to see what we've done anyway.''

''Down there? Is it safe?'' Arbuckle had no stomach at
all for crawling around under millions of tons of rock.

Dash smiled. ''I'll get my jumper. You and your, ah,
friends come along. Take your own samples and have them
assayed. Your fellows there look strong enough to knock a
little ore loose.''

Mick laughed.

Arbuckle felt trapped. He had to go down there or he'd
look like some chump. ''All right, Dash, but don't think
you can put one over on Harry,'' he said.

''I'm sure I couldn't, Harry,'' Dash said gently.

CHAPTER 51

• •

Wordlessly, Hannibal Dash handed each of his guests a
carbide lantern and led them to the gallows frame. He
lit the lamps for them while they waited for the lift. Around
them the topside men were pushing ore cars off the turning
sheet and onto the tramways that would take ore to the
shipping chutes or slack to the slackpile.

Dash had changed into a jumper and carried a canvas
shoulder bag and his geologist's hammer with its pick end.
He felt only gratitude that Harry Arbuckle had waited
eleven months to come to his own mine. The cables
whirred, the pulleys in the gallows frame spun, and then

the cage erupted like a geyser from the shaft, carrying its burden of loaded ore cars which the topsiders yanked off.

"Gentlemen?" Dash asked, directing them toward the opensided iron cage rocking on its cable.

"Is it safe in there?" Arbuckle asked, plainly nervous.

Dash smiled and said nothing. Arbuckle's two goons were waiting for the great man to take the first step. Harry peered about in terror and stepped gingerly onto the dimpled sheet of steel that formed the bottom of the cage. The rest followed. The topsiders rolled three empty ore cars on.

"It bounces. You'd better hang on," Dash said.

"You don't have to tell me, Dash. I been around," Arbuckle said.

The two goons looked sick. The counterweighted iron cage dropped suddenly, its plunge sickening, and daylight fell away except for a small receding square above.

"Jaysas," said one of the goons.

"Take me up, Dash," Arbuckle moaned.

"We'll start at the bottom level," Dash said. "A hundred fifty feet. We've been cutting out the ore from large stopes supported with square set timbering. Every timber in Goldfield has to be hauled from California. This is the level we're working now but we still have one face crew at level two. The miners work inside cubes of wood that permit us to excavate large stopes without having them fall on us."

"Yeah, well I don't need to hear your problems, Dash."

Dash clamped the corner post of the cage hard while it slowed. Above, the hoist engineer was watching a needle circle around to a number three on the face of a great gauge. He braked when the needle reached its destination. Bells rang, the cage bounced violently on its woven steel tether.

"Watch your step, gents," Dash said. The cage had stopped an inch too high.

"Let's make this quick, Dash. I don't want none of your crap." Arbuckle seemed subdued and his cockiness had vanished.

"As you wish, Mister Arbuckle." The vestibule was

jammed with full ore cars that the muckers had filled by
the shovelful all that shift. The rank odor of exploded dynamite lingered in the dank air. Around them, men yanked
the empties off the lift. The noise underground was deaf-
ening, the sound amplified by small and narrow drifts. They
followed a low, cramped drift just wide enough to let the
standard one-ton ore cars through, while behind them Dash
heard the lift crew rolling heavy ore cars across the turning
sheet, a plate of boiler iron at the vestibule, and into the
lift.

"Dash, I think I'll wait back at the lift," Arbuckle said,
falling behind.

"Mister Arbuckle, it's your mine. Look ahead there;
that's the biggest stope in the mine. We've got twenty-four
men working in that single room each shift. Now, we'll just
take some ore samples. You just chip out what you want
and put it in this bag."

"You can do it."

"No, Mr. Arbuckle, this is your assay. I won't touch this
ore. You take your samples now and have your own assayer
run them."

Arbuckle coughed. "I want ta get outa here right this
damned minute, Dash!"

They stepped into the stope and the oppressiveness of
the narrow drift gave way to airiness. Light bobbed around,
making the framework of black timbers dance and wobble.
The racket of shovels scraping up ore and sledgehammers
pulverizing it into liftable pieces yielded a kind of madness.

As soon as they entered the stope the work slowed and
then stopped while miners stared.

"Take your samples quickly, Mister Arbuckle," Dash
said so softly that his voice almost disappeared in the di-
minishing din. "Miners don't like supervisors around and
always stop working until we go away. The less ore they
muck, the less money you make."

"Yeah, well . . ." Arbuckle thrust the geologist's hammer and sack at one of the goons. "You do it," he said,
plaintively.

Minutes later, the big man returned, carrying several pounds of rock in his sack.

"All right," said Dash.

They caught the lift to the hundred-foot level. "I don't need to see it," Arbuckle said.

"This was our best stope," Dash said relentlessly, maneuvering them out of the cage. "Still have a crew in here. This gold is pocketed along a shoot. It's found in a thick sheet along both sides of a vertical fault running more or less east–west. It's distributed in particles so fine they give the quartz a yellowish cast. The quartz is in white rhyolite, the country rock here. The gold was deposited by percolation up the fault. There were some feeders but the upheavals here were so violent that they can't be traced more than a few yards. The ore here reached an incredible width, over a hundred feet in either direction from the fault." He herded his visitors along a drift again and then into a great hollow of a room, weirdly silent and dead.

"A lot of this ore ran three or four thousand a ton. But there wasn't much of that and only in this pocket. This stope runs along the fault, that way, toward your boundary line. That farthest wall there—you can't see it yet—is your boundary."

"My boundary? The rich stuff goes past my boundary?"

"Some does. That's the Yankee Doodle Claim, owned by the Goldfield May Queen Mining Company. They've got the Desert Rose next to it and the May Queen beyond that."

"You mean you chumps just quit there and didn't go in? And that's highgrade ore?" Suddenly Arbuckle was sounding indignant.

"It's not your ore, sir. And it's not highgrade there. It's routine two-hundred-dollar ore."

"Not my ore! Who's to know, tell me that."

"Well, our neighbors, for one. They come down here regularly."

"And you let 'em?"

Dash shrugged. "We check on them, they check on us.

It's a mutual system that keeps things peaceful. We can send a man into the Yankee Doodle anytime we want."

Arbuckle laughed, the first sign of relaxation since he had plummeted into the bowels of the earth. "Chumps," he said. "What a bunch of chumps."

Dash suddenly grew impatient. "If you want samples, be about it. I've got an assay running and I have to be topside in five minutes."

This time, Arbuckle grabbed the geologist's hammer and began whacking at rock. It was one of the few times in Dash's memory he had seen Harry work.

"Put those in your pocket, Harry, not in the bag with the other samples. Don't mix them. You want an accurate assay of each level, don't you?"

Arbuckle started to object and then did as Dash suggested.

Dash herded his guests to the lift vestibule again, this time pulling a bell cord to summon the cage.

"All mine," Arbuckle said. "We hardly begun. We'll go down a thousand feet, like at Virginia City. Once I get you chumps out I'll really go to town."

Dash smiled. The lift squealed to a halt and bounced on its cable. His guests squeezed on, edging around loaded ore cars which a lift man kept from rolling around while the cage bounced upward. Dash pulled the bell cord and the lift catapulted upward, popping out of the earth in a blinding burst of daylight.

"That was nothing," Arbuckle announced. He turned to his goons. "You was scared; I could tell."

Dash retrieved his hammer from Arbuckle. "All right. You go take those samples to an assayer of your choice and let me know the result."

"It ain't your business, Dash," Arbuckle said. With daylight came his truculence again. He lifted the sample bag from his shoulder and handed it to one of his goons. "Get this to the Downing Brothers and tell them Harry Arbuckle—get that, tell him Harry Arbuckle—wants it run right now."

Dash wanted to return to his lab in the worst way but he forced himself to walk Harry to his fancy machine and see them off. "You come again anytime. I'm always glad to help," Dash said.

The bigger of those louts cranked up the machine while the other yanked the choke lever and adjusted the spark. It burped into life and Dash watched his visitors rock down the yellow road toward Goldfield.

A relief flooded through him. It could have been worse. Harry Arbuckle was capable of anything. In a way, he was glad that Harry had come by. Dash's every instinct told him that the Free Lunch was petering out; that it was a shallow mine and nothing lay below. The rusty quartz in its rhyolite gangue had suddenly altered into diorite in the lower level. He and Rogers and Underwood had been monitoring the change for several weeks. If that was the case, the one-year lease had been the perfect length. Except for some lowgrade ore near the surface they would clean out the entire mine in the space of their year.

Arbuckle wouldn't believe that, though. He would harbor only one belief, no matter the facts: the Free Lunch would go on forever. That might be just fine, Dash thought. Arbuckle would be so busy trying to squeeze money out of a dying mine that he would cause them no more trouble.

A month earlier Dash, Maude and Mother Dear had made a swift trip out to a strange ridge darkened by juniper, which he concluded was five miles due east of the Silver Peak Mountains. And there he had staked out two claims for himself and another for her, next to her original, making four in all along a ledge that outcropped for almost half a mile. Then he had done some swift surveying and come up with coordinates that would be good enough to file on. Maude Arbuckle had gone to Hawthorne to register the four claims far from Harry's surveillance. The new bonanza had come at a perfect moment, with the Free Lunch dying. In a few weeks he could turn his attentions to the new ore and give the gutted Free Lunch back to Arbuckle.

CHAPTER 52

....

Olympus Prinz found Daisy in a strange mood. When she let him in late that afternoon she seemed nervous and distraught. She wore her usual shapeless shift, which clothed her during the hours she wasn't open for business.

"Here," he said, handing her the twenty-five dollars he always gave her.

She shook her head. "Not this time, Olympus. It'd ruin everything."

"But Daisy—"

"Put it back, Olympus."

He returned the money to his billfold, puzzled. "Can't you see me? Is that it?"

"Of course I can see you. I'm glad you came. I've wanted you to come all day." She smiled tenderly. "Just this once, no money, Olympus." She smiled. How oddly her gaze raked him this time. He found her studying him intently, her eyes drinking in everything about him.

"Am I different or something?"

"Oh, no, Olympus," she said. "Let me fetch the tea."

She vanished into the rear of her tawdry crib and he settled himself in the broken chair, feeling puzzled. Well, she was entitled to her moods. One of Daisy's miracles was her steady good cheer even in these circumstances. Some inner fountain of grace put a shine in her eyes and a smile on her soft lips whenever he was with her.

He heard her bustling around back there and when she reappeared, carrying her porcelain teapot and two chipped cups, she was wearing a filmy white satin wrapper that slithered over her figure with every step, pouring itself over her breasts and thighs in a way that revealed her tall, slim body.

He stared, faintly astonished as she poured tea, not bothering to clutch the white satin at her breast. He loved to look at her; at the nest of light brown hair that slid around her shoulders, at her pale face—she had become whiter and whiter in the months he had known her, losing the sun-blessed coloration she once had.

She handed him a steaming cup, a wry smile on her face.

"You're more beautiful than ever, Daisy," he said lamely, unable to fathom the change.

Her smile seemed to rise from her heart. He had never seen her smile like that, a thousand suns pouring from her lips and eyes. "I feel beautiful," she said.

They sipped tea awkwardly, silently, a few moments.

"Daisy?" he said.

"You're such sweet company, Olympus. Of the men I've known . . . I mean socially, not here . . ." Her voice trailed off, as if she had reached forbidden ground.

He desperately wanted her to continue because it would reveal what this odd moment was all about. But the ancient wall arose and she retreated from whatever she was going to say.

"The hours you spend here are my favorite times," she said.

Prinz sensed that more lay just beyond. Time ticked on and he found himself unable to say anything. Since she wouldn't talk much about herself, he always primed himself with small talk for her; Goldfield gossip, or the price of the mining stocks, or Teddy Roosevelt's latest speech, or Elihu Root's bristly new interpretation of the Monroe Doctrine, or the gaudy pressed aluminum ceiling in the Montezuma Club. He was developing his most important story of all, about the stealing of rich ores from the mines, but he sensed she didn't want to talk much this afternoon. It was barely past the supper hour and soon she would be engaged in her trade. He marveled that a woman so lovely could be un-marked by her profession.

She stood, her glances still clicking over him like a Ko-dak for some future album. He thought she probably would usher him to the door; her gift of unpaid company had expired. Instead, she simply walked to him.

"Olympus, do you want me?" she asked.

An urgent heat swept him, lifting his pulse. All he could manage was a nod.

"I want you," she said. "I always have but I needed the other—the talk—even more. You gave it to me, Olympus. You are always giving me yourself. You're the finest man I've ever known."

He swallowed, not answering.

She smiled again, the radiance in her face that drove all the sordidness and squalor away from the crib. When she smiled like that the whole world around her shone.

"Olympus," she whispered. She undid the white silken robe and slid it off and stood before him. "Come to me," she said. "I need you tonight."

In the next minutes he experienced something so strangely sweet that he knew it would rest in his memory forever. Their passion lasted only moments, for as swiftly as they united it engulfed them and left her groaning and him limp, as if a tidal wave had flooded over them. But that was only the salad.

"Olympus, I love you," she whispered in his ear.

She clung to him, held him tightly upon her as if to absorb his energy and spirit. He felt some strange heat rise from her, a glow that pierced him wherever their flesh touched, as if some fountain of pure energy and love was radiating from her into him, bestowing its blessing upon his soul. He didn't feel the usual sleepiness that came in the aftermath of love because the fierce energy of her long lean body galvanized him. He felt he had been taken to the Garden of Eden and made innocent.

"I love you, Daisy," he whispered.

She didn't smile. Instead, he discovered tears rising in her eyes, and gently wiped them away. He could not fathom what was happening but he knew that this act of love was as far removed from the lusts of the tenderloin as heaven was from hell. He smelled incense, sandalwood and bayberry, piñon pine and lavender, even though she had burned none, except what incense lay in her soul, an offering to him.

She held him upon her so long he wondered how she could bear his weight but whenever he started to slide aside she fiercely pulled him to her again. At last she released him and they stared at each other side by side, caressing and touching. These were the sweetest moments in his young life—but what of the future? He looked into the contented face of a woman he didn't possess. He saw none of the distraction that had harried her when he arrived. Her eyes were soft and tender and her gaze was imprinting him on her heart.

"Daisy? Would you marry me? I'll love you and care for you for as long as I have breath."

The contentment drained from her face. He could scarcely see her in the twilight. "Don't spoil it, Olympus," she said.

"Spoil it! I want this to last forever. I don't know who you are or why you're here. I only know I can give you a better life. Whatever it is, let it go. Be my bride. Wear white at our wedding, Daisy, because that's the color of your soul."

"Please, Olympus," she said, an edge in her tone.

"I don't understand."

"Then don't try. Just accept this. This is my love and I've given it to you the only way I know how."

"And this is the only way I may have you."

"You'll always have me, Olympus. To my dying day."

"That doesn't sound right, Daisy."

She didn't answer. She wheeled her legs to the floor and stood, smiling at him. He stared up at her nakedness, memorizing it, searing her beauty into his soul. A yearning built in him again. But she abandoned him and he could hear her washing herself at the dry sink. He dressed and waited. When she appeared again she was wearing her shift. But she didn't look the same. Some residue of their union rosed her cheeks and flashed in her eyes.

"Daisy," he said. "I feel the wall again. The woman I love is on the other side and I don't know how to find the door. All I can do is tell you that I love you and hope you'll come to me some day."

He remembered the heat of her body and wondered at it. What did she radiate? Something she exuded pierced him, balmed his flesh and soul as if it were the very fountain of life.

"I'll be seeing you," she said. That was a new expression. Usually, at the door, she said, "Come back soon, Olympus."

"I'll be seeing you," he replied.

They didn't hug at the door. She shied away from it.

"Daisy," he whispered as he stepped out.

She didn't smile and the door closed behind him, stopping that radiant energy that had bathed him. He turned and looked. It was dark now. He could stand across the street and wait for her shade to rise, signaling her willingness to have guests. But he didn't want to. For the first time, he loathed the men who would lie with her this night. They might not possess her heart but they possessed the loveliest body in the world.

He walked back to his paper, filled with a gentle afterglow alloyed with melancholia. Daisy had opened a door to herself at last but wouldn't let him past the vestibule. Maybe, sometime, Daisy would surrender and they could fashion a sweeter world out of their enduring love.

He let himself into his little printing plant and its sleeping alcove, comforted and hopeful. She had taken the first step.

CHAPTER 53

·······················

Beth Fairchild-Ross counted the hundred fifty-three dollars she had collected the previous night and knew she had enough. She could make up what Reggie had borrowed from the bank and return to her dear babies. Tommy would be struggling with his *McGuffey's Reader* now but Jimmy and Annette would be at home with Mrs. Kennicott—if she was still there. Oh, how she yearned to hug them.

The knowledge should have wrought joy in her but it wrought turmoil instead. A thousand dreads consumed her. What would Reggie say about her long absence? And her silence? How would her children treat her after she had abandoned them for so long?

What if Reggie had been arrested, tried and convicted? She had been gone long enough for it to happen. How the world would condemn her for abandoning her children in their moment of need! But she didn't think that had happened. Reggie had clipped bond coupons and had never altered any books. He had always meant to pay it right back, of course. He might be the head of the trust department but he wasn't the only one who had access to the bank's stock and bond portfolios. So how could they ever pin anything on him? Still, as long as the coupons were missing a heavy cloud lay over him. He had borrowed more than his entire annual salary.

Reggie was going to ask questions and she was going to tell him nothing. If he pressed her she would tell him a petty lie: she had gambled and won. She knew faro well enough to make it credible. Let him believe that. But the truth would go to the grave with her.

It frightened her to leave. She feared Dollarhyde would send Ned and make a slave of her if he found out. Maybe they would come and tear the money from her. They all knew she had spent little and salted away everything. The whole tenderloin knew that, and with each day she felt a noose grow tighter around her, as one slimy man after another tried to horn in. She had earned almost twice what she needed to pay Reggie's debt and had paid exorbitant sums to be left alone.

But she had been planning for this moment for weeks, her mind feverish with it. She knew what she must do. She intended to abandon everything. Calling a hack to pick up her shabby trunk would be fatal. She loathed every item of clothing she possessed anyway. The seductive peignoirs and all the rest would only remind her of her ordeal. She would simply walk to the bank as she always did and never come back. The district had eyes; they knew her habits. They would see nothing out of the ordinary.

Another dread haunted her: Suppose the bank didn't have that much currency in large bills? She utterly refused to carry a cashier's check or letter of credit or anything that might trace her Goldfield life. She had agonized about yeggs and what they might do to an unescorted woman en route home. The trains were safe enough. The danger would lie at both ends of the trip, in lawless Goldfield and in San Francisco or Oakland once she detrained and took the ferry across the bay.

She had decided upon a money belt. But even to buy one in Goldfield would alert those who bought and sold information. So she had quietly fashioned one of cotton duck with pockets all around; a slender belt that would fit under a corset.

She fingered it, trembling. She had kept it hidden from her neighbors, Sadie and Lulu, who visited now and then. But maybe they knew about it. God only knew who slipped into her crib while she did her banking. She cried suddenly, unable to stop a flood of strange emotion so complex and tangled she didn't know whether she was weeping from joy, terror, relief, or dread of what she might find at the end of her sojourn.

She had, in a way, come to enjoy Sadie in particular.

The woman was a fountain of good cheer. She had a volcanic temper that helped her subdue the unpredictable tenderloin. From Sadie, over tea, she had learned the lore of that profession—and it *was* a lore. She found out how to deal with the occasional dangerous man, how to avoid pregnancy and disease, how to turn a man away, how to deal with drunks and hop fiends, how to deal with menacing men with knives or white slavers. From Sadie she got an education in making men happy, often told in bawdy exclamation points and anecdotes that made Beth blush. From Sadie, most blessed of all, she got respect for her privacy. Sadie never asked who Beth was or why she had come to the tenderloin.

And now she would betray Sadie. She would not even trust her friend and mentor with a good-bye. It had been an ordeal to abandon Olympus two nights earlier. In those tender, intense moments she had tried to armor him for what was to come and comfort him with a love that he would always remember. She loved him dearly. In some other time and place she would gladly have pledged her troth to him.

She loved most of all his undemanding company, his acceptance of her, which made him an island of pleasure in the darkness of her days. Now she would leave him because it was not possible to take him with her through the wall and into her other life. She wept as she thought of his love, his good humor, his enjoyment of her person and finally her body in one last feverish and spiritual interlude. She wanted him in her arms as desperately as he wanted her. The memory of that last night was so sweet and sacred that she knew she would relive it over and over in the years to come.

"Good-bye, Olympus," she whispered. "You rescued me from hell."

She wondered whether she had changed. Whether she had hardened into an uncaring, too-worldly woman. What *was* she now? A slut? Forever a whore who had taken hundreds of men into her body? Could she ever wipe away the

stain? Would this terrible life stamp her face or creep into
her speech or pop out vulgarly in polite company? Would
God angrily cast her away? Would she have nightmares?
Would she reveal her secret to Reggie while talking in her
sleep?

She wondered whether she could ever find sacredness in
marriage, sacredness in chastity. She wondered if she could
face all those nice people in San Francisco again, look them
in the eye, wonder whether they knew. She wondered
whether she had any worth at all and whether her sacrifice
made any sense. Maybe it had all been for nothing.

She sat on her hateful bed gathering her courage. Then
she resolutely arose, bathed herself with a sponge, strapped
on her money belt, and dressed in her severe suit, the one
she had worn to Goldfield. She felt feverish. She stuffed
last night's money into her reticule, leaving twenty dollars
visible in case thieves might snatch it and the rest secreted
at the bottom. She peered out her window. The tenderloin
slept by day, awakened by night, and now it slept. She
stepped into a brisk bright day but it didn't cheer her. She
walked uptown and no one followed.

She entered the Nye and Ormsby Bank and approached
the pale clerk she usually dealt with. He knew her profession.

"I wish to close my account," she said. "I want the
largest bills you have."

He looked startled. "I'm not sure . . . let me see, madam," he replied. He retreated to the vault and returned with
a black enameled sheet-iron box. "You're in luck. I feared
we didn't have many hundreds. But we have some five
hundreds, and a few one thousands. Will those do?"

"Oh, yes!"

She signed the receipt. He stamped purple ink over several documents. "Normally, we require advance notice,"
he said. "But all your deposits were cash." He smiled
knowingly. "How do you want it?" That struck him as a
joke, too, and he tittered.

"Thousands and hundreds. How do I know these are true bills?"

"The paper and the engraving, madam. It's a special paper. Of course, if you'd like specie—"

"No, oh no. The bills please."

She stared at the Treasury notes distrustfully as he put them on the marble counter. She fingered them. They had that stiff feel of real money. "All right," she whispered. There before her was the fruit of months of terror and shame and hope. He handed her a little brown envelope and she pushed them in and slid the envelope into her suit coat.

"Please sign here," he said. She signed *Daisy Jones*.

He smiled. "Be careful," he said, faintly amused. She peered around her but saw no one in the sleepy bank.

She knew exactly what to do next. She entered the adjacent hotel and found the necessary room. There she transferred her huge bills to her money belt and buttoned it tight after counting them once again. She abandoned the telltale brown money envelope that most banks used and stepped into the street, peering sharply at every moving vehicle and person. No one followed her. She walked slowly to the Tonopah and Goldfield Railroad Station where the northbound to Mound House Junction on the Virginia and Truckee Railroad, Carson City and Reno, would be leaving in an hour.

She prayed no one would recognize her. Now came the hardest part, when she would be seen by many men, maybe some of her customers. She had done what she could by wearing a prim and fashionable suit of a sort not worn by bawds. She wore no paint either, and her lustrous brown hair had long since returned to its natural tint. She wore a pair of oval, gold-rimmed ladies' spectacles which she had never worn before and which effectively disguised her.

A throng had already collected at the station and the train stood idly, its engine chuffing at leisure. She found a line at the ticket window and waited her turn, dreading the wink or grin that would mean she had been discovered. She saw a man she knew and turned away from him. He was with his wife.

"San Francisco, coach," she said.

"All righty, ma'am," said the clerk, who began stamping a form. "That's thirty-seven and one half. You'll transfer at Mound House and Reno, the bay ferry's included. You have luggage?"

"No," she whispered. She paid him with hands that trembled so much she could barely control them.

"All right. This top one here, this is our ticket. Have that ready. Train leaves in twenty, boards in ten."

She bought a *Goldfield News* from a candy butcher, the better to hide her face on board. It occurred to her she hadn't eaten. But she wasn't hungry.

She boarded a few minutes later and found a window seat where she could look back upon raw, lusty Goldfield. She felt like weeping because of Olympus.

The engine ahead gathered steam in its bowels. She heard the clang of step stools being thrown into coaches and the familiar song of the conductors. And then the coach shuddered as couplings stretched, and Goldfield slid away.

Beth could not stem her tears and dabbed her face with a handkerchief for miles as she rode into the unknown.

CHAPTER 54

· ·

The *Observer* was prospering beyond anything that Olympus Prinz had hoped for it in spite of the arrival of another paper in Goldfield, the *Daily Sun*. He understood the reasons why and exploited them. He was covering ground the dailies shied from for fear of losing advertising or antagonizing readers. His Goldfield mining stock list, separating the wildcats from bona fide issues, was one attraction. Every time a new stock was floated, Prinz went to people he trusted, like the geologist Hannibal Dash, who had an uncanny knowledge of the district, and got the facts on the new company.

Another was his effort to cover serious problems with the sort of reportage that required time and effort beyond what a daily could throw into it. He had examined such questions as railroad fares, miners' wages, white slavery in the tenderloin district, the need for an infirmary, Goldfield housing, the always precarious water supply, the necessity to move the county seat from Hawthorne to Goldfield, mining laws as they applied to Goldfield claims, school requirements, even-handed taxation, mine safety, and scores of other topics.

His reportage had been so thorough that the columns of the *Observer* had, willy-nilly, become known as the best source of information about the city and its mines.

He took sides, opinionizing about everything, often with a little mockery tossed in for seasoning. They were calling the *Observer* the most bullheaded paper in Nevada and he took malicious pride in it. He was not quite on anyone's side and not quite anyone's enemy, which enhanced his prestige and certainly increased his circulation. Whenever he or Uriah Horn solicited ads from merchants, the conversation always turned to the paper's reliability.

"Well," a men's ready-made clothier told him, "your views ain't mine; I take to the *Sun* because it says nice things about this here burg and you're a regular dirt-grubber. But darned if you don't get read harder than the dailies. Mind you, I don't approve of your undercutting the wildcatters; they bring business into Goldfield. Let the buyer beware, I allus say. But it's a mighty fine chart. I see what stocks to stay away from. Everyone I know takes a gander at that list, whether they admit it or not. When I put an ad in your rag, stuff marches right off my shelves. You sold me outa shoes last week and that was just a two-column by six, too."

Hiring Horn, a serious young drifter out of Fort Dodge, Iowa, freed Prinz to get out more. Horn broke down the type, proofed pages, composed small stories and announce-

ments, sold ads, mailed bills, delivered the editions to newsboys on Thursday evenings, and was learning to set type.
But no printer's devil could substitute for the Linotype machine Prinz desperately needed.

But that was a luxury he resolutely denied himself. Instead, he had taken cash out of the till and bought visits to
Daisy. How the world would mock him if it knew! Prinz,
the sage of Goldfield, throwing away a fortune to have tea
thrice a week with a slut. And getting nothing more than a
few words and smiles for his money, too—until two days
ago.

Daisy simply wasn't a Cyprian. Olympus knew that
much. Daisy was an educated, gracious woman of good
family and good connections. She enjoyed his humor,
treated him warmly, added philosophy to his life, and most
odd of all, expressed the finest ideals. He knew little more
about her than he had the moment he met her. But he persevered. Behind that nom de guerre, Daisy, was the woman
he loved. Some day, somehow, he would pierce her veil.

Meanwhile the labor-saving Mergenthaler typesetting
machine lay beyond his reach, forcing him to set type fran-
tically to survive against dailies well equipped with the
great, clattering, smoky monsters. But that was his choice.
He mocked himself. The ultimate rationalist was the ultimate fool. He had never before sacrificed anything precious, and scarcely could rationalize it. He didn't even
believe in sacrifice; it was a deliberate casting away of a
resource. The cash he squandered on Daisy also kept him
out of an apartment and bound to his printing shop, where
he lived in a curtained alcove.

For several weeks this fall he had been preparing yet
another of his intensive stories about Goldfield. He had, all
along, avoided a topic most vexed and painful, the highgrading done by miners. It was more rampant than ever in
the mines with rich ore. The miners considered it their right
to load up with as much of the best gold they could secret
on their persons and waddle out under the angry gazes of
the managers who could not touch them without search

warrants. Mine owners estimated the losses at two to three million a year, an awesome brigandage.

But every shopkeeper in town was secretly delighted. It raised the wages of most miners from four dollars a day to at least fifty, and the more enterprising stiffs in the richer mines were toting out hundreds each day. That gold lubricated the city's economy. Goldfield boasted a whole business devoted to sewing pockets and pouches in miners' jumpers and pants, cutting little compartments into the heels of miners' brogans, gluing false crowns into miners' caps, soldering false bottoms into lunchbuckets, and hollowing out the handles of shovels and picks.

Far worse was the thievery once the highgrade ore reached grass. There, rich ore "accidentally" fell off ore cars or ended up in the slack piles mixed with country rock or dropped between loose boards at a mill. For every pound the mining stiffs smuggled out the topsiders got ten, and for every ten the topside men snatched, the straw bosses got twenty.

The Western Federation of Miners couldn't do much for the stiffs. The tough bosses in the hiring halls were getting rich faster than the stiffs. If a miner wanted a job in a rich mine he had to buy it. Any miner who wasn't willing to pay for a shift didn't get to work it. It was, in fact, a racket that bled working miners, forced them to steal, and rubbed consciences raw.

It was one of those stories that grew and grew as Prinz poked into it. No one considered it a secret. He had no trouble finding miners who boasted of their looting. He compiled the names and addresses of thirteen fake assayers who were buying the booty for half its bullion price. He talked to frustrated superintendents and owners who were stymied by law. One needed a search warrant to hunt for gold on a private person. Any manager who tried would simply trigger a wildcat strike, stop mining, and possibly suffer heavy damage to equipment. The miners considered the gold theirs, no matter what law, ethics, or religion had to say about it. No Goldfield jury would convict a miner of highgrading no matter what the evidence.

The lessees, operating against the calendar, were in a tighter spot. They couldn't afford stoppage with the clock ticking so they simply looked the other way. Losing ten or fifteen or twenty percent of their gold—no one ever knew just how much—was cheaper than not mining at all.

Prinz detailed all that in a long story with several sidebars and didn't stop there, either. He interviewed a few merchants: a café owner who coined money selling hearty meals to miners coming off shift; a clothing merchant, cobbler, and several saloon keepers who perhaps got most of the illicit gold, along with gamblers and tarts. Even the three undertakers in town were coining money selling flossy coffins and posh send-offs. Their attitude was plain: a shrug of the shoulders, a smile, a quick defense of their patrons, and an overblown, elaborate disbelief that anyone was stealing anything. One bartender argued that Goldfield was the most honest community he'd ever seen.

He interviewed a couple of ministers too. The Reverend Mr. Arbuthnot had thundered against theft to his congregation only to end his sermon with the sly reminder that gold truly belongs to whoever finds it first. Pastor Dellwig took an even more relaxed view, saying that the pocketing of ore was a time-honored part of any miner's wage and could be sanctioned by church and God. What's more, the minister added, sharing the wealth was sanctioned by the splendid doctrine of socialism, and under this new ethic endorsed by the WFM and the Wobblies, why, it was a right and duty for any man in the pits to slice the pie.

"This is gonna be some issue," Uriah said as he slid type into a stick. "I don't know how you got all this together."

"Questions. Just keep asking, and if one person's lips are buttoned try another. There's always some who'll talk. I'll be sending you out soon, Uriah, and you can take a flyer at it."

"I'd like that, Mr. Prinz. I just think you're doing the

world a favor. I'd like to do that when you think I'm ready. I'd like to dig into stuff so people can be informed.''

"It doesn't always make friends, Uriah," Prinz said as he carried a heavy galley tray to the proofing table.

"I've been looking around for something in life that does some good," Uriah said. "This is it. I just hope you'll keep on teaching me and I'll be worth my pay."

"You already are. You're picking up speed setting type; you're breaking down type as fast as anyone can. You'll be a journeyman printer soon. And the rest, selling ads, getting the papers out, why, you're helping me a lot."

"Well, I'm hoping to be an editor like you. I have an itch to help the world out some."

"This is the way then," Prinz said, studying a proofing sheet covered with sticky ink.

"I guess I always had a serious turn," Uriah said. "I always thought maybe a newspaper like this or a magazine like *Harper's* might be the place to be. My sentences get tangled up, though."

"When you know what you want to say they won't get tangled anymore. I always form opinions and let the story express them."

"So do all the rest of the editors. I guess a reader never lacks for an opinion in Goldfield," Uriah said.

At the last Prinz composed an editorial: The vile practice of organized looting, he concluded, corrupts miners, union leaders, businessmen, as well as straw bosses, mine owners and financiers. He found some justification for it in the wages and conditions of the working stiffs, who faced a long daily ordeal under the earth, always in danger, severed from sunlight and the delights of the day. But he dismissed the idea that it did no harm. The burden upon the soul and spirit of the highgraders and those who accepted what they knew to be loot was too great. It might enrich men but it was ruining their spirit and self-esteem all the more. How many men in Goldfield looked into their mirrors each morning and saw a thief?

He'd written a compelling editorial, he supposed as he

proofread his handiwork. This issue might cost him a few
ads from a few merchants—saloon men especially, who
profited most from the theft. The morticians were always
fickle but usually came back in a fortnight. He had a prod-
uct they needed, advertising space in the best-read little
sheet in Goldfield.

He locked the forms, slid them into his flatbed press, and
began cranking out the issue, a task that occupied him and
Uriah for several hours. He needed typewriting machines,
a Linotype, a rotary press, a secretary, and a bookkeeper.
That was what he was sacrificing to visit Daisy.

After the ink had dried, he and Uriah spent Thursday
evening toting papers to newsstands and cigar stores to be
sold for a dime. They carted bundles to newsboys for street
sales, and the post office for mailing, and in the end, delivered over a hundred directly to their downtown destina-
tions.

Tomorrow Uriah would spend twelve or thirteen hours
breaking down type and returning the letters to the case
boxes while Olympus billed advertisers and subscribers,
paid invoices, did some banking, sold more ads, and pondered the contents of the next issue. He already knew what
it would contain: reaction to this week's story. He hoped
he could quote a few who were spitting anger as well as a
few who liked what they read. It always kindled interest.
Maybe he could milk highgrading for three or four issues.

This issue, above all others, had drained the energy from
him. He saw Uriah off with a pat on the shoulder for the
boy's good work and settled into his narrow cot in the
alcove, proud of his achievement. The *Observer* would be
noticed.

CHAPTER 55

....

Casey Pepper didn't want to read the story. He knew what was in it. That was all anyone talked about. So, the *Goldfield Observer* was another antilabor rag just like all the rest of the capitalist apparatus he intended to blow off the face of the earth. He knew of the punk who ran it, the one with the funny name and the college degree. A college man. Casey snorted. College men were wrong even when they were right. This Prinz would find out how wrong he was soon enough.

Pepper always lived in a state of barely controlled rage. But it never paid to lose his temper. When he lost his temper he couldn't think and thinking was what he needed to do now. The rag would stir things up. It was bad enough for stiffs to go into the pits and work in darkness and danger for four dollars, risking death from cave-ins, death from premature blasts, death from noxious gases, death or injury from bad accidents, and miner's lung. And now a young California snot who had never done a day of hard labor in his life was telling them off.

Four dollars. Three-fifty for topsiders. A stiff earned just enough to hold body and soul together. How could four dollars compensate a living, breathing man with a wife and children for the risks he took in the stopes? Casey spat. That's all such arguments deserved, he figured: spit.

Now this lackey of the plutocrats was attacking the working stiffs for pocketing a little ore, as if the ore belonged to the plutocrats and not an ounce belonged to the good lads who mucked it up. Some young snot, smart with fancy words, had moralized and brayed like an ass, and might cost seven hundred miners in the district their bit of sunshine.

That was the whole trouble with private property. A few

had almost all of it and the rest got almost nothing. And if they took a little to even up the score, why, the law landed on them and the preachers and the four-eyed journalists. It'd mean that the owners would howl and the men would strike—go without rather than accept a pittance—and the politicians would send in the army the way things had gone at Coeur d'Alene and Cripple Creek.

No, by God, it wasn't going to happen. Casey Pepper wouldn't let it happen, not while he had red blood to bleed. He was a steward for the Western Federation of Miners Local 220 and that bunch was as tough as they came. But being tough didn't fill the bill. The whole rotten system needed burying.

He had quietly joined a new outfit that had just been cobbled together in Chicago by Big Bill Haywood, mostly drawn from the ranks of the WFM: the Industrial Workers of the World. These were men of vision, men who understood that the only thing left was to tear down rotten capitalism to its foundations through a gigantic universal strike and build a syndicalist state in which every man had an equal share of the world. If they could not have justice by peaceful means then they would have justice through war.

There was one thing about these few: they would act. Now was the time to do something hard and memorable and put the IWW on the map. Pepper and the others in this new outfit saw the class enemy whole. It did no good to chop off one tentacle of the octopus and let the others go.

That day, Pepper walked past the little building that housed the *Observer*, noting its false front, its rectangular frame construction, its foundation of mortared rock with two screened vents to let air through the crawl space. He noted the adjacent buildings lining the quiet reaches of Second Street near Hall, well back from the bustling business district. He grunted his pleasure.

It was funny how things happened without a word being spoken, the acts of men so attuned to an idea that no talk was ever necessary. Each man would know what to do and why. Pepper wandered into a small saloon called the Santa

Fe, strictly a miner's pub just off the edge of the Combination Mine Group on the east edge of town. The Santa Fe wasn't made for fat cats. It catered to tired men in their jumpers, men who stopped for a mug of pilsener or a boilermaker to blow the silica dust out of their throats and celebrate another day of being alive without the rock above them landing on their heads. No, it wasn't a place for shopkeepers or financiers, or women, or drummers.

Pepper ordered a mug and surveyed the bunch. No one spoke much but that rag was on their minds. This Friday afternoon the crowd was peculiarly quiet but the silence was louder than any yelling he had ever heard. He peered about through smoke, listening to the chronic coughs of miners whose lungs were rotting out from life in the pits. The plutocrats boasted that there wasn't much silicosis in Goldfield; it had good dry air and a warm climate and the miners didn't need special ventilation. Pepper's ears told him it wasn't so.

Pepper spat. He headed for a plank table in the corner and several men wordlessly followed him.

"Yes or no?" he asked.

"Yes," said Vince St. John. The rest nodded.

"All right," said Pepper. "As soon as it's dark."

That was all that was ever said.

By twos or alone they cased the neighborhood that late Friday afternoon, arousing no curiosity in those peaceable precincts. Second Street was lined with small shops and a few houses and a couple of sandy fields, one used as a baseball diamond; a bakery, a cobbler, two assayers, a tonsorial parlor, a coal and ice yard, a private home with a millinery sign on it. The street would be deserted sometime after six when the shops closed.

At the Santa Fe, Casey Pepper, along with Vince, the fiery Mex Teodoro, Mitch, Paddy, Gunter, and Wild Bill waited for dark, speaking not a word. Pepper sat and sipped and listened to the coughing. Why hadn't he ever listened to miners cough? He was so used to the sound he had never noticed it. But now he heard nothing but coughing, wheezing, spitting into brass cuspidors, and more coughing. These men were paid to wreck their lungs and go to their graves at the age of forty.

"Hallelujah, I'm a bum," sang Paddy in a gravel voice. "Hallelujah, bum again. Hallelujah, give us a handout to revive us again."

Mitch laughed. It was the new Wobbly marching song, the sacrament of the powerless. When they turned you into a bindlestiff, then you might as well sing about it.

Darkness settled. The sun slid behind the Malpais Mesa, leaving a burning blue in the west. Pepper sipped and wondered whether the IWW should take credit for this. He would leave that to the men later. At his nod, they filed out in ones and twos over ten minutes, dissolving invisibly into the night. Minutes later they coalesced on Second Street. Mitch and Gunter each carried a bundle of ten Du Pont Hercules sticks stolen from several mines. Both were veteran powder men. For safety's sake, Paddy and Wild Bill carried the fulminate fuses, pencils of copper tubing, well behind Mitch and Gunter. Pepper carried a roll of tarry Bickford fuse under his jumper. Teodoro toted a pail of scrap steel for shrapnel and Vince would keep a lookout.

A light still shown in the print shop. Pepper peered in and saw a young man in a green eyeshade patiently breaking down type in the harsh glare of a naked bulb. The others peeked in too. The boy was scarcely past his teens and was toiling deep into the night for his master.

Pepper's eyebrows lifted, making a question.

Each man nodded. It was too bad but it wouldn't stop them. The eyeshade punk inside was a tool of the plutocrat class and this was war. That was the central idea separating those in the IWW from the WFM miners. Class war. That lackey inside shared the guilt of the privileged even if he wasn't the owner, Prinz. Too bad, but it couldn't be helped. Pepper studied them all silently, just to make sure—not only that they were all agreed but that there was no traitor or stool pigeon, some weak-kneed crumb who might squeal. Not that such a fool would live long.

He saw nothing but resolve as he examined his men one by one in that shadowed glow.

"Do you want to wait?" he whispered.

"Get it over with," Vince muttered. "The longer we stand here, the worse it gets."

"That's a dollar-a-day kid in there. We could wait for Prinz. He lives in there."

"It's tough," Wild Bill whispered. "But it's now or never."

They reached some unspoken consensus. Pepper felt bad for the kid who was going to die.

The screen popped off the vent easily and with only a minor squeak. Swiftly, Mitch and Gunter inserted the long Bickford fuses into the caps and crimped them in place. Then the two of them crawled under the building, gingerly hefting their bundled sticks. For a while both worked out of sight under there, fusing the bundles and running the Bickford back to the vent. A stroller on Second kept them all flattened to the ground the next minute, until Vince whistled. At long last the powder men crawled out and nodded.

That was the signal to separate one or two at a time in all directions. They would slip into various clubs and saloons and have mugs in hand when it blew. Except for Gunter who would do the honors and go straight home after cutting across a few lots to put himself on an adjacent street even before the long fuses burned down. He barely spoke English but he seemed always to know what to do. This would be perfect: The fuses would burn invisibly for three or four minutes, hidden by the rock foundation, giving them all time to scatter. The two bundles, each weighed down by scrap iron, would blow at either end of the long building. In moments there would be no *Goldfield Observer* to torment working stiffs who asked only for their inheritance in a rotten world. Oh, some might rage, some might point at the stiffs, but no one would prove a thing.

Casey Pepper nodded and men began sliding into the night, mere shadows on an unlit street two blocks from the bustling business district. A window glowed here and there. Many places had electricity but poorer people still used kerosene. He could see the stars in the autumnal sky, peaceful observers of a sinful world. He slid away himself, after studying the ground sharply for damning things left behind or boot prints in the hard caliche. He saw nothing.

He touched Gunter's shoulder. The big man, who wore a beret, nodded. Pepper walked swiftly to First and then Main and was buying a beer at the Monte Carlo Saloon when two powerful blasts blew the *Goldfield Observer* to smithereens and the fire bells started clanging.

CHAPTER 56
....

Prinz stared in mute horror at the rubble that had once been his place of business. The blasts—they told him there were two—had leveled the little frame building, caved in the adjoining buildings, shattered glass for two blocks around, shot chunks of foundation rock right through the walls of several neighboring buildings, set the tonsorial parlor to the south aflame—passersby were only now extinguishing it with buckets of water—and blown Uriah Horn to bits. They told him in horror that Horn's head was thirty yards north and the rest of him on the roof of the cobbler's shop.

Uriah, he thought. *Not Uriah.*

Numbly, Prinz stood beside the ruin of the *Observer*, watching Constable Inman herd the crowds back while firefighting volunteers fought a perverse wind that fanned the flames and threatened to burn Goldfield to the ground. Prinz felt nothing; he was so shocked he scarcely grasped what had happened. But one thing he did understand: under that tarpaulin over there lay the mortal remains of a good youth who worked hard and wanted to succeed—and who was innocent.

After his initial rage and horror, a flood of guilt washed through Prinz. If he had steered away from controversy the boy would be alive with a bright future before him. But that didn't make sense either: without its staple of controversy, the *Observer* wouldn't exist and the boy wouldn't have had a job.

The whipping orange flame that was eating the shop next door cast weird jolts of light over the terrible scene, rendering it into a hell. People stared at him and pointed, some nodding, some waving a clenched fist. A man spat at him. He ignored them. He couldn't think anyway. He had gotten word at the Montezuma Club four blocks away, his only home apart from the sleeping alcove in the shop.

At last Inman approached him. The rangy constable looked more like a rural western sheriff than the law officer of a modern metropolis like Goldfield. "I don't suppose there's any question of motive," he said, eying Prinz. "You know anything?"

The newspaperman shook his head.

"We've got a murder. Whoever done it could hardly have missed your boy—what's his name?"

"Uriah. Uriah Horn . . ."

"Where from? You know? Any relatives around?"

"I think from Iowa. Fort Dodge, he once told me. I— he was a fine fellow, Claude."

"How come he was here now?"

"He always works late the day after we publish, breaking down type. It's a long slow job." Tears welled in his eyes. He hadn't cried since he was a boy. Ashamed, he brushed them back. "A good fellow," he said. "I'll—I'll bury him . . ." The painful knowledge that he lacked the money caught his tongue.

"You talk to anyone this eve? See anything suspicious?"

"Nothing. I quit about six, took a meal at the Louvre Chophouse—I usually do—and went over to the Montezuma. I usually do that, too." He squirmed under the policeman's quiet gaze. "I should've stayed and helped the boy," he mumbled.

Inman stared at him gently. "Prinz, let go of it. I'm trying to help. That story did it, you think? I just want you to say it or lead me in some other direction."

"It was the story," Prinz said.

"Seems kinda dumb to write something like that. Like committing suicide. Them miners, they'd do anything to keep their fingers on a little ore."

"I know," Prinz said. He saw himself now as a Stanford snot, a dabbler in huge and terrible things. He had brought it on himself and a boy had died because of it.

Inman smiled faintly. "It was a good story. I read it. Thought you were the most reckless sonofagun in Nevada. I'll say it was fair, but them miners don't see things that way. One bad word and they're out to get you. Well, darn it, I've got at least one, probably several killers I've got to track down. I don't like it. I figure there was two or three. They were after you. You live in there—I mean, you used to. That kid, he was Olympus Prinz as far as they were concerned."

"I know."

"Well, I got some ideas. That dynamite was stolen from the mines. I'll check dealers just in case some fool bought some but I just know it was stolen. Smell that smell? That's how the bottom of a mine smells. The caps and fuse, any stiff could walk out with those. There's a bunch of socialists and anarchists in that WFM, too. I'll have to talk with them. One of them, Vincent St. John, he's a wild man. Darn it, Prinz, now I got to do a lotta work."

The comment seared Prinz. Inman was blaming him for this, seeing a perpetrator, not a victim. "I—was trying to make the world a better place," Prinz said miserably.

"Better place! Jesus Christ," Inman snapped. "All right, where'll you be? You ain't got a roof over you."

"I have no plans."

"Well, let me know. It seems likely that they'll try for you, seeing as how they missed you this time. I can't keep an eye out if I don't know where you are."

"The tent hotel, I guess," Prinz said, referring to a giant

canvas establishment where newcomers could rent a cot for a dollar a night.

"Heck no, not there, that's solid WFM men," Inman said. "I'd collect your perforated corpse in the morning."

"I got space," said a listening man. "Got a dump with more rooms than I can count. You just come on over, Prinz."

Olympus found himself staring into the genial face of that scoundrel, Sam Jones. For a bad moment he wondered how it would seem, how the crusader and swindler could share a roof. "I . . ." he said.

"I want to talk to you anyway, Prinz."

"I have nothing to talk about."

"That's what I want to talk about. I got a notion I want to try out on you and see if it fits."

"I'm in the middle of the most painful thing that ever happened to me, Mister Jones. I don't know what I'm going to do. My employee's dead. I've lost everything. My business. My books and papers. My equipment. I lost everything because I'm not for sale. I'm still not for sale."

"You come on over. All I'm gonna do is ask some advice. You don't have to trust me. I wouldn't trust me, either. I'm a horse broker, know that? Reminds me of the time I sold a pair of good-looking gray trotters to a fellow. I sez to him, 'Billy, it'll do your heart good when you see those horses trot,' so Billy put down five hundred for the two geldings. Well, sir, those pretty horses wouldn't go, that was the trouble. You whip them and they'd back up. They wasn't fixable. So, Billy, he harnesses them up to his shiny new black lacquered surrey—and they don't go. He whips and they just back up. He boils over, and he sez, 'You told me those trotters trot, but they don't even move.' I sez, 'Whoa up, Billy; I didn't tell you those trotters trot; I said it'd do your heart good to see those trotters trot and that's the plain truth.' So don't trust Sam Jones farther than you can throw an anvil. You just come on over and get some sleep and figure on camping there until you know what you're gonna do. A man don't get Du Ponted every day.''

Prinz sighed. He was bone tired and so melancholic he doubted his sanity. But this was a port in the storm. ''All right, thank you,'' he whispered.

''I'll send word over,'' Jones said, vanishing into the crowd.

Prinz stared after him, puzzled by the scoundrel's disarming candor. Obviously the crook wanted something. But that bed sounded good.

''Why don't you go, Prinz? Nothing for you to do here,'' Inman said.

''I just want to look around,'' Prinz said. He wandered into the space where his building once stood, looking for things in the wavering lantern light. He saw little to salvage. The caseboxes had vanished along with his fonts. Hundreds of small a's and capital B's and italic c's covered the whole neighborhood like pebbles. Most would soon be souvenirs. The flatbed press lay in pieces all over the street. The stones, or worktables, had vanished. The newsprint was ash along with his morgue, the back copies of each edition. The invoices and bills were smoke. The *Goldfield Observer* was dead and could not be resurrected by a man with less than two hundred dollars to his name.

He had always loved ideas and had frolicked in controversy, without ever supposing it would lead to violence and death or his own deep poverty. He sighed, realizing the abstract ideas he toyed with were other men's bread and butter.

Cold pierced him. This bitter night he had tumbled from his shelf as a successful newsman in a boomtown to a wandering bum, likely to ride the rods like any other bindlestiff. It was a lesson that no debating society in Palo Alto had ever taught him.

They were taking away Horn. Some mortician with a long black wagon and a box. Two men in leather jackets were lifting the blanketed bundle into that box. Just a kid, dead at nineteen, another one drawn to some wild town on the frontier or what was left of the frontier. It was a new century now. Prinz knew he was no different from Uriah. He'd come out here to see the wild times himself before they vanished forever. A lot of people did. They'd all come to Goldfield to throw one last party.

CHAPTER 57

· ·

Olympus Prinz stared at the black crater where his newspaper had once been. In the morning he would find a mortician and buy Uriah a send-off. Let the world know that one person in Goldfield cared. Let the remains be properly buried and not dropped into the potter's field beneath the brooding brow of Malpais Mesa.

A sharp chill lowered as the last of the volunteer fire crew abandoned the lot and spectators dissolved into the gloom. Prinz pulled his duster about him.

He had to tell Daisy. He scarcely knew what to say. He would have to shorten his visits but he would still visit her as long as he had a dollar in his purse. She would be busy at this hour. It was after eleven. That's when they all left the saloons and slinked to the tenderloin. He headed south, crossed Myers, and plunged into the gaudy district, ablaze with invitation. Her shade was down. He waited in the cold, feeling the icy air eddy by. He didn't want to see the man who had bought her. He would turn his face away so he wouldn't glimpse him. He had accepted her on her terms and come to love her just as she was, the Daisy in the red-light district, the woman with some other name and some other soul.

At last the door opened and a man hurried away.

"Daisy!" he said, racing toward her.

He stopped suddenly. It wasn't Daisy. The woman was a peroxide blonde with hair humped up on top of her head, stocky as a bulldog.

"It's Sheba, hon. Come on in."

He stared, bewildered. "Where's Daisy?"

She shrugged. "That's the one before me. She walked out yesterday. Left all her stuff, too."

"My God, where'd she go?"

She looked him over. "If you aren't buying, hon, move on."

"Just tell me where she went! Give me an address!"

"How the hell should I know? Come in or get outa the door."

"Where can I find out?"

But the door slammed. He saw her shade roll up. She arranged herself in her bay window seat, tugging her gown open at the breast.

Gone. He turned miserably, wondering if he would ever see her again. Someone here would know. He would try that Palace Dance Hall. She had told him once that the owner of the cribs was there. He started that direction when the door of the crib next to Daisy's opened and a miner departed, bucking into the wind. Sadie. Daisy had talked of Sadie some. They were friends. Sadie had helped her.

Sadie was eying him, her robe tugged tightly about her. "How about it, Sweetie?" she asked.

"Sadie! I'm a friend of Daisy. I've got to find her! Tell me where she went!"

"How should I know? She just vamoosed and no one's seen her since. Dollarhyde, he rented the crib yesterday afternoon. Now, you comin' in for some fun or am I shutting the door?"

"Sadie, here's two dollars. Can I talk for a while?"

She eyed the bills. "Lot cheaper than you was paying Daisy, I guess." She sighed. "Five minutes and pay me first."

He entered the grim little crib with its olive drab walls and grease-stained furniture. She held out her hand and he put the two bills in it. "Well, what?" she asked.

"Tell me what you know. Everything."

"You some sort of detective or something?"

"No, no, no, I'm—a good friend of Daisy."

She laughed cynically. "Whores got lots of good friends. She lit you up, eh? I could light you up too, I guess."

"Just tell me everything, the smallest detail, I have to know everything."

She seemed amused and let her robe sag open at her breasts. She could be anywhere from twenty-five to forty, he thought, and she was trying to seduce him. She pulled out a cigarillo and lit it with a kitchen match.

"Who knows? No one saw her. She walked out in the morning. She left everything—not that she had much. She never spent a nickel she didn't have to. She was someone's wifey, you know. Nice, know what I mean? I never asked why she was doing tricks. Big trouble, I guess."

"Sadie, how do you know she was someone's wife? Did she say?"

Sadie laughed. "Never said. Did you ever look at her ring finger—say, what's your name?"

"Ah, Prinz. No, I didn't."

"You men. There'd been a ring there for years; anyone can see that if you look. A wifey, Prinz. She went home to Daddy."

"Where's home? Did she ever mention a city? A state?"

"Man, you sure got the hots, don't you. No. She didn't say a word. I don't ask if they don't want to say. You learn that in this life."

"Did she know the business? I mean, your business?"

Sadie laughed and then shrugged. "She was pretty dumb."

"Did she ever give you a clue? I mean, why she came?"

Sadie yawned. "I'm getting tired of this. If I knew I wouldn't tell ya. A girl needs her privacy. If Daisy wanted you to know she would of told ya. Now, time's up . . . unless old Sadie can do it for you."

"If you think of anything . . ." Prinz stopped. Sadie wouldn't think of anything. "Thank you," he mumbled. "I love her. We just talked."

"Sure, sure, you just talked. That's what whores do. Adios, Prinz.'' She opened the door, letting in a gale of bitter air.

He stepped into the street where men dodged by with averted eyes. In the tenderloin no one wanted to see or be seen. Wearily, Prinz stumbled toward the Palace Dance Hall knowing how it would end. This night had been like a trapdoor opening under his life, dropping him into a void. He pushed into a wall of smoke, rank beer odor, and the distinct pungency of vomit. A boozy ''professor'' rattled the battered keys of an upright Behr Brothers piano while some tarts steered their johns around a gritty dance floor, jamming their hips into their prospective customers.

Prinz maneuvered his way to a grimy bar where a brute with black hair parted at the center, and hooded eyes, watched his progress.

''Are you Mister Dollarhyde?''

The barkeep nodded to the left. A gray man hulked at a table next to the bar. Prinz headed that way.

''Mister Dollarhyde?''

The man blew cigar smoke and eyed the newspaperman up and down like a carpenter measuring him for a coffin.

''You had a girl named Daisy. I need to find her.''

He didn't respond.

''You know where she went? An address? Anything?''

Dollarhyde—if that was the man—blinked slowly. ''Ah, another john's fallen in love. It happens.'' He laughed softly, the worldliness in him leaking into the room.

''Sadie said she just left. Did she tell you—''

Dollarhyde laughed. ''Probably got kidnapped. Got herself sold to someone. Maybe she's in Mexico by now. Better forget her. She left her stuff. Whores always take everything including the light bulb. I figure some dude snatched her.''

''Did she ever say anything . . .''

''Wife. She was a wife. You can't hide that. That got her lots of loot, you know. Screwing a wifey. They paid good for her. Tough to lose her. I raised her rent when I found out she was doing so good. Raised her protection, too. But she always looked like an amateur, know what I mean? In it for kicks. Man. I wish a few more like her would land around here.''

"How did she go?"

Dollarhyde shrugged. "She walked out."

"Was that unusual—walking out?"

"She walked out every day. Off to the bank."

"What bank?"

"Who knows? There's three. Lissen, pal, I've got no time for lovesick puppies. Buy a beer and have a whirl and forget the broad.''

Prinz shook his head and pushed through the quiet hall. The dance was done and the hurdy-gurdy girls were pawing at the pants of their partners along the bar. Several were dragging some groggy-looking miners up a filthy stair where there probably would be a few pestilent floor mats and ancient blankets hanging between them. The professor downed an entire mug of some sort of varnish and shuddered. Prinz let himself into the cold night and sucked in the clean desert air.

He peered about him sharply, looking for footpads, but South Main Street was running out of steam this night. What did it matter if they held him up for five dollars anyway? His newspaper had died, his young employee had died, his home had died, and his love had died. His future had died, too. There was so much loss that Olympus felt only a numbness. Tomorrow would be worse. The day after that he would be wrestling with guilt and melancholia while he buried Uriah Horn. The day after that the smart young college grad with the fancy ideas and a way of jesting in print would leave Goldfield behind him, a different and more somber young man en route to—somewhere.

Prinz hurried into the wind, up a darkened Main Street lit only by blurred lights at the intersections, and turned right. Goldfield had changed, grown hard and alien and mean. He couldn't even remember what drew him here in the first place. He found Jones's big mansion where a porch light burned a welcome for him.

CHAPTER 58

· · · · · · · · · · · · · · · · · · · ·

Sam Jones himself opened to Prinz, and led him into the great, shining house.

"Nightcap?" asked Jones.

"I think not."

"Man needs sleep after an ordeal like that," said his host, steering Prinz up a winding stair. "Not a good time to palaver."

Prinz was grateful to be left alone.

"I laid out some night things. Water closet's that way. We'll put on the feedbag when you come down."

Prinz found himself in a sumptuous gray bedroom with a fourposter bed that had a monogrammed white coverlet. He felt a rush of gratitude to the old pirate for putting a roof over his head. Jones didn't know it but Prinz was grieving more losses than he could bear; a death, Daisy's disappearance which was another and worse death, and his sudden impoverishment.

He tumbled into bed and slept dreamlessly, overpowered by the blows that he had endured that evening. When he awoke at last he had no idea of the time but the sun was high and dancing off motes of dust in the air.

He found Big Sam and Delia Jones at the long breakfast table, awaiting him. He would have to endure a breakfast before he could escape.

"The cook's day off," Delia said. "But everything's ready, Mister Prinz." Much to Prinz's amazement the infamous lady produced a generous and gaudy breakfast on monogrammed china, while Jones sipped coffee and made small talk.

"You are a voluptuary cook," Prinz said to her. She looked puzzled a moment and then laughed.

Whenever she refilled Jones's china cup, he patted her

affectionately. The pair were exchanging smiles, which further mystified Prinz. Apparently two of the greediest mortals in Nevada had hit it off.

When at last he dallied politely over coffee, Jones got
down to whatever business he had in mind.

"You made any plans?" he asked intently.

"It's too soon, sir. The first thing is to bury my assistant,
Uriah Horn."

"I'll help with that."

Prinz shook his head. "It's something I need to do myself. But thanks."

"What about the paper?"

"It's done."

"Why? Lack of boodle?"

"If you mean, could I start up the *Observer* again, perhaps I could. I don't have the means to operate my own
plant. Sometimes you can print a paper in someone else's
plant. But I don't think I'll do that."

"Why not?"

"Dynamite's a persuasive argument and I got the message. I've lost . . . Uriah Horn died."

"I know the feeling. Well, Prinz, I always admired that
rag. You were the only outfit in town that stirred things up.
Rest of those sissies just smile and run the gossip."

The compliment surprised Prinz, considering it came
from a man who had been a prime target of the weekly. "I
did some good," Prinz said. "But it's over, sir."

"Naw, it's not over, Prinz. I've been thinking. That's
what I do these days. You know I sold out, didn't you?"

"You what?"

"Borden bought me out. I've become a venture capitalist."

"You sold out? That bonanza? But—if I may ask—
why?"

Sam Jones chuckled heartily. "Well, it wasn't because
I've reformed. It was an attack of thirty-eight-caliber conscience that done it."

That puzzled Prinz until Jones described his encounter

with a disgruntled customer named Bonesett and his moment of truth in the wake of his escape.

"Now don't go thinking I'm reformed, Prinz. I'm just looking for a new way to noodle the boodle outa folks. If I was reformed, I'd give all that loot back to those suckers. But I'm not suffering any attacks of conscience. I always say, God made sheep for fleecing. I mind the time I sold an outlaw buggy horse to a widow lady. Now this nag pulled a buggy all right, when you finally got him into harness, but it took three gorillas and a winch to harness him up." Jones erupted with joy at the memory. "Naw, Prinz, don't you go telling the world I'm a saint going through the pearly gates."

Prinz smiled. How could anyone not enjoy the reprobate? He was the only man Prinz had ever met who went out of the way to demolish his own reputation. But Prinz needed his grief. "I guess I'd best be putting my affairs in order. Thanks for the meal. I didn't know Mrs. Jones had such talents." The young man rose.

"Where do you think you're going, Prinz? Whoa up. You're as headstrong as a green-broke horse. We've got some business to do. I was just getting the brush cleared away."

Prinz settled himself in the commodious chair once again.

"How much do you need to start up your rag again?"

"How much do I need . . . ? Why . . . Good Lord, I can't accept money . . . Sir, this isn't the time to discuss something like that."

"Now's the time, Prinz."

Prinz stammered helplessly. "Mister Jones, a newspaper should be independent. It can't—deal in propaganda. You see, I'd be obligated."

"The devil you would, Prinz. You just run your stories any way you want. Now how much? I'll put it in your account and you can get the wires humming ordering stuff. You'll need a press and type and all the rest, right? What's that come to?"

"But, sir, I can't do that."

"All right, you can't. But how much is the ticket?"

"Why—maybe fifteen thousand for the bare bones, twenty thousand for a complete plant with a Linotype."

"We'll make it twenty."

"But, Mister Jones. I . . . please forgive me after your kindness—I can't be your publicist."

Jones chuckled. "I didn't say you had to be. You just keep on raising hob."

"You don't understand. I might want to criticize you."

"Of course. Go ahead and raise hob. There's no such thing as bad publicity."

"But—Mr. Jones, if people know you've financed the paper, they'll assume I'm your mouthpiece."

"Not if I don't say anything and you don't say anything. Not if I give you cash."

The young man squirmed with desire and dread. "Why?" he finally asked.

"Goldfield needs a conscience. I never had much of one myself but I see the need."

"It's a risky proposition. What if I can't repay you?"

"Prinz, this isn't a loan."

"Not a loan?" Astonishment boiled through Prinz. The old pirate wanted to give him twenty thousand dollars, no strings attached, to revive the *Observer*. "Mister Jones, is everything on the table? You have a grudge against the *News*, is that it? You have a little program you'll suggest I support and you'll figure I can't refuse?"

"Everything's on the table, Prinz." Amusement lit the reprobate's face. "Can't a wildcatter make a gift? What if twenty grand landed anonymously on your doorstep? Would you turn it over to the foundling home? Take it, fella. This is the first time I've ever had a charitable notion in my rum-soaked skull so take it before it fades away. You're as skittish as a six-week-old horse colt."

"Is it charity?"

Jones guffawed. "By God, you're a tough one to give money to. Me, I roll in it like a horse rolls in dust. You show me money and I'll come along like a hawg following a slop pail. I see you've got to get used to the idea. You think about it and let me know.''

Prinz sagged in his chair, discomfited. ''I will,'' he said. But he had more questions. ''What're you going to do? I mean, now that you've left the, ah, floatation business.''

''Floatation, that's a pretty good word. What I did was sell fancy, engraved, gilt-edged paper for lots of money. I was a hope peddler. Well, I'm still raking it in, all these Goldfield mines just delight to pay dividends to their stockholders. I own a piece of the Jumbo and the Florence, and they just can't wait to fill my coffers. I guess you could say I'll wheel and deal. We need a stock exchange around here; maybe I'll build one. That's the only way they'd let me in.'' He chuckled softly. ''Call me a speculator. I'm going to go for the gold. You could write, 'Mr. Sam Jones, the well-known Goldfield speculator, said today that his net worth was beyond counting but that's because he never figured out what comes after a thousand.' ''

Prinz tried sternly not to enjoy the man but failed utterly. ''Well, what're you going to tackle first, Mister Jones?''

''Parties, Prinz. Mrs. Jones is the meanest social climber in Nevada and we intend to claw our way to the top. No bowing and scraping for old Delia. She ain't gonna kiss the ten-carat diamond ring of Madam Moneybags the social arbiter to get there. She's gonna take the shortcuts. If she ain't on anyone's four hundred list she'll start her own four hundred list. If she ain't in anyone's blue book she'll write her own blue book. If she ain't in the social register she'll crank up her own. You do that by squandering boodle.

''Now first off, we're going to throw a masked Gold Diggers Ball before Christmas, a real fandango with a big string orchestra, Gypsy violinists and maybe a Hungarian or two; a trestle full of so much chow it'd feed an army—stuff with Frenchie names I never heard of; and enough free booze to float the national debt. I'll pour enough Napoleon brandy to crank up the French Revolution. We'll have a few entertainments, too. Maybe a Boor Prize. I guess you're thinking I mean a Door Prize, but I don't. Next day, we'll have us an open house and do it all again just for the ones that missed the first one. I'll go as Count Dracula, and Delia, she'll be Lady Godiva.''

"Lady Godiva?"

"Oh, quit worrying, Prinz. She'll be wearing a mask."

"I think you'll have a crowd, Mister Jones."

"Look here, Prinz. I'm Big Sam. No one that knows me more'n two minutes gets to call me Jones."

Prinz found himself rushing toward a decision, no matter that he wanted to think about things for a day or so. "All right, Big Sam," he said. "You own me."

"Well, that's a sensible young fellow. I don't own you but that's beside the point. Here." Jones reached into his suit coat, and before Prinz's disbelieving eyes peeled off twenty thousand-dollar Treasury notes from a money clip and laid them in Prinz's sweaty palm. "Do me one favor, Prinz," he said.

Here it comes, the editor thought.

"When you write up the parties, tell 'em Delia's pretty. It ain't a lie, you know."

"No, that's the unvarnished truth, Big Sam."

"Good, boy, good. Make sure you tell 'em how vulgar it was. What a pair of social-climbing fiends we are, me and Delia."

Prinz sighed. "There you go, dictating what to write."

"Well, I oughta get something outa this, Prinz."

Later, on his way to the mortician's parlor, Prinz realized that Jones's cheer and generosity had allayed his grief for a few moments. But once Prinz stepped out the door he walked into sorrow.

CHAPTER 59

. . . .

On the third of November, 1905, the Free Lunch Mine died. The face crew at the third level had run into a blank wall. A lateral fault had shifted the ore shoot out of sight. The rock going topside was mostly rhyolite with quartz but it contained so little gold it wasn't worth mining.

Hannibal Dash poked around the bottom of the mine looking for clues as to which direction the ore shoot had shifted. But he was reduced to hunches. There had been no similar shift in the levels above and he was unable to match up any structures. The values had been declining sharply for several weeks, reaching as low as thirty dollars a ton. Dash took some samples and directed his shift foreman to put the face crews on the hundred-foot level, where there might be some unexploited highgrade ore in the floors.

Topside, he gathered Rogers and Underwood in an emergency meeting to decide whether to shut down at once or try to eke out enough ore to stay profitable until the lease expired December 1. He advised against it. Labor and operating costs would turn into a hemorrhage that would erode the solid profit they had made over the eleven months they had leased the mine.

"The one thing we might try is surface mining. See whether we can find more of that highgrade that Maude Arbuckle uncovered a few feet down," he said. "But I don't think we will. She drove that shaft on a little shoot that had formed from a feeder. Sheer luck. My best advice is to shut down. We haven't time to drive deeper and I doubt there's anything down there anyway."

"Why do you say that, Hannibal?" asked Rogers. "The mines around the Golden Horseshoe are much deeper and going strong."

"Because we're at the extreme edge of the fault structure," Dash said. "Those mines, the Jumbo, the Combination, are sitting on comb ridges that were formed by the intersection of two giant faults meeting in a *Y*. Those huge faults permitted percolation that deposited all that gold."

Rogers sighed. "I'm persuaded. We've made a tidy sum here. I'll start laying off men. Any hard-rock miner can find work around here and most of 'em would like to move anyway. Nothing to highgrade at the Free Lunch." He laughed sourly.

"The union's been sending us the dregs anyway," Underwood said. "The best men get assigned to the mines they can steal the most from. Our crews these days aren't up to snuff. Let's shut it down. We cleaned it out. The year lease was perfect. Nothing to regret."

"Arbuckle's not going to like it—cleaning out his ore and leaving him with a husk," Rogers said. "I guess you'll be dealing with him, Hannibal."

Dash nodded. It would all look like another conspiracy to Arbuckle, as if somehow Hannibal Dash had known when he negotiated the lease that the mine would yield one year's worth of profit. Dash was going to have to explain it all and he dreaded it. Harry Arbuckle was about to have his income cut off. But it would be no surprise. Those samples Arbuckle knocked out of the mine and took with him should have alerted him. But they didn't. You couldn't credit Harry Arbuckle with rational thought or reasonable expectations.

With that, the lessees began dismantling their possessions. The lease required them to leave their underground works including the tramways, timbering and hoist intact, but there was plenty aboveground to dismantle. They turned the Free Lunch into a hulk, its life and energy gone, its whistles no longer signaling shifts. The bells no longer clanged and the pulleys no longer whirred. The ore cars no longer rattled along tram rails and country rock no longer roared into the slack pile.

Dash intended to wait a week before informing Arbuckle. He wanted to remove everything from the premises before that shyster Reilly showed up with injunctions and threats. But it was not to be. Two days later Harry Arbuckle roared up in his flyer, flanked by his two thugs.

"What's this? What's this?" he bawled after barging into Dash's assay laboratory. "What're you crooks up to?"

Dash stopped packing his beakers into crates. "We're turning it back to you a little early, Harry."

Arbuckle squinted, unbelieving. "Whatdoya mean, early?"

"Lease expires December first. We'll be out sooner. The values dropped—you know that. You took samples out yourself. We don't think it's worth the effort to continue."

Arbuckle roostered himself into outrage. "You're up to something, Dash. This here's a good mine. The last load goes outa here November thirty and you're gonna send me a check for it."

Dash shook his head. "Sorry. The last load went out a day ago and you won't get much for it because there wasn't much gold in it. Look, if you don't believe it, go take some more samples. I'll get a hoist engineer and take you down. Nobody's down there. You can poke around all you want."

"There's no one down there? You have a cave-in?"

Dash sighed. "Harry, we could've started punching down to the next level but we've only three weeks and it didn't make sense even if there's good ore lower down—which I doubt. I just have to say it to you: I don't think there's much ore in there. I think this mine's used up. If you want to, you can drive a shaft down a hundred feet, or three hundred feet and see for yourself. You can find another lessee or run your own company. It's all yours."

"Ya took all the gold and left me nothing, is that it?"

Dash was afraid of that sentiment. "Harry, I don't know if there's more gold and you don't know. I don't think there is."

"You knew that all along. You knew it when you shoved me into the lease. You cleaned me out. I ought to rub you out."

Dash watched the man warily, not knowing what to say.

"Look at it this way, Harry. We're letting you have it two weeks early. That's what you wanted—to get rid of us. You can lease it on the fifteenth if you want."

"Yeah, well, I'm gonna have Reilly on your heels. You sneak one ounce of highgrade outa here, you'll see me in court."

"Harry, you may wish to employ a geologist to examine the mine. You might, ah, wish to slow your spending. If you've put your royalties into good investments you'll be fine."

Arbuckle didn't reply. He plainly was realizing his income was cut off. "Don't you move nothing outa here," he said. "Not one pump, not one motor, not one cable. Let that stuff there be."

Dash thought it wise to stop his packing.

"I'm keeping these two pals of mine around here just to see you don't try nothing," Arbuckle said. "I'm gonna talk to Reilly."

With that, Arbuckle plunged outside. Dash heard the Desert Flyer sputter and cough to life and then clatter away.

He smiled. "You gents mind helping me pack?"

"Like Harry says, nothing leaves here, Dash," said the larger one.

Dash shrugged and returned to wrapping beakers in old newspapers and stuffing them into the crate.

"The mine's probably done for, gents," he said as he worked. "But I suppose Harry's got plenty of cash to pay you. Maybe you could find more ore here. The surface works are ours. That's how the contract reads. But Harry could buy it from us. I think the capital value's around fifty thousand. Then Harry could mine it himself. Hire a good superintendent and let him run it. Reilly'll tell Harry how the contract reads, I imagine, unless he quits. He's a man that likes his pay. You mind putting this crate over there and getting me another?"

Harry's two thugs stared.

"How often does Harry pay you, once a month? You'll

get paid December first?'' Dash asked. He smiled. ''Hope you get it.''

Dash toiled through the afternoon until his lab had been dismantled and crated, all under the eyes of the two goons whose names he didn't know. Then he wandered into the bleak November sunlight and found that Underwood's maintenance crews had largely completed their work. The ore cars had been gathered, ready to ship. The big pumps and giant electric motors had been unbolted from their mounts and dragged to a loading area. Cables lay coiled, ready to move. Mine timbers lay stacked. A mountain of gear, saws, axes, winches, pulleys and drilling steels had been crated or kegged. The two new pneumatic air hammers and their hoses had been lifted out of the mine and were ready to go. Desks and chairs and files were being dollied out of the rough, board and batten offices.

Dash found Rogers in his naked office huddled over the telephone. ''I've sold it all,'' he said. ''Some new leasers, Monnette and Hayes, are going to tackle the Mohawk. They got a fraction and they think maybe they'll strike something. I got better than our book value. They're glad to get it; saves them transportation and time. We've done fine.''

''If we don't have trouble,'' Dash added.

Rogers grunted. ''Wait 'em out. That's all it takes.''

The afternoon waned and Reilly didn't show up threatening lightning bolts and damnation. By six o'clock, with the light fading away, the two goons were acting hungry and unhappy. By dark they quit and maresfooted it back to Goldfield. Dash watched them go and knew that Arbuckle's empire had crumbled.

Rogers returned to his telephone. A few minutes later a half dozen trucks sputtered and coughed their way to the mine, and under the harsh white glare of a night light the teamsters winched up the gear onto the flatbeds and chugged away. Three ox-drawn flatbeds took the heaviest loads, the pumps and motors.

Hannibal Dash watched his mine come apart with mixed

feelings. A sadness had settled over him. This had been his one and only strike—the mine he had rescued for Harry Arbuckle—really for Maude, who deserved it. It was done for unless he had come to wrong conclusions. That might happen. Mining was always a crap game, which was why he enjoyed it so much.

Which reminded him of the letter from Madison snugged into his salt-and-pepper suit coat. "We are expecting you for Christmas," Melanie had written. That was her soft and oblique way of telling him that the year she had given him had come and gone. "Robert and Cecily are excited about your return. I gave them each five dollars to buy something special for your Christmas. Dean Kronhelm has listed your classes for the spring term. I look forward to seeing you, my dear."

The letter had stabbed him like a knife to the heart. Now certainly was the time to go, he thought. A dead mine. A bonanza behind him. His thirst to see a bonanza camp satiated. He could go back and resume life with his dear family. He'd admire Cecily's spring-fresh vibrancy again. He'd throw an arm over Robert's shoulder again. He'd say private things to Melanie with knowing glances of the eye rather than words again. It had all worked out perfectly.

Except that he couldn't go back and he choked upon the very thought. He loved this independent life, the fierce hunt, the mad fevers of a gold camp. Even though his heart and conscience shouted at him to pack up and leave, he knew he couldn't. He had to see what lay within the secret confines of that dark ridge where he and Maude had claims. And after that, every body of ore in the West.

That night, in the empty solace of his bed, he wept.

CHAPTER 60

· ·

From the moment Beth caught the steam ferry in Oakland to take her to the glistening city across the bay, the ache in her chest became unbearable. Little by little the white city catapulting up its hills grew larger, and so did her anguish. She loved San Francisco, its elegance, its rakish glory, its social delights. It had nurtured her, given her husband and children and a spacious frame home on Union Street. The wicked city was in her bones and she couldn't imagine life anywhere else.

If she had known what to expect in Goldfield it was because the vices of her own city had educated her. As the ferry slid into its Market Street pier she knew she had to be careful. She hurried to a hack and gave the driver her address. Horse transportation hung on in San Francisco because no flivver on earth could climb those hills even in reverse gear.

Her long odyssey was almost over but the hardest part lay ahead. The children would scarcely know her after five months. Reggie would be angry and puzzled—until she gave him the money. After that he would be puzzled and sulky. But she was assuming he would be there, not in prison. She reminded herself that she could assume nothing, not even that the house on Union Street was still the family home. It was entirely possible that her entire sacrifice— that's what she called it—had been for naught.

At her own dear home she paid the hack driver with trembling hands. A weariness washed through her, not just from a day and night and morning of travel, but from the anguish she had felt ever since she fled Goldfield. She touched her hair, smoothed her dress. Would they see through her? Would she wear her secret on her face? Had she coarsened?

She stumbled toward the alien door and let herself in with her carefully guarded key. It seemed so quiet. Everything was as it was. Then Mrs. Kennicott burst down the curved stairs, a cry upon her lips.

"It's you, ma'am! My Lord, we thought . . . we thought . . . oh, dear."

"I'm back. I'm sorry I was gone so long."

"But where were you? Where's your luggage? What . . . ?" The housekeeper's bewilderment spilled out of her.

"We'll talk about it later, Mrs. Kennicott. I'm safe. How are—"

"Oh, ma'am, they're fine now. Tommy had a bad spell of diphtheria but Doctor Alston saved him. We had to keep Jimmy and Annette with their grandparents. They're upstairs. I'm afraid . . ."

"They were hurt—by me."

"Oh, ma'am, two babies wanting their mother. Ma'am, there was nothing I could do but wipe away their tears. It was such a time. Your husband, he almost went mad with their weeping. Where oh where did you go?"

A grief beyond enduring filled Beth. "I can't tell you that, Mrs. Kennicott. Please don't ever ask. And what of my—of Mister Ross?"

"Oh, ma'am, he's endured like a saint. I don't know how he bears to live under those accusations. He just says it's a mistake and an audit'll clear him. So many people stopped by to help him past his grief when you—"

"When I left. They thought I deserted him in his moment of need. Is he in . . . trouble?"

Mrs. Kennicott sighed. "You mean charged. I wouldn't know, ma'am. He doesn't say anything to me. I think he is. I think the police . . . they've come here just to see things. They asked where this and that came from. I think he's in awful trouble, ma'am. Mercy, I hope they don't take him away. He'd die."

Beth gathered her courage and walked up the stair to the nursery, wondering what sort of price she had paid for abandoning the children she loved. Mrs. Kennicott followed, chattering about everything imaginable, as if Beth needed to be caught up with all the news instantly. Beth ignored her and opened the door softly upon her sunlit babies who were building castles with wooden blocks. She caught the glint of sunlight off Annette's light hair and noted the solemnity of Jimmy, who resembled her own father and had none of Reggie's nervous energy.

Her babies stared up at her, not really certain who she was. Beth had the awful feeling that if she hugged them she would give them a terrible disease. "Hello, dears," she said.

Neither child responded.

"Remember me? I'm Mama."

"You went away," said Jimmy solemnly.

"I'm back now. Back forever. I'll always be with you."

"All right," he said, and it wrenched her.

Annette just stared uncertainly.

"It'll take awhile," whispered Mrs. Kennicott behind her. "They're just babies, you know."

Beth kneeled before Jimmy and tried to hug him but he squirmed away. Annette let Beth draw her tight. It felt so good to hold that dear girl. Annette smiled but speechlessly.

"I'll never go away again," Beth whispered. "I'll be here when you need me." She found herself weeping.

"Mrs. Kennicott, I'll be in my room. Please ring Reg— Mister Ross."

"Certainly, ma'am."

She washed herself restlessly, found a clean skirt and blouse, and changed. But it didn't make her any cleaner.

He walked into the bedroom around noon and stared at her. He looked even more gaunt than ever. He had always had a nervous tic, something restless that burned away his flesh and left him a thin, almost frail blond man who seemed to radiate energy. He seemed much more boyish than she had remembered him, a youth in a man's body. She had never seen that in him before.

"I'm back, Reggie," she said.

"I hardly know what to say," he snapped. "Leaving me.

Deserting me when, when, things were bad. I don't even know whether we can be happy. Your note said you'd return soon. This isn't soon. Why did you go? What sort of callousness took you away? Afraid I'd blacken your nice reputation?''

His bitterness poured out. She had expected it but that didn't make it any less painful. ''Are you still in trouble?'' she asked wearily.

''What do you think? The noose tightens. I've been suspended as chief of the trust division pending the results of an investigation. The police have questioned me. No one can prove anything. I'm not in jail yet. It's a mess I can barely stand. If it weren't for those children you abandoned—I'd . . .'' Suddenly the anguish seeped away and she saw a beaten, frightened man. He looked crushed. His body had aged.

''Reggie, Reggie,'' she said softly. ''Do you trust me so little?''

He glared bitterly at her. ''You pushed me into this. Always wanting this and that. The holidays. The servants. The parties.''

''I know,'' she said. ''I went away so I could help you.'' She pulled the bills from the pocket where she had tucked them. It frightened her to have so much money.

''Here,'' she said. She handed him the bills. He studied them amazed, flipping the thousand-dollar bills and then the one hundreds. He could never know what each bill represented. He could never know that each thousand-dollar bill meant degrading herself with a hundred men.

''Will that help?'' she asked softly.

''My God, Beth. Where did you get them?''

''I can't tell you.'' She realized she hadn't given enough thought to an explanation.

''You stole them!''

She shook her head. ''Let's say I gambled and won, Reggie.''

''I must know. I demand to know.''

''You could thank me, Reggie.''

He looked ashamed. "I'm sorry, Beth. I'm sorry. This is such a shock. I don't know . . . I have to sort this out."

"Will the big bills give you trouble? I mean, making the accounts come out?"

He shook his head. "No. I can buy certain types of securities—coupon bearer bonds—and put them in the trust portfolio. And tell the auditors I found the missing assets. Now, where were you, Beth? I must know. If this is illegal we'll be in worse trouble."

"It's not illegal," she whispered. "I can't tell you any more. It'll just have to be that way. Don't ever ask."

"I must know! You can't just leave me for five months and return with a fortune."

"Reggie . . . look." She held up her bare left hand.

"The ring. I don't know how you converted a half-carat ring into five thousand dollars."

She felt tears welling. She couldn't endure this.

He saw her anguish. "I'm sorry, Beth. We'll straighten this out later. Whatever you did, you did for me. For the children. Some day you'll tell me. Gambling isn't the whole story. You were gone too long. I was bitter. I thought you'd simply abandoned me. Everyone else did too. It's going to be hard for you, what people are thinking. There was a lot of nasty gossip when you left."

On and on he went, his nervous energy fusing and burning him.

"Just take it and get your accounts right!" she cried.

"All right. I can do it this afternoon. I'll need to go to some securities brokers where I'm not known. In Oakland, I guess." He clenched the big bills nervously. "You've gotten us out of a jam," he said. "I'll see you about six-thirty."

That was as close as he came to gratitude. He wheeled away, leaving her in her silent sun-drenched bedroom. She collapsed on the bed too distraught to think. It hadn't gone well. He hadn't an inkling what she had done for him. He thought it had been the spin of a wheel or turn of a card. No wonder he wasn't grateful. It was all aces and kings and chance that brought this reprieve to him. She knew that and yet everything within her cried out for thanks.

Her mood lightened after a bit. She rubbed away her tears. Reggie would be cleared. He would stop pressuring her for answers. Her children would be her own again when she spent time with them. In an hour or so Tommy would return from school and she would begin to win him back. She and Reggie could resume the old life, be with friends. More carefully, of course. But she had won. She had given her family a gift beyond their imaginings. She had not been discovered and never would. She had traveled to hell and returned safe. It was going to be all right after a while even if she didn't care for Reggie very much. He wasn't half the man that Olympus was.

CHAPTER 61

....

B ig Sam looked dashing in his Dracula costume, Delia thought. He was limping around inside of a giant black cape fastened at the neck by a woven gold clasp. A black silk stovepipe hat perched precariously on his head. He absolutely refused to wear a mask, though.

Her Lady Godiva costume had been a trial because no one in Goldfield had any notion of how an eleventh-century countess dressed herself. Her deft seamstress had whipped up a lush winecolored velvet dirndl and a puffy gold lamé blouse and a black bodice that Delia had laced over her curvy bosom. To this she added a gaudy tiara of paste and rhinestones. And on a little stick she carried a tiny black mask that barely covered her eyes.

The appointed hour of seven came and went without a soul appearing at the door. All was ready. Big Sam had employed half a dozen lackeys and had contracted with the Palm Grill to cater the event. The dance hall had been festively decorated with greens imported from distant peaks.

A trestle table groaned under its load of viands: meats of every sort, vegetables, pastries, fruits, salads. Another lengthy linen-covered table served as a bar, where row upon row of bottles, and every exotic liquor, might be found. Three mixologists imported from the Northern Saloon stood ready in their white aprons to dispense refreshments.

The string orchestra, a dozen Gypsies or something, squeaked and sawed, tuning up their fiddles.

The parquet floor gleamed beneath the crystal chandelier.

"Oh, Sam, no one's coming," she cried. "We're being snubbed." They had invited the entire membership of the Montezuma Club, a total of a hundred fifty-three, and their escorts as well. "They despise us!"

Sam laughed. "That's more fun than having them all show up. I think that would take the cake. That'd make every paper in the West, I reckon."

"Well, there's always tomorrow," she said, resignation filling her. Tomorrow would be the open house at the Joneses' and all of Goldfield was invited.

But then the guests began arriving. Outside, a bedlam of carriages, chugging automobiles, and whickering horses signaled that Goldfield's elite would come, probably gawk, and no doubt return home with a lot of wicked gossip about the Gold Diggers Ball. But Delia didn't mind that. She liked Sam and that was all that mattered. She also tried to adopt his point of view: If people snubbed the Joneses, that made life all the more amusing.

But they traipsed in, some of them sporting gaudy costumes, and others merely in formal gowns and suits, bearing small masks. The orchestra struck up a waltz. Serving girls in black dresses and little white aprons circulated, bearing silver trays of hors d'oeuvres. For all her bravery, Delia was gladdened that the party had started. Sam tugged her from one couple to another, introducing them to her.

"This here's Senator George Nixon, and behind him George Wingfield and May," he said, scarcely giving her time to welcome her guests. "And over yonder, that's Al Myers, and come on over and meet L. L. Patrick and Harry

Ramsey, and that looks like Hubbard and Winslow over there . . ."

She knew a few of the names. They had come. And more still flowed through the door. They dizzied her. These people owned and ran the gold mines of Goldfield: the Combination 1, 2, and 3; the Hazel Queen, the Golconda, Red Boy, Wonder, Mammoth, Goldstone, and Victor; the Sandstorm, Rustler, Side Line, O.K. Fraction, Clermont, Lucky Boy, Slim Jim Fraction, Grizzly Bear; the Red Top, and the Florence Group; the January, February, Mohawk, and the great Jumbo, which had yielded a million dollars of ore in four months.

On and on they came, men whose names had become legend in Goldfield, along with their ladies: Charles Taylor, Frank Ish, Dick Colburn, George McClelland, Con Crook, and Tom Lockhart. Why, there were fifty million dollars at her dance. Even some from Tonopah had come. She met Tasker Oddie, the silver king, and Patrick McCarran, a lawyer from there.

She met them all and waltzed with many. She introduced herself to wives, mistresses, and a few she suspected were former madams. Women were still in short supply in raw Goldfield and their dance cards filled instantly. Delia scarcely got the chance to meet them before some dandy whisked them off to the dance floor for a turkey trot or a polka.

She met the saloon man Tex Rickard, and Shanghai Larry Sullivan, the very one that Goldfield's women gossiped about. She met George Graham Rice, a wildcatter who made Sam look like a choirboy. So the sports and demimonde of Goldfield were showing up too, whether or not they had been invited. It amused her. Sam wouldn't have counted it a success without a few tarts and crooks for leavening.

The orchestra paused, letting people refresh at the punchbowl, and started up again, this time with Christmas airs. She accepted a dance with George Nixon, scarcely imagining that she, Delia Biddle Jones, would whirl through a polonaise with a United States senator.

"It's a beautiful party, Mrs. Jones," said her partner. "A coming of age for Goldfield. And it's only the beginning."

She wondered whether he referred to Goldfield or her parties. He and that former tinhorn George Wingfield seemed to have a pocket full of money and they were buying up some of the mines. She eyed Mrs. Wingfield who was dancing with someone or other and looking unhappy. It was whispered that May Wingfield lived in common law sin with Wingfield. Delia studied her sharply, wondering if such things showed in a woman. She decided they did. May Wingfield looked as if she had seen too much of life.

She danced with Wingfield, the pale, bug-eyed gambler who was said to be the senator's front man. Something cold exuded from him, as if even a dance was a calculation.

"I grubstaked your husband," he said as they turned around the dance floor to a two-step.

"You did? I never heard of it."

"He showed up at the Tonopah Club half starved and I donated five silver dollars. That was the beginning of Samuel Jones. Look at him now."

"I'm sure Sam is very grateful," she said, feeling his cold hand upon hers.

"We'll see," he replied as the polka faded away.

That young attorney from Tonopah, Patrick McCarran, caught her up and steered her into the crowded floor. She liked him intuitively. He smiled and led her nimbly through a turkey trot, which was the rage.

"Mrs. Jones, I came all the way from Tonopah just because I heard you would be Lady Godiva. Your beauty's as legendary as her ride on the white steed," he said.

"Oh, Mr. McCarran, you're naughty. I didn't say I'd do the ride; I just said I'd play her. I looked it up. She was a countess, the wife of Earl Leofric of Mercia. She told him she would ride naked through Coventry if he lowered taxes on those poor people. She did, and he did. But of course no one peeked, except one. I don't suppose you'd be that one, now, would you?''

"Mrs. Jones, how could anyone help it? A beauty like you?"

He laughed and she laughed too. He was an adorable man and a natural politician. When the dance ended he thanked her and headed for the bar.

She spotted that awful Harry Arbuckle mounding up a plate of pastries, along with a blond slut whose skirt was slit up to her hip, or almost. That was too much.

She slid over to Sam, who was enjoying his Crab Orchard bourbon and a Hilt's Best cigar with some of his cronies. "Throw them out," she whispered.

"Aw, Delia, what's a party without Harry Arbuckle and a whore? As long as you're not gonna ride naked on a white horse, she'll have to do."

She glared at him while he guffawed. There were times when Sam got on her nerves. This wasn't the respectable social life she dreamed of. How could she ever be the queen of Goldfield married to a man like that? Maybe this wasn't the California Social Register but it didn't have to be the Goldfield Tenderloin, either.

No one seemed to mind. A vast democracy permeated the place. Men of means gathered in knots, talking shares and ore values. The sports collected separately, argued boxing and horses and gawked at the costumes. She introduced herself to people whose names she couldn't remember, fancying that she had natural abilities as a hostess.

At midnight Count Dracula hushed the fiddlers and subdued the increasingly roisterous crowd.

"The vampire will have a word," he yelled.

"Go suck blood," retorted a young sport.

"Doin' that all my life, feller. Now, Mrs. Jones and me, we sort of figured we should add a little entertainment to all this chowing and waltzing. We'll call this little item, Manna from Heaven, since that's about what it is. Now I want you all to gaze skyward, not at that thousand-dollar cut-glass chandelier with the electric lights, but at them little blue boxes up there, the ones with the ropes attached.''

He waited a moment. ''There ain't a soul in here with an ounce of greed,'' he said. ''We're all a respectable lot and rich enough to preserve our dignity. I can't even bend over, that's the kind of dignity I got. Now, since we're none of us greedy, I imagine all you folks'll go right on dancing, right on the money, and just ignore what's happening because it ain't very couth. Nice folks like us don't grovel around grubbing up money.'' He waited for the chuckles. ''All right, are you ready?''

He paused, deliciously, and then pulled two velvet cords. They tripped the latches and green bills showered and fluttered to the floor, a blizzard of dollars. Men shouted. Women yipped. Gentlemen hopped and snatched. Women crawled up backs to grab. Smart fellows got down on their knees and grubbed. Two ladies squatted and clawed.

''A five!'' some lady bawled. ''Five dollars!''

Delia watched, amused, as the gentle veneer that had dignified so many in that ballroom vanished and men and women did a lunatic dance, snatching bills. She glanced at Sam, who smiled benignly, his eyes verifying something he had always known about the mortals he had traded with all his days. The boxes contained five hundred ones and a sprinkling of fives and tens. He would reload them and do it again tomorrow night. He winked at her and she winked back.

Harry Arbuckle got one and ostentatiously touched a lucifer to it and lit a cigar. An odd performance for a man rumored to be in bad shape, she thought. His slut squealed and yanked the burning bill from him.

Around Delia crazed guests shoved and elbowed and kicked shins, along with the servants. A handful stood by and smiled, among them Senator Nixon and that mine leaser Hannibal Dash, who was always a gentleman. But it was Count Dracula who enjoyed it the most. She spotted the delight in Sam's face and knew what he was thinking. This was the triumph of the wildcatter and the gold digger at their Gold Diggers Ball.

CHAPTER 62

· ·

Hannibal Dash tried to put off Judgment Day again. "Dear Melanie," he wrote, using a newfangled fountain pen. "The press of business keeps me from returning to Madison for Christmas. I would like instead to invite you to come here. Goldfield is a booming, attractive city. I am able to settle you and Robert and Cecily in a spacious home with all the amenities. I have a rich new claim that requires location work. Now that our Free Lunch lease has expired I will begin the new project. I'm expecting you. My love to each of you, Hannibal."

He enclosed another cashier's check and mailed it with a heavy heart. He could not return to the stuffy life in academia. Not after this wild, free time and his first great triumph. He knew what the result of this letter would be and it saddened him. She was rooted as deep as those old oaks in Madison and he could not chop down the tree.

That done, he set to work. In the space of a day he outfitted himself with five burros and packs. Then he loaded up chow, water cask, canteen, a bag of barley, a new wall tent, kerosene for the lantern, his field assaying equipment, a field office, two shovels, a pick, an axe, a crowbar, a maul, and sundry other items including a revolver. He scarcely knew how to use it but the desert harbored two-legged rats of the sort Maude had driven off a few weeks earlier.

He set off before dawn, not wanting to be noticed or followed, and headed west over a route that Maude had showed him around the foot of Montezuma Peak, past a malign salt marsh, heading for the brooding ridge where they had measured and staked the four claims weeks earlier; two for her, and two for him. He wasn't an experienced desert traveler but she had showed him what she knew and his numerous field trips as a geologist helped. In spite of December frost, he slept warm in a good bedroll at a water hole at the foot of a long hogback halfway there.

He found her at the ridge late the second afternoon. Or rather, as he led his reluctant burros up the last slope she materialized from behind some cedar brush, her little carbine in hand. She wore her tattered bib overalls, a flannel shirt, a sweater over that, a pair of ratty gloves, and a straw hat anchored to her graying hair with a faded red bandana.

"Maude, you look prettier every day you spend in the desert," he said.

She cackled. "You can try that stuff on me later. We got a lot to do."

Indeed they did. They had to erect six cairns around each claim, plus a seventh at each discovery site. Later they were going to have to excavate a ten-foot-deep shaft into the pay rock of each. Neither of his former partners, Rogers or Underwood, could help this time. They had subleased a corner of the Mohawk and were driving a new shaft back in Goldfield.

He and Maude toted rock until the early December darkness overwhelmed them and then she led him and his burros, along with Mother Dear, down to the permanent camp at the rincon. By the time the night chill had lowered over the silent wild, he had erected his new tent beside her ragged one, watered all the burros, put them out on pickets where the dried grass rose thick, and organized his gear.

She had sonofabitch stew for him when he showed up at her cheerful fire; at least that's what she called it. He gathered it could be anything. Her version included the beef he had carted out, pinto beans and chili peppers, which he spooned into his hungry body, barely warmed by the cedar-fed fire.

"There's not much rock up there," she said. "And it's not broke up, either. It's a back-breaker just to haul a single piece of rock a hundred yards to one of those piles. Sometimes I use a tarp and just drag it. You're in for it.

Locating four claims is enough to turn a city man back into a bookkeeper.''

"I'm used to outdoor work. Have you had any trouble?''

"Two-legged varmints? If I had I would of told ya straight off. I don't sniff a mortal around here closer than twenty miles as the crow flies. I dowsed for water and didn't get a twitch of the rod, so this is it. Two miles up to the claims, two miles back, every day for a month.''

He told her about the demise of the Free Lunch and Harry's dark suspicions that it was all somehow a plot. "It's down to ten-dollar ore, Maude. The good ore ran out when the lease did. I don't think there's anything deeper. We decided not to try.''

"I know how Harry thinks. You had it all figured. Gut the mine and leave it. It was a plot to rook him. I can read his mind. It'll never occur to him that the mine's plumb out of pay rock," she said. "Is he broke yet?''

"I can't say. He owns the Texas Saloon, I think. It could be enough.''

"The day Harry makes a profit from a business, that's the day Harry croaks," Maude said. "That shyster of his'll snitch it, you just watch. He'll be back to mooching drinks again before you know it.''

They heard the bark of a coyote and an answering one in the thick darkness, and paused to listen.

"Maude, I think you should divorce Harry. Get it over with. He's dangerous. He'll maneuver to get a piece of this.''

"Yes, you're right. I'll get around to it.''

"Maude—he sent a man after you. He wanted your ledge. That man might even have killed you. Don't wait.''

"Well, that's Harry for you. Hannibal, you've got to understand Harry. He's sort of pathetic. He can't think like other people. He's so crooked and twisty he thinks everyone else is, too. He's not even in the real world much.''

"All the more reason, Maude.''

"Well, I will some day. It's not that I like him, mind,

it's that he's so pathetic. Now just don't press me. I'll do it when I'm good and ready.''

Dash contemplated the flames, trying to fathom that. She didn't seem to grasp the danger she put herself in, coddling that old fool. ''You like him, I guess,'' he said.

''Like him! The day I married him I did, but the second day it was all over. It's just that he sort of wore down into something I understand, like a river cobble.''

''Why, then?''

''Just leave me be, Dash.''

They toiled hard for eight days, loosening rock, dragging it to the cairns with a tarp, and erecting the markers that would tell the world that the gold-bearing ridge had been claimed and legally located. Mostly they said nothing, laboring comfortably through the short winter days and staring amiably into the little juniperwood fire each night. He admired her strength; she did more than he and had more energy.

A storm blew in as Christmas approached. The cold air lowered and an icy wind whipped the pay ridge. They quit early, too numb to continue, and fled to the rincon. That night snow whirled in, heaping swiftly around their little camp against the wall of a great cliff. Dash shivered in his bedroll, unable to sleep, while the tent snapped and flapped. His feet turned into icebergs and the feared he was courting a sore throat and catarrh.

''Dash,'' she said outside his tent in the middle of the night. He crawled out of his blankets and found her outside, barely visible.

''Are you cold? You city fellers don't know much about staying comfortable.''

''I'm so miserable I don't know how I'll make it to dawn.''

''You fetch your bedroll and that kerosene lantern and move in. My outfit's plenty warm.''

''Warm?'' He wondered how it could be warm.

He put a match to the wick of his kerosene lamp, collected his bedroll, poked his bare feet into unlaced boots, and stumbled through a drift while she led the way. He pushed open the flap and discovered that Maude had a four-footed visitor. Dash pushed Mother Dear aside and settled into his bedroll. He wondered if Mother Dear were going to step on him in the night—or worse.

"Don't take notions, Dash," she said.

"I have none, Maude."

"I don't like that love stuff. Harry hasn't been in my bed for ten years. I keep a knitting needle handy just in case he tries. Once I thought I'd enjoy it; that's what a girl thinks. But I never did. Maybe it was just Harry, but I'm too old even to think about it now. If you don't know what you've missed, then I guess you aren't missing a darned thing . . . Well, you've stopped shivering. This is nice. Your teeth were knocking so bad I thought you were a castanet. I got Mother Dear in here and that always does the trick."

"I'll leave the lamp on, Maude. It takes the chill out."

"Mother Dear's enough. You'll see. She puts a little frost on the canvas with all her breathing."

"It does feel warmer, Maude. I was so desperate I was about to get up and try to build a bonfire out there."

"You'll warm up. I got the walls anchored down with rocks, too. There's no wind sliding in. But it's mostly Mother Dear. She throws heat like a blast furnace," Maude said. "I've gotten through cold like this plenty of times and this rincon's perfect. Tomorrow I'll rig up a half-shelter. I'll build us a hot little fire right in the corner of the cliff. The rock just throws the heat at you in an open-sided shelter. You wait and see. It's not up to an injun lodge for heat but white men aren't entirely dumb. We'll lay off a day, see to the burros, and maybe it'll blow over."

He felt her presence in the cramped tent, and knew she wasn't sleeping either.

"How come you're out here, Hannibal," she asked. "Why aren't you back in Goldfield sinking your profits into a good mine or two and sitting on your butt?"

"I like it here. It might be a bonanza. We'll have to dig and see."

"Then what, Hannibal?"

"Well, I guess we'll lease it or run it."

"No, I don't mean that. You're married, aren't you?"

"Why do you ask?"

"I just figured it. You look married. If I'm being too nosey just shut me up."

He thought awhile. "I'm married," he said. "I've a wife in Wisconsin and two children in high school. They want me to return. I miss them."

"You ditched them."

"No, not really," he replied defensively. "I asked them to come out here. Melanie—that's her—just wouldn't. They like it there. I send them money and . . ."

She laughed. "You ditched 'em. This is more fun. Me, I'm just going to keep on if this don't work out. I fancy a little cottage is all but I don't seem to get one. A little cottage in Goldfield and a little gold to run it. If this is a bust I'll just start again. There's a lot of country to poke around in. No one's hardly looked at Arizona, and maybe I'll go on down to Mexico. Lots of silver and gold down there. The Esperanza, that's the biggest gold mine that ever was. I think I'll just find one of those for myself. I got the eye and I can dowse."

He laughed. "Dowsing. If you think you can find minerals by holding a stick—"

"That's how I found this ledge!"

He subsided. "Well, probably it was something else at the edge of your mind. Soon we'll find minerals with well-drilling, bringing up samples. That's what gasoline engines can do."

"You're hooked on mining, Hannibal. Don't tell me you aren't. You ditched 'em in Wisconsin. The pair of us jokers, we might be married, but not very much, and not to each other."

Her candor offended him. "Maude, I've never stopped caring about Melanie and—"

She laughed. "I know," she said. "I sort of like to have that darned Harry around just to pick on. You and me are partners in crime, Hannibal. Next thing you know, we'll be down in Durango or Chihuahua or some place chopping rock out of hillsides. I'd hate to be married to me—or you.''

PART III

. . . .

The Pearly Gates

And the twelve gates were twelve pearls:
every several gate was of one pearl: and the
street of the city was pure gold, as it were
transparent glass.

—Revelation, 21:21

Children are innocent and love justice, while
most adults are wicked and prefer mercy.

—Gilbert K. Chesterton

There is an evil which I have seen under the
sun, and it lies heavy upon men: a man to
whom God gives wealth, possessions, and
honor, so that he lacks nothing of all that he
desires, yet God does not give him power to
enjoy them . . .

—Ecclesiastes 6:1

CHAPTER 63
. . . .

Olympus Prinz spent a week at Brown and Company on Mission Street, the San Francisco jobber that supplied printing equipment to newspapers throughout the West. It took him only half a day to master the motordriven Hoe rotary printing press and folder that would permit him to run his weekly editions in a few minutes. The making of stereotype plates that could be wrapped around the printing drum was utterly new to him. The rest of his time had been spent mastering the Linotype. He sat for hours at the great, clattering monster, setting and justifying lines to cast into lead slugs that rested in galley trays, while the beast swiftly sorted out each letter and returned it to its casebox. Since he would be far from help he had to learn how to service the beasts as well, wipe away the ink, and make the endless adjustments that would ensure a cleanly printed page.

He stayed with his older sister, Annemarie Thiessen, and her husband Alex, who lived on Montgomery Street within sight of Coit Tower. Alex was an importer of wicker furniture, mahogany and teak, and they lived comfortably in a tall frame house with splendid views of the bay from its upper windows.

"You ought to stay for the holidays," she told Prinz. "You hardly know your nephews, and besides, what does Goldfield have to offer?"

"At the moment, not a lot," he said. His new building being erected on the site of the wrecked one wouldn't be ready until early 1906. And it would take two weeks before the press, Linotype, and a half a boxcar of equipment would arrive at the new office of the *Observer*.

He didn't much like San Francisco. After he had wrested a master's degree in philosophy from Stanford he had sickened of academic life and become a cub reporter for the

San Francisco Chronicle, and then a journeyman reporter. In his three years there he could scarcely remember a day when he felt warm. But the city itself troubled him. Beneath its glittering beauty, its lusty materialism and its voluptuary appetites, lay a hollowness and desperation he had never experienced in sedate Palo Alto.

It had occurred to him then that the gaudy white city rose not only on the western rim of the nation, but the western rim of Western Civilization as well. The great western migration, in which hundreds of thousands of Yanks had pulled up stakes and headed west to fulfill their dreams, stopped abruptly there on the shore of the mysterious Pacific. The city brimmed with people who had run out of West to flee to and were forced to confront their failures—or escape into booze or turn themselves into hop fiends. His reporting had taken him everywhere, and everywhere he saw mortals without roots, wallowing in their darkness, devoid of spiritual strengths, hating virtue most of all, as if decency were to blame for all their ills. He had never seen so much human wreckage nor so much secret despair in a single city.

Once or twice he had reported stories from the Barbary Coast, some of the cruelest waterfront turf in the world, where a man might be flattened by a doctored drink and find himself a shanghaied slave on a whaler, his fate no longer his own and his life reduced to nothing. After three years his aversion to the hollow city had overwhelmed him and he scraped together his ancient printing equipment and chose Goldfield as an experiment.

"You must come with us to the Gilberts' ball on New Year's Eve," Annemarie insisted. "I can arrange it. They're always wanting bachelors anyway."

"But I haven't a tuxedo—"

"This is Frisco, dear. Those can be rented."

Thus Olympus, in rented plumage, found himself being drawn up Nob Hill by a laboring pair of trotters and deposited with his sister and brother-in-law at a gracious portico of an alabaster mansion. Tomorrow, thank God, he would head for Goldfield.

There, amidst the quiet splendor, he met the gowned and bejeweled company and his grand dame hostess Nina Gilbert, who had inherited shipping and coffee fortunes. And there, while the string orchestra played a waltz, Mrs. Gilbert introduced him to Mr. and Mrs. Reginald Fairchild-Ross, he a nervous, energetic blond man of the sort who might be seen in a straw boater and white blazer, and she . . .

His heart failed him. She stared, ashen, on the ragged edge of collapse. He saw a plain gold ring on her finger.

"It is a pleasure to meet you, Mrs. Fairchild-Ross, Beth. And you sir," he croaked, wondering if he was babbling.

"Mister Prinz . . ." she whispered.

"Well, I'll let you young people get acquainted," said their hostess, abandoning him.

"Prinz, may I get you a drink?" asked the husband. "Say, are you all right, fellow?"

"Yes, yes, I'm fine," he said.

"Well, I'll get you a sarsaparilla," said the husband.

Olympus could not think of a thing to say. He stared helplessly at her while she shivered. Then she seemed to recover, perhaps because her husband had left them.

"Mrs. Fairchild-Ross, if your card isn't filled I'd like the Old and New Year Dance," he babbled.

She nodded numbly and handed him her dance card and her little pencil. He wrote his name there, reserving the dance that would ring in the new year.

"Excuse me," she said and whirled away. He watched her flee toward the bannistered stair that would take her to the upper reaches of the house, a vision of slim loveliness, floating in her ball gown.

She vanished somewhere up there. He stood shaken, so torn with love that he couldn't think while the orchestra spun sweet melodies.

The husband returned. "There you are, Prinz. Where did Beth go?"

"She excused herself, sir."

"Well, she'll be back. What do you do, Prinz?"

"I—nothing at the moment," he said. He would not say Goldfield.

The man laughed. "I wish I could do nothing. I'd take a boat to Tahiti."

They talked awhile more and then Ross abandoned him for more entertaining company. The man had made conversation as if it were a duty while all the while his gaze darted toward friends, flicking from one to another. Olympus hadn't liked him much but couldn't say why. He was just the sort that women adored, intelligent and witty, but probably not schooled beyond the sort of mental shoe polish that would let him shine in all seasons.

Olympus wandered in a daze while the orchestra played on. The formal waltzes and mazurkas had come first but as the evening progressed the music did too, and the parquet floor was filled with two-steppers and turkey trotters. He saw no sign of Beth, Daisy, Beth, and felt a certain relief. It had been too much for both of them. But he ached to see her, ached to open one door after another throughout this altar to the gods of money, until he found her. He yearned to know *why*.

Eleven came and went with no sign of her and at eleven forty-five he knew he wouldn't ever see her again. His night had turned bleak and he regretted coming. He should have gone to Goldfield. He spotted Annemarie and Alex chatting with friends and having a grand time.

Then Beth materialized, pale and solemn before him just as the orchestra plunged into the New Year's Dance. His heart raced once again. Neither could speak.

"Mrs. Fairchild-Ross," he said. He took her into the whirl and found her light and supple and feathery in his hands, her movements matching his perfectly as if some primordial knowledge connected them. He yearned to say something, anything, but knew he couldn't. The question that lay in his mind languished there because he could never ask it. She eyed him now and then, assessing him solemnly, coming to some sort of conclusion. The strings sounded sweet and the crowd's excitement rose as the old year ticked away.

But he was barely aware of that. She squeezed his hand and he squeezed back. She squeezed again, conveying something as primal and sweet as love, and he squeezed her fingers tightly, replying with fervor. Her hands found his arms and he felt gentle pressure there. Hesitantly he slid a hand to her back and pressed her to him. She smiled.

Then suddenly the new year arrived and the band stopped. She hugged him fiercely, her hands clutching him tight and then releasing him just as swiftly. They clutched again, the moment swallowed by the hilarity around them, and then it passed. She glanced warmly into his eyes, smiled, and thanked him. He let go, and it was like letting go of life. He watched her drift back to her husband and join two other young couples there.

That was all. She was everything he had ever suspected when he knew her as Daisy, and more. She was a dream he would forever dream. On his deathbed he would remember only Beth.

He eased toward Annemarie.

"You danced with Beth Fairchild," she said, in a tone that suggested disapproval.

"She's a lovely woman, Annemarie. Is she a friend of yours?"

"Friend! I won't have anything to do with her. What she did she'll never live down."

Olympus gaped. Beth Fairchild-Ross's secret wasn't so secret after all. "Well, yes, but—" he said but she cut him off.

"Leaving Reggie just when he was in trouble, falsely accused of embezzlement and about to be arrested. How could she? He runs the trust department at the bank. Did she stay with the poor man and support him during his ordeal? Stay with his children? No, she vanished, God knows where, and the moment his accounts were cleared and they found the error, she returned. Oh, it makes me burn."

"I see," said Olympus.

CHAPTER 64

∙∙∙∙∙∙∙∙∙∙∙∙∙∙∙∙∙∙∙∙∙∙

The whole human race disgusted Harry Arbuckle. They had all quit him. He sat in his accustomed place in the Texas Saloon listening to the quiet. Usually about now Freddy Glidden, the tonsorial artist, came in to shave him. It had been a great morning ritual. Arbuckle got himself a shave while enjoying his morning eye opener and listening to the Goldfield gossip from his pals. He always tipped Freddy five dollars just to show the world that Harry Arbuckle was a generous man. Five clams for a ten-cent shave. But he hadn't seen Freddy in three days and his jowls were peppered with stubble. The bum should shave him the rest of his life for what he got outa old Harry.

But that's how it was. He'd bought so many beers for all of Goldfield they should pay him a pension for life. Instead, they quit him. Those gorillas he paid to keep order around the joint—why, first time he couldn't pay them they ditched him just like that. Adios. They never thanked him for all the beers and whiskey and schnapps he'd bought them, or the bowlers and suits and ties, or the free meals he bought the whole crowd every noon and evening, or the stuff he gave them, stickpin headlights, solitaire rings, all that. Why, they had only to ask and old Harry got them anything they wanted.

Gone. The bums. The whole human race. The only fellow in the dump was Max Faust, the barkeep. He said he'd stick as long as he could pay himself out of the drinks. But Faust, he was gonna take off any moment, too. There hadn't been six patrons wander into the Texas the last two weeks. Bums, the whole lot of 'em.

"I suppose you're quitting me too," Arbuckle said.

"You pay me and I'll stick."

` "I'm temporarily overdrawn. Lots more soon. I'll make it worth your while."

"Yeah, well, it better be soon, Harry."

Bums. They came and told him he was overdrawn, just like that, a week or two after the last dinky check came in from those crooked leasers. Pay up, they said, or we'll get a lien on this place.

Arbuckle had never heard of a lien but Turner Reilly got it all squared away. Harry hocked his headlight diamond and his pinky ring and that took care of it for the moment. After that it just got worse. His girlfriend Mabel walked out on him. She took on airs after he said he couldn't give her a little folding money. She always wanted greenbacks so she could indulge her little habit over at Hop Fiends Gulch. Just the day before she was telling old Harry she loved him forever and sparking him until he was cross-eyed. She was worse than Ethel and Billie combined. They'd all just used him. They knew old Harry was a generous man and they took advantage. Like the whole human race, buncha bums.

Arbuckle sipped gin and bitters and sulked in his chair. Those leasers, Dash and all, had done him in. They'd told him the Free Lunch was played out so they could buy it cheap. They'd connived it. That Dash, the geologist, he had them mine the bum stuff and keep back the good so they could steal the mine. All them assay reports, they didn't mean nothing. That was just part of the scheme. A man'd have to be a chump not to see that.

He had put Turner Reilly to work finding new leasers and for a few weeks it looked pretty good. Reilly herded one outfit after another out there and let 'em look it over, take samples, all that. But not a one of 'em wanted to lease the mine. Arbuckle knew exactly what was happening. It had all been planned that way just to make Harry think the mine was dead.

That mine was loaded with gold but they had figured out a way to drive old Harry out of it. Even Reilly was in on it. Harry paid the man five grand a month retainer and all he ever got was a lot of double-talk. That day when Reilly walked in with an offer to buy the Free Lunch for a lousy thousand dollars, Arbuckle knew right then and there that Reilly was two-timing him. A thousand dollars! Reilly said that it came from the outfit next door, the May Queen, and they just wanted it for the shaft. They could get at their ore easier.

That reminded Arbuckle that Dash wouldn't cross the boundary line to go after that highgrade ore. The thought had heartened Harry for a while. He could get a bunch of stiffs together and quietly pull out the highgrade. The chumps wouldn't know the difference. But he couldn't find any stiffs even though he'd put word out.

Arbuckle nursed all these hurts along with a gin, as he had for several weeks. Another bad morning drifted by. Outside that door Goldfield boomed and bustled. Fifteen thousand people, they were saying. Richer than Midas. But not a soul dropped in to lift a mug with old Harry. Then the doors did swing open and Turner P. Reilly, Esq., stepped in looking as dapper as ever.

"I knew you'd be here, Harry," he said, pulling off white gloves and unwinding a scarf. "We've a little business to do."

Business these days usually meant being gouged by someone or other. Just last week Harry had sold his Desert Flyer at forty cents on the dollar to pay for electricity, firewood, water, and all that stuff.

"It's my retainer, Harry," Reilly said. "You're a month overdue. You'll want to pay for January, too. I've made a little arrangement here. You might just look at these."

"Tell me. I don't feel like reading."

"Well, Harry, it's a deed I've drawn up as a discharge of indebtedness and payment for next month. Now, I've had the Texas Saloon appraised. Its fair market value is twelve thousand. Nice location, two-story building. Really quite valuable. That makes it a wash, doesn't it? Twelve thousand in real estate for my ten thousand retainer through January thirty-first, plus expenses."

"What? You gonna take this away?"

"Now, Harry, you owe it. We're half through January."

Harry's bile rose. "What did you ever do for me? Did you sue Dash like I asked? No. You just twiddled your thumbs. You shoulda won me ten lawsuits by now."

Turner Reilly paused solemnly, his steady gaze upon Harry. "Harry, I was set to follow your detailed instructions but when I interviewed Hannibal Dash, I learned a few things you'd neglected to tell me."

"Like what?"

"Dash had a valid, signed and witnessed option to buy the Free Lunch. He said he would exercise it immediately if we filed. Of course I altered my strategy. We certainly didn't want him to take it away, did we?"

"That's all a pack of lies. I never signed a thing. Maybe I was drunk."

Turner P. Reilly, Esq., gazed kindly. "Whatever you say, Harry. Dash explained a few other matters. It seems that Maude found the gold. She dug it herself. Dash helped you relocate at the last second—after you'd let all of Goldfield know. Dash paid for a pair of lawmen, Earp by name, to drive off some claimjumpers. It seems you knew all this but neglected to let your attorney know. Harry, my friend, there must be utter candor between an attorney and his client or else there can only be . . . shall we say, embarrassments in court."

"That's all horsepucky, Reilly."

"Well, sign here. This'll convey the Texas Saloon to me in fee simple. You'll retain me to the end of January."

"I suppose you'll kick me out, too." Arbuckle had converted the entire upstairs to a suite.

"No, I have a little rental agreement here. You'll not owe a thing until February first. After that, a simple hundred a month, payable on the first of each month. You just initial that and we'll be done for the morning."

"Why should I?"

Reilly sighed and rubbed up the shine on his patent leather shoes. "It'd be embarrassing to you if I had to resort to litigation, Harry. This way, no one will know."

"Why should I retain you, anyway?"

Turner Reilly smiled. "Because I'm valuable. My researches have uncovered scores of items you found useful. In fact, Harry, I know something right now that could turn your life around. Something so important that you could be on easy street once again."

"Well, tell me, you shyster."

"Tut tut, Harry. If you've discharged me, I have nothing to tell you. I don't work for nothing. You sign and I'll share my enterprise with you."

Sulkily, Harry took the fountain pen that Reilly handed him and carefully scrawled his signature across the documents. Then Max Faust witnessed.

"All right, what's the big deal?" Arbuckle asked.

"Why, part of my duty is to check claim filings in Hawthorne. And keep tabs on your estranged spouse. Well, the clerk and recorder has it on record that four mineral claims have been filed west of here, on a ridge near the Silver Peak Mountains. The claimants are Maude Arbuckle and Hannibal Dash. I thought you'd like to know, Harry. Isn't that what you pay me for?"

"Maude?"

"You are legally married to Maude, I take it, and entitled to community property?"

"Maude? She found something?"

Reilly shrugged. "Who knows, Harry? A claim doesn't make a bonanza. Maybe we should find out."

"Yeah, find out. That shady bum, Dash. Cheating me and Maude."

Reilly stared contemplatively out the grimy window. "People are certainly greedy, aren't they? You know, the longer I practice in a gold town and see all this gold fever around me, the more ashamed I am of mankind. Out there somewhere—there's a description of the claim, so we can find the place—there they were, your own wife and her paramour, ignoring you. Fortunately I meet enough decent and honorable people in my daily life so that my law practice doesn't get me down.''

''Yeah, well go after them.''

''There might not be enough time, Harry. My services end in a fortnight. And you'll owe me rent. But I'll do it. Trust your counselor.'' With that, Turner P. Reilly donned his scarf, his duster, his homburg, and his white gloves, picked up his walking stick and departed the precinct.

Maude. The thought electrified Harry. That Maude, she was holding out on him. He felt lower than he had ever felt in his life. He'd given away everything he had but no one repaid. He'd married Maude when she was a desperate old maid but she'd betrayed him. He'd treated the whole town of Goldfield not just once but thousands of times.

Now he was done for. Great tears welled up and he turned away from Max Faust. He couldn't stop the flow that boiled hotly from his eyes. If only someone would understand how it was. If only God would punish all those who'd cheated him, beginning with Maude. But Harry found himself alone in the world, afraid of the future, and so desperate that pain clutched his chest. No one cared. He would be an outcast the rest of his life. Harry rubbed his tears away and sat in his chair, waiting for a friend.

CHAPTER 65

Not until well into January 1906 did Hannibal and Maude finish the cairns that bordered the four claims. By then they were down to flapjack flour. They had even labored through Christmas, prying rock from outcrops and hauling it on the backs of burros great distances. When Hannibal had suggested resting on the holy day to renew their spirits, Maude had resisted.

''Gold was one of the three gifts the wise men brought the Christ Child,'' she said. ''All those high and mighty people who think we should scorn gold because it's nothing but metal, I guess they never read that in the book. I guess if gold was good enough for Jesus, it's good enough for me, so let's keep at it.''

She obviously thought it was an unanswerable argument. There was nothing to make a feast of anyway so they had put in the usual day, from the moment the cold winter sun arose to the time they had to stumble down to their rincon camp in evening darkness. It took a lot of work to locate a mining claim and the worst was still ahead. They had only forty days left to drive a ten-foot shaft into each claim, a task they weren't equipped to do either by experience or stamina. They would have to get help and it wasn't going to be easy to find when powder men could steal fifty or a hundred a day.

Thus, one February evening, they headed back to Gold-field. When they reached the abandoned Free Lunch Mine Maude released the burros, knowing that Mother Dear would keep the others close to the old shack. The mine sheds sagged in a pale moonlight, looking forlorn.

"I'll move in here," she announced and set about cleaning her old shack with an ancient broom.

"But Maude—this is no place to stay."

She glared at him. He understood at once that she didn't think it would be proper for the two of them to be wandering about Goldfield. What had been acceptable to her out in the desert would be scandalous in town. He realized she didn't have a cent, not even enough for a meal. She was utterly alone in the world and dependent on him.

He had no cash but drafted a check and handed it to her.

"What'm I gonna do with a hundred dollars?" she asked.

"You're in rags. Your boots are falling apart. You need groceries. You need tools. You need a ribbon in your hair, a bonnet, a bowl of fruit, and a steaming hot bath at a boarding hotel."

She looked stricken, as if he had said something terrible. "Well, I'll pay it back when we get that claim going," she grumbled, not resisting. "I guess there's scrap wood around here to cook with."

"We'll go back to the ridge soon," he said. "Lots to do. But Maude, enjoy life. You scarcely know how. Or had the chance."

"Don't you run my life for me, Hannibal Dash," she said as he left her. "I never took a lick of charity and I won't start now."

It struck Dash that in his short sojourn away, Goldfield had transformed itself once again. Power lines erected by the Nevada Power, Mining and Milling Company marched across the desert to a new substation. The Catholics had finished their church on Cedar Street. The State Bank and Trust moved into a building next to the Miners Union Hall. The union had built a hospital, St. Mary's. The big, wooden Goldfield Hotel had opened on Crook Avenue. A fine baseball diamond and stands stood west of town. The Downing Brothers had built an assay office on North Main Street. A grade school was rising on Cedar Street. And that was just the beginning of change. He spotted new saloons, a photographic studio, several new office buildings, and a gaggle of restaurants.

It amazed him. He knew it had been going on all along but he had scarcely noticed. He let himself into his little house and threw open windows to freshen the stale air. It had always been just a camping place.

He found a few letters waiting for him. One, a thick envelope from Browning and Browning, attorneys-at-law in Madison, he could guess at. Another was from Melanie. A third was from Cecily. That one faintly surprised him. He set them aside for a while while he unpacked his gear, debating whether to go eat a late meal somewhere or face what was in those envelopes.

He opened the one from his daughter and confronted a tidal wave of hurt. She had expected him for Christmas but now she knew she would never see him again. He had deserted them. He didn't care about her. She felt orphaned. Why had she been born if he cared so little? She had knitted a scarf for him for Christmas and had bought him a new shaving mug too. She had waited eagerly for him to walk in the door. She had baked Christmas cookies each day before Christmas so he might have some fresh ones. But when Christmas had passed, and New Year's too, she knew. She had wept, but she would never weep again. And good-bye forever.

Dash read it, feeling wave after wave of guilt and love pour through him. He should never have left; it had always been a selfish lark. He knew that if Cecily felt such hurt, Robert would feel it even more. But Robert had maintained a proud silence that no doubt had turned into bitterness toward his father. Both his children were already strangers.

Dash sighed, knowing he had little defense except the most illogical one of all: he had come to Goldfield because he had to, because an overwhelming need had torn him out of his comfortable academic life and hurtled him into a world of excitement, adventure, gain, pain, and struggle.

He read Cecily's tormented letter once again, noting where the pen had hesitated, where she had written over a word, usually chosing a more severe one. Her pride had wilted under his neglect. He could see the frightened, scorned young woman blaming herself for his indifference. But it hadn't been her at all. How could he ever make her understand that? He did love her, just as he loved his son and wife. He loved them all! Maybe he could find words to comfort her, though he doubted that anything short of returning to Madison would do that.

He turned to the one from Melanie. In that soft, flowing hand she wrote with rigid emotional neutrality. The holidays had come and gone; the new year was upon them. The children went about their studies in a dreary spirit. The year she had given him was long past. She had come to an understanding of Hannibal and had seen an attorney.

The letter from Gideon Browning, an old friend of the Dashes, was simple and pointed. Mrs. Dash wished for legal separation and maintenance for life. The papers, if Dash agreed to them, would avoid litigation and be approved by the Dane County district court. Mrs. Dash would receive five hundred a month—merely a continuation of Dash's own payments—even after the children's majority. Mrs. Dash would continue to have dower rights in Dash's estate.

The letter from Gideon reflected none of the long and amiable friendship they had shared. There it all was on paper; the life he had casually thrown away just to scratch his itch. Gideon had steered her away from divorce for obvious reasons: there was a real question of who was deserting whom, especially since Hannibal had invited her west.

Dash read everything a second time, feeling drained. He had known something like this would happen. But knowing it was coming didn't lessen the torment he felt as he absorbed all that in his dreary cottage. He remembered the amiable times in Madison, outings on Picnic Point of Lake Mendota, lifting little Cecily from her crib to hug her, attending academic dinners in formal attire to hear one or another university president or regent pronounce lofty ideals and spell out the progressive impulses that had governed the university from its inception. Madison was no backwater college but a formidable university, with a formidable faculty. He had been a part of that and had made his own large contributions.

He could go back. There would be wounds to heal but he didn't doubt that if he closed up his affairs in Goldfield, returned to the big house on Langdon Street, and resumed his instruction of geology, it would all pass by. Melanie would study him for a few weeks and one day return to his arms and they would be lovers again.

It tempted him. He could return a moderately rich man, having achieved an amazing success in Goldfield. There would be plenty of money for summer travel, for Melanie's pleasures, for the children's schooling and lives, for retirement after a life of dedication to glacial geology, maybe to write the standard work in the field. All he had to do was let himself die and return to the somnolent rituals he had fled.

He had been harried to the crossroads and all he grasped as he contemplated the mail was the psychic pain. He knew he needed time and rest before he could come to any decisions.

He dug out his salt-and-pepper suit and put it on, finding it baggy. The relentless toil and bad food had shrunk him. He walked through a chill Goldfield evening, noting that the boom town never slowed down, and climbed the stairs to the second-floor Montezuma Club. There, ignoring the scrutiny of his many friends who hadn't seen him in weeks, he cashed a small check and retreated into the night in search of a place to luxuriate. Goldfield's energy reached him, galvanizing everything inside of him.

He chose to dine at Victor Ajax's La Parisienne. He loved the cuisine and would go there even if it was in the heart of the redlight district. Once he would have shrunk from going to such a place. This time, out of some small defiance of convention, he hurried there, enjoying sights he had never seen or even imagined in Madison. He devoured a splendid T-bone steak smothered in onions and surrounded by sautéed mushrooms, new red potatoes, California asparagus, and a glorious spinach and bacon salad. With all of this he imbibed three glasses of Kentucky whiskey, two more than his normal intake. The little celebration quieted his spiritual pain for the moment but he knew it would roar back in the gray light of dawn.

He left about ten. The beckoning tarts didn't tempt him but neither did they offend him. He waved and laughed as they sat in their crib windows inviting the world into their rapacious arms. Goldfield roared and caroused. The thunder of boots in the dance halls, accompanied by the tinny pianos played by the perfessors of the keyboards, radiated a raw energy to him that he soaked up as if it were the essence of life.

He didn't go home. He returned to the Montezuma Club, his ears thirsting for news of bonanzas, ore values at the January or Jumbo, highgrading, union troubles, deals, share prices of the Combination mines, busts, new mills, new railroads coming up from Bullfrog and Las Vegas, new shafts, new apex litigation. He had not heard a word in two months, an eon by Goldfield standards. One day one king, the next day a new king, and everybody having fun in the process including the losers.

There he learned that George Wingfield, former Tonopah tinhorn, was becoming one of the largest holders of Goldfield mines along with his business partner Senator George Nixon; and that Harry Arbuckle had lost the Texas Saloon to Reilly and was back to cadging drinks and meals, sleeping on pool tables or in the sawdust of the dives, as if three hundred thousand dollars had never happened. He was starving, they said, because no one quite believed it.

Dash registered that somberly, hoping Maude's heart would not be too soft when she found out. Then he slid into the night, knowing he could no longer evade the decisions he had to reach. Who was he? A quiet, settled academic with a loving family? Or a restless, driven explorer and adventurer who came alive only when he was out in the remotest reaches of the world, risking everything, pitting his wits against the universe? And could those two parts of him ever be reconciled?

Even before he let himself into the dark cottage, he knew what the answer had to be. And it deepened his loneliness.

CHAPTER 66

All Olympus Prinz had to do was start in, yet he couldn't. He wandered helplessly through his shining shop, admiring the Hoe press and the Mergenthaler Linotype, the stereotyping and engraving equipment, the worktables called "stones" in the trade, the handset display fonts, and all the rest. The shining place beckoned him to plunge in, work faster than ever because of the Linotype, and produce the *Observer*. He wouldn't even need a printer's devil for a while. He could sit down at that rattling monster, set justified lines of type at breathtaking speed, and melt it all down again when he was done.

But he couldn't. He had returned from San Francisco in a somber mood and found himself half-paralyzed. He oversaw the installation of the equipment, paid a duty call on Sam Jones, settled into the new apartment at the rear of his plant, and wandered through Goldfield trying to grasp its inner life which he had known so well. During his month away, Goldfield had grown. Three stores, a beanery, an office building and two saloons had opened. New cottages lined Greenwood and Francis streets. Yet it remained a raw frontier town, a relic of the Wild West that had long since vanished. It seemed odd that a full-blown frontier mining camp flourished in the new year of 1906.

He tried not to think of Beth but she filled his soul. She had been born with grace: grace of body, grace of mind, grace of spirit. She had social grace and private grace. She had grace in desperate moments and grace among her friends. He had discovered her grace when she was Daisy and scarcely imagined he would find it in a girl of the Line. She had an easy grace when he had talked with her over tea, as if they were old friends and he wasn't paying for her time. Her grace was innate, unbought by merit, as if it were her destiny for everything to come out all right.

He relived the midnight dance when she felt so light in his arms, as if she belonged there and always had. He recollected the carefully elegant way she dressed and looked in her own milieu, so comfortable and at home among her friends. He had watched her with her husband and sensed a subtle wall between them. He wished she would abandon Reginald and flee to Goldfield. But he knew what she had invested in her husband and knew the price was so high she would never consider another. It wasn't her life as Daisy that posed the stumbling block but her marriage and commitment to an embezzler she loved. Those who had used Daisy had never possessed Beth, but Reginald did and always would whether he deserved it or not.

Reginald Ross didn't deserve it, Prinz thought. That sort

of callow sport would not grasp the depth of Beth's sacrifice and suffering if he were told the story.

Prinz tried again to drive his inchoate longings away but couldn't. Sometimes they turned starkly physical and he remembered one stunning moment of passion and wished there could be more. But the next moment he was always glad he hadn't become her steady lover. He couldn't have endured the pain. He meandered through his shop, looking at the gleaming machinery as if it belonged on another planet but his mind was always on Beth.

He knew perfectly well why he couldn't bring himself to begin. The new *Observer* required a voyage of the soul. He plunged into a bright winter day and hiked toward the cemetery in the barren flat below Malpais Mesa a mile from town. The sun glared at him heatlessly, making the naked wastes even harsher than usual. The various sects and societies had carved up the burial ground and erected gates announcing that the Knights of Pythias lay in this plot and the Latter-Day Saints in that, the Catholics over here and the Masons over there. Heaven had been parceled out and fenced in except for the rear corner where Prinz found the new grave of Uriah Horn along with the unmarked mounds that hid girls of the Line, heathens, and darkies.

The boy had died because of Prinz's reckless reportage and it had become a sorrow he could scarcely endure. He didn't know much about his printer's devil. Uriah had been studious and serious, not some fast young slicker eager to spend his paycheck. Nineteen years old, innocently breaking down type when the dynamite blew. And dead, an act of callousness by those who perceived the poorly paid youth as a class enemy.

Constable Inman had stopped by the day that Prinz returned and told him it wasn't hard to figure out who had done it. The IWW bunch. But he didn't have an iota of proof. It was easy to pilfer dynamite from any mine. It was available to anyone in the pits, not just the powder men. He and his officers had talked to all sorts of close-mouthed miners and learned almost nothing. Even so, the constable had admitted, scratching his head, it had to be those radical Wobblies. He could name a dozen, ones who divided up the world into classes and friends and enemies. But they had good alibis and he couldn't prove a thing.

Prinz had nodded. Men who had killed once would kill again. The death of Uriah and the demolition of the old plant hung over the revived weekly paper. It wasn't hard to see what was coming in Goldfield. The town seethed at the brink of labor war. The Wobblies would not stop until they had their One Big Union and that meant absorbing the Western Federation of Miners Local 220. And it meant crushing the American Federation of Labor craft unions too.

On the other hand, the mine operators were determined to stop the highgrading that was costing them millions of dollars. They intended to install changing rooms where workers would doff their mining clothes and hang them in one locker, then don their street clothes which would be stored in a locker across the room, all under the eyes of a supervisor. It would slow the theft all right, while it humiliated men who toiled in the pits.

Prinz could either write about those things or avoid them. If he wrote about them he would probably be blown to bits or shot. If he didn't write about them he would destroy his own soul, and know himself as a coward. He wasn't a fearless man and he didn't laugh at death or scorn danger. Far from it. He was desperately afraid. He cherished his young and unfinished life and wanted it to continue intact. He cherished his limbs, his eyes, his ears, his whole body, along with his well-trained mind. The question was whether he cherished his soul as much, because if he didn't write about these thunderous storms looming over Goldfield he might as well be dead.

He stood mutely at the grave, but he was coming to an understanding. If he shirked his duty now this boy's death would be in vain. If he resolved to use his intelligence, his ability to inform, with courage in the face of danger, then Uriah's death would no longer be a random act of violence in an uncaring universe. If he chose to endanger himself for a good cause, Uriah's young ghost would stand beside him. If he picked up the cudgel and fought, then Uriah's death would no longer fill him with guilt.

"Well, Uriah," he said to the silent mound of yellow earth, "I'll probably be joining you before I know it."

He walked back to town, thinking that there were fates worse than death, among them living with self-condemnation. A man could know of his own cowardice even if no one else on earth suspected it. He hadn't thought much about what it meant to be a man, perhaps because he had never found himself in a circumstance in which he could choose what he would be. He was being put to the test and he would not fail.

The skeptic in him mocked all that. He could publish a prudent little paper, duck the issues, entertain people with the wit he had been born with, and the sky wouldn't fall on him. The old *Observer*, after all, had contained doses of wry humor that sometimes teased and often mocked the world. Why not stick to the thing that had worked?

He knew the answer to that. His ordeals had changed him and the paper would change with him. The new *Observer* would be more serious and more charitable.

That afternoon he sold ads, going from merchant to merchant as he had done before. Some hesitated, obviously fearing that the violence that had destroyed the *Observer* might be visited upon them. But they could hardly say no, and by the end of the day Prinz had sold plenty of space and added five new accounts. He put on his new printer's apron and set to work, building ads from display type, ruler lines, and Linotype text, even while he swiftly reviewed the topics he might choose to cover in the first issue of the new paper.

There was the question of conspicuous consumption. He had been reading Thorstein Veblen's penetrating and sardonic book about the American rich, *The Theory of the Leisure Class*, and saw in Goldfield some conspicuous examples of extravagant spending to garner prestige—

particularly the recent parties hosted by Sam and Delia. He set that idea aside for the nonce. He would bite the hand that had rescued him, but not in the first few issues.

He wanted also to do some issues on the tenderloin and the miserable lives of its girls. That would take work and delicacy. He had no intention of moralizing about it the way other papers did periodically. Those editors had scarcely bothered to talk to any of the women there, some of whom were not there by choice. Neither did he want to invite ministers to use his columns to anathematize the soiled doves and condemn them to eternal damnation. No, he would do better, and maybe Goldfield would come to understand itself and the lusts that drove it. Maybe such a study would even generate some mercy for outcasts. His education was a gift from Daisy, who talked often about the life of its inmates with humor and charity and that innate grace that neither abandoned standards nor condemned those who didn't measure up to them.

In the end, he chose the topic that had harried him all afternoon, the topic that could only be described as suicidal for a lone editor trying to put his little weekly back on its feet: Goldfield's looming labor crisis.

That evening, after he had pulled off his apron and wiped the metal counters clean with solvent, he retired to his apartment strangely fulfilled. He knew he had made the right choice even if it was the dangerous one. How odd that his happiness was the fruit of a spiritual choice and not some material thing. He hadn't come to Goldfield to get rich but to write about a wild mining camp that was an anachronism in the twentieth century. He had come to discover its color, its craziness, its vitality, its uproarious fun. Maybe it would inspire him to write like Bret Harte.

And now, thanks to an impulsively generous old pirate he had his chance again. But there would be a difference because of what he had learned about Beth: Before, he had intended to mock barbarous Goldfield. This time he would write about the glittering city with respect. Everyone there, even poor Harry Arbuckle, was his brother or sister trying to cope with the fears and terrors of being alive.

Painfully, Prinz settled himself before the Linotype and began to compose a credo he would box on the front page. It was a beginning.

CHAPTER 67

· ·

Maude settled into her shack at the Free Lunch and waited for Hannibal to find some powder men. Someone had to punch some ten-foot shafts into that ledge fast or she and Hannibal couldn't locate.

She didn't mind living in the old shack. She swept it clean, cooked up a mess of beans, and made herself at home while she waited for Dash. Then one afternoon she spotted Harry moseying around the Free Lunch. From her window she watched him fool around the headframe, picking up rock and dropping it into a burlap sack. Then he trudged out toward the loading chutes, looking for chunks that got knocked off. He was finding some, too. Out at the ore bins he poked around, picking up this and that. The old fool hardly knew good ore from bad. She ought to go help him.

She'd wondered how the cuss stayed alive and now she knew. He'd gone back to picking up the crumbs, toting a bag back to one of those crooked assayers and collecting a few coins for it. He looked comical out there in his purple chalk-striped suit and black bowler, teetering from one heap to another, poking around for the leftovers. It sure looked like a dawg's life to her.

He was so intent on it that he paid no attention to the shack, not even noticing the curl of blue smoke drifting from its stove-pipe. She debated whether to let the old cuss go or maybe just help him out. She had the eye, and she could fill his sack with a few cents' worth of ore. She sort of wished she'd thought of it herself but as long as she had twenty of Dash's dollars unspent, she didn't see the need.

She pulled on her new coat against the January chill and wandered over there, thinking to help out.

He saw her and paused. "What are you doing, spying on me?" he asked.

"I thought I'd help, Harry. I've an eye for ore."

He glared, suspiciously. "There's tons of highgrade down there but I can't get at it. I know what you and your pals are up to. You busted me so you can buy the mine for a song and clean it out."

She sighed, watching the stiff wind flap his baggy, unpressed suit. He hadn't shaved in a week and his flesh looked puffy and bloodshot.

"Have you had an offer?" she asked.

"Yeah, them people over there want it." He waved in the direction of the May Queen. "They offered a thousand. They said they just wanted it for the shaft so they could get to their ore, but I'm not that dumb. My attorney, Reilly, he came over with the deal but I told him to go to hell."

"Harry, you should take it."

"There you go, nagging again. Reilly'd just use it to pay his bill."

"I'll help you look," she said. "We should start over there, around the hoppers. Not here."

"I know what I'm doing. You just want to steal it."

"I don't need that ore, Harry."

"I know you don't. You got some fancy claims. I heard about 'em. Reilly, that's what I hire him for. They're mine, you know. You owe me them claims after what you did to me."

"They're mine and they'll stay that way, Harry."

"The devil they will. I'll put Reilly on you and he'll skin you alive. You and me are married and don't forget it."

She pushed back a wind-whipped wisp of gray hair. "Do you remember, Harry, when I asked for a little cottage? That's all I wanted from the Free Lunch."

"Don't you sass me. I should take a horsewhip to you

for what you did to me. Look at me. Cleaned out by them crooks."

It was all bluster, as usual. She'd heard it all her life. "Let's go look for ore," she said. "You're showing some enterprise and that's good."

She led him over to the hoppers, where ore had tumbled into wagons that took it to the mills. Chunks of unoxidized quartz lay everywhere, gleaming subtly. She plucked them up, studied them, dropped them into his opened sack while he watched her.

"You sent a man after me," she said.

"I know what you're up to, Maude. You're trying to pin something on me. What do you take me for, some chump?"

"He followed me out of Goldfield and watched. He tried to take my claim from me. I shot him."

Harry squinted at her, surprised. The wind reddened his veinous cheeks, ruined by booze long before.

"That was when you had some thugs with brass knuckles and revolvers, and you thought you could hire someone to steal my claims. I sent him away."

She found a good, fist-sized piece with visible gold specks filtering through the rusty quartz. "Here," she said. "It's worth two bits."

"That's enough. I can't carry all this."

She faced him. "If that ledge pans out, I'm going to have my yellow and white cottage with a big front porch and enough to enjoy life. I'd like to plant a tree there, maybe a McIntosh apple if there's enough water, and a rambling rose. I think I'll have a washerwoman. I can cook but I sure hated to pound sheets and hang them up for two dollars a week. Yes, I'll have that, Harry. I earned it. But if I buy my cottage you'll pester me all the time. I don't know what to do about that."

"I'll do more than pester you, Maude. I'm moving in. You got no say about it and you know it."

It was always the same. She turned her back to him and walked to her shack, not caring whether he followed. He didn't. She wondered why she didn't divorce him. She should have long ago. She certainly had grounds: nonsupport, desertion, cruelty, adultery—all would work. And Hannibal would lend her the money for it. He wanted her to. But she just couldn't. She liked to remember those times when they prospected alone on the desert, and Harry was a better man.

After all these years she had come to understand Harry Arbuckle not as a bad man, but a sad one. She guessed that if she ever got her little yellow cottage and a bit of cash from the ledge she'd share a bit with the bum. Not that she wanted him around: she'd drive him away with a shotgun if she had to. But she'd send him something because he didn't know how to be a man and no one could ever teach him.

She wished God would lean out of heaven and touch poor Harry, just send a little shock through him that would clear his mind and let him see himself. But maybe that wasn't a good idea either. If God ever gave Harry a conscience, Harry would die of shame. No, it was better just to let things lie and hope that some day, when Harry was starving or drunk, or lying in a gutter, his guardian angel would say, "Come on now, Harry. You're going to wash up, dust yourself off, and start working on your soul. From this day on, you're going to be a man. You brought hell up to earth and now you're going to send it back down where it belongs. And the moment you do, Harry Arbuckle, you'll find the happiness you never had."

But that was fantasy. She reached the shack and turned. Harry had started to town with his gleanings slung over his shoulder.

Pretty soon he'd run out of scavenged ore. What would he do then? She smiled, not knowing why. She ought to despise him for making her life miserable. But she didn't. Poor old Harry, she thought. The Devil got him.

The next day Hannibal Dash showed up with two young men he introduced as Ned Stickney and Harcourt Warren. The pair sure didn't look like powder men, she thought as she surveyed their white shirts, cravats, and suits.

"Maude, I met these gents at the Montezuma Club and found out they're looking for a lease. They're not new to Nevada—they've leased some silver operations at Austin—but they're new here and not having any luck finding a claim to work," Dash said. "They've got a proposition for us and I want you to hear them out."

"You set yourself on that cot and I'll whistle up some tea," she said, bustling about as she glanced at the two fellows. The pair looked scarce out of their trundle beds.

"Mrs. Arbuckle, we're interesting in leasing the four claims on that ridge," said Stickney. "We've got some experienced men in Austin, put out of work a few days ago when our lease expired. We've got a little capital—not a lot, but we can raise more. What we proposed to Mister Dash—and want to propose to you—is that we do your location work for you. Bore the four shafts ten feet. That telluride ore'll be ours—the pay for the shaft work. You'll get your claims located out of it. And if the values look good ten feet down we'd like a two-year lease on all four claims, usual terms, twenty-five percent royalty on all milling ore that reaches grass."

"Two years?" she said, eying Dash.

"That's a long lease, Mrs. Arbuckle," Warren said. "But we're up against it out there. Nearest town is twenty miles away. Silver Peak. We've got to start from nothing. Scrape a truck road twenty-five miles to the rail spur. Bring in a whole town."

"How long until you start mining?"

"Oh, we think we can start in April."

That seemed a long time to wait around for some cash to come in. But the man had a point. That ridge was out in the middle of nowhere and a lot had to be done.

"You mind if I talk to Mister Dash, gents?" she asked.

"Of course not," Stickney said, herding Warren out the door.

"I shoulda loaded your burros up with some of that telluride and brought it in to live on," she said to Dash. "Only we were getting pretty hungry."

"You were hoping for money a lot sooner."

"I guess I could do some washing again, Hannibal. Me and those Howard scrubboards and Fels Naptha are old friends. Maybe I could scavenge around here. That's what Harry's doing. He gets fifty cents or a dollar out of it."

"Maude, they're extended to the limit but maybe I can get five hundred out of them against future royalties to you."

"What if they don't like my claims and work yours?"

Dash thought about that. "I suppose you could give me half of your claims and I could give you half of mine," he said.

"Now there's a corker, Hannibal. All right. I'll do it if they'll advance me a little."

"And if they don't?"

"Lord, Hannibal, I know how to get along. I just need a little hope money to go on."

Two days later Maude signed a thicker mess of papers than she'd ever put a nib to before. She and Dash became joint owners of the claims and Stickney and Warren leased the claims. She got a hundred dollars out of it in advance; that was the best they could do. She figured she could make it last until April and if she couldn't, that wouldn't even slow her down.

"Now I got dreams again," she told Dash. "Life's hardly worth living if you don't have dreams."

"You've got more than dreams this time, Maude. You have a future."

CHAPTER 68

....

Sam Jones felt a little silly wandering around the Montezuma Club in the outfit Delia had bought for him. But he didn't want to hurt her feelings so he wore it. And anyway, what difference did it make what an old pirate wore?

She had handed him a blue double-breasted blazer, some white flannel pants, and a visored cap that looked like it belonged on the noggin of a railroad conductor.

"There you are, Sam. I want you to wear it," she'd said.

"That stuff? I'd look like a ticket collector."

"It's a yachting suit and you'll look nice in it."

"Yeah, but I don't have a yacht."

"Well, you wear it. It's time you learned to dress nicely. This is what William Vanderbilt wears—I saw it in *Harper's*."

"I don't care what Vanderbilt wears. I'm not Vanderbilt and I don't wear stuff like that."

She'd pouted and he'd surrendered. If she wanted to dress him up to look like a circus majordomo that was her privilege, he guessed. She wasn't happy in Goldfield in spite of the high-flying social life and he was trying to humor her all he could. So far, no one in the club had heckled him.

He was an investment capitalist now and the Montezuma Club was his office. It was splendid how things worked out. All those parties they'd thrown had finally melted some ice among the upper crust, and most of the club members had become pals. In a club like the Montezuma he didn't have to hunt down opportunities; they just seemed to drop in his lap. There were always mine owners and entrepreneurs wanting capital for this and that, and he enjoyed listening to them. Once in a while he'd taken a plunge in some outfit or another and the results weren't half bad because he was a pretty shrewd judge. But mostly it was fun. He'd sit in his big black leather wing chair and the daily parade would start.

Windlass Borden found him at his usual post one April morning. Jones thought that Borden looked a little haggard.

"Morning, Big Sam," Borden said, and Jones intuited that this was not entirely social. Borden was going to put some business proposition on the table.

"Morning, Windlass. How blows the wind?"

Emil Beerbohm appeared with a glass and a bottle of Dr. Thatcher's Liver and Blood Syrup on a silver tray. Borden poured a dollop into the glass and chugged it down, wheezing slightly. He pushed the cork back, and Beerbohm vanished as swiftly as he had arrived.

"Well, Sam, not too brisk. I'm taking a beating from the Sullivan Trust. That's what I want to talk to ya about. Need a fresh start."

Jones already knew the answer to that. He wasn't going to finance Windlass Borden's wildcat company, especially against the L. M. Sullivan Trust Company. Shanghai Larry Sullivan had been around Goldfield quite awhile, and had put together a wildcat outfit that made Borden look like a blushing virgin. Sullivan and his partner George Graham Rice were a pair of bottom-feeding carp who had hit it big. The Sullivan Trust Company occupied the old National Club on Crook and Main and employed a whole army of shirtsleeved clerks to handle the boodle.

Like Borden, they advertised wildcat Goldfield stocks from one end of the Republic to the other, but unlike Borden, they employed brassy tactics. Somehow or other they had lined up Governor John Sparks as chairman of the board of several of their wildcats and had heavily exploited the name. Any rube in the country would buy into a company run by Nevada's governor.

"I need boodle, Sam. I need new advertising, too. Yours isn't working so good anymore. You come back in, be a silent partner, fifty-fifty, and we'll show Sullivan how it's done. We'll just recapitalize the whole outfit. If half isn't enough, take two thirds.''

"Windlass," said Big Sam genially, "I'm outa the business and I'm invested up to my eyeballs anyway."

"For old times' sake, Sam. I gave you your chance when you landed in Goldfield. I even lent you ten bucks to get started."

"Windlass, I never forgot and I paid you back."

"Sam, I'm broke."

"Broke? How'd that happen?"

Borden sighed. "Women, mostly. The more they cost the better I like 'em. I bought into a deal at Rhyolite that fizzed out. But that's not what sunk me. I just got suckered at the stock exchange and I owe John S. Cook Bank eighty-seven thousand on a margin call."

Jones whistled. That was a lot of loot.

"I thought it was a rich deal, Sam. It looked good. I was watching the Goldfield Nevada Boy Company. It's got four good mines, you know. Every day that stock was climbing, so I asked around, real quiet. I found out they hit highgrade in the Utah—that's one of the mines. And I spotted this little item in the *Goldfield News* that confirmed it. I knew a killing when I saw it.

"So, Sam, I sold everything I had and went to Cook. He lent me some boodle on margin. I started buying, quietly, you know? I picked up Nevada Boy at a buck twenty-six, on up to a buck seventy-one, until I owned a hundred-fifty grand of that stuff."

Borden sighed and drained his liver tonic. "Two days later it had dropped to seventeen cents. I owe Cook more than I want to think about. You know what happened? Some Boston sharpers in the exchange had done it with wash sales. They'd planted the newspaper item. They got me and a lot of others, too. My God, Sam, they got Windlass Borden. I'm plumb ashamed of myself. I'm gonna go belly-up if I don't get help."

Jones found certain moments unpleasant and this was

one of them. "I can't help, Windlass. I'm outa that racket for good."

Borden sighed, and stood. "Flossy's already left me. I told her I couldn't give her this month's three grand and she was out the door. Going back to running a cathouse." He looked beaten. "Well, Sam, I'll figure out something."

Sam felt sorry for him and wondered whether he would have shared the same fate if he had stayed in the racket. A wildcatter got too sharp for his own good. It was probably the end for Borden. He'd skip town and the debt. Sam watched him retreat, doubting he'd ever see the old con again.

He'd hardly lifted the *San Francisco Examiner* when George Hayes plumped his porky carcass into the seat vacated by Windlass.

"Want to talk to you, Big Sam," he said.

That meant money. Jones signaled Emil Beerbohm for booze. "You've run out of cash," he ventured.

"Well, yes. We've been driving a shaft since last fall and we're coming up dry. We took in a couple of Chicago partners who put up five thousand but they won't spring for any more."

Hayes and his partner Monnette, both of them mining engineers, had leased ground on the Number 2 Mohawk and were having the same luck as the others who'd tried it. The two Mohawk claims lay next to bonanza mines in the Golden Horseshoe, including the Combination, the Jumbo, and the Red Top. But nothing of consequence had been discovered there.

"So you want more capital," Jones said.

"We're tapped out. I hate to give up a lease like that. We think we'll hit pay ore a little deeper."

Sam knew all that. The deeper Hayes and Monnette had driven without finding ore, the farther the Mohawk Company stock had dropped. It was selling for thirty cents which Sam thought was a good risk. He'd been buying all he could grab, which now came to twenty thousand shares. Jones didn't need to think this one over.

"I'll lend you five thousand against ten percent of the net production, or you can make me a fifth partner," he said.

"I was hoping you would," Hayes said, straightening the three hairs left on his shiny dome. "Let's make it a loan. That's what my partners wanted me to ask for. The ten percent sounds about right, considering your risk. It's not one we can pay back if we keep hitting low tenors."

Jones didn't need persuading. "George, that mine being right there on the best ground, I can't hardly go wrong. But I've gone wrong lots of times. It's all guesses. Let's go on over to the Exchange. I'll need to sell some stuff to come up with that."

They walked the two blocks to the Goldfield Mining Exchange which was operating in a basement while it awaited the completion of permanent quarters. Bedlam greeted them. Shirtsleeved traders hawked their wares. Buy and sell prices appeared on blackboards and vanished just as fast. Sweating men transferred shares, took notes, yelled hoarsely, bumped into each other, and dodged the mobs. When the Exchange had opened in October it listed over eighty Goldfield mining stocks. But the number had grown almost daily. Brokers from placid places like San Francisco and Philadelphia had emigrated to Goldfield to catch some of the lucre and con any suckers they could, sometimes the same victim several times in a row.

Jones found John Loftus, one of the most active curb traders in town, and unloaded ten thousand shares of Sandstorm Mining Company stock. It had produced steadily but wasn't yielding much. He netted seven thousand out of that. He bought another five thousand shares of the Mohawk Mining Company, which was largely owned by George Wingfield, Al Myers, George Nixon, and John Cook, all men he knew. Then he drafted a check to Hayes for five thousand, and dated it April 10, 1906. It would be a handshake deal, like most of those in Goldfield.

"There you are, George. That should take you another

hundred feet.'' He smiled. ''Your Mohawk outfit has more Georges than Buckingham Palace.''

Hayes reverently tucked the check into his breast pocket. ''I knew you'd go for it, Big Sam. You're a plunger.''

''I'll sink money down any rat hole,'' Jones mused. ''I've put money into lame horses, unhappy women and barren mines. Sometimes it pays off. Say, Delia and me, we're having a little wingding on Saturday night. You gotta come dressed like a soldier—she does that, you know. Costumes. Maybe you'll have something to celebrate by then.''

CHAPTER 69

. . . .

More and more that spring, Big Sam Jones whiled away his time in the Montezuma Club. It had been decorated as lavishly as the Washoe Club in Virginia City and occupied the entire second story of the Palace Building. Its ceiling flaunted chased flowers and trailing vines. Terracotta wallpaper graced the walls, while the floor was constructed of matched and dovetailed eastern oak. Its commodious couches, chairs, and tables were fashioned from oak the shade of ebony, richly upholstered in leather or heavy satin.

There Jones could sup, talk gold, make deals, do some curb trading, or enjoy the club's constant entertainments, which recently included an Italian pianist, baritone soloist, professional whistler, and vaudeville acts borrowed from the Arcade and the Mint theaters.

On April 17, scarcely a week after George Hayes had borrowed cash to continue his probe into the Mohawk, the portly mining engineer hurried across the club and dropped into one of those sumptuous couches beside Jones.

''We hit it!'' he said, catching his breath. ''A real, fat, heart-thumping bonanza.''

Discouraged after six months of digging deeper, they had

started a drift at a higher level and found themselves in solid highgrade with no boundaries.

"Well, George, you'd better catch your breath," Jones said. "It's only gold."

"It's so rich we'll send it out under guard," Hayes boasted. "Sam, that cash you lent us made the difference. We'd of thrown in the towel. Now you're going to see the best mining ever done. The lease expires on January eleventh and we're going to run three shifts full-blast right to the wire. It certainly stirs the blood, eh?"

Jones allowed that it stirred his, considering that he now possessed ten percent of a bonanza.

The next day an earthquake reduced San Francisco to rubble, and Jones read horrifying expresses about fire, death and disease. A few days later he learned that his erstwhile partner, Windlass Borden, had vanished while owing the Cook Bank a huge sum on a margin call. The bank shut down the Borden Trust and confiscated its assets. A few days after that, it became clear that the Mohawk bonanza might be the most awesome in the history of gold mining. Hayes and Monnette's miners were blasting thirty thousand dollars of gold a day out of a magical chamber the size of a small room, and every bit of it was highgrade. There was no country rock, only rich yellow-tinted ore stretching in every direction, which all went to the smelter without sorting.

Jones tried to buy more Mohawk stock but they told him that George Wingfield got there first. He and George Nixon already had a large chunk of the million shares, and Wingfield was the president of the Mohawk company. Jones supposed that if he was getting rich, the Tonopah tinhorn was minting ten times as much.

Big Sam watched amazed as his twenty-five thousand shares, which he had accumulated at prices ranging from seventeen to thirty cents, topped two dollars, then three, and continued climbing as the scope of the Hayes-Monnette bonanza lit fires in the Goldfield Stock Exchange. Some of the ore was so rich that Hayes bagged it and shipped to the Selby Smelter under armed guard.

In June, Hayes concluded that he could never mine all that gold before his lease expired, so he subleased a fraction to the Mackenzie Company. The sublessees immediately began operations at what they called the Frances-Mohawk, and these were as profitable as the Hayes and Monnette lease.

Sam's Mohawk stock hit four dollars a share and he was a hundred thousand dollars richer than he had been in early April. The share prices continued to ratchet upward so fast that each month would add another hundred thousand to his worth. His share of the lessees' net earnings was filling his coffers at the rate of two thousand dollars a day.

Jones had become so rich he hardly knew what to do with himself or where to stuff the loot. He distrusted banks so he invested some of it in other good mines and stowed bars of bullion in his own safe. And the money didn't slow down. Hayes was excavating a huge underground cavern out of solid highgrade, without hitting country rock, adding men as fast as the mine could absorb them.

Goldfield celebrated. A new wave of fortune-seekers crowded in, drawn by the electrifying news. In one of those convulsions that periodically transformed the boom town, Goldfield shed more of its original wooden buildings and remade itself in stone and sometimes even imported brick.

Hayes didn't dare curb the highgrading, lest the powerful Western Federation of Miners, now combined with the Wobblies, shut him down. Mohawk gold fattened the purses of the tinhorns like Arizona Slim, Johnny Behind the Ace, Pay-back Billy, Stud Poker Tom, Faro King Mike, or Set-'em-up Denver, whose oilcloth faro, poker, black-jack, and chuck-a-luck outfits sopped up the booty the lucky miners hauled from the foot of Columbia Mountain. One veteran hurdy-gurdy dancer in the tenderloin was earning five hundred a night just from corkage. Sluts laid their fortune in Hayes-Monnette gold and banked the profit. Goldfield was on a gold binge.

But Hayes and Constable Inman found a way to stop at least some of the hemorrhage. Inman started raiding the quack assayers and confiscating the ore heaped up in their laboratories—easily identifiable as coming from the Mohawk. So at least some of the lost ores were being recovered, ten thousand here, fourteen thousand there, and Jones was getting his piece of it. His five-thousand-dollar loan had turned into the most profitable venture of his life.

The news of Sam's improved fortunes didn't escape Delia, and she renewed her campaign to move to Newport Beach.

"I'm so lonely, Sam," she said at breakfast one spring morning. "Couldn't we go now?"

Jones eyed his beautiful bride sadly. He had given her everything she had asked for except the one thing he couldn't give her for a while. She delighted his eye and still managed a big grin for him now and then. But he could sense that Goldfield was wearing thin for her, along with the big parties, and the rowdy café society of a mining camp.

"Delia, sweetheart, we'll get out there in a year or two. Those mines are slippery as eels and I've got to watch them every day. Miss a trick and your paper profits evaporate. You just hang on awhile—you're young, your life's hardly started—and pretty soon the time'll come when it's right to go. These mining camps don't last long. Then we'll shake off the dust and have a lifelong toot."

It didn't seem to please her. She made a moue and fiddled with her fork.

"We've an anniversary coming up in a few weeks, Delia. I was planning a little holiday for us in San Francisco—but the city's rubble. We could go to Los Angeles a few days but it means taking a stagecoach down to Bullfrog and the railhead."

She mulled that. "Two years is a long time, Sam, in a godforsaken hole like this."

She seemed as determined to get out as ever. For a while there it had seemed to him it would all work out. The parties had kept her occupied and amused. She had thrown theme parties, each with a motif. One was Mexican, another was French, and another had been a minstrel night. She had met countless people but had befriended none of them. She had turned down invitations to join the Goldfield Women's Club and the Ladies' Aid Society, as if these worthy organizations were somehow beneath her.

He knew she was lonely, most of it self-imposed, and he ached to help her. He had invited other couples to dinner at the Palm Grill thinking that perhaps Delia would do better in more intimate circumstances. But Delia had simply smiled at Claribelle Hayes, or made polite table talk with Martha Ransom, or listened attentively to Eloise Park. No friendships ever blossomed from these meetings and Jones sensed none ever would. Delia's eyes were upon California and nothing else would ever count.

"Delia, honey, Goldfield's treating you fine. You've got everything you want and then some. All you gotta do is decide to enjoy it," he replied. "It's all in your noodle. How'd you like a race horse? I'll get a blooded filly from Lexington and have her shipped out here, and you can have yourself some fun."

"Prominent people don't race horses, Sam."

"Well, I never said I was a prominent person," he replied, wheezing at the thought.

About the time of their first wedding anniversary, he sensed a change in her. She turned cold and resolute and crisp, as if she had decided upon some large change in her life which she had yet to announce to him.

"We've got old Number One to celebrate," he said on their anniversary, wondering how she'd react. "Let's go hear Julius Goldsmith play his fiddle."

"He's not a fiddler, he's a violinist, can't you ever get that straight? I'm tired of the Palm Grill. It's a bore. Couldn't you take me on a trip to Europe?"

"Tenderloin's just as good," he said. He summoned a hack, had them driven to Victor Ajax's La Parisienne, and bought the full two-dollar dinner for them both while she glared. A bottle of wine in a cut-glass decanter materialized, followed by raw oysters, clam chowder, broiled bass, a salad, fricassee of veal, banana fritters, prime rib, broccoli, potatoes, sugar cookies, sliced pineapple, Swiss and cheddar cheese, almonds, Kona coffee, and claret, all of it on bone china or pewter salvers, and laid upon snowy linen and served by sweating Italians in tuxedos. She ate lustily, no matter her mood. He had to credit her with that. When it came to intake, whether of food or drink or gold, Delia couldn't be matched.

"Feel better?" he asked afterward.

"I wish you wouldn't smoke those cigars around me."

Jones sighed. The marriage was plainly becoming tenuous. "Well, if you won't give the place a chance, I guess you ought to go where you want," he ventured.

"What does that mean?"

"I mean, what's stopping you? If you want to nip off to California, you got ticket money right there in your handbag."

She began to weep. "You just want to get rid of me. I'm just a joke to you. You've treated me cruelly from the beginning," she whispered, her voice just low enough not to carry. "You called me a gold digger. You told me I'm too . . . too *obvious* to be accepted by nice people—whatever you meant by that. You insulted me and my family. You seduced me and ruined my morals and my reputation. You made me miserable. I never knew if I was your wife or just your little slut. I hated sleeping with you, you're so crude. You rejected all my wishes, even the simplest ones, like living in some civilized place. I've never been so wounded and ashamed and angry in my life."

Tears leaked down her cheeks while she caught her breath. "You're a beast. No decent person would ever associate with you. You're so far beneath me and my family I don't know what I ever saw in you. I tried to give you some—respectability. Some gentility. You don't even know what those mean. You wouldn't know how to be a gentleman if your life depended on it. You're never home.

You're always at the club. You never take me anywhere."

Those beestung lips drooped into sullen anger now. "I want a divorce. I'm going to get one and I'll throw the book at you, too. I'll tell the whole world what you are. Just wait until they see the charges. You're a swine. I'm going to take you to the cleaners, believe me. If you thought I was a gold digger, then you haven't seen anything. If you thought that all I wanted was gold, why did you marry me? Wait until the judge hears about all that. When I get done, you'll be cadging drinks like that Harry Arbuckle. And you'll be a soprano."

"I was hoping I could make you happy, Delia," said Big Sam, sadly.

CHAPTER 70

....

A deputy sheriff dropped the summons into Sam's lap while he lunched at the Montezuma Club. Jones knew what would be in the manila envelope. Delia had moved out and this would be the first fruits of all that. He'd been expecting to be served.

He finished his filet because there was no reason to dig into the papers until he had satisfied his belly. Then, over Irish coffee, he perused the papers, using his new spectacles. He'd reached an age where he couldn't see a blasted thing closer than a yard away.

He had to admire Delia. She had employed the young Tonopah fellow, Pat McCarran. When it came to gold digging, Delia was no fool. McCarran had represented that crazy woman, May Baric, against George Wingfield just a few weeks before. The woman lost of course, but Delia sure knew where to go to find a divorce lawyer.

Delia wanted a divorce, having lawfully shared bed and board with Jones "in excess of a year." She wanted half his holdings, fifty thousand dollars of attorney fees, and alimony of five thousand dollars a month. She had filed a notice of *lis pendens*, to tie up his holdings and prevent him from hiding or dissipating them until the case was settled.

Jones sighed, sipped coffee, and took a gander at the complaint. Delia had settled on cruelty, not a bad choice given the remaining options of nonsupport, desertion or adultery. He studied the three pages of accusations, enjoying her creativeness. A woman that inventive surely deserved something out of it.

He had, he discovered, cruelly demolished her reputation. He had mocked her constantly, intending to humiliate her. He had always ascribed the basest of motives to her desire to marry him. He had ruthlessly disparaged her origins, threatened her with social ostracism, and abused her in the marital relationship. Not only that, he had beaten her repeatedly, forcing her to take to her bed for weeks at a time.

He sighed, sort of wishing it were true. Now he would have to live up to this new reputation.

Worse, he had conducted himself in an uncouth manner, refusing to behave like a gentleman. He had been niggardly about funds, forcing her to endure privations in spite of her social station.

On and on it went, a Sears Roebuck catalogue of complaints, some of them even true. Sam rubbed his jaw, wondering if he looked like Bluebeard. Next time he passed a mirror he would check.

"Pretty good," he said to no one, and shuffled the papers back into their cocoon. He was sorry to see her go but he had been expecting it and knew he couldn't change anything. He had given her his love and as much of his wealth as she wanted.

Jones would get around to yakking with lawyers pretty soon but for now he wanted to play the game his own way. He supposed that might be foolish, but he enjoyed danger, and if he lost his entire boodle he would just have the fun of trying again. A horse trader was always holding something or other by the halter.

He chose to walk over to Second Street, even though it'd devil his bum leg. The spring breezes and the exercise would do him good.

He turned into the entry of the spanking new offices of the *Observer*, and discovered a comely young brunette lady with her hair ribboned into a ponytail, who apparently served as a general factotum.

"Tell Prinz it's Big Sam," he said.

"He's rushing to complete an edition," she said.

"You just tell him it's Sam. I can see him back there diddling the keyboard of that type machine. What's your monicker, honey?"

She didn't budge. "I'm Sara. You may call me Mrs. Hartwig."

"I never knew anything about women but I think you're the prettiest Sara in Goldfield."

She surrendered after a frosty moment and shortly Olympus Prinz poked into the front office, wiping his hands with a grubby towel.

"Olympus, you got an office around here?" Sam asked.

"Well, if it isn't Sam Jones. I suppose you've come to see what your loot's bought."

"Naw, my teapot's whistling."

Puzzled, Prinz motioned him back to a corner alcove where a battered desk groaned under exchange papers and unidentifiable clutter, including some butcher paper with fragments of doughnuts stuck to it.

"Old Delia's coming after me with a gelding knife," he said, dropping the envelope in Prinz's hands.

"You want me to read this?"

"Heck, yes. Blot it up."

Jones waited patiently while Prinz studied the document. The editor smiled faintly. "I always knew there'd be strings, Sam."

"What do you mean, strings?"

"You want to keep this out of the paper. That's common

enough. Powerful men have a way of arranging it. Not a word of May Baric's suit against Wingfield ever got into a Goldfield or Tonopah paper. Every editor in town knew what Wingfield could do to him. He could shut me down. I didn't publish it either, because I'm a semicoward these days. I can still smell the dynamite.''

Jones guffawed. "Prinz, keeping this stuff out of the rag isn't what I have in mind. I got no reputation to lose. I want you to run it, full bore, front page, big fat headlines. If you won't do that, I'd like to buy an ad and put her in, the whole kit and kaboodle.''

Olympus Prinz blinked and stared. "Sam . . ." he muttered, trying to figure that out.

Jones just smiled. "I'm just trumping her, Prinz. She and her shysters are thinking I don't want all that bad publicity. Heck, McCarran's already sent a letter to my lawyers—you know, Crecelius, O'Brien and Swinny—suggesting that maybe the whole thing can be settled quietly and Judge Lovely'd go along with it up there in Hawthorne, without it coming to a reputation-busting battle. All I had to do was sign on the line.

"Only, Prinz, I don't play that game. I'm a wildcatter and a horse trader, and there ain't nothing gonna dip me in perfume. Old Delia never got that straight and she don't have it straight now. She thinks money is what makes a person respectable. I probably got more loot than Crocker and Huntington and they wouldn't let me through the door on Nob Hill. Now, is this little suit news, or ain't it?''

"Oh, it's news, Sam.''

"You got anything half as entertaining in there?''

Prinz sighed. "No, I'm starting a new series on the water supply. It's still lousy, we still have outhouses polluting the wells, and people are still dropping dead from typhoid.''

"Well, typhoid's got nothing on rich people's divorces. You're talking to an old promoter, Prinz. Lead with the scandal.''

"I don't use my stories to promote the paper, Sam. I

know it sounds crazy to you, but I've a passion for facts and figures.''

''Well, that's why you're half broke all the time. You got born without a sense of promotion and that's a lack in a businessman.''

Prinz sighed and shook his head. ''You sure about this? You won't regret it? These are unproven allegations, Sam.''

''That don't matter a bit. You just do the story. Delia's the one who'll be sorry.''

''I'm not following you, Sam.''

''Well, Ignatius Benedict O'Brien's telling me we'll ask for an annulment—nullity of marriage he calls it. He says she tied the knot for the wrong reasons, looking for boodle instead of wanting a family and stuff like that, and misrepresenting herself about fifty times an hour, talking about wanting an itty-bitty cottage. He thinks he can make it stick. If we weren't properly hitched, she gets an annulment and nothing, instead of a divorce decree and loot.'' Sam relished the thought, remembering his long talks with O'Brien after she had vanished the other morning.

''Uh, Sam, are Delia's accusations true?''

''Oh, here and there, depending on what kind of spectacles you got on. Like my being a wildcatter with Borden.''

''Sam, you heard that Borden's dead, didn't you?''

''No!''

''The earthquake. He was in some basement den of an engraver who'd done time at Sing Sing for forgery, when it caved in on him. He had some stock certificates with him, and they weren't his wildcats, either. They found him under the rubble.''

Jones felt a momentary pang. ''I always knew old Windlass'd graduate cum laude. I'm sorry. I wouldn't wish that kind of death on anyone.''

Olympus Prinz eyed Sam wryly, saying nothing, an odd grin pasted on his face. ''You told Delia you were a wildcatter?''

''Of course. Some while after we got stuck in double

harness. That's what drew me, you know. She was the dog-gonedest gold digger. I told her I'm an old wildcatter and she was a first-rate Nobel Prize–winning gold digger, so we made a match. She was itching to get into good society, but I said we'd fetch us some horselaughs from those blue bloods if we tried. I told her it's more fun just to be ourselves but I guess she never cottoned much to the idea. Don't get me wrong, Olympus. I thought she'd be a delightful wife, and real pretty, too. The truth of it was that I fell for her. Loved her. Thought she was a regular Gibson girl.''

Prinz was making notes at last.

"'She's a headstrong filly and just threw the bit. Now you can quote me. You tell your readers I said she's right, I called her a little old champion gold digger after we got hooked to the double-tree. I didn't want to marry some old fudge who'd bore me to tears.''

Olympus leaned back in his wooden swivel chair and sighed. ''You mind leaving these documents so I get them exact?''

''Let her rip,'' Sam said.

The next day, the *Observer* sold out in an hour and the editor had to run off another five hundred and sold most of those, too. Ignatius Benedict O'Brien called, horrified, but Big Sam paid him no mind. It was a great Barnum and Bailey kind of day.

CHAPTER 71

••••••••••••••••••••••••

Hannibal Dash sent the papers back to Gideon Browning unsigned. He didn't want any part of a deal like that, half married with heavy responsibilities but none of the rewards and comforts of wedlock, his future in bondage.

He knew why they were trying it. When it came right down to it he wasn't the one who'd deserted. She was. She

wouldn't come, even after he'd acquired a young fortune
and invited her. If she wouldn't come then there'd be a
clean divorce.

He spent the early months of 1906 helping his lessees
set up. Almost magically, they built a tent city out there,
using big wall tents erected on wooden floors, with good
stoves in each. They chose a flat near the pay ridge and
hauled in the water. They scraped a truck road up to Silverpeak, too, and soon were hauling the ore out and supplies in, employing twenty men in all.

In the space of a fortnight they completed the location
work on all four claims and Hannibal saw to it that the
claims were patented. As fast as word leaked out, about
fifty prospectors and adventurers clawed over the ridge,
claiming everything for two or three miles in all directions.
But Hannibal doubted the place would come to much. He
had studied that ledge with all the skills he had mustered
and he thought the pay ore wouldn't extend much beyond
the original claims.

Ned Stickney reported good values, with the gold running over three hundred a ton and an additional eighty dollars of silver at the outcrop but declining slightly ten feet
in. Not a Golconda, at least so far, they all agreed, but a
solid operation. Dash's own structural analysis suggested
that a two- to three-foot-thick sheet of the telluride ore inclined into the ridge at about a thirty-degree angle. Stickney
and Warren were driving two inclined shafts right on the
ore.

"You going to give this place a name?" Stickney asked
on one of Dash's trips out there.

"I hadn't thought of it."

"Well, we'd like to call it the Pearly Gate. The streets
of heaven are supposed to be paved with gold, aren't
they?"

Dash laughed and agreed. Some sort of American genius
had gone into naming the country's gold and silver mines
and he had taken endless delight in reciting his favorites.

In Goldfield he checked on Maude almost daily because he was worried about her safety. Harry scavenged the Free Lunch constantly, finding enough ore to keep himself going. But that would come to an end soon.

"Oh, he comes over and tells me he's gonna get even with me and this and that, but it's just his usual caterwauling," she told Dash one day.

"Maude—when your royalties start coming in he'll get serious. He'll put Turner Reilly on it and between them they'll tie you up," Hannibal replied. "Look, Maude, if you insist on marriage, at least protect yourself. Set up a trust fund he can't get his paws on. It's easy. I'll have my lawyer—"

"You're not gonna spend one more cent on me! I owe you too much as it is."

"Maude, please do it."

There must have been something in his voice, he thought, because she suddenly nodded.

"I guess if I want that cottage and a little to live on, I should," she said.

In the space of a March week his attorney, Porter Crecelius, set it up and she signed the papers. The royalties would flow into the Maude Arbuckle Trust and the Carson City bank trustee would release whatever she needed to buy her dream cottage, furnish it, and begin to enjoy a comfortable life after decades of desperation and hardscrabble living. Hannibal rejoiced.

With the most pressing of his affairs out of the way, he took stock. He was moderately rich and shortly another venture would begin to pay. He enjoyed Goldfield. Its raw vitality fed him. It was time, he supposed, to settle down. Goldfield would stay at the center of the mining world for years to come. He might venture anywhere, Mexico, Colorado, Brazil, but he would call Goldfield home.

The strange, crazy city filled with gold-mad people radiated a palpable energy. It was hard for anyone to remain unhappy for long in a bonanza town. Widows were turkey-trotting and two-stepping a few weeks after their bereavement. He had never been in a place like this, oozing optimism. Even the bindlestiffs riding the rods into town and flopping at the Miners Union Hall on Main managed to panhandle cheerfully. Some were comics.

Dash hunted for an appropriate house, astonished by the prices. Sheer demand had doubled and redoubled the value of everything but not all the carpenters in Goldfield could keep up. People sojourned in the dollar-a-night tent hotel until they could rent a room for twelve hours a day.

But at last he found a handsome frame house on Sundog Avenue and bought it for four thousand cash from a mining engineer leaving town. He would have to add a shed for his assay laboratory, but all in all, he was pleased. The high ceilings dispersed the summer heat while the several stoves made winter warmth easy. It had running water and a water closet, unlike most Goldfield homes. He contracted to have his assay lab constructed, bought wicker furniture, hired a woman to make drapes and another to clean, and moved in one sunny May day.

He heard nothing from Melanie or Gideon Browning but he kept sending her monthly checks along with notes describing his successes, the new house, and life in Goldfield. The whole business was hanging and he wished it would come to some sort of end. It occurred to him that they were waiting for him: it would be up to him to divorce her. She couldn't. But something within him resisted and he made no move. He would live on hope as long as he could.

In June the first royalty check rolled in from Stickney and Warren. It came to three thousand five hundred. Elated, Dash trotted out to the Free Lunch to tell Maude she had that much in her trust.

She was watering the geraniums she had planted around the shack, making them prosper even in the wilting desert heat.

"Well, Maude, it's time for you to buy your cottage," he announced. "You've got thirty-five hundred in the bank."

Maude squinted at him, set down her watering can, and

stared. "That's more'n I ever made in all my life put together," she said.

"You can buy a lot more than a cottage for that, Maude."

"I know. I hardly know what to do. I guess I'll just stick with a miner's cottage until I believe it."

"Come on, let's go look. I'll rent an automobile and we'll go poke around. I drove one once and I can do it again."

"Hannibal Dash, I wouldn't get into an automobile with you driving. You'll hit a telephone pole."

"Well, we've a lot of town to cover."

She surrendered, hairpinned a gigantic straw hat to her head, and walked back to Goldfield with him.

"I don't know if I want to do this. Maybe I should share it with Harry," she said.

Dash hoped to God she wasn't serious.

"How do I know I won't get taken? Maybe there's none for sale. Town's always full up anyway."

"We'll find you a cottage or a lot, Maude. I know a fellow. He built my lab in back of my house and he'll put a cottage up for you. Just tell him what you want."

"Hannibal, you're pushing me too fast. I think I should wait a few months and see how that mine pans out. Maybe it's just a ledge that'll quit before I get a house paid for."

He stopped cold in the middle of Columbia Street. "There's a reason to buy now, Maude. Some promoters around here are talking about putting Goldfield on the map with a world champion boxing match. I think it's crazy, myself, but Tex Rickard's in the middle of it and so is that wildcatter."

"Jones, you mean?"

"No, George Graham Rice and his Sullivan Trust, and Shanghai Larry Sullivan. It's a scheme to jack up the price of Goldfield stock and if they succeed there'll be another rush. We've passed the fifteen thousand mark they tell me at the club, and a world champion prizefight'll turn this town even crazier than it is. If you want your cottage, Maude, buy now."

"I don't approve of prizefights. That's the devil's business. Not even Harry'd pound some innocent fellow until he passes out."

"All right, but just find the courage to take the next step now."

She did. They found a sun-blistered white place with shiplap siding, a broad veranda supported by ornate white posts, two bedrooms, a commodious kitchen, a two-holer in back, and a white picket fence around it. The price was fifteen hundred. A miner and his family were pulling out.

"It doesn't have plumbing, Maude. But the main's in and you can put it in."

"I never had tapwater in my life and I won't get fancy now, Hannibal. But I expect I could find some young rascal that'd daub some yellow on it."

"Is this what you want, Maude? You could do better."

"This here's my very dream. I'll just sew up some curtains, broom it out, get a little Monkey Ward furniture and live like a retired madam. I think I've gone right through those Pearly Gates."

It seemed a pitiful little house to Hannibal but he didn't argue. She could afford much more but if this was her dream, then he could only help her realize it. It took the morning to arrange matters with the trust department of the Carson City bank but after a flurry of telegrams and Dash's own guarantee, Maude found herself the owner of the only real house she had ever owned.

A fortnight later he helped her move in, shove the stiff new furniture around, fill the lamp reservoirs, connect the White Oak cookstove to the stovepipe, and pile up a load of firewood she'd bought from the Paiute woodhawks.

"Maude, there's something that needs doing. You'll want a deadbolt on both doors to keep Harry out."

"Oh, fiddle, Dash. He's harmless. I'll just give him a dime and shoo him away if I don't want him around."

He could find nothing more to say on that topic.

CHAPTER 72

•••••••••••••••••••••

Mostly, Harry Arbuckle felt sick. He got so dizzy he would have to sit down sometimes. They threw him out of the saloons now unless he could show them some coins. It made him mad. He had made all those saloon keepers rich once. He could have bought and sold them. Ingrates, that's what they were.

He had flopped at the Miners Union Hall. Any stiff could flop there. But the wooden floor bit at him and he didn't sleep much. He never did. His suit stank but it was all he had. This morning, like all the others, he trudged out toward the Free Lunch wanting to scavenge some ore before the heat was up. In the middle of summer you couldn't even walk around those slack piles without frying yourself.

It wasn't his mine anymore. Turner Reilly made him sign some papers taking it away. That bum had never done a thing except bleed him white. Millions and millions of dollars down there and he couldn't get at it. He itched to go down there and claw loose some of that highgrade but there wasn't even an electric motor to run the lift—and no one to run it anyway.

In the early light he clawed through the rubble again but he didn't see any more quartz. Those crooked assayers, they were saying the stuff he brought them didn't have any gold in it. He felt sick and winded, and sat panting on a heap of rock, smelling his own stink. At dawn he'd puked up everything he'd scavenged from the swill behind the Palm Grill. His heart hammered. Old Harry was dying and none of those bums he'd given so much to would help him. Not even that bum of a barber, Freddy Glidden, he'd laid five-dollar tips on once.

He hunted some more but his eyes had gone bad. He found a piece of quartz and slid it into his pocket. The assayer would just laugh at that. He'd been hungry for so long he hardly knew what a full belly felt like. He stumbled around the loading chute and then the tailings, looking for a nickel's worth of gold. But it eluded him this August morning. He gave up. Maybe he could borrow a drink or two. Someone would remember old Harry Arbuckle this afternoon. You couldn't hardly borrow a drink at eight in the morning.

He shuffled back to Goldfield, feeling pebbles push through his worn-out soles. It was a long walk out to the mine and it made him dizzy all the time. He got as far as Alloy Street and saw them building the prizefight arena in the big gulch west of town. Tex Rickard and them were staging a big fight between Battling Nelson and Joe Gans for the lightweight championship of the world. The purse was supposed to be thirty grand. It was supposed to put Goldfield on the map and drive up the price of the mining stock.

Arbuckle snorted. He coulda put up a hundred purses like that. Seven thousand seats, they were saying. He drifted that way. Maybe some of them carpenters would remember Harry Arbuckle and give him a dime.

He passed a yellow cottage with white trim and there was Maude watering a little rosebush. He stared, amazed. He had lost track of her. She had vanished from the shack and he thought she was out prospecting, cheating him outa his half. But there she was, looking real good in a simple white cotton blouse and a long gray skirt. She'd drawn her sleek gray hair into a bun.

"Come in, Harry," she said. "I've been expecting you."

"Yeah, well, you owe me."

She didn't reply. He followed her up the steps to the veranda where some white wicker chairs rested in the shade, and through the front door into a gleaming little place, with waxed wooden floors and white enamel and shiny new furniture.

"This here's mine. You've been holding out on me."

She didn't reply but eyed him carefully, reading the grayness of his flesh, his emaciated frame, and the sagging, filthy suit. She led him into the kitchen where a nickel-plated cooking range stood.

"I'll start a breakfast, Harry," she said. "There's a pitcher and a washbasin out there. Maybe you'd like to wash while I fix you some vittles."

Numbly he retreated to the summer kitchen, found a porcelain basin, a filled pitcher and some Ivory soap, and scrubbed the crust of filth from his stubbled face. Then he collapsed into the kitchen chair. A cup of coffee steamed before him. He sipped, eying her lithe grace and the sparkling little house while she stirred some oatmeal. It rankled him. She'd been holding out, not telling him about this.

She placed a large steaming bowl of the oatmeal before him and some fresh milk from the ice chest, and a spoon.

"It's not fancy but it's filling, Harry. You need it."

He wolfed it down. He'd get around to what he was going to say after he got his belly full.

But she chose to talk while he ate. "This is mine," she said. "It's held by a trust for me. It's not yours and never will be, so forget what you're thinking."

"I'll get Reilly on you," he muttered between bites.

"Harry, that man never did a thing except bleed you to death. I'm in a partnership with Hannibal Dash. I found a ledge and we developed it. Some leasers are working it."

"Well, half's mine. It's all mine. You owe me, Maude."

She shook her head serenely. "No, Harry. The money goes into a trust at a Carson City bank. You can't touch it. The lawyers tell me that you'll never get a cent. You deserted me, you know. You left me in the shack and wouldn't share the money. That's one reason you'll never get anything if you go to law. There are other matters that would interest a court—adultery and nonsupport. Taking my half of the Free Lunch."

He finished the oatmeal. It felt amazingly good inside of him. "I knew you'd cheat me. Everyone cheats me," he said. "They all took old Harry. You and Dash were the worst."

She ignored that and dropped his bowl into a dishpan. "The royalty payments have been pretty nice," she said. "I have all I'll ever need. It's a good ledge, mostly gold with some silver. I found it by dowsing. Hannibal could hardly believe it." She laughed. "We're partners in a mining company, Dash Mining and Exploration. He's incorporated it. No, Harry, you can't get that, either. My share's in the trust. He's going to finance mining ventures, stuff like that."

Bitterness welled up in Arbuckle. "After all I done for you, you just leave me out in the cold."

She didn't argue but she smiled at him, her gaze meeting his until he looked away. He never could meet her gaze and it always riled him.

"I coulda bought and sold you and Dash fifty times."

"You could go to work, Harry."

"That's for chumps. What do ya want me to do? Clean out spittoons and mop floors?"

"It would be an honest living. I washed and cooked for two dollars a week—and fed you with it."

He laughed harshly, not knowing what to say. He felt sick and weary, ready to croak. That was all that was left of him.

"There's a tub in there and some hot water in the stove reservoir. Do you want to clean up?"

"What good would it do?" he asked, truculently. "You'll just kick me out afterwards. Some woman you are."

"I don't plan to let you live here. That's true."

"Some wife you are."

She ignored that. "That suit should be burned. I'll walk over to Main Street and get you some things while you clean up."

"I don't want your charity!" he snarled. "Just gimme some money and I'll go. Get your purse or I'll bust your arm."

She eyed him somberly a moment and reached some sort of conclusion. "I think not," she said softly. She drew hot water from her reservoir and toted the bucket into the lavatory. He heard her adding cold and fussing around in there.

"All right, Harry," she said.

It galled him but he followed her in there. The tub steamed. His old straight-edge and shaving brush rested on a dry sink. A Turkish towel lay on a chair.

He bathed, washed the filth out of his hair, and scraped away a week's stubble, feeling somewhat better. His dizziness lessened. When he was drying himself the door opened and some new duds landed on the floor, a ready-made blue shirt and denim britches. He dressed himself, hating her for it.

She was in the kitchen again. "I know what you're up to," he said. "Don't think you'll put one over on me. I'll get my half."

She served him a steaming bowl of beef stew and he devoured it while she watched thoughtfully. "You look nice now," she said. "I've thought about you a lot, Harry. You know what? I'm not mad at you. Not even for trying to steal my ledge. Not even for taking my share of the Free Lunch Mine. It's because you don't know any better. No one ever showed you how to get along with folks. You think everyone's trying to hurt you, steal from you, cheat you. But that's the mirror, Harry. You're just seeing people like you see yourself."

He was getting mad again, but he wanted that stew down him before he landed all over her.

"You got that from your folks; your pa, your brothers. Some things are just plain lacking in your tribe—love, kindness, caring about others."

"That's chump stuff. Now you cut out the nagging. I knew if I walked in here you'd cut me to ribbons."

She paused, as if wondering what to say. "Maybe I'll support you, Harry. It depends. Are you interested?"

He hated her power over him. "Go to the devil," he snarled.

"Every morning I'll have one dollar for you and a breakfast ready. Does that interest you?"

He nodded sullenly. He could eat a couple of two-bit meals and still have enough for some beer with the fellows. "What's the strings?" he asked.

She smiled. By God, she still looked pretty when she smiled. Her face had tanned so dark it looked almost mahogany but her blue eyes shone and her slimness made her handsome.

"Harry, the deal is, you and me are going to church every Sunday. You skip out and you don't get your dollars that week."

"Church! Them weaseling crooks?"

"I've been thinking about this a long time. I mean, what kind of church might help you."

"You can go ta Hades," he snapped. "I'm getting outa here."

"That's the hitch, Harry."

He needed that dollar a day. He'd likely croak if he didn't get it. Maybe he could string her along, fake it. He'd get even after he figured her out some. "Yeah, well, Maude, you always ruled the roost."

"I've been trying a few out, Harry. Every Sunday for six weeks now. There's those hellfire and damnation ones but I'm not taking you there. You grew up in the middle of hellfire and damnation. They haven't got a proper notion of the Good Lord and they'd do you a lot of harm. I've been looking for some preacher that knows about God's love and forgiveness and mercy and all that—and I got one.

"It took some hunting, though. Half of them want to threaten you with an angry God. You don't need that. This one fellow, he's worth a try. You're gonna be here at nine every Sunday, Harry, and you're gonna have a quarter handy to put into the plate, and you're gonna sit quietly and learn a few things about good people and saints and God. Maybe you'll blot up something, maybe you won't, but I don't know what else to do."

Arbuckle felt like a man being led to his hanging, but she slid a silver dollar into his palm and smiled. "See you for breakfast, Harry," she said.

CHAPTER 73

....

Hannibal Dash rented a suite in the new Nixon Block and launched his Dash Mining and Exploration company. He had refined his dreams into a workable plan that would give him joy the rest of his days. He wanted to supply venture capital to promising mines; not really to grubstake prospectors but to develop mineral assets on a scientific basis. He intended to employ new drilling techniques to pull samples from deep in the earth.

Dash believed that Rudolf Diesel's powerful engine could be used to run drilling rigs that would bring up ores for assay and evaluation. Why, some day, a mine's managers and backers might have a clear idea of what reserves lay under their claims long before the shafts and drifts and stopes were dug. Operators would know not only where the ore lay, but what its worth might be, and what sort of country rock they would be dealing with before they began digging. Mining would become less risky and better grounded in known realities.

But he had not forgotten Maude and her dowsing stick and in a moment of whimsy he designed a company emblem that featured the forked stick. He gave Maude a third of the stock and invited a colleague, the brilliant metallurgist Francis Bosqui, who had unlocked the secrets of milling Goldfield's fractious ores efficiently, to buy the other third.

Immediately Dash's firm prospered. He found himself out in the field much of the time, studying the structural geology of various potential mines. He organized a drilling crew and set it to work, mastering rotary drilling and all the lore associated with a new technology. In the space of a few months he had analyzed several claims, done assays on the samples taken from the cores brought to the surface, and written reports for grateful mine owners. In one case he supplied venture capital for shares in the new mine near Rhyolite. It wasn't foolproof investing but it certainly beat the sort of fevered gambling in shares on the Goldfield exchange. Meanwhile Bosqui was developing profitable ways to mill the low-grade ore mounded into mountains around the Goldfield mines.

Dash's life blossomed in ways he had scarcely imagined. He loved the fieldwork and after his fill of it he loved to return to his home base in Goldfield. He loved the outdoor life, the field assays, living in a sheepherder's wagon, wrestling with the drilling, the balky motors, the drill bits that wore out too soon, the stems that broke off, the rock too tough for his bits. Each job offered challenges and dangers. But when he could show his clients the assays drawn from lodes at various levels over several acres of ground, he felt a deep satisfaction.

He was pioneering, innovating, designing equipment ad hoc, and becoming something of a legend without even realizing it. He learned to chart strata from his bore samples, determine the strike and dip of an ore body sight unseen, plot contour maps of underground formations, all of which earned him the sobriquet, the Wizard of Goldfield. Often he took shares for payment, giving him interests in proven mines in Goldfield, Weepah, Diamondfield, Southern Klondike, Gold Reef, Divide, Gold Mountain, Lida, and Palmetto.

Sometimes he rared back in his office chair, loaded the battered desk with his feet—something he never would have done a few years earlier—and pondered the events that had enriched his life. He had always done fieldwork as an academic geologist but now he was doing it for profit. In a few months he had acquired a larger reputation in mining geology than he had won in all his years in academia. He was getting rich without trying. His life as a mining consultant and entrepreneur was endlessly diverse and challenging, while his life as a professor had been monotonous and cramped. *Mining and Scientific News* had gotten wind of his drilling techniques and there had already been two pieces about him which had excited the whole world of mining and surprised the schools of mine engineering that had been caught flatfooted.

He smiled guiltily. He owed his new reputation as a wizard of technology to a middle-aged woman who found ores by dowsing for them. Which reminded him it was time to pay a call on Maude. He intended to look after her, not because of any debts—her share in the new company was making her rich, too—but out of sheer love and admiration.

He walked up to Alloy Street and found her at home. She wasn't quite so spartan now. When she gadded about Goldfield she wore sprightly straw hats garlanded with ribbons or silk flowers. And she'd been known to wear turquoise necklaces now and then. But she was still Maude, content in her cottage, and he knew she would never change.

"Maude," he said, sipping Earl Grey tea in her parlor, "there's more money in your trust than you'll ever spend. You'd better squander some."

"I'm giving Harry a little," she said.

He disapproved. "Maude, I don't understand it. I thought you'd given up on him, after all he did and didn't do."

"Oh, I gave up on Harry about a week after we got hitched, Hannibal. But you know, he just needs a little mothering. I get him into church on Sundays now, but I can't say as it's doing the cuss any good. I keep watching him like you watch the crucible in your assay furnace. I reckon it'll burn the dross outa him sooner or later but what if there's no precious metal in there?"

"I don't know how you do it."

"Bribery. I give the old cuss a silver dollar a day. It's the only hold he has on life. He'd croak without it. So I just herd him into a pew on Sundays or he doesn't get the pocket silver for the next week."

"What does he say?"

"He sets there like a lamb and after we get out and he's wrung the hand of the preacher, he tells me he knows what

I'm up to and it isn't gonna work. He's on to me, he says."

"No results."

"Not one blasted thing. You'd think twenty hours in a pew listening to a preacher should peel a few layers off that old onion, but I don't see it. Maybe I should turn the screws a notch and make him come to church potlucks too."

"Maude, he'd scare off the congregation."

"Now, Hannibal, don't you go poking fun at him. He's just a pathetic old fellow who didn't get taught right. I got it in me to keep after him. He flops in the Miners Union Hall, gets his morning breakfast and a wash-up from me, and I give him his dollar. They let him into the saloons now because he's not bumming drinks and he's pretty subdued, at least that's what Tex Rickard told me last week. Harry sits real quiet, sips a mug, and sometimes some miner or other even buys him a beer."

"Well, don't let him stay in here. I'm afraid you'll go soft and he'll start to bully you."

"Ha!" she said disdainfully. "That's my business, Hannibal, not yours. I'm thinking of letting him flop on a cot in the summer kitchen. He'd stay cleaner. But I don't want him hanging around and I told him so. If that attitude vaccine he gets in the pews ever took, I'd maybe let him come back. That high-collared preacher, Ralph Dillon, he's a nice cuss without any hellfire stuff in him but he can't get old Harry inoculated. I gotta give you credit, Hannibal. It's the trust fund that did it. He knows he can't get at me. He doesn't even grumble about it anymore."

"Maude, is that it? That's his life now until he dies?"

"That's it, Hannibal. He got too twisted up inside. I'll just take care of him and plant him out there with the Presbyterians and put a picket fence around his grave. That's all I ever wanted from life."

Dash discovered tears on her sun-stained cheeks and felt he was taking communion in church. If Maude were truly fulfilled by her life in Goldfield and taking care of Harry, it was the humblest fulfillment he had ever heard of and the most selfless, too.

"Maude," he whispered, "did anyone ever tell you that you're the most beautiful woman in the whole world?"

"Oh, darn you, Hannibal."

He had intended to tell her how some drilling over in Rhyolite was going; that he was on the brink of investing in that mine, based on some initial assays at one hundred, two hundred, and three hundred feet. He had intended to tell her that Francis Bosqui was ready to take some milling ideas out of his lab and try them on a huge pile of ten-dollar-a-ton ore on the Florence for Tom Lockhart; he had intended to tell her that the Dash Mining and Exploration company had distributed a profit of ninety-nine thousand dollars in the past three months and her trust fund was thirty-three thousand richer.

But all of those things could wait. She dabbed her cheeks with a plain old bandana and smiled.

"Love is what you give to someone who doesn't deserve it," Hannibal said. "Love's what you give when there's not the slightest chance of getting anything back. Maude, everything you've invested in Harry is pure gold."

He took his leave. Life had never been better except for his loneliness. Nineteen six had been a banner year and it was only two-thirds over. If Goldfield had been crazy before, it was mad now. The Battling Nelson—Joe Gans championship fight on Labor Day had attracted thousands and driven up Goldfield stocks. A fine frenzy gripped the town. Nelson had made the Ladies' Aid Hall his head-quarters while Gans headquartered in the Merchants Hotel in Columbia, and for weeks the propaganda blasts and betting had bemused Goldfield. Hannibal had scarcely paid attention to boxing his entire life and the forty-two-round fight seemed brutal to him. But rowdy, sporting Goldfield had loved every moment, howling to the heavens when Battling Nelson's low blow forfeited the match to the black champion. They told him that more gold and loot had been bet on that bout than the entire value of several Goldfield mines and he believed it.

In the weeks that followed, his Goldfield portfolio had

nearly doubled in value and he had the saloonman Tex Rickard, that wildcatter George Graham Rice and his partner in crime Shanghai Larry Sullivan to thank for it. The stock exchange had gone berserk, with curb trading day and night, before and after regular sessions. That was the crazy thing about Goldfield, he thought, as he ambled home. Luck reigned, and virtue had little to do with it.

He turned into his walk and saw a familiar elegant slightly overweight woman sitting patiently in the wicker chair on his veranda.

"Why, Melanie," he said, his heart racing.

CHAPTER 74

················

Delia Jones waited restlessly for the verdict. She sat in Clyde Lovely's golden oak courtroom in sleepy Hawthorne, hoping for favorable results. Heaven knows, Patrick had tried hard. She decided to be philosophic about it. Even if she didn't get all she wanted, she would still have a lot. If she got only half the alimony she asked, it would still be two thousand five hundred a month. If she got only a quarter of Sam's assets, it would still be three hundred thousand dollars. That wouldn't be the same as six hundred thousand, but a lady could make do.

It had been a perfectly awful trial, in which she found herself called all sorts of evil things, from gold digger to grass widow to social climber. That nasty attorney of Sam's, Ignatius O'Brien, would pay! The only person who had truly enjoyed the whole thing was Big Sam himself, who had lounged on the other side of the court having a grand time. She hated him for it. Thank heaven it had all been said in Hawthorne, miles and miles from Goldfield. There had been a clamor to move the seat of Esmeralda County to Goldfield, which was the largest city in Nevada, but so far the legislature hadn't complied.

Judge Lovely emerged from chambers in his black robe. He was bald and reminded her of a brown hen's egg decked in gold-rimmed glasses. He had enjoyed the whole spectacle almost as much as Big Sam, which made her mad, but Patrick said not to worry; he was a fair and intelligent man.

"Will the Joneses come forward please," he said.

Delia and Big Sam approached the bench.

"All right," he said, "I've come to a decision. I'm ruling against Mister Jones's petition for an annulment. From the evidence presented here the last three days, I've decided the following: It's true that Mrs. Jones misrepresented herself, true that her sole purpose was to gain wealth and prestige; true also that she had no intention of contributing anything to the marriage, such as love and caring for her spouse, conception of children and childrearing, the achievement of domestic duties, or even ordinary companionship and private comforts. However, Mister Jones married her with his eyes open—the testimony supports that—and that made a valid contract of it with the color of lawful wedlock. I herewith rule against annulment."

Delia felt a vast joy build in her. Sam wasn't going to get away with that! McCarran winked at her.

Clyde Lovely consulted some notes, and plunged in again, while the court reporter scribbled. "I am granting Mrs. Jones's petition for divorce," he said, "although there really are few grounds other than ordinary incompatibility, which Nevada law does not recognize. It is plain from testimony that Samuel orally abused Delia, calling her such things as a gold digger and social climber. I've concluded that his comments—well supported by testimony—constitute the necessary cruelty to support my decision. I herewith grant Mrs. Jones a divorce, effective now."

McCarran winked again. Delia felt a thrill of delight. She knew what she would do. Just as fast as she could she would flee Goldfield, find a gorgeous home beside the yacht basin, and begin to meet nice people instead of these raucous barbarians left over from the frontier. She'd meet socially prominent men and she'd remarry. Who could resist her beauty?

"Now, the matter of property arises," the judge droned on, and Delia listened attentively because this was the crux of the matter. "This couple has been married barely a year. Testimony establishes that Mrs. Jones received somewhere between forty thousand and fifty thousand dollars in that time to spend any way she chose. That is a formidable sum, more than a miner in any Goldfield mine would earn in a lifetime."

Delia didn't like the sound of that, but of course Lovely was just supplying the reasons for paring down her demands. She knew she'd soon be off to California, a very rich woman.

"It's also been established that Mrs. Jones kept back some and is comfortably fixed. Given the brevity of this marriage and its purely fiduciary nature, at least for one partner, I see no reason to divide Mister Jones's assets. I herewith rule that Mister Jones is entitled to keep his assets and dispose of them as he chooses."

That hit hard. Delia wanted to protest but instead she clenched her fists.

"Given the brevity of this marriage and the unquestioned generosity of Mister Jones toward a wife who gave him little in return, I believe and rule that Mister Jones's obligations are fulfilled. I see no reason whatsoever for him to pay alimony. The argument that he should maintain her in the style to which she was accustomed fails upon the fact that she wasn't wedded long enough to become accustomed to anything."

Delia felt faint.

"As for attorney and court costs, since each party is both a plaintiff and defendant, I rule that court costs shall be divided evenly and each party will bear his or her own legal costs." He smiled amiably. "That's it. Court costs will come to seventy-five dollars each. Copies of this judgment will be mailed to you shortly."

Delia felt as if she had been kicked by a horse. She

hadn't gotten one thin dime out of it. All she had was a divorce decree and a debt to her attorney.

"Sorry, Delia," McCarran said. "It was a tough one."

"Oh! Appeal this!"

He grinned slightly. "You're lucky to get a divorce out of it instead of an annulment," he said. "You're free. You've got some cash in the bank. You can do whatever you want with your life."

Delia stared at her attorney, the judge, at Big Sam who was shaking O'Brien's hand, at the courtroom full of males, and saw at once that this was simply another male conspiracy.

She approached Big Sam. "Well, you got what you wanted," she said.

Big Sam looked troubled. "Well, Delia, I didn't expect this. I thought you'd get something."

"If it'd been a woman judge you'd be out your entire wad and begging on the streets like Harry Arbuckle," she said.

"Delia, I want to take you to the Palm Grill tonight. I've got reasons. Will you? It's important."

She eyed him skeptically and nodded. It'd be a free meal.

"I'll pick you up at seven, then," he said.

Wearily she took the Tonopah and Goldfield Railroad back, said good-bye to McCarran at Tonopah Junction, and stepped off her coach in the dusk of a September evening at the Grand Street station. In a black mood, her mind still resisting her defeat, she hired a hack to take her to the St. Nicholas Hotel, where she had lived since abandoning Big Sam.

Her small dreary room offered little comfort. She had a little money. Thank God, she had stuffed some of that cash into an account at the Cook Bank. But it wasn't a lot and all it did was buy some time.

She washed railroad cinders out of her face in the common lavatory down the hall and returned to her room wearied. She wanted a stiff drink.

She slumped into the hard bed, wondering what to do.

She could go back to Los Angeles and clerk somewhere, barely surviving. Or she could stay here and try it again. Not all the rich men in Goldfield were as disgusting as Sam and plenty of them lacked a wife. She was simply going to have to start over and find another. She had assets, a beauty that made men pant, a beguiling way with them, and a gorgeous wardrobe, the best in Goldfield. The honeybees would soon be buzzing around. She was in a city with ten men for every woman. Not half the members of the Montezuma Club were married.

All right then. She was young and free and she was going to find just the right man this time, someone with a college background and not some lout off the dirt roads. Maybe a fine young mining engineer or a rich lawyer like Turner P. Reilly. She didn't want to live in this disgusting town one more day but there weren't a lot of rich single men anywhere else.

She studied her wardrobe, looking for something enticing. She owned daring clothing she would never have dreamed of wearing not long ago and tonight she would wear something that would turn a lot of eyes her direction. If you've got it, flaunt it, she told herself.

An hour later she was washed, lilac perfumed, bejeweled, and slightly painted. She wore a clingy white silk dress that concealed nothing and revealed her lacy chemise. Its white accented her peachy flesh. She might be dining with Sam but she would be dressed to catch the eye of everyone else.

Big Sam picked her up on time, looked her over with a wry knowing smile, obviously reading her intent, and escorted her up the street to the restaurant they had frequented so often. She wondered why he was taking her out. She was wearied by the brutal day and wished she hadn't accepted. He seemed uncommonly silent and tired. She sensed the divorce had hurt him more than he let on. He cared about her; he just didn't care enough to give her the thing she wanted most, she told herself.

At the Palm Grill some substitute maître d' escorted them

to Sam's familiar table. Sam seemed at a loss for words for once, and they sat through a cocktail without saying much. He looked as if he wanted to say a lot but she was glad enough that he was keeping his mouth shut. She swore she'd walk right out if he made fun of her anymore.

She wasn't hungry and picked at a chicken before pushing the plate away. He wasn't hungry either, apparently, because his tenderloin plate remained almost untouched. At last he dabbed his lips with the linen napkin and settled back in his chair. He didn't light his usual Havana and she felt grateful. She loathed cigars.

"Well, Delia, I'm sorry."

Irritation bloomed in her. "Is that all you wanted to say?"

"No, it's not. You know, I didn't like that verdict."

She gaped. "But you won everything."

"Aw, Delia, it wasn't any fun seeing you get nothing. Made me feel bad. This is a big mean world." He faltered, fumbling for words. "Aw, heck," he said, and pulled something from his suit coat. "I never figured you'd get nothing out of it."

He handed her a check payable on the John S. Cook and Company Bank. She stared unbelieving. He was simply giving her a hundred thousand dollars.

"Sam!" she gasped.

He guffawed. "I had to give John a call to cover it. Sell some stock tomorrow."

"Sam! Sam!"

"All yours, sweetheart. I always told you I loved you. Take it from an old wildcatter. Go out there to California and start over. That's what we all came here for—to start over."

"Oh, Sam." Tears welled up and flooded down her cheeks.

"People take this gold stuff too seriously," he said. "You invest that at five percent and you'll do nicely."

She choked back the sobs that wracked her. "Thank you, Sam."

He turned serious. "It's because I love you. Love's worth more than gold and you don't have to dig for it. I hope you find what you want in life. I thought I had."

CHAPTER 75

· ·

Hannibal Dash scarcely trusted himself to speak. Melanie surveyed him, faintly amused and definitely curious. Beside her rested a small valise.

"Won't you come in, Melanie?" he asked.

"I believe I will."

She stood, still eying him as if he were a final exam she was grading. He pulled open the door and motioned her in, and she responded. She had come at a good time. The summer inferno had vanished and these autumnal days were mild and bracing.

"I'll show you the house," he said crazily, not knowing what to say. This wasn't as large as their great frame house on Langdon Street and it lacked any view at all. Goldfield had no views unless one counted the cone of Columbia Mountain or the dark mass of Malpais Mesa.

He led her into the parlor and she peered serenely about, seeing the desert light gauzing through the curtains. He had furnished the house with oriental wicker, most of it cream colored, which seemed perfect for this hot, dry climate. By her standards it was austere but he couldn't help that. His interests lay elsewhere.

The waxed hardwood floors glowed in the bright light, radiating illumination back upon her. She wore a dove-gray velvet suit and a pleated and starched white blouse with a cameo at her throat, all of which complemented her gentle face and large soft eyes. Except for a little thickening she was as exquisite as ever and very like the glorious Melanie who had once walked up an aisle to marry him. He felt an odd and utterly inappropriate rush of desire. But he pushed that aside and led her through the library, dining room, the kitchen and pantry, a second parlor, and finally a pair of spacious, high-ceilinged bedrooms upstairs, flanking a water closet. Fortunately the place gleamed thanks to his part-time housekeeper who cooked his breakfasts, cleaned, and then left. He ate lunches and dinners elsewhere, usually the Palm Grill.

"It certainly is different," she said when they had completed their tour. He scarcely knew what to say. They settled in the sunny front parlor where the hot, dry breezes were toying with the gauzy curtains.

"Did you have a good trip?" he asked politely.

"It was hard."

That could mean anything, he thought, and they lapsed into awkwardness again.

"This life agrees with you," she said, surveying him once again. "You look ten years younger. You've lost weight. You're tanned. You've a shine in your eye."

"You look beautiful, Melanie."

She smiled, perhaps bitterly. It was hard to know.

"That's an assaying lab in the back," he said. "I'm in the mineral exploration business. I have two partners and four employees."

"It is what you want to do," she said.

"Yes."

"I would like to see this place—Goldfield—if you would show it to me."

"It's not very pretty, Melanie. Not like . . . Madison."

She smiled for the first time. "It certainly isn't. I don't suppose I'll ever get used to it."

He studied her, afraid to speak. But then he led her out to his new ivory-painted Winston phaeton and settled her in it. He retarded the spark, adjusted the choke, and cranked. It took a dozen hard yanks and he was getting sweaty and testy when it coughed to life. He ran around and advanced the spark and pushed back the choke.

"The seat's hot from the sun," she said.

Perversely he drove her toward the mines along gravelly roads that twisted between giant heaps of yellow tailings, past ore chutes, mine heads, gallows frames, poles burdened with electric power lines, rough shacks housing engines that hissed steam, on and on, through the Combination mines, the Jumbo and Florence and Red Top, where man had forever obliterated the natural beauty of the earth.

"Show me the Mohawk," she said. "It's a famous place."

He did, pointing to Hayes and Monnette's feverish leasing operations that were yielding a bonanza every day. "It's the richest mine in the United States," he said.

"Mines are not very pretty."

"Nothing in Goldfield is."

"I thought the desert was. From the train it looked endlessly hostile and beautiful, harsh and naked. It made me feel very small and insignificant." She had to speak loudly, straining her soft voice to be heard over the clatter and rattle of the machine.

He drove back to town, chugging up Main Street and down Columbia, scaring teams and saddle horses.

"I have offices there," he said, pointing to the impressive Nixon Block. "Dash Mining and Exploration. And an equipment lot and warehouse north of town."

"Do you like what you do? Oh, why do I ask? Of course you do."

"I've never felt more alive, more challenged, more—on top of the world."

She didn't say anything for a while. Then, "Why is it so crowded? The streets are full of men."

"Not much housing. They live in the saloons. Eat and drink and socialize there." They passed the Louvre, the Texas Saloon, the Hermitage and Northern and Palace and Mohawk saloons.

"There are certainly lots of saloons," she said neutrally. "I would think it'd debase the people."

He wanted to tell her that Goldfield wasn't Madison, and people here elected Honest John Sparks, not Robert La Follette. But he didn't. "People do what they want," he said.

She turned and fixed him with her soft gaze. "That's what attracted you."

"Uh, Mel, I'm too busy. Those places are full of sporting people, tinhorns . . ." He censored himself after that.

She laughed pleasantly. She hadn't laughed until then. "You wouldn't go into one anyway, Hannibal. I'm afraid I would be embarrassed to meet them," she said. "But then again, maybe I should meet a few. Are there gamblers in them? You know, faro and keno and poker and green tables?"

"Yes."

"I'd like to see some but not now. Show me the tenderloin."

"Oh, Mel, you don't want—"

"I've never seen one. I've never been in a wild town before."

He eyed her doubtfully but she had the steely don't-cross-me look he knew all too well. "All right," he growled, steering the Winston south on Main. They chugged past hurdy-gurdy dance halls and grubby saloons and little buildings with women's names on them, and Victor Ajax's La Parisienne.

"My, my," she said. "I don't see anything very wicked. Where are they?"

"Just getting up now."

"I hadn't thought of that," she said. "You must take me through at night."

"I'd rather not, Melanie."

He emerged at the south end. "Beyond there is Hop Fiends Gulch," he said, savoring the shock in her face. He turned toward the Goldfield Brewery.

"Oh, those poor creatures," she said. "Is there no ladies' society to help them?"

"Ladies' Aid Hall. Goldfield Women's Club."

"Are there . . . things I might enjoy? Library?"

"Not yet. But the Turkish bath has books. Some vaudeville theaters—Arcade Music Hall, Mint Theater. We're on Keith and Albee's Orpheum Circuit."

She made a face. "What does one do for uplifting entertainment? Is there a repertory theater?"

He was enjoying this. "Well, last week we had the Cozad Dog, Pony, Monkey and Goat Circus."

"Oh."

"On the Fourth of July we have drilling contests, singlejacking, doublejacking. This summer a couple of stiffs won a big prize by doublejacking steels forty-one inches into Vermont granite in fifteen minutes."

"Oh."

"We had the world lightweight champion boxing match here on Labor Day. It went forty-two rounds. It was decided by a low blow. The preachers all preached against it."

"Were there many women watching?"

"Lots. This is Goldfield, Mel."

"What else do women do?" Her voice had acquired a razor edge.

"Women christen new mines with champagne."

"There don't seem to be very many. Is there society? Will I make friends?"

He laughed. "Not the sort you knew in Madison. You will need to be democratic, if that's the word. Openminded. You'll need to be open." He steered north again past the Presbyterian church, which she surveyed with oozing satisfaction, and Pickles Moving Company. He clattered west past the Goldfield Plunge and Turkish Bath Company, the incomplete Nevada Hotel, the post office, the State Bank and Trust Company, the Goldfield Steam Laundry, and then north past the baseball field, and finally back to his home on Sundog. She seemed bemused and he couldn't read her thoughts.

"It's like living in Casablanca or Bombay," she said. "It will be very hard but the danger and discomfort should add some spice to it. I think I like the desert. How far are we from anything?''

''You're in a godforsaken corner of the universe. Abandon hope, all ye who enter here.''

''I was afraid you'd say that. Hannibal, what does Goldfield have that Madison doesn't?''

''Dreams,'' he said. ''That's what the unsettled West gave this country. People came west with dreams. It's the place of beginnings and second chances. The failed farmer could come out here and homestead. The failed merchant could start over. The starving widow could come west and open a boarding house. We've always had dreams in this country. We could always pick up and go west. Most fail but that never mattered. The West is really the graveyard of hundreds of thousands of dreams but no one ever regretted coming west and trying. It was the dream that counted, the golden chance, the virgin shimmering unknown land, the newness, the breathtaking possibilities that the frontier offered—there for the taking. Goldfield is full of people with dreams. It's the last gasp of an era. I . . . had to come to the place of dreams.''

She absorbed that for a minute. Then, ''But you didn't fail at the university; you didn't need to start over,'' she said, hurt edging her tone.

He couldn't answer. ''How are the children?'' he asked.

She fixed him again with those soft eyes. ''Robert is a freshman and majoring in geography. He is quiet and angry and determined. Cecily is boarding until . . .'' She stopped.

''Until you return?''

''Oh, Hannibal,'' she said. ''Until I send for her.''

Something sweet in the ether dissolved an ancient pain in Hannibal. ''Are you hungry?'' he asked.

''I've been hungry for most of two years,'' she said, her composure disintegrating like petals falling from a wilted rose. He helped her out of the silent car and she dusted the grit off her velvet skirts furiously. ''I should have worn a duster,'' she said.

''We'll rest a little and I'll take you to the Palm Grill for an early dinner,'' he said. "It's a little like some places in Madison.''

"I hope not,'' she said. "I don't want anything to be like Madison.'' She turned to him. "I want everything to be new.''

In the airy parlor the terrible, towering wall between them tumbled into the twilight. "Oh, Hannibal!'' she cried as he opened his arms to her. "Oh, Hannibal, hold me, hold me.''

He did and the world was made right.

CHAPTER 76
....

Olympus Prinz studied the sensational stories in the dailies and knew how he would be spending his time the next few weeks. A holding company, Goldfield Consolidated Mines, was being formed by George Wingfield and Senator Nixon. It would be capitalized at fifty million dollars and would issue five million shares of stock at a par of ten dollars.

The constituent mines supporting the capitalization included the Mohawk 1 and 2; the Red Top and Jumbo mining groups, newly acquired from Charles Taylor for $1,330,000; the January and February groups, acquired by the purchase of nearly all the stock of the Goldfield Mining Company; and the Laguna group. The new company was nearing the acquisition of the Combination mines for a reputed $2,580,000, a move that would quiet the apex litigation between the Combination and Mohawk.

There wasn't a whole lot more to be gleaned from the *Sun* and the *News*. Which was fine with Olympus. He would do the real story while the dailies scattered their energies writing up funerals and weddings, store openings and burglaries. His weekly *Goldfield Observer* wasn't the paper it had been before it had been dynamited. Gone was

Olympus's mockery and humor. He had converted the paper into a virtual magazine, studiously examining Goldfield's proliferating problems. Its very seriousness had gradually won it a readership in a town with a sensationalizing frontier press. No one had threatened the plant or him, perhaps because he covered all sides of every issue.

All this, he knew, was a direct result of his own maturing. The explosion, the death of Uriah Horn, and the loss of the woman he loved had scored his heart and whittled down his conceit. He sometimes wondered whether Beth even lived; whether she had survived the earthquake. He had no news and preferred it that way. Annemarie and Alex, thank heaven, had survived and were living in Oakland until an overworked building contractor could rebuild their home.

He had done well all year, blessed by the industry and savvy of Sara Hartwig, the young widow he had hired as a general factotum. She turned out to be as gifted and determined as Uriah, swiftly mastering the bookkeeping, proofing, circulation, and advertising sales. He sometimes eyed her speculatively, wondering what lay behind her soft brown eyes. Some day, when she was well past her grief for her Joseph, who had died of diphtheria, he would find out.

Well, he thought, the Tonopah tinhorn had finally been dealt a royal flush. The Mohawk company had turned out to be the biggest bonanza in Goldfield. The cash rivering in from the Hayes-Monnette and Frances-Mohawk leases had made Wingfield a major player like Charles Taylor, Alva Myers, and January Jones. The man owned a few lesser mines and probably a lot of stock. But it was the Mohawk, and only the Mohawk, that was fueling his new ambition.

The reports troubled Olympus. The fifty million seemed much too high. The Goldfield Con was obviously floating some of the most watery stock outside of wildcat properties. The announced purchases, plus the unannounced price of the January and February groups, probably came to around five million. Was the Mohawk thus worth forty-five million?

Wingfield and Nixon's Goldfield Con was offering to trade its shares for the shares of its constituent mines: two Goldfield Con for one Mohawk; one Goldfield Con for two Red Top or two Jumbo. One Goldfield Con for five Laguna or five of the Goldfield Mining Company which operated the January and February. The Laguna deal puzzled Olympus most of all. The Goldfield Con prospectus had valued the claim at two million dollars even though several leasers had yet to extract an ounce of gold from it. Wingfield was trading watery stock for shares in great mines. Some people were going to be hurt.

None of which made the dailies over the next few weeks. Olympus enjoyed that. He would have the real story all to himself. The next days he interviewed mining engineers and geologists at the Montezuma Club over lunch. The man he counted on for answers was the Wizard of Goldfield, Hannibal Dash, whose drilling techniques had revolutionized the way reserves were calculated.

"What's the Mohawk worth, Hannibal?"

"I did some drilling for them so I can't reply without breaking confidences."

"Well, is it worth forty-five million including known reserves?"

Dash smiled. "I can't say. But it's nowhere near that."

"What about the Laguna? Wingfield threw that into the pot and it's valued at two million."

"I can answer that. Its only value is its proximity to good mines. But that could change."

"What would you value all the Goldfield Con properties?"

"Oh, twenty-five to thirty million. But there's a lot I don't know. There's a few million in lowgrade ores aboveground that'll be milled eventually. My partner Francis Bosqui's developing the means to work them profitably."

"May I quote you?"

"Why not?" asked Dash.

"Do you think people who trade their stocks for Goldfield Con will come out all right?"

"I'd rather not say, Olympus."

"Well, what do you think the Goldfield Con stock will sell for in a while?"

"Four or five dollars."

"Ah," said Prinz. "I knew I could count on you."

He got the same story from a dozen more experts. But he got quite the opposite view from the bonanza-maddened traders at the stock exchange. The news had triggered a massive bull market in Goldfield stocks, most of which had doubled in weeks. Mohawk had risen to $17.75 a share. Everyone in the country, it seemed, wanted a piece of that awesome mine.

Traders lived on hope but Prinz didn't want his story based on that fragile commodity. There was nothing left but to interview Wingfield himself. He grabbed his notebook and pencil and headed for the Nixon Block. A pair of clerks guarded the outer office but he could see Wingfield in the posh inner sanctum, staring into space and manipulating a stack of silver dollars. The man sat in a quilted swivel chair behind a walnut desk. Flocked red wallpaper rose from the oak wainscotting and a crystal chandelier hung from above.

"I'd like to see Mister Wingfield," he said.

"Who's calling?"

"Olympus Prinz of the *Goldfield Observer*."

"He's busy, Prinz."

"I'll just take a moment," he said, walking past the startled clerk. Wingfield watched his progress without a trace of emotion. The tinhorn was as dapper as ever in his starched white shirt, cravat with a headlight diamond on it, and white suit. His blunt, thick fingers dealt with the silver dollars with surprising delicacy.

"Prinz, it's all in the prospectus," he said, amiably.

"I'd just like a few figures, George."

"It's the best thing that could happen to Goldfield. I'm quieting an apex suit that could throw miners out of work."

"How'd you come up with fifty million capitalization?"

"Prinz, I can't explain the complexities of mine finance now. I've a meeting—"

"Sure, George, but what about some quick figures: You've bought several mines for somewhere around five million. And even that involves exchanging shares, not cash. I'd just like you to run through your mines and reserves, and come up with your capitalization . . ."

Wingfield's deft fingers cut the silver into four piles of five and shuffled them together. Then divided the pile into halves, and shuffled the halves like cards. "Trust the market," he said at last.

Prinz wasn't put off. "You're assigning a two million value to the Laguna group—"

Wingfield rose and steered around his beeswaxed desk. "Nice to see you, Prinz. Consolidated's the hope of Goldfield. I'm looking for a quarter century of prosperity. It's a conservative investment largely funded by eastern financiers. Baruch, heard of him? Bernard Baruch's lent us some capital. Now consider this, Prinz. Instead of repayment in cash, he's taken an option to buy shares. That should tell you everything the two-bit gossips and lobsters missed."

"I'll report it," Prinz said, feeling the pressure of Wingfield's hand on his elbow.

The interview didn't come to much. But he had gotten a few additional leads. He was getting good at that.

For two days he composed his stories. He quoted his experts, described his interview with Wingfield, tracked prices on the stock exchange, talked about reserves, delved into the share trading. When he had covered everything he could track down, he knew he had the story that the dailies had slid past because they didn't want to tangle with Wingfield. The man was reputed to carry a small revolver and occasionally terrify people by poking it into their bellies. Prinz reported, also, the unspoken premise of the consolidation. Goldfield Con was going to take on the Wobblies. One big company intended to crush the one big union and install changing rooms.

He printed his usual thousand six hundred copies and impulsively ran another hundred. The press hummed quietly into the winter twilight. Sara Hartwig helped him run a hundred-odd copies through his address stencil machine for the post office and then she left. The rest he would drop in bundles to his newsboys and his retailers, mostly tobacco shops, some of the larger dramshops, a one-armed old newshawk who peddled papers on Crook and Main, and some miscellaneous accounts he hand-delivered, such as the copies he always took with him to the Montezuma. It usually took three hours to bundle them, load them into a wagon he rented each week, and drop them off.

He was loading the wagon at his delivery door when three men materialized out of the dark. One stuck a shiny little revolver in his ribs and Prinz kissed his life good-bye. But the man didn't shoot. Two of them herded Prinz into the plant while one of the others drove the wagon away.

"You sit there," one said.

Prinz watched them run each of his page forms over to the type-melting pot at the Linotype machine. They loosened the wing nuts and threw the type into the pot. It smoked as it melted.

Prinz knew better than to yell.

After they had melted down the pages they unbolted the cast stereotype plates from the press and melted them down also. Then they collected the stereo matrixes used to cast the curved press plates and hacked them to bits. They weren't missing a trick—so far, he thought.

One of them headed for the morgue, where two issues lay, ready to be inserted into a bound annual edition of the paper. These they picked up, studied the date, and pocketed. The larger of the two headed for Prinz's desk and shuffled around until he found Prinz's reporting notes. He grinned. He tore them out of the pad and touched a kitchen match to them. They burned slowly, adding to the smoke.

They hadn't missed a trick.

"I've a message for you, Prinz," said one. "Your rag just went outa business."

Prinz's mind swarmed with possibilities: print it on another press, fight, defy.

"You'll be leaving town," the thug said. "It's healthier."

CHAPTER 77

Getting rich was even more fun than being rich, Big Sam Jones thought. He couldn't spend all that boodle if he tried. But getting rich gave him his daily dose of excitement. In the space of one month, November 1906, his Mohawk shares had jumped to $17.75, and his twenty-five thousand shares were worth over four hundred thousand dollars. But everything else had leapt upward too and he was a million dollars richer than he had been a few months earlier at the time of his divorce. He usually wandered over to the stock exchange and sat through the first session just to see his holdings balloon another twenty or thirty thousand dollars.

One December day he discovered young Prinz standing before him at the Montezuma Club. "I want to see you, but not here. I can't be seen with you," Prinz said.

That sounded pretty good. "Your office?" Big Sam asked.

"No, not there. Could I meet you at your house in ten minutes?"

"I'll see you there," Jones said.

A few minutes later, in the quiet of Jones's parlor, Olympus Prinz spilled out an amazing story of research, publication, destruction, and a threat.

"Wingfield," Jones said. "His paws are all over this one. A lot subtler than the Wobblies but much more dangerous. You want to keep on? I'll help. We'll publish in Tonopah or someplace and slip 'em in."

Prinz shook his head. "I'm not ready to commit suicide

or spend the rest of my life fighting lawsuits. Or end up in a hospital with busted limbs, or end up blinded or deafened. I'm here to give you your equipment back.''

"Oh, heck, Prinz, that was a gift and it's yours.''

"Take it back if you want it, Sam. I never really felt I owned it.''

"Prinz, you could take that equipment and publish somewhere else.''

Prinz sighed. "I don't know what I'll do. I've an offer for the whole plant. The *Chronicle* wants it.''

"Well, sell it. I hope you'll keep on editing a rag somewhere. You got guts, and the world needs newspapers with guts.''

Prinz looked troubled. "Sam, think about what I've told you. The watered stock. You're one of the biggest shareholders in town and Wingfield's gonna move on you. They've got a majority interest in a lot of mines and they'll force you to cash in your shares for Goldfield Con's watered stock. It'll be like stealing half of everything you own.'' Urgency filled Prinz's face.

"That's a good point, Prinz. I guess I'll go do something about it. Thanks for the tip.''

Ten minutes later he showed the editor to the door and swiftly extracted a sheaf of stocks from his safe.

By the time the opening bell announced the next session of the Goldfield stock exchange, Jones had three trusted brokers selling off his entire Goldfield holdings in small amounts. He watched amiably until his bum leg hurt too much. By the end of the afternoon session he had transformed over half his holdings into a million and a quarter of cash. In spite of the heavy selling, the prices never faltered.

The evening session went the same way, frenzied trading and plenty of buyers. Sam unloaded all the rest and found himself possessing two and a third million dollars. It would take a month for the accounts to clear and then he would be sitting on the largest liquid fortune in Nevada. He hadn't had such a memorable day since his divorce. And he had

Olympus Prinz to thank for it. He didn't know what he would do with all the loot. Maybe buy the Hawaiian Islands, or the Union Pacific, or Palm Beach, Florida.

The sale turned out to be adroitly timed. The next day an express messenger arrived at the Montezuma Club with a message for Jones. Mr. Wingfield wished to see him, and the express man was to drive Mr. Jones to the Nixon Block.

Cheerfully, Jones limped down to the lacquered hack and was whisked up the block. Straightaway he was ushered into Wingfield's royal suite. The young tinhorn—he was not far into his thirties—smiled and motioned Sam to a wing chair while his fingers marched silver dollars into arcane patterns. On the rear desk, beside the telephone, was a copy of the *Goldfield Observer*. Jones had to admire the fellow: there he was, one of the richest men in Nevada and young enough to enjoy it; and a principal owner and vice president of a company that held eighty percent of the gold mining stocks of Goldfield.

"I've heard rumors, Big Sam," Wingfield said.

Jones shrugged. "You never know, do you?" he replied. "What are the rumors?"

Wingfield laughed lightly. "I grubstaked you a couple of years ago. It was five dollars."

"I haven't forgotten," Sam said. He dug into his pants and extracted a double eagle. "I was ready to eat rats. This'll pay you back with a three hundred percent gain."

Wingfield slid a thumbnail across the gold, scoring it slightly. "I like higher returns, Big Sam."

"Well, three hundred will have to do," Jones said.

Wingfield frowned slightly. He took gold seriously. Funny how they all took gold seriously. A fella could hardly have fun dickering for gold because they all got solemn, like ministers talking about God. Easy come, easy go, wasn't in the gold traders' book of life.

Wingfield opened a teakwood cigar safe and offered Big Sam a cheroot. Sam thought it smelled mighty fine. Wingfield sniffed his own and ran a delicate tongue along it, moistening the rounded end. Then he nipped it with a silver cigar-cutter and lit it with a gizmo that magically burst into flame.

"I've enjoyed your success in Goldfield, Sam. So has George Nixon. He says there's no one in the country that used the United States mails like you, unless maybe it's Shanghai Larry Sullivan and George Graham Rice, as he styles himself."

Big Sam waited, alert.

"It's been good for Goldfield," Wingfield said. He puffed, while Sam watched the orange worm circle the end of Wingfield's cigar. "We thought you'd like to share in our new company. We'll buy your Mohawk straight, one for one with Goldfield Con. Twenty-five thousand Mohawk for twenty-five thousand Con."

"Last I knew Mohawk's almost double Goldfield Con, George. Eighteen dollars."

Wingfield smiled. "As I was saying, Senator Nixon always had a warm regard for your success. He's rising all the time. A powerful man in the Senate."

Now it was Jones's turn to enjoy himself. "Why, George, that's mighty kind. You just send my regards to the senator. Delia and me, we used to enjoy his company at our dances."

A faint annoyance crept over Wingfield's face only to evaporate in a smile. He reached into the drawer, extracted a Goldfield Consolidated stock certificate for twenty-five thousand shares, and shoved it across the waxed desk.

"You gonna make me a director of Con?" Sam asked.

"It isn't planned."

"I oughta be a director. All you smoothies need someone with a rough edge."

Wingfield laughed lightly. Jones had never heard a male laugh so lightly.

"Well, I might just buy this. What's it worth?" Jones asked.

"Your Mohawk."

"Nothing to trade, George. I unloaded every share I own yesterday. I guess it'll all sort out when the accounts are settled. This is a dandy cigar. If that's it, I'll be moseying along."

Wingfield stared.

"You mind if I borrow that *Observer*? Mine didn't reach me this week."

Wingfield glanced at it, at Sam, and out the window. "I like horse brokers," he said.

"Delia doesn't. She just couldn't cotton to a horse trader. She's down at La Parisienne these evenings, examining bachelors. You ought to look her up. She's wanting to marry someone respectable like you."

But Wingfield rose to dismiss him with a languid tinhorn's hand.

Big Sam Jones limped home. That was about as much fun as he'd had in one piece. The burg looked different to him, somehow. Everything seemed the same: the mobs on the streets, the hilarity, the boodle in everyone's pocket, the variety theaters running two shows a night and matinees. But it wasn't the same. Nixon and Wingfield and their cohorts had gotten a lock on the town in a few breathtaking weeks.

The old mining gossip, the wild rumors, the risks, the leasers hunting down mines to work, the tinhorns at the stock exchange peddling dreams and greed, the ones that went bust like Arbuckle and the ones that walked off with the loot like Hayes and Monnette . . . it was all changing.

It was going to be a company town, with company stores and company scrip and company rules and company officials in the courthouse. It wouldn't be much fun anymore. It wouldn't be greedy, bawdy, raucous, demented, feverish and delightful. There'd be no more Gold Diggers Balls. That was the whole trouble with gold. They all took it too seriously. Now, at last, it was time to leave Goldfield. Jones thought he would put up his rock pile—plenty of new-mint millionaires to buy it—and go somewhere.

Maybe Newport Beach, he thought cheerfully.

CHAPTER 78

············

Olympus Prinz spent his last hours in Goldfield at the Montezuma Club watching a Wobbly rally in front of the Miners Union Hall up the street. The combined Industrial Workers of the World Local 77 and the Western Federation of Miners Local 220 were on strike. George Wingfield had lost no time cracking down on highgrading once he put together Goldfield Consolidated. His little army of thugs had nabbed three ore-laden miners in the Mohawk and that had opened the ball. Now the One Big Union and the One Big Company stood face to face at last.

Prinz didn't doubt that Wingfield was watching from his offices up Main Street. The new king of Goldfield intended to crush the Wobblies just as they had been crushed at Coeur d'Alene and Cripple Creek. But at the moment the densely packed miners looked formidable enough with their bloodred flags flapping in the December wind and their clenched fists punching the sky as they listened to Vincent St. John address them from the balcony of the union hall.

The Wobblies owned the county. They had elected the Goldfield town commissioners and most of the county's supervisors in the November election. They had drawn Western Union telegraph messengers, waitresses, clerks, laundresses, and toiling people from all walks of life into the One Big Union. They had won a raise for the telegraph messengers and were striking for a five-dollar-a-day wage for the miners and an absolute end to talk of changing rooms.

They had strangled the *Goldfield Sun* for its anti-Wobbly stance with a newsboy boycott. Prinz had watched all that with dismay: It wasn't just a ruthless capitalist who was shutting off information he didn't like. The Wobblies were at it too. Wingfield, who favored the *Sun*, had even gotten into a shooting match with some Wobblies over that. The red flags of trouble were flapping. The *Observer* had been doomed; Wingfield had merely gotten there first with his growing army of mine security thugs, some of whom looked like jailbirds. The only papers left in Goldfield were town-booming pussycats.

Prinz couldn't hear the oratory through the window but he knew the rhetoric; he'd heard its harsh cadences in Goldfield often enough. It was the language of radical socialism, reduced from abstractions of equality to everyday immediacy: food on the table, no more starvation, no more wage cutting and abusive hours and insecurity and company scrip for pay; no more indignities upon the suffering and humble poor; no more plutocrats and magnates, no more children toiling in the pits when they should be outside at play, no more desperate women without pensions driven to a shameful life on the Line to survive.

And no changing rooms. The gold in the ground was for everyone, not just mining magnates. The gold belonged to the people! It was time to tear the rotten system down and build a syndicalist new order where working stiffs owned the production of the world.

Prinz watched skeptically. It all seemed a romantic dream to him, devoid of what theologians called original sin. The Wobblies would fail. Wingfield wouldn't succeed either. The changing rooms, if he got them, would scarcely slow down the theft. Most of the ore was stolen aboveground anyway. Top handlers shuttled an occasional car full of rich ore to the slack pile where the stiffs could furtively snatch the booty out of the waste rock. Every man in the mills knew how to snatch good bits of ore or secret some concentrate on his person. Most of the railroad workers in the state knew how to pocket good ore. Shipments of highgrade had shrunk dramatically en route to smelters.

Hayes and Monnette had lost a million dollars of highgrade ore, it was being said. And over at the Little Florence, a fabulous eight-inch-thick seam of ore that was almost half gold and worth $250,000 a ton had been melting away into the sturdy canvas pockets of miners' jumpers in spite of guards and radical security measures.

Prinz felt glad to get out. Henceforth there would be no place in Goldfield for a newspaper devoted to printing the hard realities. He didn't doubt that some of those men standing in front of the huge red banners at the union hall were the very ones who had nearly blown him to bits and killed Uriah. Casey Pepper, another of that bunch, was haranguing the miners now, his fiery words and gestures a palpable force even behind the glass window of the Montezuma Club. The giants were going to wrestle here in Goldfield and this strike would only be a preliminary bout. No matter which side won, the bonanza days and wild times would be over. There would be a company town, sedate, secure, and close-mouthed; no longer the cheery, generous abode of tinhorns, speculators, con artists, bawds, and endlessly cheerful adventurers whose preoccupation was simply having a good time. George Wingfield was going to make Goldfield *dull*.

Prinz turned away from the window. He had seen enough of red banners and armed miners, heard enough of angry rhetoric. He'd already seen too much of the Goldfield Consolidated Mining Company, too, more subtle and ruthless than the Wobblies and less inclined toward the smallest generosities that gave life its sweetness. There was this about the Wobblies and the stiffs: let them find a hungry man or a homeless one and the man got fed and a free flop in the union hall. The WFM had built a hospital, took care of its injured, helped its widows, fought for its children. It gave them something sterling that no Tonopah tinhorn running a fifty-million-dollar corporation could ever match.

Prinz thought that socialism was visionary and would strangle the world if its coercive visions of absolute equality became reality. On his last day in Goldfield he knew that he favored market capitalism but despised most of the capitalists. It would be something to cart with him into his next venture.

He pulled out his Keystone silver watch from its nest in his vest and knew it was time to head for the station. He was going to Oakland, where he would stay for a while with Annemarie and Alex, who were still waiting to return to the wicked city across the bay. Olympus had asked himself whether he could ever work for others after running his own newspaper, and knew he wouldn't if he could help it. Thanks to Sam, he had a nest egg to invest in the Bay Area. Along that eastern littoral of the bay, Berkeley, Oakland, Richmond, and Alameda were blossoming into amiable towns in their own right—towns where an enterprising and fair newsman might build a solid weekly. He was going to try.

His two years in Goldfield had matured him. He had started as a smart alec, writing humor at the expense of others, a West Coast mirror of that colorful young fellow Henry Mencken with the *Baltimore Sun*. But that had blown apart with the dynamite. All of 1906 he had written penetrating, balanced stories that exuded an innate respect for others, the weak and foolish, the strong and admirable alike. Goldfield had given him a different sort of gold, a honing of his skills, a maturing of his judgment.

He had never dared to ask Annemarie about the Rosses; whether they had survived and how they and their little ones were faring in devastated San Francisco. He did not want to betray Beth's secret even with a casual question. He knew Beth did not belong to him and he had the moral courage to recognize that and let the matter rest. But that could not keep him, when lying abed and awake many long nights, from remembering how it was to sit with her at tea, to hold her in his arms and feel her love radiating up to him in a union that was meant to be from the foundation of the universe. Remembering how it was to talk with her in wild Goldfield, the place where everyone had a dream and some dreams came true.

As soon as he got settled in the Bay Area he would send for his lovely Sara Hartwig, she of the lively mind, the bachelor's degree in English literature, the fellow journalist who wore his gold engagement ring.

EPILOGUE
....

With the triumph of Goldfield Consolidated Mines Company in early 1907, Goldfield passed from a nineteenth-century frontier mining camp to a twentieth-century company mining town. The years 1907 and 1908 were boom times for Goldfield, when most of its major buildings were erected, the population expanded, and production increased. Gold production continued to climb through those heady times, reaching a peak of $11,200,000 in 1910, slightly less in 1911, and after that slowly declining to about one and a half million in 1918. Small-scale production continued into the 1950s and tailings are being reworked to this day. Close to a hundred million dollars worth of gold, valued at a little over twenty dollars a troy ounce, was extracted from the district, along with a little silver and other metals. The official figure is about ninety million, but that does not count lost records or highgrading.

Goldfield's acute labor difficulties culminated in a Wobbly strike in late 1907 that the mine operators countered by pleading with Gov. John Sparks for military protection to quell massive disorder. Eventually, Theodore Roosevelt sent in the army, and the radical Wobblies, looking up the barrels of two Nordenfeldt-Maxim machine guns, retreated. Later, a federal investigation commissioned by an uneasy Roosevelt, who suspected he may have been gulled, concluded that there had been no significant disorder or reason to bring in federal troops. Calling in the army had been a ploy to reduce wages. But by then the mine operators had won, the Wobblies were crushed, and Goldfield became a docile company town.

Goldfield shrank to a town of one or two thousand and eventually was burned down by fires in 1923 and 1924. The 1923 fire, probably started by a Prohibition-era still, destroyed most of the town including Main Street businesses. The 1924 fire finished off most of the rest. A 1913 flood pouring off of Malpais Mesa had cut a wide swath through town. Today only a few buildings stand amid a vast wasteland of headframes and mountains of tailings.

I chose to end the novel at the point when the fun vanished, and the rowdy, wild, scheming frontier town, with all its bonanzas and dreams, was largely swallowed up by the Goldfield Consolidated Mines Company. George Wingfield had won and went on, as his biographer puts it, to become the Owner and Operator of Nevada. After 1906, Goldfield wasn't the same.

AUTHOR'S NOTES

....

The central characters in *Goldfield* are all fictional but some peripheral characters, such as George Wingfield, George Nixon, and Patrick McCarran, are historic. All scenes depicting them are purely fictional. In the case of George Wingfield, I believe they are in character, even if fictional.

Beth Fairchild-Ross is fictional but her story is based on a true episode involving a Bay Area woman who chose the only way open to her to salvage her husband's career and reputation. The original story can be found in Frank Crompton's *Deep Enough: A Working Stiff in the Western Mine Camps*, reprinted by the University of Oklahoma Press.

Delia Favor is fictional also, but she is based on a vivid description of the gold diggers who arrived in Goldfield en masse, written by Sally Zanjani in her brilliant and magical study, *Goldfield: The Last Gold Rush on the Western Frontier*, Swallow Press. This novel owes much to Zanjani's comprehensive and delightful depiction of Goldfield and its denizens.

Wyatt and Virgil Earp and their wives arrived in Goldfield in the spring of 1904, almost twenty-three years after their famous 1881 shootout at the OK Corral in Tombstone. Virgil became a security officer at the National Club and then a deputy sheriff, while Wyatt became a pit boss at Tex Rickard's Northern Saloon. Earlier, Wyatt had operated his own Northern Saloon in Tonopah. On October 20, 1905, Virgil succumbed to a second bout with pneumonia at age sixty-two. Wyatt left for California shortly thereafter. Their depiction here is fictional.

The author is indebted to the staff of the Nevada State

Library for unearthing massive amounts of material about Goldfield.

I have generally hewn closely to historical realities and times, as they were ably documented in Hugh A. Shamberger's encyclopedic *Goldfield*, an amazingly comprehensive study of the town, complete with maps, charts, tables, dates, and scores of photos. In a few instances I have taken minor liberties for story purposes.

—Richard S. Wheeler
February 1994

WESTERN ADVENTURE
FROM TOR/FORGE